Elegant Sinners

Elegant Sinners

Terry Ward Tucker

Summerhouse Press
Columbia, South Carolina

Published in Columbia, South Carolina
by Summerhouse Press

Copyright © 1997 by Summerhouse Press

Manufactured in the United States of America

Summerhouse Press
P.O. Box 1492
Columbia, SC 29202
(803) 779-0870

This book is a work of fiction although it is set in a real place. Any
character resembling a known person, living or dead, is purely coincidental.

Library of Congress Cataloging-in-Publicaton Data

Tucker, Terry Ward, 1947-
    Elegant sinners / Terry Ward Tucker.
       p.   cm.
    ISBN 1-887714-15-4 (alk. paper).
    I. Title
PS3570.U359E44   1997   97-23930
813′ .54--dc21   CIP

10 9 8 7 6 5 4 3 2 1

FIRST EDITION

for Margaret Earle Patterson
my kitten-eyed Greta

and Ingrid Tucker Patterson
my rose-lipped Ingie

Acknowledgments

I thank God for leading me to the river of creativity and offering me a drink. Thanks go also to my mother and father, Margaret and Ward Tucker; brother, Jay Tucker; daughters, Greta and Ingrid Patterson; nephew, Henry Tucker; and grandmother, Thelma Pitts. And then there is Tony Summey, who is good in every way and finds the good in the rest of us.

Others who helped bring forth *Elegant Sinners* are: Robin Sumner Asbury, my publisher, and her assistant Rebecca Roberts; Julian Bach, my literary agent and mentor; Ben Robertson, computer man extraordinaire; Lindsay Pettus, dear friend; Dr. Michael Rowls, my captain; Dr. John Griffin, fellow author and friend; and the citizens of Lancaster, South Carolina, my home town. I give you all pieces of my heart.

—*Terry*

Elegant Sinners

A dance begins. A tradition repeats.
Shimmering mirrors multiply a hundred flaming tapers
into ten thousand reflections of light.
Couples whirl in a vision lovely, weightless, without blemish.
Who are these ghosts who haunt Southern lore?
Ladies and gentlemen?
Gods and goddesses?
Or, are they and their progeny
nothing more than elegant sinners?

Prologue

December, 1996: I have not seen the skyline of Charleston for a year less two days, nor crossed her bridges, nor swum her bays, nor witnessed her red sunsets. Twelve months. You'd think I could have put the memories of this aloof city behind me by now. Yet in an eyeblink, in a heartbeat, they can all come rushing back—incidents, people, places. Every day the details of what happened to me there, of what it was like to be an outsider there, run through my mind like a movie. I cannot stop it; it plays itself out again and again, and none of it ever changes.

There is no discernible beginning to my story. One must jump on board in the middle—of a life, a marriage, of a dizzying rush of events that lead to the destruction of several human bodies and more human spirits. I've told these dark secrets to my innermost soul hundreds upon hundreds of times. I will tell them to you only once.

The autumn we signed the lease on the beach cottage near Charleston was the seventh autumn Stuart and I had been together, and over the course of those dispiriting years, I'd watched him go through a metamorphosis. Oblivious to his own indoctrination, unaware he was being trained in the art of satisfying a neurotic, he had joined me in the worst of my habits. He believed, erroneously, he was expanding as an individual, moving in a broad arc as an enlightened man toward a richer interpretation of life.

He believed this fiction as a direct result of his relationship with me, for I was an expert liar. Notions of leaving his work at Boston University and starting a consulting business of his own, of living on a remote island near Charleston, South Carolina, of not working a regular job—Stuart thought he had come to these brave decisions alone. He never made the connection between the subtlety of suggestion on my part with the blossoming of an unorthodox idea in his own head. He always had to "talk me into" the latest outrageous scheme, be it selling the houseful of antiques his grandmother had left him so we could quit our jobs and move south, or giving up his tenured position as a professor to try something less dull and predictable, or borrowing money indiscriminately to support a failing business effort. I had to say no to his proposals a good long time before finally giving in. Stuart was required to fight to get his way. This was necessary so that blame could be affixed properly should an idea turn sour later on.

Unlike my first husband, who told me after eight months he could no longer deal with my intense need to live on the edge, Stuart made a splendid foil. He was the product of a mother whose most daring deed was to bake a chocolate soufflé from a recipe she had concocted herself, and of a father who'd devoted his whole career to the hometown savings and loan. All very stable and safe. It was I who presented Stuart with a kaleidoscope of life, I who interfered with his predestination of becoming the youngest dean of the English department at Boston U. by inflaming his mind with stories of my own free-spirited parents and their lifelong war with the commonplace. But my stories were not altogether true. They concealed the real character of those two irresponsible fools who left me as a helpless child to live out my life hampered by emotional wounds they had inflicted.

At the age of six, I was put in the care of a maiden aunt while my mother and father took two years off to sail around the world in a vessel they had built with money that should have been spent on me. On the morning they departed Boston Harbor, my aunt took me to the municipal dock to watch these two romantics christen their boat *The Beautiful Ghost Dream*. Sometimes I still want to believe that had it not been for the great storm that arose on the Indian Ocean their second autumn out, they would have come back to get me. It happened off the coast of Australia, a smashing, murderous hurricane that, in its first horrifying hour, splintered *Ghost Dream's* main mast and sank her ten miles offshore. With her, the little boat took down all my parents' worldly possessions, their hopes and dreams.

My father had finally fulfilled his destiny of becoming an abject failure, leaving nothing but a small rag of a daughter tucked safely away in the home of her only sane relative. My mother died of exposure two days after the storm, an hour before a fishing boat spotted the bit of wreckage that had kept her and her husband afloat. My father wrote to tell us of the tragedy, and that he was not coming home. The memories of my mother were too painful, he said. He never wanted to see Boston again.

"But what about me?" I cried to my aunt. "Doesn't he want to see me?"

His letter, and the rejection it contained, became an indictment against a child's self worth, the beginning of a private journey of fear that drove her as she grew older to accomplish more and more, to prove again and again that her fragile life had value. It was the reason for the endless testing she put to her own abilities, to determine whether or not she deserved to keep on living. I have now realized, after years of introspection, I will always be that child, continually searching for the ultimate foe, my final destroyer. Then at last my father will have been right—his daughter's life was worth nothing, her efforts of no consequence, her existence barren of meaning.

Even as a child I forced myself along this path to self destruction, down and down a terrifying spiral that gained momentum daily. But somehow my journey did not turn desperate until I realized I could not stop. By then I was unable to deliver myself from the bondage of growing up in the house of an upright spinster aunt, who blamed my father one hundred percent for the death of her only sister. With me as a gallery of one, she convicted him daily with words burned raw from hatred, assaulting my unformed child's soul with repeated executions of his spirit.

Then, after four years of silence, letters began to arrive from Australia. My father, it appeared, had had a change of heart. I was unfamiliar with his personality, and did not know that most of what he wrote was pure fabrication. I believed every word of every letter, all his sugared stories of the life we would share together when he finally saved enough money by working at a shipyard in Sydney to build *Ghost Dream 11* and sail home. Those letters, infrequent as they were, sustained me for seven years. They expunged all guilt from this man, who surely owed ten lifetimes of guilt to me and to my mother. But the spell of the letters had turned him into Aladdin, and me into Scheherazade, my young heart overflowing with poisoned stories I told to no one but myself.

My aunt nearly lost her mind trying to convince me of the man's treachery, but the dreams he spun were too lovely to be destroyed by simple truth. The magic of what might be, what could be, what was promised to be, gilded completely the starkness of life's realities. I became the main character in a play I created myself, the princess in a fairy tale with a hundred happy endings. But on the morning I turned seventeen, my hopes were crushed when I was asked by the fates to grow up all in one day. A cablegram arrived from Australia informing me that my father had been killed by a collapsing scaffold in the shipyard. My aunt said I told you so, that she knew he'd never come back. And I hated her until the day she died for being right. *Ghost Dream 11* did not come home, nor did my father, and I never healed from the wound.

It was not possible for Stuart to understand these origins of my neuroses, though he honestly believed he could. In fact, he spent inordinate amounts of energy playing therapist/lover to me. But my problems were too deeply rooted for armchair therapy. Moreover, he did not realize the danger to himself of involvement in my certain downslide. Unwittingly he contributed to his own destruction. Innocently he joined me in mine. His entanglement in the unfair dynamics of a relationship with a half-sick woman soon became permanent. Only once, I think it had to do with the sale of his grandmother's furniture, did he look me squarely in the eyes and say he felt he was being controlled in sly ways, but could never pinpoint how or when.

He declared me a master manipulator, yet did not seem to realize these same feelings had been communicated to me eventually by everyone I had ever been close to, including most recently the elderly clients to whom I had sold writing projects when we'd first moved to Charleston. I discovered early on that Old Charlestonians compete with each other fiercely in every area of their lives, and on their peninsula of extravagance and wealth, the stakes could be exceedingly high. I used all my powers as a psychological seductress to make myself irresistible to these Southern innocents so ignorant of neurotic duality. I made myself a bauble they could brag about over cocktails, a new curiosity, a fad, an expensive distraction. After all, few people anywhere were important enough to have need of a professional ghostwriter. But how far my game would go I could not guess. How many players would finally die I could not predict. For the pawns were ignorant of the rules, and I was careful not to let them learn there was really only one requirement to keep the game in motion—the necessity of proving again and again that even a child of a father like mine could accomplish incredible things, of which surviving Charleston was the most incredible of all.

Part One
Arlena

Chapter One

"Arlena, you're running late," Stuart said the third time. "It's ten after nine. Want me to start the car?"

I could have strangled him. He in his t-shirt and shorts telling me in my suit and high heels I was late. It was too much. He was too much. I decided to ignore him.

"Arlena, sweetheart, if the swivel bridge doesn't stop you, traffic into town will. You know Southerners think hurrying is a crime against nature."

That did it. I clenched my teeth. "Will you stop with the two-minute warnings, Stuart? I'm nervous enough with the car on the fritz. *And* my side hurts *and* my head hurts *and* I'm hot."

No breeze at all came off the ocean that morning. Nothing made up for its absence. Not ceiling fans. Not wide open windows. Nothing. The September sun had already heated our tiny bedroom, the chamber of sweat, Stuart called it. I stared at my face in the dresser mirror, searching for a small sign of confidence in the dark eyes looking back at me. All I could see was my lipstick starting to melt, oily evidence of the scorching day ahead. I hoped to God it would be the last of an unseasonably tortuous heat wave. Maybe cooler weather would make me less irritable.

Unable to control himself, Stuart began rushing me more instead of less. His urgency made my thoughts jump around crazily. They crashed into each other and broke up into anxiety. It was frightening. It killed off all reason. I wondered why the Valium I'd secretly swallowed in the bathroom had not taken effect. Stuart knew I could dissolve emotionally at any moment, yet he was helpless in the face of it. The look in his eyes bordered on alarm. He was afraid I might work myself into another crying jag, the kind he'd seen so frequently, the kind that would exhaust me for days. Once more he tried to reassure me.

"We're lucky old lady got-rocks came through again," he said too cheerfully, referring to a phone conversation I'd had the day before with Miss Fanny Peregrine, my best client. She had agreed to pay me early. The reminder of a potential check made me feel better. Stuart picked up on this slight change in mood and pushed for momentum. "Maybe we can spread some cash over the bills," he said. Then, "Look at you, Arly...you're sweating. Come on the porch. Cool off."

I allowed him to try to help me, to pull me through the sitting room toward the screened porch, but not without making a detour every other step to grab papers and cram them into my briefcase.

"Okay," he said as we stumbled into the glorious sunlight that flooded the porch each morning. "Look at that blue ocean. Breathe the sea air."

I did neither. I was too busy fumbling with the briefcase. It slipped when I tried to force it closed, its contents spilling to the floor. Stuart and I bumped heads trying to catch things as they fell.

"Look what you made me do now," I snapped. "There's sand all over this porch. What if it gets into my dictaphone? Oh no, my pages are out of order. I'll never get them straight."

We were both on our knees sorting through papers, though my stack only seemed to get more mixed up. "Take it easy," Stuart said. "Who cares about a little sand? Not when half of South Carolina's gorgeous beach front is right in your own back yard."

I snatched the papers out of his hands and crammed them back into the briefcase. "What's the matter with you?" I said. "Has your brain shut down? We're in debt, terrible debt. Three notes overdue at the bank, a month behind on our rent, no health insurance, no life insurance, nothing. And the car...you know the car might not make it through the week. Sometimes I don't think I can stand it, anymore." My voice was trembling. I could feel myself getting desperate. "Stuart, you have a Ph.D. I have a Master's. For God's sake, what's wrong with us?"

"Nothing, we're fine. No one is forcing us to live like this. Consulting for me, freelancing for you. That's it. No more canned jobs. No more canned bureaucracies. But we have to give ourselves time. Neither of us can attract blue-chip clients overnight. How many times have I begged you to be patient? Two years isn't very long ...."

"Stop right there, big boy. I'm not listening to *that* speech again. You got away with moving me to this backward little place, but I stopped listening to what a great idea it was a long time ago. We never should have left Boston and you know it. Now get out of my way. I have to find the keys."

I slammed the briefcase shut and used Stuart's shoulder as a brace to haul myself to my feet. He stood up slowly and stepped back. I sneaked a quick look at him as I pulled couch cushions out and shoved chairs aside in my ritualized quest for the keys. He caught my glance and took advantage of the show of weakness.

"Guess you've forgotten the good old days," he said, calling up our four vacations on Sullivan's Island before we finally decided to move there. He did not mention that I was the one who'd pushed hardest for the move. "Falling in love with the island," he went on. "Falling in love with Charleston ...."

"Give it up, Stuart. You can't make me feel guilty for expecting to eat regularly. Why don't you stop trying to put snakes in my head and *help me find the freaking keys.*"

The shrillness in my voice startled us both. Stuart did not speak. He stood motionless and stared at me with weary eyes. Where did he get the strength to keep going when there was never enough money? Not enough to buy himself a decent dress shirt. He'd been wearing the same tie a year. I turned away to avoid his eyes and resumed my frantic search. But Stuart would not be defeated. For the millionth time he deflected my chronic black mood. "Why don't you look in that trash bag you call a purse?" he said when it became obvious I was getting nowhere with my search.

"Will you leave me alone, please? I'm going out to look in the car. Maybe I left them in the ignition."

"Arlena, you're not paying attention. I saw you put them in your purse, last night, I saw you. Here, look for yourself." He jerked the purse from its almost-permanent home on the back of the Boston rocker, and held it upside down over the couch. The keys tumbled out. He grabbed them and jingled them in my face. "Bingo," he said. "Now tell me you're sorry for every little thing."

I lunged for the keys and missed. "Yeah, yeah, yeah," I said, "whatever you say. Just give me the keys and let me go. Miss Peregrine might not pay me if I'm late."

"Go ahead. No one's stopping you. But I'll carry the keys.

You'll carry the briefcase. We don't want to risk another search, do we?"

I turned on my heel and marched through the house, Stuart right behind me. He continued to talk; I continued to ignore him. "It wouldn't matter if you were a month late," he said. "Miss Peregrine would still love you. Yesterday, when I dropped off last week's chapter pages at her humble little mansion on the harbor, she wasted half my morning telling me what a precious darling girl you are. Never mind the chapters were a week overdue. Of course, it was clear to me she'd confused you with someone else. But did that matter to her? No-o-o. All she wanted was to bore me with an hour-long soliloquy on how you've given her better things to contemplate than pills and old age."

"What things?" I said, wheeling around.

He bumped into me and stepped on my foot, which helped my mood not at all. "Good grief, Stuart, get off me. What was Miss Peregrine talking about, anyway?"

"How the devil am I supposed to know? You're the one who works for her. Maybe that elephantine manuscript you helped her put together last year, the one we've been using as a doorstop. She probably thinks some fool might still publish it. What was the name of it again? *Tarnished ...Tarnished ...*?"

"*Tarnished Honor*, smart-mouth, as if you didn't know. Now give me the keys. I hate being late."

He widened his eyes and smiled wickedly. "*No*," he whispered.

I hesitated a split second, weighing whether it was worth exhausting myself just to get my way. Usually, it was. But on this particular morning I felt so tired.

"All right, you win," I said in my most controlled voice. "You may drive me, but only to Mount Pleasant. Then you must get out of the car and drop into a very deep hole."

By the time I got to the car, he was bent over the steering wheel, a race driver gunning his engine. I fell into the passenger seat and we roared down Atlantic Avenue, my door still half open. It didn't close until we veered right to avoid an overweight jogger.

Stuart had become totally obnoxious. "I always love it when we're on our way to schmooz Fanny Peregrine," he shouted. "She's so deliciously rich."

"Will you stop yelling—I'm twelve inches away. And stop driving like a maniac. I want to get there in one piece, on time, for once. Are you sure Miss Peregrine wasn't upset that last week's chapters were late?"

"Nope—too busy raving about your la-de-da writing class at Southern Prep. She's tickled clear through her shriveled little aristocratic soul you decided to teach there again this year."

"She'd better be. I would never have agreed to do it if she hadn't insisted. It surely wasn't the pay, or the kids. They're worse than the Marquis de Sade. Stuart, watch the road. We're weaving."

"Hey, a couple hours a week at hoity-toity Southern Prep won't hurt you if it makes our dear Miss Peregrine happy. Our dear *rich* Miss Peregrine. And there've been plenty of times we needed that extra two hundred bucks at the end of a dry month."

"I don't care. If it weren't for Raven FitzSimons, I wouldn't go back. Last year, she was the only kid in the school who treated me like I was human. The rest of them acted like creeps. Oh, no. Is that a sailboat in the channel? Look, the bridge is opening. Slow down."

"Well, so much for being on time, precious-darling. Now you're going to sweat your pretty little ass off for fifteen minutes while the biggest triple-master in the whole of South Carolina drags her expensive hind-end, on no wind, through the middle of this rusted-out bridge...."

"I swear, Stuart, if you don't shut-up, I think I'm going to scream. You get on my nerves so bad."

"Scream all you want. That sailboat ain't hurrying, particularly not for some pseudo-sophisticated school teacher—excuse me, some pseudo-sophisticated private school teacher of adolescent snoblets in attendance at the prestigious Southern Preparatory School of Old Charleston. I don't know what you expect from those inbred brats, Arly. They're just teenagers. They can't help it if their addresses are all south of Broad Street. Parents and grandparents of kids like that wouldn't dare let them soil their Birkenstocked feet on the steps of a public school. Why, they might have to walk next to *black* children, God forbid. It's no wonder they're warped. They've had it drilled into their heads since the day they were born that Southern Prep is God's gift. This is old stuff we're talking about. Elitist stuff. Traditions of superiority that go back before the War Between the States. Yankees like us will never understand Southern attitudes about that kind of thing."

"I told you, I don't care. It's provincial and offensive, and the only reason you're defending it is that you're on the payroll, too. I may quit to make a statement—in spite of Raven, in spite of Miss Peregrine, and most of all in spite of you...if I don't die of heat prostration on this bridge first."

"Stop showing off. You can't afford to quit. It'd be suicide for yourself and murder for me. Admit it, the last thing you want is for Southern Prep's Board of Directors to start looking for a new fundraising flunky to replace little old me, even if the job is only a half-assed consulting gig. And you can't ignore what Miss Peregrine wants. She's too rich to ignore."

"I hate the way you talk. Miss Peregrine is a person, not a caricature. And she's not a money machine."

"Well, aren't we high and mighty, precious-darling-girl. Forgive me for having to be concerned about something as indelicate as money."

I glowered at him, but decided it expedient to let him have the last word. It was too sticky hot to fight. I could feel the humidity in my lungs. Instead of wasting more energy sparring with Stuart, I decided to kill him off in my mind. I pictured him sinking beneath the waters of the great Intracoastal Waterway that rippled along before us. He sank without a struggle on the bow of the boat, the slow-crawling sailboat that seemed to have one purpose on earth—making me late to Miss Peregrine's.

Stuart scrutinized me. I sighed and paused to let him know I had conceded the moment, then said less sharply, "Oh, Stu, you know how odd Miss Peregrine is. I don't understand her at all."

Skeptical of my rare surrender, he shot me a look to make sure I was not planning an ambush. Satisfied more or less I wasn't, he propped his head on the car seat and closed his eyes against the heat. The sailboat bobbled along slowly. Once more I envisioned it breaking apart and sinking beneath the waves, only this time I did not make Stuart go down with it. This time I let him stay beside me in the car.

Again I spoke calmly. "It's as if, well, as if she's tough and fragile at the same time. And I feel so sorry for her, having to live with that nasty housekeeper. She's the meanest woman I've ever met in my life."

Terry Ward Tucker

He cracked his eyes and looked at me sideways, then decided against remarking on who was the meanest woman *he'd* ever met in *his* life. "Louisa Hill?" he said after a pause. "Louisa Hill is a saint."

"How would you know? You've never even laid eyes on her."

"True, but anyone who could stand Fanny Peregrine twenty years is more than a saint. I don't know how you've stood her fourteen months."

"You don't mind cashing her checks, though, do you, smart boy?" I was about to let him sink again with the boat. "No one should have to put up with a crank like Louisa Hill. She's horrible, goes out of her way to make Miss Peregrine look senile. Look there, the bridge is closing. *Drive.*"

"Maybe we ought to let the guard rail go up first. And maybe stop wasting time worrying about crazies. Miss Peregrine is a tough old bird. She can take care of herself."

"No, you don't know what you're talking about. She's tired and weak. She's turned into an old, old woman just in the last few weeks."

"Forget it. You can't solve everyone's problems. We have enough of our own. Don't think about anything when you meet with Miss Peregrine but getting paid and getting out."

Stuart was right and I knew it, but I also knew he didn't care about Miss Peregrine, not the way I did. He couldn't. He hardly knew her. I was the one who'd worked for her over a year, three mornings a week, hour after tedious hour. And all that time I had watched her grow more and more frail. To Stuart, she was just another client. To me, she was Miss Peregrine.

"What time do I have to have the car back?" I said.

He didn't answer until he'd pulled the Romeo onto a side street off Mount Pleasant's marsh bank. "The only appointment I have today is with Bill Martin," he said, squinting against the white glare of morning still shimmering above the marsh. "It's at two, here in Mount Pleasant—you'll make it back in plenty of time. But the appointment isn't the problem. *Money* is. We have to get Miss Peregrine's check to the bank by one. I've already written a few of our own against it. Hope they haven't bounced yet. Can you make it back home by twelve-thirty?"

"I'll try. What are you going to do while I'm gone?"

He shook his head. "I don't know what to tackle first. Guess

I'll write Bill Greene's sales promo for Sea Bird Condos. He might hire me to write his whole marketing plan, if I cut my price again."

"So do it. We need the money."

"You *do* it," he said as he helped me into the driver's seat. "You're supposed to bring home the big bucks today."

I saluted him through the car window as I revved the motor, then turned and began rummaging through the glove box.

"What now?" he said.

"My side hurts. I'm looking for my Darvon in case I get in trouble at Miss Peregrine's."

"Under the seat. Look under the front seat. When are you going back to the doctor about this? You can't ignore pain forever. You'll be down with a fever again."

"I'm fine, I'll rest this afternoon. It only hurts when I'm tired."

"I don't like it, Arly."

"I don't, either, but I can't think about it now. I have to go to this meeting. It means money."

He gave me one more hard look, then gripped the door handle as if to hold back the car. I began talking in a singsong. *"Stuart, the car is moving. Let go of the door."*

He scowled and stepped back. "After Miss Peregrine, you're going to rest," he said.

I held up the Darvon bottle and rattled it. "Yeah, me and my little friends plan to stay in bed all afternoon. Want to join us?"

Stuart was not amused. From the way he was looking at me, I was glad I hadn't mentioned the Valium. He said no more, but his face showed the same fear that had been gnawing at him for months. He was afraid we had lost perspective, that we might get permanently hurt if we did not stop taking chances. But therein lay the problem. I had become addicted to the risks, more than to the Darvon or Valium. Worse, I had introduced Stuart to the same rush.

As I drove toward the city and my meeting with Miss Peregrine, yet one more meeting where I'd have to make something impossible happen, something like collecting an undeserved check, I fought back the panic of full-blown anxiety. My heart ached cruelly deep inside my chest. It felt like the unraveling of my soul. *Too much, too much,* I thought. *I'll rest after, I'll sleep. That's all I need, one good night's sleep.* But even as I talked myself down, I became stunningly aware that the drama I had started in Charleston—indeed, the drama of my entire life—was completely out of control.

Chapter Two

"Come in, come in, child," said Miss Peregrine. "You're letting my air conditioning out. I can't afford to cool the whole battery. And don't think I haven't noticed you're late again."

Miss Fanny Peregrine pulled me through the front door of her Old Charleston mansion. Gooseflesh jumped up on my skin as her fingers dug into my bare arm. I shivered. The air in the foyer was freezing compared to the sweltering heat outdoors. I hunched against the cold and swore at myself for leaving my suit jacket in the car. I'd taken it off earlier to keep from soaking it in sweat on the drive over from Mount Pleasant. The Alfa Romeo that Stuart and I had coddled along forever was much too sporty for anything as common as air conditioning. We had long ago surrendered ourselves to Charleston's killing heat. Many days, dozens of days, I longed for a cool sleek station wagon and the suburban life that was supposed to go along with it. I was thinking about suburbia as I followed Miss Peregrine's labored steps from her cold foyer to her colder parlor.

"So, how's that old cesspool, Sullivan's Island?" she croaked, then cackled at her own irreverence. As always I swallowed the bait.

"Miss Peregrine, why do you go on like that about Sullivan's? You know it's beautiful out there. You've told me over and over how you spent half your childhood roaming the island beach."

"Beautiful, my ass. Nothing but sandspurs and frogs and lizards and snakes and rats and ...."

"Stop, please. I have to live there the whole winter."

"And I don't feel one whit sorry for you. You could have found a reasonable place right here on the peninsula, and for less money. Why in God's name anyone would want to live in one of those miserable, broken-down, sway-backed beach houses is beyond me."

"But, Miss Peregrine, I ...."

"Don't 'but' me. I've known Lucretia Middleton since she was a snotnose brat playing with the pickaninnies up and down Water Street. She was reared to be a lady. Sorry to say it didn't take. Grew up to be a blood-sucking vampire bat. It's a sin for you to pay her a pocketful of rent money every month for that pile of rotten lumber she calls a house. Hell, she ought to pay you, to stay there and keep the bums out. I'll bet it doesn't have proper heat ..."

"Yes, it does, an oil furnace."

Miss Peregrine pretended not to hear. She grumbled on as if I hadn't spoken. "Lucretia's horse-thief of a father left her that cottage thirty years ago and a hell of a lot more property in town. Trouble is he didn't put aside enough money to help her keep any of it up. But that's not unusual in Charleston. People in this parsimonious town make me sick. Can't tell a rich man from a poor man so much play-acting is going on."

"Miss Peregrine, I know you think Sullivan's is shabby, but Stuart and I want to live on the water, and the only way we can afford to do that right now is to rent something during the winter months when things are cheaper."

I felt close to tears for the second time that morning. Miss Peregrine was unrelenting. "I do not think Sullivan's is shabby," she said, irritated by my lack of discernment. "I know paradise when I see it. It's the people I can't stand, all those pretentious socialites from town who own property out there. Most of them are insensitive fools who wouldn't recognize a natural treasure if they tripped over one on their way to a garden party. Sullivan's Island is nothing but a dollar mark to boneheads like that. They wouldn't hesitate a minute to cut it into quilt squares and build peach-colored high-rises up and down the beach. No one of quality owns at Sullivan's, anymore."

"I don't know, Miss Peregrine. I guess you're right, but a few nice people rent out there during the off season. Right now it's like a neighborhood instead of a summer place. That's why Stuart and I love it so."

The old woman sniffed and put her chin in the air. "You don't fool me," she said, her eyes narrowed to accusatory slits. "You like it because no Negroes live close by. You Yankees are no better than tartuffes. I am glad to report that Southerners never mince words about prejudice. But you, you'd rather live in a lowdown shack in a stinking sand pile than associate with Negroes, all the while talking your liberal talk. A hurricane ought to blow you off the island for being so two-faced."

I gave up. I did not feel strong enough to debate racism with a self-avowed racist, especially one who had the power to make me examine my own motives.

"Miss Peregrine," I said, "would you like me to make you a cup of coffee?" I was trying to change the subject. I needed her in a better mood before reminding her about my check. But I had to be careful. Miss Peregrine did not like to be patronized.

"No coffee. I'm supposed to take my medication with fruit juice. Come on. You can help me get some."

We retraced our steps through the antique-filled parlor to the massive curving staircase in the hallway. But we did not walk up. Instead, Miss Peregrine opened a closet door opposite the stairs. Inside the former closet was a four-by-four elevator. We stepped inside. I reached out to steady my feeble companion for the ride, but Miss Peregrine was in no mood to be helped. She pressed the button labeled Level Two, and we waited in silence as the elevator wheezed its way up to the kitchen.

A year of negotiating the strange floor plan in Peregrine House made it seem a little less odd for the kitchen and dining room to be located on the second floor, but the idea of an elevator in a private residence still struck me as peculiar. There was no question about Miss Peregrine needing it. Four stories and endless stairs were too much for her eighty-six-year-old legs to manage. When the elevator stopped, its automatic door opened onto the kitchen. Miss Peregrine held the door back with her walking cane and nudged me out. I refused to move without first securing her elbow.

"*Tycie, where are you?*" she shouted in her usual unladylike manner, then mumbled something under her breath about darkies and loafing. There were times in Miss Peregrine's home I felt as if I had stepped backward into another century. Had the movement accomplished so little in this place?

"Yes ma'am, Missy Peregrine, I'm coming," Tycie called out. I could hear her gimpy feet shuffling through the pantry on the far side of the kitchen. "Well, look who the wind blew in," she said when she saw me. I smiled. Tycie was my favorite person in all of downtown Charleston, the only true lady I had met in that neighborhood of mansions south of Broad Street. A real aristocrat. From what I had observed, every white person in every house claimed aristocracy, but not one had Tycie's delicate high cheek bones or narrow hands and feet. I considered her of royal lineage, perhaps the great grandchild of an African chieftain.

"Hello, Tycie, how are you?" I said.

"Fine, just fine," she answered. "Glad the good Lord done give me another day to praise Him." She rolled her eyes toward an invisible heaven beyond the ceiling.

I helped Miss Peregrine into her favorite kitchen chair, then walked across the room to hug Tycie. I would have walked the whole distance had she not met me halfway. "It's good to see you, Tycie," I said as I patted her skinny shoulder. Bits of white fuzzy hair stuck out around the edge of her blue headcloth. I wondered how old Tycie was. I wondered if she knew.

"Tycie," Miss Peregrine said, "get my jar of peach brandy out of the pantry."

Tycie stiffened. I saw the whites of her eyes. "You ought not to make me do that, Missy Peregrine. Your cousin said for you not to drink no more of that brandy."

Miss Peregrine rose from her chair and stood erect. She cracked her walking cane across the kitchen table. Tycie and I jumped. "Tycie, do what I say and get my brandy right now. And don't tell me another word Louisa Hill has uttered. She is my housekeeper, not my cousin, and I'm thinking about firing you both."

"Oh, Missy Peregrine, don't hit the stick. I'll get the brandy, I'll get it now."

Tycie hobbled to the pantry in a pitiful attempt to hurry. Her humiliation made me sad. She was old and did not deserve it. I despised seeing her mistreated, but not enough to challenge a stick-wielding tyrant who had promised me an early paycheck. I considered disappearing into the pantry along with Tycie. For all I knew, Miss Peregrine was planning to fire me, too. I glanced at her, hoping she would not catch me looking. She remained standing, eyes closed, eyelids twitching. Slowly, too slowly for someone in real control, she eased herself back into her chair. I could bear the silence no longer and began talking in the falsetto voice school teachers use with difficult little children. "Well now, maybe we'd all feel better if we had some good, cold juice."

"Get my pills," Miss Peregrine said flatly.

Thankful for something to do, I scurried to the cabinet. There were thirteen pill bottles. I knew. I'd helped open them many times before.

"No, no," Miss Peregrine said when I began collecting the bottles. "Get the plastic bag, up there." She pointed with her cane to the upper part of the cabinet. I felt around on the top shelf for a bag. When it tumbled into my hands, the sight of its contents shocked me. It was transparent and quite large, fully as large as a bread bag, and a quarter-full of candy-colored pills and capsules.

"Why did you put all these pills together?" I said. "It's bad to mix ...."

Miss Peregrine snorted. "Got tired of hurting my old arthritic fingers on those curs-ed child-proof caps," she said. "Now put those bottles back on the shelf. I'll need them later to get my prescriptions refilled."

"But I'm afraid you'll get your pills mixed up. What if you took the wrong ones?"

I was accustomed to my private collection of Darvon and Valium tablets, even my lovely Percodans, but the pill bag had a dangerous look. What could Miss Peregrine be thinking to mix her medication like that? I watched her pick out tablets and capsules and line them up on the kitchen table.

"After all these years I ought to know what medicine I'm supposed to take," she said, poking at the pills with a trembly index finger. "Besides, it's none of your damn business what I do. Is that thirteen?"

I made a quick count while she poured a glass of orange juice from the carton Tycie had left on the table. "Looks like it," I said. "Let me count again to make sure."

But she did not give me a chance. I stood by, helpless, as she scooped up the pills and tossed them into her mouth. She held the juice glass high in the air and mumbled a toast, then tilted the glass and washed down the pills with a long, gulping drink.

"What did you say, Miss Peregrine? I didn't hear you."

"Mud-in-your-eye, what else?" she said.

"Oh, mud-in-your-eye." I nodded and smiled as if this and everything else in the South made perfect sense. Then, deliberately and slowly, I pulled a chair away from the table and sat down to rest. I placed my hands in my lap and breathed evenly, concentrating on staying calm. My side ached in rhythmical cramps. I grimaced and tried to force the pain from my mind. I did not intend to let Miss Peregrine get the best of me, not this morning. There was the check to collect, the client relationship to preserve. I knew that my relationship with Miss Peregrine had to remain one-sided. Petty anxieties of mine were of no concern to her. She did not care about my feelings any more than she cared about Tycie's. We were hired help. Nothing more. We knew our places.

"Arlena," Miss Peregrine said, jerking me out of my reverie. "Look in the icebox; see if Tycie sliced any cantaloupe." I stared at her a moment before rising to follow orders. It was amazing how spoiled she was. "Well," she said, "do you intend to get my cantaloupe or not?" I stared another second, perhaps a bit too defiantly, then slid back my chair with a disagreeable scrape.

"Pour," Miss Peregrine said matter-of-factly as I set two brandy snifters on the miniature tea table next to the parlor fireplace. We had moved downstairs for our work session after she'd finished her breakfast. I'd hoped the food would improve her disposition. It had not.

"Miss Peregrine, I have to drive back to Sullivan's when I leave here, across two bridges. Maybe I shouldn't be drinking ...."

"I said *pour*," she repeated.

I poured.

"How are plans for your writing class coming along?" she said, changing the subject as capriciously as a child.

Oh no, not that, I thought. I hated talking about Southern Prep. "Well," I began stoically, "the semester doesn't start for another week yet, but if last year is any indication, I'm sure everything will go fine. I want the kids to participate in competitions again this year. Maybe we'll have another short story to place in the literary society's student contest. Last year, the story Raven FitzSimons wrote came in first."

"Dear, dear Raven. Thank the Lord she doesn't take after her mother."

I kept quiet. Raven FitzSimons's mother was Miss Peregrine's personal attorney. It would not do to start voicing opinions about fellow employees.

"Still working for that old codger, Grayson Pinckney?" she said then.

"Yes," I answered, though resentful at being quizzed.

"I approve. Grayson is quality. What about Caroline St. Cloud?"

"No, I delivered her book of reminiscences to the printer last week. I can't believe it's done. Mrs. Cloud's illness made it difficult for her to recall everything she wanted to put down."

"And the dear thing probably wanted to record nothing but the truth, unlike Grayson Pinckney, who I'm certain has lied magnificently through hundreds of pages. Well, darling, I'm glad you did not give up on dear Caroline. She is my cousin twice removed, you know. There's a great deal of therapy in writing one's memoirs."

I studied Miss Peregrine's face. Occasionally she surprised me. I wondered how much more insight she was hiding behind those cloudy blue eyes and pleated wrinkles.

"How many sets of reminiscences have you worked on here in Charleston?" she said.

"Fourteen."

"That's a prodigious amount of boredom for one young lady to survive. I cannot see how you stood it."

"I was paid to stand it, but I'm hoping to get ahead enough someday to spend more time on my own projects. I don't suppose you'd consider financing one or two?"

"I'd consider it," she said, but I knew she would not. She was too busy thinking about her own manuscript, *Tarnished Honor.*

"Have you heard anything from New York?" she added.

I detected a measure of calm easing into her voice. I hoped it was the brandy. "You mean about your manuscript?"

"No, I mean about our manuscript. Did you forget I gave you half-ownership? I had to do something, or you'd never have had the fortitude to finish the tome."

"I haven't forgotten, Miss Peregrine. It was a generous thing to do, but the story is yours. It will always be yours."

"Don't be saccharine, Arlena. And don't flatter me. You know I'm not generous. I gave you half the copyright to light a fire under your tail to do a good job. I may be old as Adam, but I'm not stupid. And don't think you can change the subject and make me forget what I was talking about. *Have you heard anything from New York?"*

"No, but it's only been four weeks. Sometimes it takes months to get rejected."

"*Tarnished Honor* won't be rejected. Too juicy, too much spice. And you wrote it far better than I expected you to. Sometimes I think you have more spunk than you let on."

This was definitely the brandy.

"Thank you, Miss Peregrine, but I've tried to warn you, Charleston gossip might not be of interest to New Yorkers."

"Oh, they'll like what's in *Tarnished Honor*. Good title, too. Half a brain could see the commercial value."

I had no intention of telling Miss Peregrine the New York facts of life. Maybe allowing her to rattle on would hasten her mellowing mood.

"Everyone likes to see rich people laid bare," she said, "especially if they're pompous asses like Old Charlestonians. That's why tourists parade through here every day in those asinine mule carriages. They think they might get a glimpse of what goes on behind the doors of a mansion. Well, *Tarnished Honor* gives them more than a glimpse."

Miss Peregrine chuckled at the delicious prospect of creating a stir with her manuscript. She held up her snifter for a refill. I poured, again. It was clear she did not want to work. I was relieved. I'd grown tired of the endless dictation. It had not been enough to slog through four hundred pages of quasi-fiction. Now she wanted memoirs. Banal, boring memoirs. Somnambulistic memoirs. But for the desperately needed paychecks, I could not have mustered the self discipline to keep going.

As for *Tarnished Honor*, once it was done, I found myself actually proud of it. The story itself was simple—Miss Peregrine's personal account of life in wicked Old Charleston. But she had been fearless in the telling of it, explicit, naming names. So explicit, in fact, that she felt compelled to keep the whole project a secret. Supposedly, she had been working on her memoirs. If pressed, I was to say she was moving along slowly because of her advancing age.

I didn't think as highly of *Tarnished Honor* as its author did, however. For example, I never had the slightest hope of seeing it in print, a fact which nagged at me somewhat. It was, I think, the closest I had ever come to guilt. Yet this changed nothing. I continued to let Miss Peregrine think there was a chance it might be published. She had no way of knowing I had lied about contacting New York—indeed, had not written the first letter. It was my professional opinion that trying to sell *Tarnished Honor* would be a waste of time. But I knew Miss Peregrine would not listen to me. She never had before. Nonetheless, I sometimes questioned my own motives about leading her on. Was I taking advantage of an old woman's vanity? Or giving her something enjoyable to do with her diminishing time on the planet? My answers were different on different days, depending on how badly I needed money. Not once did I turn down a paycheck out of guilt. Not once did I tell Miss Peregrine she was wasting her time and money. I did not know or care where she came by her grandiose ideas. All I wanted was to work, to get paid. It was necessary. How else could I earn enough money to help Stuart with the grim business of making a living?

"Miss Peregrine," I said brightly to get her mind off *Tarnished Honor.* "I brought two more chapters of your memoirs today. Would you like to take a look?" I was trying to call attention to how hard I'd been working to justify asking for an early check.

"Hell, no. I don't want to see that pabulum. The museum board only asked me to write it to oil the water for next year. They're hoping I'll give them another stack of money when their fund-raising drive rolls around."

"All right, then. I'll leave them here on the tea table. It won't hurt to wait until Thursday to go over them." I glanced at my watch. Half past eleven. I had to do something about the check. Miss Peregrine was already showing signs of drowsiness.

"Do you have changes on the pages Stuart dropped off yesterday?" I said. "I can look at them while you write my check if you want. You told me you didn't mind paying me early this time."

"Your check is already drawn," she said. "It's in the secretary drawer, over there. You'll have to wait until tomorrow to deposit it, though. I haven't told Jeannette to transfer monies to my checking account yet. But don't worry, I'll tell her this afternoon."

I tried to be unobtrusive about taking the check from the drawer. Fifteen hundred dollars. Life or death. Stuart would be ecstatic. He wouldn't like having to delay making a deposit, but he'd be grateful for any reprieve. Beans and wieners would go down easier one more night knowing there'd be cash for tomorrow.

Miss Peregrine's voice interrupted my thoughts. "I haven't proofed a page of that memoir rubbish," she said.

I heard her words, but for a moment could not process them. The trauma of asking for the check had caused a momentary lapse in brain function. I recovered quickly and walked to my usual chair. With much officiousness, I began riffling through the papers in my briefcase. "It's best to make corrections together," I said. "It won't be a burden that way. Then next time Mrs. Heyward calls from the museum to ask how you're coming along on your memoirs, you can tell her you're making progress.

"If she asks me that question one more time, I'm going to ask her if she's still sleeping with the plumber. Susannah Heyward is an ugly old bat, worse than Lucretia Middleton. I'll bet her husband hasn't kissed her twice in thirty years. Wouldn't surprise me if she were paying the plumber to sleep with her."

I snickered, then cleared my throat to cover the sound. Miss Peregrine's coarseness spared no one. I was afraid she might come after me next. "Oh, Miss Peregrine, you know Mrs. Heyward adores you, and the other board members do, too. You're the only living founder of the Charleston Fathers Museum. That's why they fawn all over you."

"Hypocrites," Miss Peregrine said. "They don't care if I live or die. It's my money they want. And why? To support their precious façade, that's why—the façade of false Southern pride that's eating this city alive." She leaned her head back on the silk-tufted settee and closed her brandied eyes. "I'm weary of false pride," she said. "I'm weary of hypocrites."

I looked at my watch and thought of Stuart pacing the porch. I hoped he'd hung onto the few dollars change from yesterday's trip to the grocery store. We had a few wieners in the refrigerator and a package of buns in the cupboard, but no gasoline at all. One more crossing of the Cooper River Bridge, and the Romeo would be on empty. I moved quietly from the chair to the settee when I realized Miss Peregrine had fallen asleep. "See you on Thursday," I whispered into her ear. "You rest now, and thanks for the check."

She opened her lizard eyes to two slits and smiled almost imperceptibly. I squeezed her gnarled hand in mine, placed an afghan across her knees, then tiptoed toward the tall French doors that opened off the parlor to the foyer. Just inside the foyer, I set down my briefcase and pulled the glass-paned doors shut as quietly as their squeaking would allow.

"What are you doing?" a voice behind me rasped. It was the voice of Louisa Hill. I jerked around and banged my arm against the grandfather clock that dominated the large foyer. Its metal workings clanged. I touched the wooden cabinet to try to stop the noise. It did not help.

"*What are you doing?*" she said louder.

"Miss Hill," I breathed. "You frightened me. I...I was just leaving. Miss Peregrine is asleep."

"Yes, well, I came all the way home from my church meeting to check on her. I hope you didn't exhaust her again."

"No, no," I said, moving closer to the front door. "I'll just come back on Thursday at my regular time. I...I'll see Miss Peregrine then."

"If she decides to cancel, I'll call you," the woman said in her noticeably northern accent. I tripped over my own feet backing out the door.

"That'll be fine..fine," I said, but she ignored my stammering and slammed the door in my face. I blinked and tried to focus on the ornate brass door-knocker that had jumped so suddenly into my line of vision. I shuddered as I stared at it, my back crawling the way it always did on encounters with Louisa Hill. Again she had turned a simple exchange of information into a hostile confrontation, only this time her offensiveness was more intense than usual. Its presence penetrated the heavy wooden door. I could almost smell it.

I shrugged my shoulders in frustration. I couldn't believe I had allowed myself to be intimidated by this woman. If she were no more than a paid housekeeper, why didn't Miss Peregrine restrain her? The polished brass kick-plate on the lower part of the door caught my eye. It gleamed in hot noonday light. I became faintly aware that my neck was starting to sweat. I leaned toward the door to rest a moment before turning to face the heat. Not a smart move. I bumped my head on the door-knocker. Why not? I thought, as the pain in my head mingled with the pain in my side. Why not deal myself one more blow? Then I remembered Miss Peregrine, imprisoned in a mansion with no one to buffer her from Louisa Hill but an aging black servant. It was a sobering thought, more than enough to curb my own self-pity. I focused again on the closed door and whispered an unheard good-bye.

Chapter Three

"Did you get the check?" Stuart yelled from the kitchen window as I angled the Romeo into the driveway. Before I could yell a retort, he burst through the back door like a football player and came running down the outside steps two and three at a time. I watched the ends of his necktie flutter in the midday breeze. It was like him to be in a hurry. Any day I expected him to charge through the same door, and tumble, fanny over teakettle, down the same steps.

"What ever happened to *hello*?" I said.

"No time. Have to get to the bank by one."

"Forget the bank. The check is postdated."

"Postdated? Fanny Peregrine gave Southern Prep fifty thousand dollars last year. I know. I was the one who drafted the request letter from the board. Why would she want to jerk you around for a measly fifteen hundred dollars?"

Stuart pulled me and my briefcase out of the Romeo and climbed in himself, then leaned into the rearview mirror and began adjusting his Windsor knot. I sailed the check through the car window, and watched with pleasure as he scrambled for it.

"Take it," I said. "I'm going upstairs to lie down. I hurt so much I can't think."

Stuart shouted after me as I made my way up the treacherous steps. "Hey, you," he said, "you on the stairs. I love your beautiful behind."

I gave him a look before slamming the door. It was good, very good, that he'd be gone for a while—I could swallow my Valium in peace.

It was after four when I began the slow agony of waking up from a drugged sleep. I had been dreaming of the foghorns, low and sorrowful, that had sounded before dawn. Stuart and I had lain in bed and listened to them—ships in the harbor warning each other mournfully of position, speed, and course. Deep in our chests we'd felt the vibrations of their enormous engines. The cottage had felt them, too. Occasionally a loose window pane would rattle, or a whole window box would bounce around in its casement.

A cold wash cloth helped me shake off the bad dreams. Two mugs of coffee gave me the courage to pack a blanket and my transcribing things into a canvas tote, and walk up the beach toward the lighthouse to find a peaceful place to work. I had been at it for two hours when Raven FitzSimons came running toward me from the point. Her long blond hair blew about wildly as she darted back and forth playing dodge with the brazen seagulls who patrolled our beach daily. She did not look like a girl who should be called Raven, not this fair-skinned, aqua-eyed beauty. But her name was not intended to suit her appearance. It was a family name, probably the surname of a grandmother or a great-grandmother. To Old Charlestonians, the naming of names was a tradition, one of many they used to darken the lines between themselves and ordinary people.

By birth and upbringing, Raven FitzSimons was an aristocrat. The trouble was she had no taste for the life, and went through her social paces reluctantly. It did not matter that her mother, Jeannette FitzSimons, had been deserted by her husband and was forced to exhaust herself daily working as a third-rate attorney for difficult clients like Fanny Peregrine; nor that the FitzSimons family had limped along five years in reduced financial circumstances caused by the divorce; nor that Raven was uninterested in high society. None of those things mattered if one lived south of Broad and had a name like FitzSimons. As long as certain appearances could be kept up—the right schools, trips, clothes and such—Raven would be included in age-old social rituals so exclusive that they required guarding by the most viciously territorial beasts in all of South Carolina, the genteel ladies and gentlemen of Old Charleston.

Raven planted herself at the edge of my blanket and dripped salt water on my legal pads. "Hi, Mrs. Prince," she said. "What were you listening to on that tape player just then? You were in another world."

"Cripes, Raven. Back off. You're ruining all my stuff."

"Sorry...didn't mean to. I came out to walk around a little. Nothing is going on in Charleston. It's deader than a nail."

I switched off my Dictaphone. It would be useless to try to work with Raven around. "So, what's new in the mountains?" I said to her after a hug. "You were in Flat Rock all summer, right?"

Raven plopped down cross-legged in the sand and put on a melancholy face. I summoned my patience.

"I spent three whole months reading psychic stuff," she said. "Spirit guides are helping me now. They're showing me how to become a better person, so I can be reincarnated at a higher level next time."

I stared at Raven. For a second I wondered if she were serious, but then I remembered her personality. Of course she was serious.

"That's nice," I said, "and did you sail or play tennis or anything else mundane?"

"Yes, I did all the correct things. Aunt Lucia made me. She's like Mother, except she still has money. I do wish she had children of her own, and would stop making me go to Flat Rock every summer. The mountains bore me to madness."

"I should think the natural setting would free up your psychic awareness," I said. I meant to be facetious. Raven missed it.

"Yes, well, it does help when you're meditating, but it's hard to keep your mind on spiritual things when you're surrounded by shallow people."

"I'll bet your mother was glad to see you when you came home."

"Are you crazy? All she does is work and complain about the zillions of sacrifices she makes for my brother and me. I hate it. Mills left for Virginia last week. He said he was going to visit his roommate's family in Charlottesville until school opens. But I know he skipped out early to get away from Mother. This is his last year at UVA, you know. He'll finish in May."

"And what about you, Rav? What will you do after this year?"

"Mother thinks I'm going to Sweet Briar, like she did. But I'm not. I think I'll go to California and study Zen or something."

I laughed. "Not before you graduate from high school, I hope. Somehow I don't think your mother is ready for Zen. Oh dear, look at those black clouds rolling in. Shouldn't you be heading home, Raven? It's getting late, and I don't like the idea of your driving the bridges after dark."

Raven pretended not to hear. I tried again. "Don't you have

to be home in time for dinner? Or supper? Or whatever it is you guys call it down here."

"Not me. Mother is working late again, same as last night and the night before and the night before that. Same as always."

"Oh, now I get it—we're feeling sorry for ourselves again. Let's fall down and be miserable. Forget sunsets and oceans and music and flowers. Forget everything. Just lie down and wallow in manure."

Raven put her hands on her hips and nodded vigorously. "Yes, I'm going straight home and do just that, and I know where to find more of it than anyone could ever want. The Tourist Carriage Company keeps a ton over on Market Street. They get it out of those stupid leather diapers the carriage mules wear. Stinks about as bad as my mood."

"Go home," I said. "Write a smelly poem for writing class next week. You sound inspired."

"I'm going, I'm going," she said, then leaned down and brushed sand from her khaki shorts. "You may as well know now, though, I'm coming back tomorrow. I hate the thought of spending a single minute at home."

"It's a deal," I said, struggling to a standing position and making a show of gathering my things in my arms to try to hurry her up. She gave me a quick hug before sprinting toward the public path to the street.

I shivered as I watched her run in the direction of the dunes. It was cooler now than when I had first come on the beach, and too dark for safety. Already I could make out the lighthouse beam on the north end of the island. It crawled majestically across rooftops and sand. It swept over the ocean, touching and lighting the double row of rock jetties that formed the ships' lane to the harbor. The beach would be dark tonight except for the measured circling of the beam. Banks of purple clouds had already obscured the moon. I looked up at their billowing duskiness as I hurried up the beach to beat the night. Only once did I turn to glance at Raven as she ran in the opposite direction through the gathering gloom. Her youthful gait made me remember my own fatigue. It had been a difficult day. I felt old and tired, despite my long afternoon nap. Old and tired and paranoid. More cruel inroads had eaten their way into my already wormy self-confidence. I suspected that everyone around me knew I was slowly caving in.

As I trudged toward the cottage alone, half frightened of the deepening dusk, a familiar voice whispered to me from the recesses of my mind. It was a voice I knew well, one from my childhood that still haunted me. All my life I had resisted it, though sometimes it roared in my head: *I am the voice of self doubt, Arlena. I have come to devour you. Living on a beach and writing, indeed. Using alcohol and drugs. Five and six drinks a day, eight and ten pain tablets. Stuart has no idea how bad it is. He does not see.*

Stuart stepped into the twilight of the porch with a drink in each hand. "A perfect spritzer for the lady," he said, bowing before my chair. "Want to take a moonlight stroll?"

"You're such an optimist, Stu. The moon hasn't been out all week. Please, just sit here with me and relax. I'm exhausted from this morning—all that worry about the check, then dealing with Miss Peregrine. She started out by calling Sullivan's a cesspool the second I walked through the door."

"More like Charleston is the cesspool," he said. "Have you walked by one of those carriage mules lately? They don't smell like roses."

"Believe me, I know. Miss Peregrine complains about them all the time, but then she complains about everything, especially what goes on out here on Sullivan's. She's always grumbling about her blue-blooded neighbors milking this place for rent money every summer. And she despises the younger people who've inherited property out here—says they don't have the foresight to protect the natural environment. They'd sell loggerhead eggs for the hope of a dollar bill."

"Well, precious-darling, the two of us have done worse than that for the hope of fifty cents."

"Can't you ever be serious?" I said. "Miss Peregrine doesn't care about money. She has a ton of it. And she doesn't care about real estate. It's the environment she worries about, the abiding value of nature. And all she can see in every direction is greedy adult children and grandchildren of her peers taking advantage of things they didn't earn. She's convinced they're too stupid to realize that someone, sometime, is going to have to take the responsibility of preserving South Carolina's coastline, particularly the beach and marsh areas. Property owners on Sullivan's don't take care of their cottages, much less the beach. Miss Peregrine gripes about them constantly."

"And what difference does it make?" Stuart said. "Let's say she's right—and for the record, I think she is. Too many people play slum landlord out here. But it wouldn't matter if they let every house rot where it stands. The bottom line wouldn't change a peso. Believe me, these people know what they're doing. It's the land that's valuable, not these termite-infested cottages. And it'll command even more attention when some well-heeled developer comes out here and starts poking around. We'll have high-rise heaven for sure then."

"Sometimes I wonder about us, Stuart. We talk, but we don't *talk*. I spend ten minutes explaining to you that Miss Peregrine rejects the idea of money being the only important thing, and you miss the point entirely. That's exactly what's she's afraid of, owners selling out and letting developers rape the island. Don't forget, families who own cottages out here have houses in town, as well. Big houses they've inherited and can barely afford to maintain. Some of them have lived in those mausoleums south of Broad three, four, sometimes five generations. And it doesn't matter if they're dead broke, they're intent on keeping up appearances. Miss Peregrine is convinced they'd do anything to protect their interests downtown, sell Sullivan's out to the Philistines themselves, to New *Yorkers*, for heaven's sake."

"Yeah," Stuart said in a yawn. "I know all about that crowd. It's the same clique I put up with at Southern Prep, that revered academic institution known affectionately in the area as The-South-Is-Gonna-Rise-Again Academy. A bunch of fancy names on the roll, but the board has to hire an inexperienced outsider like me to write their tiddledywink fund-raising brochures. Money, or lack thereof, is forevermore the problem with these people. Every year, the same old questions: Will there be enough dough to open the doors of the school one more term? To buy athletic equipment? To buy books?"

"Exactly," I said. "Now bring me another spritzer, please. I need to get some sleep tonight. Mr. Pinckney and his memoirs will come early in the morning. He likes me in his office at nine sharp."

"Honored to oblige, ma'am," Stuart said in his worst Southern drawl, "but wouldn't ya'll rather have a mint julep?"

"No, thanks, I'll save it for tomorrow. Mr. Pinckney will probably serve me three or four, all before noon."

Terry Ward
Tucker

Chapter Four

"Send her up," Grayson Pinckney bellowed through his intercom when the receptionist announced my arrival. *"I've grown faint from the anticipation of seeing her."*

"Is he always like that?" I asked when she clicked off her machine. "Always," she said. "Never serious."

"Maybe he's tired of being serious after practicing law half a century."

The receptionist pursed her lipstick lips and looked disgusted. "Must've gotten tired of it a long time ago. I've been here ten years, and he was exactly the same way the first day I walked in this office. You'd better hustle. He'll be hollering your name all over the building on the P.A. system next."

I hurried toward the stairs and ran up without thinking what it would do to my colicky side. "Come in, come in, you beautiful rose," Mr. Pinckney said, his deep bass rolling through the secretary's office and down the narrow hallway. "I've been waiting for you, pining for you. Ask Lillian there if you don't believe me."

I glanced at the bespectacled woman, who looked up from her computer monitor long enough to wink. Without slowing down, I walked into Mr. Pinckney's office, around his desk, and gave him a huge hug. He liked that kind of thing, and I made certain he got what he liked. Mr. Pinckney paid me well each month. I was glad he was not the false-fronted, financially-strapped type Miss Peregrine complained about continually, although sometimes it was difficult to tell among Old Charlestonians. Miss Peregrine had said she approved of Grayson Pinckney, that he was quality. It was the single nonderisive comment I had ever heard her make about any of her neighbors south of Broad.

In August Mr. Pinckney had tipped me five new one-hundred-dollar bills, which I had concealed guiltily from Stuart. It was the only way I could pay for all my pills and doctor visits. I couldn't tell Stuart I was seeing three different doctors and collecting pain prescriptions from all three. He had seen me through a terrible infection in my side over the winter. I didn't want him to have to go through worse. Dear sweet unsuspecting Stuart. He was a careful, observant man who knew almost every detail of my life. But I was cunning about my pills. Not even Stuart could catch everything.

"Am I still your favorite gentleman client?" Mr. Pinckney said.

I coughed. He had hugged me too hard. "Yes, sir, still my favorite, but I think you should know, my only other client right now is female—Miss Fanny Peregrine."

Grayson Pinckney laughed and struck his desk with his palm. "Next you'll be recording the ghoulish memoirs of one Louisa Hill, Fanny's ill-bred housekeeper. She's a worse biddy than Fanny, I'm told. I understand that's what happens to women when they live too long without male attention."

He took out his handkerchief, wiped laughter tears out of his eyes, and motioned me toward a chair. "Sit," he said, clearing his throat. And I knew all talk of ridiculous old ladies was dismissed from our conversation.

"Get out your recording machine, girl," he said. "Today I feel like talking about the seashore—boyhood trips and such. I'll tell you a few things about handline fishing and slopping through pluffmud. My mother used to take me to Bluffton two weeks out of every summer to visit our poor relations. That's where I learned about females and sex, but we won't put that part in. Wouldn't want to upset Miss Roz."

"That would be a mistake," I said. "She might leave you to take care of Pinckney House alone. Then you'd be out the best wife in Charleston."

"Not such a joke as you might think, my pretty, but it wouldn't be just housekeeping she'd leave me with. That daughter of ours is thirty-nine years old, married eighteen years, and her good-for-nothing husband has never had a job I didn't hand him on a platter. Ignorant fool still takes up space right here in this building, not to mention that he and Caroline have lived with us at Pinckney House since the day they were married."

This was not the first time Mr. Pinckney had told me about his daughter and son-in-law. He complained about them at every opportunity. Jonathan Priolieu, the disappointing son-in-law. Margaret Caroline Ashley Pinckney Priolieu, the disobedient daughter. She was the sort of adult offspring Miss Peregrine enjoyed lambasting, the not-too-bright variety whose only ambition in life was to stay in good graces with moneyed parents. Miss Peregrine raked Caroline's type unmercifully in *Tarnished Honor,* exposing several generations of the rotting society that had spawned her.

Mr. Pinckney forgot between meetings he'd already told me certain things. Or maybe he did not forget. Maybe he was grateful to have someone listen to him, even if he had to pay for the courtesy. Mr. Pinckney was the best client I'd ever had as far as process was concerned. He was very good at dictating and a natural raconteur. Unlike Miss Peregrine, who spouted gore and gall, Mr. Pinckney told lighthearted, whimsical stories about his boyhood days in the gigantic residence on South Battery Street known as Pinckney House. The house still stands on High Battery of Charleston's broad and historic harbor. It presides over White Point Garden and South Battery Street, four doors down from the mansion of Fanny Peregrine, midpoint in the surprisingly long row of magnificent homes fronting South Battery.

Early in our relationship I offended Mr. Pinckney about Pinckney House. Nine times I called it "Pink" House in the first chapter of his reminiscences. He was incensed that anyone could be so stupid. He scratched out all the "Pinks" and scrawled "Pinckney" in large letters at the top of every page. I did not have the courage to tell him the problem was with his Charleston accent, not my spelling. I would have sworn he'd been saying "Pink" all along. Miss Peregrine hooted when I told her about it. "Vainglorious old fool," she said. "Thinks it's his family name that makes him a man of respect, a common affliction among our kind, child. But let me assure you, Grayson Pinckney needn't worry about his good name. In this town he's known as a man of pure character, and that wouldn't change if his name were Schwartz.

"*Enough,*" Mr. Pinckney said at twelve sharp. "Shut off your talking machine and let's have a drink." He turned to the credenza behind his desk, which I knew from other sessions was stocked with expensive liquors. "Hope you're not too much of a sissy to drink your whiskey straight up."

"I shouldn't be drinking at all, sir. Don't you want me to get this tape transcribed today?"

"It's noon already. I think you should follow my example and take the rest of the day off. Work can continue without me for a change. Let those young bucks downstairs wrestle with legal matters. As for you, sweet rose, I want you to be my guest at Pinckney House for two o'clock dinner. Miss Roz will be delighted to have you."

I watched Mr. Pinckney pour whiskey into two shot glasses. One he handed to me, the other he tossed down. I took a burning sip and tried to keep from shuddering. Mr. Pinckney poured himself another. From college days through eight years of career life, I had yet to come across a people who knew how to drink with the same relish and style as highborn Charlestonians. It was a study in socially accepted excess.

Dinner at Pinckney House. I'd have to call Stuart and arrange a later pickup. "Thank you, Mr. Pinckney, but I have a few errands to run before I can break for lunch. Would you like me to come back here when I finish, or go straight to South Battery?"

"Here, at half past one. That'll give us time to take a turn around White Point. I understand there's a regatta in the harbor today. Maybe we can catch the finish."

I turned up my shot glass for a last try at swallowing fire. Definitely an acquired taste, like the entire Southern way of life.

"I'd better run if you want me back that early. Don't work too hard while I'm gone."

Mr. Pinckney jumped to his feet and rushed around his desk. I knew his purpose. "See you in an hour," he said, and took great advantage of the opportunity to kiss a young woman on the cheek. I submitted with a minimum of grace. I tried my best, but Grayson Pinckney made it impossible for me to leave in a businesslike manner. Much blocking and handshaking helped. Mr. Pinckney pretended he didn't like this. But I knew he did. It was my duty to maintain propriety. He expected it, almost as much as he expected to have the pleasure of undermining my efforts. It was an unspoken agreement.

I waited for the elevator door to slide shut, then took a small bottle of Valium from my skirt pocket. My plan to spend the afternoon working had been sabotaged. What harm could a few pills do now? I swallowed two tablets, stepped off the elevator at the basement level, and started toward the water fountain at the far end of the hall. My stomach turned a little as I walked. The bitterness of the Valium made me feel nauseous. I hurried faster toward the end of the corridor where the water cooler hummed peacefully against the wall. I leaned into it and drank a long minute before realizing someone was watching me.

Oh my God, it's that idiot, Jonathan Priolieu. No wonder Mr. Pinckney hates him.

"Hello, Mr. Priolieu," I said casually, trying to cover my surprise. "Thought I'd get a drink before going out in the heat."

"Call me Jonathan, and why bother leaving just yet? The building is pleasant on these lower levels, cool as vanilla ice cream. Why don't you come visit with me a while, in my office."

He pointed toward his door, but made no move to step aside. I did not have to wonder why his office was on the farthest back hall. Mr. Pinckney despised him. "I'm sorry, Mr. Priolieu, I'd really like to, but I'm in an awful hurry. Maybe another time."

"Maybe," he said. "Then again, maybe not. Maybe I want to talk to you now."

I stepped back and made contact with the wall. My breath caught in my throat.

"Mr. Priolieu, I have to go," I said.

"Jonathan," he whispered. "Say it. I want to hear you say my name."

"Jonathan," I said without moving.

"Good. Say it again."

"Jon—athan." My voice cracked.

He placed both palms flat on the wall, one on each side of my head, then nuzzled my cheek and ear. His breath reeked of bourbon. The feted smell settled into my stomach, making my nausea worse. "Please, I have to work here," I said. "Mr. Pinckney is my boss."

"Don't worry," Priolieu mumbled in his sickening accent. I smelled his breath again. "It's always done in Charleston. The Holy City isn't nearly as holy as everyone pretends. And for all you know, a well-placed word from me to Miss Roz might do you more harm than if you spent a little time in my office. If you don't be nice to me, I might tell her how fond the old man is of his solicitous little ghostwriter. She'd make him get rid of you in a second."

"Please, I can't, I'm sick."

"Don't fret yourself. I'm a patient man. We'll work this out eventually." He kissed me hard on the mouth, grinding my shoulder blades into the wall, then stepped aside and swept out his right arm in a false gesture of politeness. At that moment, if I'd had a gun in my pocket, Jonathan Priolieu would have been a dead man.

Chapter Five

A blast of hot air burned my face. It invaded my lungs as it rushed
into Grayson Pinckney's office building through the polished walnut door off Broad Street. The door had stuck when I first tried to
escape, like a tightly vacuumed refrigerator door on a hot day.
But my anger at Jonathan Priolieu gave me strength. I tugged at
the brass pulls until the door sprang open with a loud sucking
sound. Gauzy heat flooded the reception area, reminding me piti-
lessly I was still in sultry Charleston.

A short walk down Broad Street to the corner of Meeting
brought me in sight of the Mills House Hotel. It was *my* hotel,
refuge from the burning sidewalks and unbreathable midday air
of a Southern city laboring through early autumn. The Mills House
and its grandeur made me glad Stuart and I had moved to Charleston. Within the sanctuary of its lobby, I forgot the city's cruelty to
outsiders and remembered her exquisite beauty, the heartbreaking
physical beauty of symmetry and color, order and light, line and
grace. Each time I entered the hotel, I felt with renewed force the
understated emotion of lowcountry ambiance. For me the feeling
was almost erotic, though I knew the Southern fullness of it could
never be wholly experienced by a woman whose maiden name
was Giello.

I planned my agenda as I approached the hotel: call Stuart
from the lobby pay-phone, tell him I'd ride the bus home later,
grab a few minutes of rest in the lounge area of the ladies' room.
A good plan. The Valium would have a chance to calm the nervousness brought on by Jonathan Priolieu.

As my heels clicked in rhythm on the sidewalk, I shielded my
eyes from the midday glare. Even with sunglasses, my retinas
ached. On clear days brilliant beams of light poured down on

Charleston. Light bounced back and forth flamboyantly between high buff walls of historically correct buildings. With burning intensity the unfiltered light baptized common chimney pots on rooftops and shone luminously on spires of great churches like St. Philips and St. Michaels. No spare beauty, this. It was generous and profuse, far too extravagant for the needs of one small city.

Ten long strides across the black and white marble squares of the Mills House lobby took me to a wide, portrait-lined hallway. At one end was the opening to the Grand Bar, at the other, a series of carved doorways to restrooms and small parlors. I was moving toward the restrooms when an unfamiliar voiced hailed me.

"Miss Prince, Miss Prince," a man called out.

I whirled around in a huff, not bothering to cover my irritation at being discovered in my only secure hiding place in downtown Charleston.

"Miss Prince," Dr. Croomer Calhoun said again as he stepped through the gilt-edged doors flanking the golden salon. I saw the luxurious bar shining at his back, all brass and crystal and mirrors. It looked inviting. For a moment, the tanned and handsome Croomer Calhoun looked inviting, like a gentleman of privilege and breeding. But despite his charm, I could not warm to him the way I could to Grayson Pinckney.

I knew that at this time of day Calhoun should be drinking martinis at the Carolina Yacht Club on East Bay, or wearing tennis whites on the courts of the Charleston Country Club. My confusion disappeared when a leggy girl occupying one of the banquettes in the distant bar waved and smiled a knowing little smile. Ah, now we know what Dr. Calhoun does with his Wednesday afternoons, and the lady in question is too drunk to care about discovery. I had the feeling I should have already been aware of Calhoun's indiscretions. He did not seem concerned about my seeing him in a compromising position with a woman a third his age. With him, philandering was obviously nothing new. Perhaps his wife no longer cared. Perhaps she gave tacit approval as long as he kept his women away from people who mattered socially.

"Excuse me, Miss Prince," Calhoun said, his words echoing in the uncarpeted hallway. "I've been wanting to speak to you about Miss Peregrine. As a matter of fact, I was going to call you this evening, but here you are in the flesh, and looking as lovely as ever, might I add. You're positively stunning in white."

"It's *Mrs.* Prince," I said, ice on my words, "but you may call me Arlena if you like." I looked him straight in his blue patrician eyes, then enjoyed it immensely when he faltered at my offer to shake his hand. He was accustomed to kissing women, not shaking hands with them. But he would not be kissing me.

There was a difference in how I had to deal with Croomer Calhoun and Jonathan Priolieu. Both disgusted me equally, but I had to treat Priolieu with restraint. His position in the Pinckney family gave him power. I could not insult him, nor expose him to Mr. Pinckney, not if I valued my job. But of Calhoun I had no fear. There was nothing he could do to hurt me. In fact, I was certain that days, perhaps weeks, went by without his even thinking of me. And when he did, I suspected I flitted in and out of his consciousness like some irritating insect with no purpose in life but to stir up venomous creatures like Louisa Hill and Jeannette FitzSimons. These were the women who hounded Calhoun endlessly about every concern of Miss Peregrine's. His role as her physician made him a perfect target. Out of respect for Miss Peregrine's age and social standing, he ministered to her by way of house calls. She was the only patient ever to receive such attention in all his thirty years of practice. He also visited her socially at fitting intervals.

Dr. Croomer Calhoun, Louisa Hill, Jeannette FitzSimons. These were the three who surrounded Fanny Peregrine, her house of scalene personalities—one male swimming alone against a tidal wave of unpredictable emotion from two frustrated females who fluttered about Miss Peregrine like harpies. If Calhoun wanted to continue attending Miss Peregrine, and collecting those fat payments for his services, he had to fend off Louisa and Jeannette. He understood this. What he could not fathom was why a new harpy had to appear out of nowhere, before his very eyes. One in the disturbing form of an insolent northern female who demanded he shake her hand for God's sake, a lowborn woman who knew instinctively that he had no power whatsoever. A woman whose foreign name made him think disturbingly and lustfully of prostitutes and princesses, but whose eyes froze his blood with icy stares, and whose body language threatened to emasculate him if he took one step too close. A woman whose name was Arlena Prince.

Miss Peregrine valued the members of her entourage. She said they were like her children, no matter how unattractive. Soon after I began working at Peregrine House, the "children" sent out small and large signals to let me know I was unwelcome. I was made to feel like an interloper with impure motives. As weeks went by, I recognized the elements of a campaign. There were open snubs from Louisa Hill, snide phone calls from Dr. Calhoun, difficulties with my paychecks perpetrated by Jeannette FitzSimons. But Miss Peregrine protected me. I did not deceive myself into believing she was noble enough to look after me because she was bighearted. I knew she did it to maintain her own independence. But the queen had to be judicious with her favors if she did not want to estrange the members of her court, particularly not the self-proclaimed prince of infidelity now standing before me in the entrance to the Mills House Grand Bar. He was, after all, the most respected physician in all of Old Charleston, the revered Dr. Croomer Calhoun.

"It's about our Miss Peregrine," he said again, his tone smooth as oil. I braced myself for a confrontation. He continued. "I want to know why you keep pushing her to continue those mindless reminiscences? Have you no mercy? Don't you think the poor woman is too old to be exhausting herself?"

I started to answer. Calhoun bared his teeth in a false smile and stopped me. He said, "I'm sure the board members of Charleston Fathers Museum had no idea how draining this project was going to be. If they had, they'd never have asked Fanny to embark upon such a thing, not at her age. Jeannette and Louisa are beside themselves. They're worried sick that she's working too hard and might make herself ill. We are all of the opinion, Miss Prince—excuse me, *Mrs.* Prince—that you don't understand the situation. Frankly, I think you're ignoring the seriousness of Fanny's physical condition."

"Is that so?" I said. "And what else do you think?"

"Oh, please don't be offended. Surely you realize we all love Fanny. And now that she's old and feeble, we simply cannot allow anyone to take advantage of her. I'm afraid she's been showing signs of Alzheimer's these last months. It seems to be getting worse. Every time I visit Peregrine House, Louisa and Jeannette have a different tale to tell about her forgetfulness. Do you think, considering her health, that it's wise to keep after her to go on with this work?"

Croomer Calhoun made me sick with his veiled questions that

were actually demands. *Who does he think he is?* I thought. *He's not talking to some Southern belle trained to obey men. A well-dressed dandy with lace on his drawers will never get away with ordering me around, not with two Valium tablets and an ounce of whiskey in my gut.*

"I don't mean to be rude, Dr. Calhoun," I said, "but I find it distasteful to discuss Miss Peregrine's condition behind her back. Besides, she is my employer—not Jeannette FitzSimons, not Louisa Hill, and certainly not you. Until she tells me she no longer needs my services, I will continue to work for her. And by the way, I take direction from Miss Peregrine only, no one else, so you can fold your suggestions ten different ways and stick them where the moon doesn't shine."

I wished I had not said it. Oh, how I wished I had not. But it was too late. Croomer Calhoun's aristocratic jaw dropped open. I flashed my eyes at him one more time, then turned and stomped away. He did not move, just stood frozen in the hallway of the beautiful Mills House Hotel.

Chapter Six

"Come into the inner sanctum, you sweet summer rose," Grayson Pinckney thundered when I appeared in the doorway of his private office. I had returned to go to two o'clock dinner. "If I may gaze upon your blushing cheeks and florid lips one trembling moment, I will gladly spend the rest of my life a thorn upon your slender stem."

"Well, kind sir," I said with a simper, "I cannot be a summer rose, for summer has fled. The stain upon my cheek is not eternal youth, but a burn from the Carolina sun. I am but mortal woman, you see—weak and susceptible. I beg you not to tease me unless you wish to break my heart."

"Break your heart? No, no, sweet lady. I'd fall on my own sword first." He then administered the ritual kiss, this time upon my hand.

"But Mr. Pinckney, it's been rumored you've made a career of breaking hearts. Some say hoards of weeping women are scattered over every state and several foreign countries, pining away their lives just for you."

"It isn't true. You're the only woman I've ever loved, except for my good wife, Miss Roz. I'd give my right arm for the privilege of running away with you."

"I believe you, but may we go to two o'clock dinner first? I understand they put out quite a spread over at Pinckney House."

"Splendid idea. Lillian, tell Caesar to bring the car around. We've decided to go tooling."

Mr. Pinckney lifted his gold-knobbed walking cane from the umbrella rack and hooked it over his left arm. Then, with his right hand at my elbow, he guided me expertly toward the hallway. I felt I was in the presence of an endangered species when I spent time with Grayson Pinckney. He was a good man, warm and kind to the core of his being. Sometimes I longed to fall weeping on his shoulder and tell him all my problems. Instead, I walked before him through Lillian's office and played the role of lady. When we stepped into the corridor, several young attorneys fell into two straight lines on either side of the hallway. They were a double row of tin soldiers. Mr. Pinckney nodded and called each by name. They responded in turn. I walked ahead and did not acknowledge the young men. Being escorted by Grayson Pinckney had its benefits.

Mr. Pinckney's patter may make one think he'd be a problem for a woman in a close place like an elevator. Not true. He said nothing; I said nothing. The elevator became a neutral space that could not be violated by a gentleman of Mr. Pinckney's code of honor. I had been learning about that code for several months, and the more I learned, the more I admired the man who lived it.

As we rode to the ground floor, I studied Mr. Pinckney's profile. The chiseled definition of his features showed not the faintest hint of jowliness so common among older men, and his white wavy hair made age a friend instead of an enemy. I thought Mr. Pinckney's hair beautiful in contrast to the deep tan of his face and neck. He wore a navy-blue blazer, gray trousers, and a starched oxford shirt. The whiteness of the shirt made his skin a warm bronze color that was repeated subtlety in the burnished gold of his Citadel college ring. But best of all was his posture. He stood tall and erect, chin tilted upward at the slightest angle. As I looked at him, I stood a little taller myself. There was much to learn about presence and carriage from a man like Grayson Pinckney.

When the elevator stopped, Mr. Pinckney checked his pocket watch and gave me a wink. Neutral space had been cleared. He was back in control. "Wonderful, just enough time for a stroll around the battery. Are you game?"

"Yes, sir," I said, smiling.

We walked to the back door of the office building where we met Caesar, Mr. Pinckney's black chauffeur of the last forty-five years. Caesar pushed the office door open to an awning-shaded parking area where a silver Cadillac sat idling. "Good morning, my man," Mr. Pinckney said and slapped Caesar on the back.

"Morning to you, too, sir," Caesar responded as he helped me into the car. I slid across the cool softness of cream-colored leather seats. The air conditioner was on high, a luxury unheard of in the Alfa Romeo.

"To the battery, Julius Caesar," Mr. Pinckney commanded, his words a military bark. In less than a minute the long car traversed the length of Broad Street and stopped perpendicular to East Bay. The Exchange Building stood directly in front of us.

"Fourteen of my Pinckney relatives were held prisoner in that old building during the American Revolution," Mr. Pinckney intoned solemnly as Caesar negotiated the corner of Broad and East Bay. "One was my great-great-great-great-grandfather. The city was occupied by those greedy-assed Redcoats at the time."

"Really? As I recall, my own great-great-great-great-grandfather was still picking olives in Sicily." Mr. Pinckney looked at me sideways, but decided against making inquiries into my parentage. He continued his speech.

"In the next century a passel of Yankees came south to stay with us a while. The weasels threw a different set of my relatives into the clink. Now that I think of it, I must be the only Pinckney in three hundred years not to insult some foreign contingent and go to jail."

"You call Yankees foreigners?" A smile twitched at my lips.

"Or worse," he said. I heard Caesar chuckle.

"Well, you're still young. Maybe you'll find a reason yet to go to jail for honor."

Mr. Pinckney slapped his knee in agreement, then leaned forward and began pointing out landmarks. From the pride in his voice you would have thought everything belonged solely to him. Rainbow Row, Adgers Wharf, Tradd Street, the Carolina Yacht Club. All reminded him of some anecdote or relative. All reaffirmed his heritage.

We turned right on South Battery and cruised to the corner of King. There we observed the grandeur of Pinckney House from the angle of tourists and understood why they flocked to see it. Four mansions down stood Peregrine House. The sight of it triggered some primitive response in my brain. I saw in a frightening vision the people close to Miss Peregrine: Louisa Hill, Jeannette FitzSimons, Dr. Croomer Calhoun. I imagined them riding monster horses around and around on a black carrousel that played music out of tune. The skin on my arms prickled. I jumped when Mr. Pinckney's voice vibrated through the Cadillac directing Caesar where to park. Already I knew that every act in Charleston had a proper execution. I was about to be instructed in the proper way to stroll High Battery.

It was a familiar walk to Grayson Pinckney. A daily walk. His lungs thrived on the rich sea air, his eyes and heart on the unchanging view. White sailboats dotted the harbor, lining up to race. Mr. Pinckney steered me to the corner railing of the sea wall to catch a better view. I put up a hand to shade my eyes from the sun. Hundreds of glittering points and needles reflected off every wave. The effect was dazzling, like Charleston herself, and every bit as severe and unyielding.

I looked at Mr. Pinckney and wondered how he withstood the glare. He stared straight ahead resolutely through unblinking eyes. Small beads of perspiration gathered on his forehead. It was a blistering time of day in the city. I was glad for the ocean breeze that whipped our hair and clothing. It tempered the heat and softened the fishy odors of the harbor. Compared to the broiling streets of the business district, High Battery was the most pleasant place in Charleston.

"Can you see Sullivan's Island?" Mr. Pinckney said. I strained my eyes but could see nothing. He pointed. "There, beyond Morris Island and Fort Sumter. Look for the lighthouse."

"Yes, yes," I said, happy to have spotted something, anything.

"I've spent many a summer day on that old island," Mr. Pinckney said. "When I was a boy, my family used to take the ferry to Mount Pleasant—*The Commodious and Pleasant Sappho.* We'd get off at the public docks, then take the trolley out to the beach. It went as far as the Isle of Palms, but Mother didn't like going over Breach Inlet on a tressel. Too rickety. Those were the days when there weren't so damn many bridges and automobiles."

I did not interrupt Mr. Pinckney. Sometimes at odd moments like this he'd give me nuggets to liven up his memoirs that he could not recall in the more constrained setting of his office. I made mental notes.

After a pause, he addressed another subject: "Fanny Peregrine called me yesterday," he said. I thought I detected a note of purpose in his voice. "She wanted to make an appointment, at my office, of all things. I can't imagine why. She knows I'd come to see her at Peregrine House any time she wanted. I even offered to send Caesar around to pick her up and bring her to Pinckney Building, but she said you'd be driving her. Strange—Fanny seldom calls me, except to twist my arm about contributing to some charity. I wonder what the old eagle has on her mind."

"I don't know," I said. "She hasn't asked me to drive her anywhere."

Mr. Pinckney was visibly shocked. His face grew red. For a second I thought he was angry. Then I realized he was embarrassed at having betrayed a confidence. He began stammering. "I, I thought...well, naturally I thought if you'd been engaged to drive her to my office, you would know she had an appointment. She *said* you were driving her. Damnation, I never should have mentioned it at all."

"Don't worry, Mr. Pinckney. If she asks me, I'll just say yes and let it go at that. I won't say another word—promise."

The ethically upright Grayson Lockwood Pinckney, IV, did not feel better. He winced and moaned as if in physical pain, then suggested we might create less trouble for ourselves if we went quietly along to dinner. And though neither of us ever brought up the conversation again, I thought it a glorious thing to have a man like Grayson Pinckney in my debt.

Stepping into Pinckney House was like stepping into an abode of royalty. Peter opened the door. Peter opened the door for everyone who had reason to visit the Pinckneys. He had done so for three generations. When Peter appeared before us in all his black shining beauty, Mr. Pinckney gathered himself up to his full height, stood at attention, and clicked his heels.

"Mrs. Prince, meet Peter. He is the same Peter who welcomed Miss Roz and me home after our month-long honeymoon in Europe forty-five years ago. Today he welcomes you."

"I'm honored," I said.

Peter bowed slightly, while I resisted the impulse to try to shake his hand. "Good evening, missy...Mr. Pinckney," he said with an easy-going grin, and I knew from his demeanor he'd been introduced in the same manner a thousand times before.

Miss Roz came floating in. I was surprised by her appearance. Too tall, too big, too plainly dressed. She should have come off as unattractive, even homely. But she did not. She, like Mr. Pinckney, had a special quality that made itself apparent immediately. She was handsome if not beautiful, and appeared to be completely unaware she was two inches taller than her husband.

"You must be Arlena," she cooed. "Grayson has told me so much about you. Hurry, come inside—get out of that dreadful heat. Peter, take her jacket and suitcase, please. Put them in the guest closet. Grayson, darling, will you join Arlena and me in the parlor? We ladies do so enjoy a bit of masculine conversation."

"Of course, dearest, but let's not bore the girl. She came here to be refreshed, not bored. And for heaven's sake don't ask who her people are. They don't go into that kind of thing where she comes from. She'll think we've never been out of the county."

"Oh, Grayson, everyone knows Charlestonians still travel. It's those hillbillies from the upcountry who never leave the farm. They're so backward. Why, my friend Ellen Ruth Gervais told me she heard that some of them who live north of Columbia—up around York and Lancaster—still have those dreadful parties called pig-pickings. I was absolutely mortified. Pig-pickings, indeed...and going on in our fair state. Sometimes I think those of us who live in Charleston are the only souls left in South Carolina still holding up the banner of culture."

"There, there, Roz," Mr. Pinckney said. "Let's not dwell on unpleasant things. Mrs. Prince didn't come here for that, either."

"Perhaps she came to have a drink," a voice interjected from the hallway. "May I pour you something, Mrs. Prince?" I flinched. The voice belonged to Jonathan Priolieu.

"A Perrier would be nice if it isn't too much trouble," I said through a strangely taut throat. The tension of the day was closing in at an inopportune time. Relax, I thought. These people are trying to be kind. Ignore Priolieu and relax.

"Hell no, don't give her any of that bottled branch water," Mr. Pinckney said. "Make her a gin and tonic. She needs to loosen up and enjoy herself. This gal works like a man, Miss Roz. True grit, she has."

"I'm sure, dear...true grit. Now then, I suggest we all slip out to the piazza. The harbor breeze is delightful out there, Arlena, even in the heat of the day. And I do want you to see the garden. It's on the museum tour of historical homes. We're so very proud of it. Old Mrs. Pinckney, Grayson's mother, designed it forever ago. Grayson was still a yard child in nappies, I should think."

Miss Roz took my arm and walked me to a white wicker paradise on the harbor side of the house. Fluted columns a foot in diameter stood at intervals along the three open sides of the piazza. The columns were stark white, whiter than the fleecy clouds floating in the sky above. Gigantic hanging baskets of pink and white impatiens swung gently near each column. There was no railing. The porch was bordered instead by pots and pots of geraniums and forest ferns. They were arranged on a low terrace of graduated shelves. More pots sat in corners, beside chairs, and on either side of the beveled glass doors that opened off the parlor. They marched up and down porch steps and lined brick walkways through the garden. They hung prettily from low branches of trees in the side yard. Never had I seen so many blossoming plants in September.

"Too bad the garden isn't at its best," Miss Roz said. "That's why I keep all these potted ladies around this time of year. You'll have to come back in the spring to see the azaleas."

I nodded, mouth open, eyes wide, trying to look in every direction at once. The flowers, the harbor, the garden, the colonnades, the furniture. Miss Roz smiled. She was pleased by my reaction to this fantasy world, though to her it was not a fantasy. To her it was simply home.

My drink came via Jonathan Priolieu. Then Miss Roz suggested we sit down and chat. As we were arranging ourselves in cushioned wicker chairs, Caroline Pinckney Priolieu arrived. She fluttered onto the piazza like a lovely brainless butterfly. Miss Roz introduced me to her, whereupon I spent several hopeless moments trying to express how much I had enjoyed having her son, Jon Priolieu Jr., in my writing class the previous year. She did not know what I was talking about, and the whole explanation got so confused, Mr. Pinckney lost patience and began swearing.

"Caroline," Mrs. Pinckney said to her daughter in an effort to smooth things over, "Arlena is the young lady who is helping your father with his memoirs. You remember—I told you about her last week."

"Yes," she said, smiling warmly, though her tone smacked of condescension. "My, my, my. I can't believe you have time to teach school, too...and let me guess, you have a husband and no household help at all. Women like you make me feel positively incompetent. I can barely keep my own closet straight, much less manage a career. I do admire you, Mrs. Prince."

Her voice went up and down like an upper register scale on a piano. I did not realize until later that she had insulted me. The deprecating language of cloistered Charlestonians is a subtle thing. These people can rip out your insides with the most exquisite politeness.

"Dinner is served, Mrs. Pinckney," said a hump-shouldered black woman who had shuffled out to the piazza.

"Thank you, Wilhemina. We'll be right there."

Everyone filed into the house behind the diminutive black major-domo. The dining room was a picture, enchanting in every detail. Matching French chandeliers hung above a long mahogany table that was surrounded by ten heavy chairs. Miss Roz told the servants to draw back the brocade draperies and let in the autumn sun. The result was stunning. Yellow shafts of outdoor light set the chandeliers aflame. Refracted color trembled within a thousand teardrop prisms as a delicate overlay of sunlight slid silently over the room. It shimmered and glowed in a golden wash just outside the human plane of vision. The air seemed almost liquid.

Mr. Pinckney helped Miss Roz and me with our chairs, Jonathan attended to his wife. We bowed our heads for a blessing asked by Mr. Pinckney, not one word of which I understood through his accent. Wilhemina and a younger black woman in identical dress served at table. They brought bowls and terrains of food from the sideboard and served in orchestrated courses. Never, had I tasted anything more delicious. She-crab soup, cucumber salad drizzled with raspberry vinegar, squash pie, tomato aspic, scalloped shrimp, spoon bread, and three kinds of pickles. Mr. Pinckney sat at the head of the table, with me at his left near the corner. He guided me through the meal like a father might guide an inexperienced child through a first visit to a fine restaurant. I loved Grayson Pinckney that day. I loved him for his sensitivity and manners. I loved him for taking care of me. Everything went swimmingly until Jon Priolieu opened his vindictive mouth.

"I understand you do an extraordinary amount of memoir work, Mrs. Prince. Didn't someone tell me the other day you work for Fanny Peregrine?"

"*Miss* Fanny Peregrine to you, Jonathan," Mr. Pinckney said.

"Sorry, sir. It certainly is *Miss*. Well, Mrs. Prince, is it true? Is the grandame of Old Charleston one of your clients?"

"Yes," I said, and for the first time felt a subject was opening up that I might be able to discuss.

"Must be fascinating, compiling the old biddy's life story, what with her checkered past."

My ears pricked. Priolieu's words were out of line. I looked at Mr. Pinckney for help.

"Fanny Peregrine's past will not be discussed at the dinner table, Jonathan," Mr. Pinckney said, "and you will refrain from referring to her as a 'biddy'." Miss Roz and Caroline stopped their side conversation. There was an uncomfortable silence.

"Oh, Daddy, don't be tedious," Caroline said. "Everyone knows about Miss Peregrine. It's common knowledge in Charleston."

"That's right, sir," said Jonathan. "And anyway, it was her father who behaved like an ass, not Miss Peregrine. I'd say he ruined the poor woman's life, making her give her child away like that." Then, in an aside to me, "Your old Miss Peregrine had a baby in her younger days. Isn't that a shocker? The gossips say it was sired by a Yankee. Frankly, I've always thought that was the reason her father made her give the poor thing away. Heartless bastard, he must have been."

My throat constricted dangerously. What Priolieu had said could not be right. He was talking about Miss Peregrine, *my* Miss Peregrine. I looked back and forth between Priolieu and Mr. Pinckney.

"I...I didn't know," I said. "I didn't know Miss Peregrine had been married."

"*Married*," Priolieu said. "If she'd been married, he wouldn't have made her give up her baby."

"*That's enough*," Mr. Pinckney bellowed and slammed the table with his fist. Every dish clattered. Priolieu held up his wine glass in retreat, though it was too late. I was already undone. A single tear escaped as I leaned over my plate. I saw it make a tiny splash on my sterling silver fork. Wilhemina, oblivious to everything but service, was taking away my dinner plate when the first sob escaped my throat. She jumped back in fright. Caroline Priolieu shouted at her husband.

"You beast," she said. "Now you've made her cry with your vicious talk. How could you?"

Miss Roz flew around the table and helped me out of my chair. She walked me to the south parlor and seated me in a cushioned wingback so that I might weep in comfort.

"Oh dear, oh dear," she said as she thrust a napkin into my

hands. Mr. Pinckney's voice boomed from the dining room, threatening Jonathan Priolieu with a throttling.

And I cried. I cried deep loud racking sobs that depressants and fatigue had set free. Caroline Priolieu rushed into the room carrying a stack of handkerchiefs. I took them gratefully and buried my face in lavender. Still, I cried. Mrs. Pinckney became distraught. She hovered, apologized, offered me water, declared her son-in-law an uncivilized boor, and begged me to sip some brandy. Caroline Priolieu proclaimed herself mortally embarrassed by the whole incident and said she might cry herself if I did not soon stop.

"Dear God in heaven," she said, "here it is my female time of the month and the world goes mad. Every hair on my head is standing out on end."

Then I found myself laughing and crying at the same time. Mrs. Pinckney and Caroline laughed with me, and we knew the worst was over. I was humiliated at having created such a scene in the home of Grayson Pinckney. Every time I thought of it, I had to fight breaking down again. Over and over I told Miss Roz how sorry I was to have ruined her beautiful dinner. Caroline declared it Jonathan's fault entirely and offered to drive me anywhere I wanted to go. I asked to be taken to the Mills House. I lied and said Stuart was to meet me there. As we rode toward the hotel in Caroline's black Jaguar, she assured me Jonathan was not as bad as he seemed, he'd been bullied so long by her father that every so often he popped out in warts and disgraced the whole family. After she dropped me off, I staggered along Church Street and made my way to the bus stop. The skin on my face felt swollen and dry, as if stretched across my cheekbones. When finally I entered the safety of the Sullivan's Island Transit, I sank gratefully onto the front seat and closed my burning eyes. Good grief, I thought as I was falling asleep, socializing in Charleston is work.

Chapter Seven

"Missy, wake up. The bus has stopped." I heard the voice from far away, too far to bother heeding. "Missy, this is Sullivan's Island. You always get off here."

"What?" I said to the disembodied voice. I struggled to drag myself up from the deep sleep known only to those who use depressants. Focusing on the voice, I realized it had a wrinkled, black man's face, one I had seen many times before on the Island Transit. The owner of it was looking at me as if he thought I might be dead.

"Oh, yes, thank you," I said. "I didn't realize...thank you." I picked up my briefcase and stumbled off the bus, fighting the disorientation of sleep. As the bus pulled away, and I started the short trek to the beach cottage, my attention was arrested by Raven FitzSimons calling to me from across the street.

"Mrs. Prince, Mrs. Prince, wait," she piped in her flute-like soprano. She was running toward me, hair flying, eyes shining.

"Hi, Rav," I said. "What are you doing out here again? Don't you ever stay at home?"

"I hate home and I hate Charleston. Come on. Let's take a walk before it gets dark. You can put your stuff in my car. Croom and Jon Priolieu Jr. are running on the beach, training for cross-country. I'm waiting for them. You remember Jon—he was in the writing class last year."

I cringed, thinking of the conversation I'd had with his mother a few hours earlier. Though Jon Priolieu was a nice enough boy, his name grated because of his father. So did that of Croom Calhoun Jr., Dr. Croomer Calhoun's son.

"A walk sounds great," I said. "Have you seen Stuart?"

"Yes, jogging toward the cottage when we first got here. He

said he was on his way home to make crab salad for you. How do you get him to do stuff like that? Croom won't do a thing for me."

I pushed on toward the dunes without answering. It felt wonderful to be back on the island. I breathed in the ebb tide muskiness of mud flats and decomposing sawgrass. Fecund marsh smells mingled with the sweeter fragrances of oleander and newly cut grass. Every odor was tinged with ocean salt. I inhaled again and remembered a remark Stuart had made the day before. He was right. The air on Sullivan's Island did have rejuvenating properties.

"You look tired, Mrs. Prince," Raven said as we tromped through the shifting sand of the dunes.

"A long day, sweetie, but don't worry. I'll turn back into my frisky old self when we get closer to the water. This soft sand slows me down."

Raven took my arm and helped me along, like an adult daughter helping an aging mother.

"And how is dear old Croom?" I said. "Horny as ever?"

"Uh-huh, that's Croom all right."

I clucked my tongue. "Raven, I've told you before, Croom will only go as far as you let him. Don't you want to finish high school and go on to college?"

"You can't give me advice," she said. "You were barely twenty the first time you got married. You told me that last year, remember?"

"And I also remember telling you what a mistake it was, an eight-month-long mistake. Wouldn't it be wonderful if I could convince you not to fall into the same hole?"

Raven patted me on the arm in mock reassurance. "You can stop worrying," she said. "The last thing Croom Jr. wants to do is get married. His father would kill him. The man is intent on Croom going to medical school, the same medical school he went to, of course. Nope, Croom can't get married, not if he plans to live out his natural life."

"Marriage isn't the only thing, Rav. You and Croom could hurt yourselves in other ways."

"Ohmygod, you think I might get *pregnant*. No way, Mrs. Prince. Croom and I know everything about sex. We'd never scandalize two upper-crust families like the FitzSimonses and Calhouns, not that it would be anything new in Charleston. It happens every generation. I'd bet my life five or six unwed mothers-to-be were on the first ship that sailed into the harbor, packed off to the New World to keep from embarrassing their families back home."

I had to laugh, though my heart stung for Miss Peregrine. Indeed, it had been happening for generations. "Maybe so, Rav, but I'm not concerned about your families. I'm concerned about you. I don't want to see you get hurt. You could injure your body, your emotions."

"My body and emotions belong to me. I'll do with them what I want."

"All right, case closed. If you want to let Croom make a mess of your life, go right ahead."

"Croom isn't the problem, Mrs. Prince. It's my mother who drives me up the wall. I'm supposed to be coming out this year. Can you imagine? *Me*, a ditsy debutante. Mother is going crazier by the day. The closer the winter social season, the crazier she gets. All she talks about is Cotillion and tea dances and the St. Cecilia Society. I don't know if I can live through it. Maybe it would be easier if my father were around. I was barely twelve when he left, and now I'm seventeen and haven't seen or heard from him since the day he walked out."

"You can make it without him, Raven. Both my parents left me when I was a lot younger than twelve."

"But we don't even know where he is. Mother stopped talking about him years ago, about the time I started wearing bras and shaving my legs. I think she took a look at me one day and saw herself at the same age. Sometimes I think she's trying to re-live her life through me. That's why I have to go through the debutante thing, and go to school at Southern Prep, and spend my summers at Flat Rock."

"Somehow I have trouble feeling sorry for you, young lady. Your life isn't exactly torture. Other girls would kill for your opportunities."

"Oh, *please*, you sound like Mother reciting guilt trip lecture number nine hundred and ninety-nine, soon to be a thousand. Doesn't anyone understand anything? It would be great if all those things really were for me. But they aren't. They're for her. Last night I caught her looking at an old photo of herself and my grandfather at the St. Cecilia thirty years ago. She was studying the *dress*, for crying out loud. After she passed out from her nightly booze, I took a close look at that picture, so I'd know what kind of dress she's going to try to make *me* wear."

"You're exaggerating. She only wants what's best for you. That's what all mothers want."

"Not mine. Mine wants tradition. This is a woman who plopped out of a two-hundred-year-old cookie cutter, the same one I plopped out of. Our lives were all sewn up before either of us was ever born. But those things don't bother me as much as they used to. I concentrate on higher things now. Our true selves aren't bound up in the physical world, you know. This earthly plane is a small fraction of our total existence. Mother can't get to my inner being, no matter what torture she dreams up. My soul is thousands of years old. It knows everything in the universe. You ought to try meditating, Mrs. Prince. It's cosmic. Might keep you from getting so tired."

"Wise old Raven," I said. "And what does Croom think about cosmic things?"

"Are you kidding? Croom never thinks about things like that. He's so shallow."

"He doesn't look shallow right now," I said. "He looks like something out of *GQ*."

Croom and Jon Jr. ran toward us on the beach, sweat glistening on their chests. They were perfect specimens of well-formed young men, statues of Greek athletes come to life. Raven was unimpressed. She proclaimed them foul-smelling and tossed them the towels she was carrying. She would have handed them over on the end of a long stick if one had been available. The boys said hello to me with formal courtesy, then Croom began sending messages to Raven with his eyes that he wanted to leave, fast. He knew I didn't like him, nor his attitude toward Raven. But a boy like Croom Calhoun did not have to pay attention to the disapproval of outsiders.

"Ready to go?" he said to Raven after the barest of conversational niceties.

"Sure," she said. "Just let me rinse the sand off my feet."

The boys and I waited in silence while Raven ran to the water. They did not know what to say to me. I'm sure they considered me a boring oldish female with nothing but English grammar in her head. I forgave them because they were still boys and had no way of knowing they would not consider themselves old at age thirty. We said our good-byes when Raven returned, and I watched as the three beautiful young people trotted effortlessly toward the dunes. It occurred to me that in thirteen short years they would all know what it was like to be thirty. That alone would temper the arrogance of Croom Calhoun, Jr.

"What took you so long?" Stuart called from the porch as I walked up the beach path toward the cottage.

"I'm not late," I said. "I've been gone eleven hours and seventeen-and-a-half minutes. Isn't that a normal work day around here?"

"Pretty normal, I guess. Raven dropped your stuff off fifteen minutes ago. She said you were on your way."

"Oh no, I forgot everything. I left it all in her car. Did she bring my briefcase?"

"Yeah, yeah...shoes, too. Now hurry up. It's past my dinner time."

Stuart had turned on every lamp in the cottage. The windows glowed with yellow storybook light. I thought I might cry when I saw how warm and cheerful they made the house look. Then I remembered the crab salad and realized I was ravenous. The crying spell at Pinckney House had used up my two o'clock dinner. Stuart always made okra soup and yeast rolls to go with crab salad. He found his recipes in lowcountry cookbooks. My stomach churned with hunger.

"You have enough time for a quick shower," he said. "I'm putting the finishing touches on dinner now. Maybe I can find some candles. We're having your favorite tonight."

"*You're* my favorite," I said, and hugged him with surprising strength from someone so exhausted. I thought dreamily of a warm shower, then dinner, then collapsing on the porch swing with a spritzer and my favorite wool blanket. All because of Stuart. All the comfort I had in the world was because of Stuart. The evening passed quietly and peacefully, and I was soothed by the routine of home. It would have been perfect save one small blotch in the form of a late evening phone call.

"I'm sorry, she's sleeping," Stuart said into the phone. "I'll ask her to call you first thing tomorrow. Yes, thank you, good-bye."

"Trouble?" I said when he came back to the porch. He paused a second before answering.

"Couldn't tell for sure," he said. "It was Jeannette FitzSimons, Raven's mom. Sounded like she had a case of the ass. What would she want with you at this hour?"

"Please, Stu, I can't deal with it now. Maybe in the morning."

My plea was so pitiful that he put his arms around me and rocked me to ease my shivering. "That's funny," I said through chattering teeth. "I didn't even realize I was cold."

Chapter Eight

I awoke to an insistent Stuart kissing and groping me under the covers. It had been weeks since we'd made love, by silent mutual consent. Discontent has a strange way of needing to be nourished. Stuart fed his by brooding—I fed mine by denying myself simple comforts such as sex. But biology betrayed me. When awake, I could easily say no to Stuart's half-hearted advances and my own stirrings. Sleep, however, released the truth, the surprise of which flowered in the darkness of my body like some exotic deep-sea plant. Sleep brought dreams filled with sensual temptations that rendered me defenseless. In dreams I found myself in the arms of pagan gods and dark princes. Jonathan Priolieu was one.

Jonathan—who tasted of bourbon and cigarettes and smelled of expensive cologne. I wanted his hands, his hands dragging me downward to the floor. In light, I spurned him. In darkness, in dreams, I accepted his every invitation to meet him secretly in the basement of Pinckney Building and go with him behind closed doors while other partners argued cases in antiseptic courtrooms. The dreams always had the same sequence of events—Jonathan pulling me into his shadowy office and turning away briefly to lock the door, myself murmuring for him to hurry with the lock and take me quickly, down and down to a place we both knew too well, a place where our bodies burned with lust and our consciences knew no guilt. How long since I'd wanted Stuart like that? How long since he'd wanted me? I closed my eyes and let him love me in our marriage bed, hoping when he was finished and asleep again, that he hadn't heard me call him Jonathan.

The next time I woke up, I was disoriented and panicky. A ringing phone had set off alarms in my head. Stuart had disappeared. I got out of bed and walked on unsteady legs to the bedroom door. From there I could see Stuart, phone to his ear, standing by the telephone table on the other side of the sitting room. I watched with interest as he signaled me to be quiet.

"Yes, Mr. Pinckney," he said. "How are you this morning?" Then he held the phone two feet from his ear. Across the room, I could hear Mr. Pinckney's voice rumbling through the earpiece.

"Fine, thank you," he shouted. "I'm calling to ask after your lovely wife. We're not scheduled to meet this morning, but if by luck she's coming into town, I'd like to see her."

Stuart mouthed words to me desperately. *"Do you want to talk?"* I shook my head.

Mr. Pinckney again. "Are you there, Mr. Prince? I'm having trouble hearing you."

"Yes, I'm here, but Arlena isn't. She usually calls in for messages around ten. I'll tell her you called."

Stuart stared at me with big anxious eyes. He was rattled at having to deal with Grayson Pinckney alone.

"Fine, that's fine," Mr. Pinckney said. "Do what you can."

"Certainly, sir. I'll make sure she calls you sometime this morning."

"Splendid. I'll look forward to hearing from her. Thank you very much. Good-bye."

"Good-bye," Stuart said and hung up the phone. He stood for a moment without speaking, nervously combing his fingers through his hair. Then, still frowning, he said, "Does he always talk that loud?"

"Always. So what time is it? Seems late."

"Nine-thirty. I decided not to wake you. You were dead on your butt last night. And after this morning, I thought you could use some extra rest. Frankly, precious-darling, I thought I was in the wrong bed."

I ignored his smirk. "I hate it when you make decisions for me."

"And *I* hate it when you get up in a rotten mood. Now tell me what's going on with Pinckney? Why is he trying to chase you down?"

"Probably wants to apologize."

I turned then and went into the bathroom to avoid further explanation. Stuart followed. I closed the door in his face, but he didn't seem to notice.

"Apologize? What for?" he asked through the door.

"Nothing. I had a little trouble with his son-in-law, that's all. It wasn't important. Forget it."

"No, I want to know what's going on."

I opened the bathroom door to another of his frowns, which irritated me no end. "Nothing is going on," I said. "Everything is great. Now let's talk about something pleasant for a change. Do we have enough cash to go out for breakfast? I need a cup of coffee before I start transcribing."

"I have a few dollars in my pocket," he said, obviously dissatisfied I had brushed him off so forthrightly. "But we probably don't have time. You have to call Jeannette FitzSimons back, and Mr. Pinckney."

"I'm not calling either one. Today I'm not going to do anything but what I want to do. Those high-assed aristocrats south of Broad expect me to jump every time they belch, but this is one day it isn't going to happen. Consider it a revolt."

"Think again, Arlena. These are paying customers you're talking about."

"Jeannette FitzSimons doesn't pay me a dime, and Mr. Pinckney doesn't pay me enough for what I do." My voice was too loud. A quaver had crept in. Time for my first Valium.

"Maybe not, but he's steady," Stuart said, "and FitzSimons is connected to Peregrine."

"How much do you think I can stand, Stuart? Do you want me to let these people eat me alive? Like they do their stinking oysters?"

"No, just return their phone calls. Humor them. It isn't too much to ask. I don't know why you're making such an issue."

I took a deep breath. Stuart looked hopeful. I decided to give in. Besides, I had a private errand to run that could only be taken care of downtown. "All right," I said, pretending he'd beaten me down. "Look up FitzSimons's number."

He sighed with relief, pulled a slip of paper from his shirt pocket, and held it in the air. "I wrote it down when she called last night," he said.

I walked heavily across the room and jerked the paper from his hand. The house shook on its pilings. Stuart looked at me with a half-grin. Usually he teased me about rattling lumber. This morning he did not have the courage.

"At least I walk with purpose," I said. "I wouldn't want to sneak around like a cat and frighten people like you do."

He shrugged and stuffed his hands into his pockets, then watched silently as I punched in the number.

"This is Arlena Prince," I said to the female voice that answered. "I'm returning a call to Mrs. FitzSimons."

"Please hold," the woman said in a Southern nasal twang. Her two syllables sounded like six. I mimicked her in an ugly whisper. "*Ple-e-se ho-o-ld.*"

Stuart narrowed his eyes, attempting to control me from the other side of the room.

"Mrs. Prince?" a different voice said, also nasal, also with rotten diction.

"Yes, this is Arlena Prince, returning a call from last night."

"Jeannette FitzSimons here, and thank you for calling me back so promptly. I hate to ask you to do this, but could you drop by my office today? I need to speak with you about Miss Peregrine."

"That would be difficult. I'm busy with deadlines."

"Yes, we all have heavy schedules, but I thought you'd be willing to take a few minutes out for the sake of Miss Fanny."

"Oh, don't misunderstand. I'd do anything to help Miss Peregrine. It's extraneous things I try to avoid, things like unnecessary meetings."

"Yes...well, I'll be in my office all day, through lunch. Feel free to come in unannounced if you happen to change your mind. We're going to have to talk eventually. I just thought it would be better to get it over with now rather than wait for an emergency."

"If it's that important, I'll see what I can arrange."

"How nice of you to work me in. I'll look forward to seeing you, around noon, perhaps. Good-bye."

I slammed the phone down on the table top and let loose a cascade of words. "I can't believe she has the gall to summon me like that. It's infuriating. And I'd bet a hundred dollars Miss Peregrine doesn't know a thing about it. Louisa Hill and Croomer Calhoun will probably call next, to demand their own pro rata share of my time."

I paced back and forth to add drama to my snit. Stuart was a good audience. "Look," he said, "now that you know you're going, why don't we make it as easy as possible. I'll call Mr. Pinckney and tell him you'll stop in around eleven. That'll put you at

FitzSimons's office by twelve-thirty or one. That gives us enough time now for coffee at Mama Chloe's, if we hustle."

I did not feel like *hustling*. I felt like staring dejectedly at the dirty straw rug that had been unsuccessful for too many weeks at keeping sand off our feet. "Once I'd like to spend a whole day doing what I'm paid to do," I said sadly. "Why do these people think manuscript pages appear by magic? Mr. Pinckney is expecting a whole new chapter next week, a polished chapter."

"And he'll get it," Stuart said. "We'll write it over the weekend. Perk up. Things aren't that bad. At least you have clients to raise hell about. Time was you had none."

"I think I was better off then. I'll be taking the car, right?"

"Sure, I'll stay here and write marketing letters. We need a new project pronto. The coffers are empty again."

I nodded, though I wasn't listening. I was thinking about my errand. I'd noticed the night before that my pills were running low. Something had to be done about getting more, and fast.

I stepped into Pinckney Building at two minutes of eleven. The receptionist was on the phone. She covered the receiver and whispered that Mr. Pinckney was expecting me. I went up on the elevator to find Lillian on the phone, also. I waved to her as I tapped softly on the door of Mr. Pinckney's private office.

"*Come in,*" he shouted.

"Good morning, sir." I was worried about facing him. Maybe he'd thought it over and decided he didn't want to work with an unstable female who cried her way through dinner. Maybe this was the morning he would fire me.

"Come in, dear. You look much better than you did yesterday."

"I'm fine, Mr. Pinckney, just sorry for what happened. Please tell Miss Roz I'll return her handkerchiefs as soon as I've washed them."

"Thank you, thank you. She'll be glad to hear you're all right. But you owe us no apology. It is we who should apologize to you. I regret anything was said in our home that could bring you to such bitter tears."

"It wasn't your fault. I was over tired, maybe a little sick, but it definitely wasn't your ...."

"Quite right," said a voice at my back. "I'm the one to blame, and for this I'm truly sorry."

I turned to see Jonathan Priolieu standing in the office doorway. My face grew warm. "I hope I didn't startle you, Mrs. Prince. Why-oh-why has it been my fate to trounce upon your tender feelings? Can you find it in your heart to forgive me? If not, I shall spend the rest of my life a miserable man."

"*Enough*," Mr. Pinckney said. Jonathan's face went redder than my own. Mr. Pinckney turned toward me and spoke more softly. "Arlena, I asked Mr. Priolieu–Jonathan–to apologize to you in person, though I wish he had sounded more sincere. I hope you don't mind my presumption."

"Yes, I mean, no. I mean, it wasn't necessary, but thank you."

"Good. All right, Jonathan, she's letting you off the hook. You may go."

"Very good, sir. Good day, Mrs. Prince. I hope you'll give us another chance to entertain you at Pinckney House ..." He was about to say more, but Mr. Pinckney cleared his throat and gave him a scalding look. Jonathan fled.

"The man is a horse's ass," Mr. Pinckney said when the office door clicked shut. "I begged Caroline not to marry him. Offered her a year abroad, clothes, fancy car, anything. But it's difficult to bribe someone who already has everything. So she married the idiot, and now she has a son by him. It makes me sick to think of Jonathan Priolieu as the father of my grandson, my only grandson. Looks like it would make me dislike him less. Every day I get out of bed and promise myself I'm not going to let him upset me, and every day I get mad enough to beat the living hell out of him. If I were ten years younger, I'd do it."

Between meetings with Mr. Pinckney and Jeannette FitzSimons, I took care of my secret errand. It did not take long. The people I had to deal with were in a bigger hurry than I. "Thank you," I said when a doctor whose name I did not remember handed over my fourth Valium prescription in six months. I studied the prescription, but could not decipher the handwriting. "Excuse me," I said. "Is this refillable?"

"Two times," he said and handed me a bill. "Pay on your way out."

"Oh, I forgot to mention the headaches. Sometimes they're unbearable. Do you think Darvon or Percodan might help?"

"Percodan is strong. Have you used it before?"

"Once," I lied.

"No, twice." He was looking at my chart. After a brief study, he wrote something on a prescription pad. "This is Darvon," he said, ripping off the top sheet. Then he scribbled something else on the next page. "Percodan. Take it only if the pain is bad. It can work on the brain. Be careful."

"Are these refillable, too?" I said.

"Yes, same as the Valium. Pay at the desk by the door."

The thought of his hundred-dollar fee churned the wave of anxiety that was chilling my insides. And the prescriptions would be a hundred more. I felt lightheaded when I thought of Stuart juggling rent and utility bills just to keep us in groceries. If Mr. Pinckney hadn't tipped me in August, I wouldn't have had the cash for my current medical errand. Taking it out of monthly money wasn't an option. We were far too pressed for that. And if I'd told Stuart why I needed it, how much and how badly my side ached, he'd have tried to make me stop seeing my new doctors and go back to the ones who'd treated me over the winter. He might have tried to make me stop working. Thank goodness my new doctors asked no questions. As long as I paid them in cash, they'd write any prescription I wanted.

The one I was seeing on this particular day ran his clinic out of a rundown building on King Street, two blocks from Hampton's Pharmacy, a conveniently impersonal sundries store where I was able to get my prescriptions filled quickly and anonymously. The whole ordeal, doctor visit and prescription purchase, took less than an hour and yielded enough pills to last two full weeks, six counting refills. After that I'd need more money to pay a different doctor across town. The three hundred I had left over from today's expenditure would finance refills until then. But six weeks was a long time away. I could not think about what would happen then, not when I had to face Raven's mother in fifteen minutes.

"Well, Mrs. Prince," Jeannette FitzSimons said when I walked into her unkempt office. "You decided to come after all, and on such short notice. I'm honored. Your reputation precedes you, I have to say. My daughter, Raven, is still rhapsodizing about your English class of last year. And Miss Peregrine, as you know, is thoroughly charmed by every little breath you take."

Jeannette FitzSimons sat behind the most cluttered desk in the most cluttered office I had ever seen in my life. She looked like an aging Raven, a graying bulging nearsighted frumpy Raven. I took a seat opposite her and prepared for battle.

"Actually, it was a writing class," I said. "I'm not certified in English."

"Whatever...you know how teenagers obfuscate. Most of the time I couldn't tell you what Raven is studying. But enough of that. You're here to talk about Miss Peregrine.

"No, Mrs. FitzSimons. I'm here to listen. *You're* here to talk."

FitzSimons straightened in her chair and dropped the superficial friendliness. I had succeeded in making her angry.

"Yes," she said, nostrils flaring unattractively. "I want to appeal to your sense of fair play, if you have any, that is. Miss Peregrine isn't well, you know that. You also know her judgment isn't what it should be, yet you continue to encourage her in this ridiculous writing project. You flatter her, play to her vanity, tell her the work is good when you know very well it isn't. The fact is, she's been working on these reminiscences over a year with very little progress. Her friends and family agree, you are taking criminal advantage, bleeding an old woman of her money. Some have suggested you harbor notions Svengalian in nature. I am asking you now, in clear and simple terms, to leave the employ of Miss Peregrine at once."

I was staggered. Now I knew why Raven hated to go home. "*Svengalian*," I said in a voice hoarse with rage. "You accuse me of your own crime, Jeannette FitzSimons. Yours and Louisa Hill's. I won't be intimidated by either of you, and I won't stop working for Miss Peregrine, not until she dismisses me herself. You'll have to find someone else to bully."

The perfect oval of Raven's face sprang into my mind as I

uttered those last few words, though I dared not mention her name. I couldn't tell Jeannette FitzSimons how close I was to her daughter.

"Eloquent, Mrs. Prince, but ineffective," FitzSimons said. "However, there's one small detail you're forgetting. Every member of Southern Prep's Board of Trustees is a personal friend of mine. Aren't you planning to teach there again this year? And isn't your husband a paid consultant to our development program?"

"Is that supposed to be a threat?"

"Call it whatever you like."

"*Coercion,*" I snarled. "*That's* what I call it." Then I turned and stomped out of the office, slamming the door in my wake. Thank God, I thought, as I stepped from the building into the cleansing sunlight of the street. Thank God I have my new cache of pills.

Chapter Nine

"Would anyone like to read something you wrote over the summer?" No one in the class stirred. My eyes moved row to row. I was intimidated by the cold expressions and expensive clothing. Why didn't I get a job at Catholic High on Calhoun Street? How did I end up in this wasp nest called Southern Prep?

"I'd like to read," a male voice said from the farthest corner of the room. It was Croom Calhoun, Jr.

"Great, Croom," I said, though his offer seemed odd. He had never volunteered before.

"Do I have to stand up?"

"No, but read loudly enough for everyone to hear."

He cleared his throat and began:

Early morning is a time of magic in Charleston. In the gray time after the light has come and before the sun has risen, Charleston seems to hang suspended out of time in the silvery light. The street lights go out and the weeds are a brilliant green. The corrugated iron of building roofs glow with the pearly lucence of platinum or old pewter. No automobiles are running then. The streets are silent of progress and business. And the rush and drag of waves can be heard as they splash. It is a time of great peace, a deserted time, a little era of rest. Cats drip over the fences and slither like syrup over the ground to look for fish heads. Silent early morning dogs parade majestically, picking and choosing judiciously whereupon to pee.

The class snickered. I waited a long moment before saying anything. For the first time since we had known each other, Croom and I looked directly into each other's eyes. The other students grew uncomfortable with the silence and began changing positions in their desks. I glanced at Raven. She lowered her eyes and stared at the gold eagle on her Southern Prep notebook. I looked back at Croom.

"Is this supposed to be a joke, Croom?"

"I don't know what you mean," he said.

"Yes, you do. You know exactly what I mean." He shifted in his seat. I paused before continuing. "All right, I'm trying to understand. At first I thought you wanted me to think you wrote that piece. Then I thought you were playing a trick on the class. But now I have to think the trick was meant for me."

"I don't know what you're talking about."

"Croom, we both know that passage is from *Cannery Row*, Steinbeck, except for the places you hacked it up. At first I didn't intend to say anything. I didn't want to expose you. But I missed the point. *You* wanted to expose *me*. You wanted to make me feel foolish in front of the class. Well, you succeeded. I do. I feel foolish because I didn't realize you disliked me so much. I'm sorry for that, Croom."

His cheeks were blood red and so were mine, but age was on my side. It would be difficult for a seventeen-year-old boy to outwit an adult. Croom was at a disadvantage, yet he came at me again.

"Yesterday at dinner my dad said you don't know any more about writing than he does." A giggle rippled across the rows of desks. I kept my composure.

"That may or may not be true, Croom. I'd never challenge anyone as erudite as your father, though I'm flattered to be the subject of your family's dinner-table conversation."

"Dad says you're a vanity publisher, that the writing is a come-on."

I felt dizzy. I had to fight to stand firm. "He's confused about nomenclature, Croom. Vanity publishers charge writers for the manufacture of their books. They talk them into paying for printing costs by leading them to believe there's a market for their work. But family histories and personal memoirs are not marketed. They're private publications, done for the purpose of preserving social history to keep threads between generations unbroken." I breathed slowly. "Your father is right about my being unpublished personally. But if I were, do you think I'd be teaching a writing class at a small private school in South Carolina, a school with the distinction of paying its faculty less than any other school in the state? Seriously, do you think I'd be doing that, Croom?"

He narrowed his eyes, then scrambled out of his desk. Its metal feet clattered as a notebook slid off its slanted surface and fell open on the floor. Croom glared at me, his face a thunder-cloud. I maintained steady eye contact, which, being a boy, he could not return. He averted his eyes, reached for the notebook, and blustered out of the room. The sound of the door slamming behind him was enough to let me know he would not be back. I looked at Raven. She was weeping softly.

"Mrs. Prince, wait up," someone called from among the hoard of young people hurrying up and down George Street. But these were not Southern Prep kids. These were college students on their way to classes on the College of Charleston campus downtown. I turned to see Raven in the crowd, waving frantically with one hand, gripping a wayward bicycle with the other. I waved back half-heartedly and did not smile. I wasn't happy to see her. She rolled the bike clumsily along the sidewalk, trying with slow progress to catch up with me. I waited until she got closer to start lecturing.

"What are you doing here, Raven? Did you skip out of school early? I just left you at Southern Prep not an hour ago."

"I'm cutting the rest of the day, okay? And if the headmaster calls my mother and rats on me, it won't matter a dip. She'll just tell him I'm sick, like always. She's afraid he'll kick me out if he finds out I cut all the time. Then her only daughter wouldn't be a student at *fabulous* Southern Prep."

Raven's disregard for authority didn't surprise me. For all her innocent look, she was extremely cunning. "You may be able to skip school, chicky, but I can't skip work. Hope you aren't plan-ning to spend the afternoon tagging after me."

"No, I'm on my way out to Sullivan's, if I ever make it home with this stupid bike so I can pick up my car. But I wanted to tell you something first. I...I wanted to tell you I'm sorry for what Croom did in class. It was a dirty rotten trick. He can be a real creep sometimes."

"Don't worry about it. Sometimes things like that happen with students."

Raven bit her lip. "You have to watch Croom, Mrs. Prince. He's like me in ways. If he gets mad, he won't keep his mouth shut. You made him look stupid today in front of his friends. He might try to get back at you."

"How did it get to be my fault he acted like a jerk? Guess that's Southern Prep for you, huh. Look, I didn't mean to embarrass Croom. Really, I didn't. And surely he has better things to do than swear out revenge on a poor plebeian school teacher. Now, turn around and take a good look at that building across the street. It's the College of Charleston Library, the quiet and lovely place where I intend to spend the rest of my day. I have work to do. Get it? *Work.*"

I walked past Raven toward the library. She followed. "Mrs. Prince," she said breathlessly as she trailed me with her bike. "Please don't make Croom mad, anymore. Things could get out of hand. He and his father might talk behind your back and ruin your reputation. Then you'd never get anywhere in Charleston."

"My reputation is safe enough, dear, not that I give a flip one way or the other. What you don't understand, Rav, as intelligent as you are, is that most people don't care what the dignified citizens of Charleston think. You grew up here. It's your whole world, but it's not mine, nor a lot of other people's. Hundreds of kids not much older than yourself and Croom live and work and go to school in this area—at the Air Force Base, medical school, nursing school, The Citadel, and several other colleges and tech schools. They came here from all over the country...Iowa, Kansas, California, and I'd bet not ten of them know your vacuous little society south of Broad exists. And if they did, they'd think it ludicrous. Grow up, Raven. There's a universe out there."

She looked at me with confusion and pain in her eyes. This was the girl who spoke of cosmic awareness, but did not bother to look beyond Broad Street. I stopped walking and turned to face her. "Why did you mention Croom's father just now?" I asked. "Is there anything I need to know?"

She blushed and turned away. "Well, sometimes I listen in on my mother's phone conversations. The other night I heard her talking to Dr. Calhoun, about you, some problem you'd caused with Miss Peregrine. Dr. Calhoun sounded disgusted, like he didn't want to be bothered with it. Everyone knows he doesn't like my mother, but he has to talk to her because of Miss Peregrine. He and Mother take care of business things for her. Anyway, I heard Mother telling him about some terrible thing you'd done. Whatever it was, she was mad as a hornet about it."

I felt a flutter of fear in my heart, an unexplained warning that alerted me to the presence of danger. I do not know why I ignored it. Raven interpreted my silence as disapproval.

"I don't care what you think about my eavesdropping," she said. "You'd do it, too, if your mother were like mine. You ought to thank me for trying to help you. I don't want you to get fired from Southern Prep."

I gave Raven a quick hug. "I understand, sweetie, but you've already helped enough. And you have to stop worrying about me. I'm a big girl. I can take care of myself."

She sighed and hugged me back. "Please be careful," she said, blinking wetly, her larkspur eyes shining with new tears. She wiped them away with her sleeve, then climbed on her bike and pedaled down George Street. I would not let myself watch her go. I turned away, shrugged off the little drama as best I could, and walked across the street to the library.

I started up the great concrete steps, but something occurred to me half-way up, something more interesting than Raven-loves-Croom. I paused on the tenth step, thought for a moment, then turned and walked smartly back down. There was something I wanted to find out, something that had been nagging at me since my dinner at Pinckney House, and the only place I could think of that might have the information I wanted was the South Carolina Historical Library on the corner of Chalmers and Meeting, four blocks down from the Mills House Hotel.

I walked too fast and paid for it later with pains in my side. It was a long way from George Street to Meeting, but I didn't care. I crossed the cobblestones of Chalmers and walked up a different set of library steps. But this was no ordinary library. This was the library designed by Robert Mills, South Carolina's most famous architect. It had survived earthquake, tornado, hurricane, flood, and fire. Now it would have to survive a search by one determined female Yankee.

Not just anyone could enter those hallowed halls, only recommended, dues-paying members of the South Carolina Historical

Society, of which I was one, thanks to Miss Peregrine. I rang the bell next to the bolted front door. A fussy matron peeped out, looked me up and down, and checked over my shoulder to make sure no one was with me. Then, reluctantly, she pushed open the door. I explained my reason for being there, whereupon she helped me fill out the correct forms, and told me where to sit and wait while she searched the sequestered stacks for my request.

"Here it is," she said triumphantly on her return. In her arms was a huge rectangular package wrapped in brown paper and tied up neatly with string.

"We store all our important *Bibles* like this," she said, emphasizing the word *important*. "This is one of our newer acquisitions."

"Miss Peregrine told me she had allowed you to catalog it."

The librarian looked pleased. "Miss Peregrine brought it in herself, five years ago. She told us she knew she was getting on in years and thought it time to dispose of such things properly. As far as I know, it hasn't been touched since."

"Thank you," I said.

The woman shifted the enormous weight of the *Bible* from her arms to mine. "Be careful with it," she said in a tone. I could not respond to her. It took all my strength to heft the *Bible* to a table.

The binding strings were tied in bow knots, which made them easy to undo. Carefully and quickly, I opened the *Bible* to its middle, the way I had been taught to find *Psalms* in my childhood. But today I was not looking for *Psalms*. Today I was looking for the genealogy pages with its handwritten records of births and deaths. There were dozens of names, most with the surname, Peregrine, but one stood out like blood on white satin. It was the last name on the list—Constantia Elizabeth Peregrine. Beside it was a brief annotation. I recognized Miss Peregrine's hand:

Constantia Elizabeth Peregrine
b. 1 May 1926. d._____. Illegitimate child of Fanny
Hampton Peregrine (b.3 April 1910. d._____). Constantia Elizabeth
was born secretly in Schenectady, New York in 1926, and was turned
over by her grandfather, Smythe Hampton Peregrine (b. 17 November
1890. d. 7 October 1950), to Our Lady of Grace Foundling Home.
There she was offered for public adoption. The child's father was Grayson
Lockwood Pinckney III (b. 2 May 1900. d. 14 August 1943). This
entry was set down by Fanny Lockwood Peregrine, Constantia Elizabeth
Peregrine's birth mother.

I calculated quickly. If she were still alive, Constantia Elizabeth Peregrine would be over seventy years old. I'd hoped Jonathan Priolieu had been wrong about Miss Peregrine's past, but he was not, save one important detail. The baby's father was no Yankee. He was a Pinckney, father of Grayson Lockwood Pinckney IV. That made Miss Peregrine's child Mr. Pinckney's half-sister. I wondered if he knew about her. One thing was certain, Jonathan Priolieu did not, or else he would have said something the day I was a dinner guest at Pinckney House.

I read the entry again and took pleasure in Miss Peregrine's decision not to let her child go nameless and unrecorded. By including her in the *Bible*, she had given Constantia Elizabeth her rightful place in Peregrine family history.

"You're a tough old bird, Fanny Peregrine," I said to myself. "I wonder what other secrets you're keeping."

Chapter Ten

"You shouldn't be going," Stuart said, his nervousness palpable. I ignored him as he followed me room to room on my race around the cottage. My shoes were on the porch, jacket on the bedroom doorknob, blouse over a towel bar in the bathroom. It was a disorganized effort at dressing.

"I mean it, Arlena. I have a bad feeling about this."

"I don't care. I'm going anyway. Miss Peregrine is expecting me."

"No, she isn't. Why do I get the feeling we're not communicating? I told you—Louisa Hill called after you fell asleep last night. She said Miss Peregrine asked her to cancel your session for this morning. Did you hear me? I said *cancel*, c-a-n-c-e-l."

"Surely you don't believe a word that woman says. Where is my hairbrush?"

"Haven't seen it. Use mine. It's in the bedroom on the dresser."

I pushed past him to get to the bedroom, but stopped short when I saw myself in the dresser mirror. Leaning forward, I frowned at my own reflection. "I look so sallow," I said under my breath. "What happened to my tan?"

I smeared on lipstick and extra blush, gathered my hair into a ponytail, and gave it a few swipes with Stuart's brush. He sat on the bed and watched.

"What difference does it make if she's lying?" he said. "No use in confronting her. Let old lady Peregrine do it. She will sooner or later."

"Sure, and in the mean time, the witch gets her way again. But not this time. This time I'm keeping my appointment. If Miss Peregrine wants to cancel, she can tell me when I get there."

Stuart became exasperated. "You should call before you go, to confirm," he said.

I laughed. "That's a terrific idea. I'll call and Louisa will answer and tell me another pack of lies. Then I'll be right back where I started from, only worse. At least this way I can pretend you forgot to give me the message. What are you so worried about, anyway? Most of the time you don't mind if I risk life and limb for a buck."

Sarcasm put barbs on my words. Stuart's expression made it obvious I'd pricked his conscience. "Look," I said less caustically, "I've been given orders, issued ultimatums, practically threatened with banishment from the state of South Carolina by Miss Peregrine's so-called *friends*. It's time I defended myself."

"It's a mistake," Stuart said. "I know it is, but I refuse to let it ruin my day. Go, joust with windmills, but don't come home complaining to me when you get your arm cut off."

He slammed out of the house through the porch door and caught himself as he stumbled down the concrete steps. I watched, suddenly unsure of myself, as he ran along the path to the ocean at a pace much too fast for simple exercise. I pretended not to care, and turned my attention back to dressing. Any remorse over attacking Stuart was relegated to a lockbox in the depths of my soul. It was the secret place I had been stashing all my troublesome emotions of late. I noticed it was getting crowded.

Tasks completed, I left the house and went forward to challenge Louisa Hill, avenge unfairness, unmask evil motives. But by the time I stood before the grand front door of Peregrine House, my great wave of courage had subsided. If Louisa Hill was willing to slam doors in my face, she might be willing to do worse. I backed away from the door without touching the knocker. Looking around to make sure no one was watching, I walked to the left of the house and opened the wrought iron gate to the back yard. Behind the gate was a brick drive. It curved past a row of overgrown azalea bushes and continued to the door of an old fashioned carriage house at the back left of the garden. Quickly I walked to the ancient structure and peeped in a low window. Miss Peregrine's black Cadillac sat alone and gleaming, close to the far wall. Louisa's car was absent. I turned from the window and again looked over the house and grounds. Everything seemed friendly now that I knew Louisa wasn't at home. Birds sang in the garden, gray squirrels chased each other up and down Judas trees, and somewhere in the distance, a windchime tinkled.

My courage returned. I walked to the back entrance of the mansion and rapped on the door. No answer. "Tycie, it's me—Arlena. Let me in." Still nothing. "*Tycie*," I shouted and reached for the doorknob. It turned in my hand. Gently, I pushed it forward , and watched half frightened as it swung open. "Tycie, where are you? I'm coming in," I said.

A draft caught the door and slammed it behind me; my heart skipped into double time. As I desperately scanned the area for a place to hide, a raucous buzzer sounded in short and long bursts somewhere toward the front of the house. I panicked and clamped my hands over my ears, then squatted on the floor to wait for something terrible to happen. Nothing did. The buzzer stopped as abruptly as it had started and was replaced by a loud clanging sound. I tried to stay still, but the muscles in my legs began burning. I shifted on my haunches. A minute passed without disaster. A second minute. Then, by willpower alone, I subdued my fear and talked myself out of panic.

This is senseless, I thought. I am cowering in a musty storeroom like a rat. I shall stand up straight, walk through the house, and find out what is going on. Miss Peregrine would want me to. She'd do it herself if she were able.

I stood up, moaning softly as my calf muscles rebelled. When I found the courage to creep into the hallway, I began a timid walk down several back corridors, in and out of a series of odd-shaped rooms, through the study, the parlor, and finally the archway of the foyer. My footsteps sounded amplified on the hardwood floors. At the bottom of the staircase, I stopped for a moment and listened to the clanging. It was louder now, coming from somewhere in the upper stories. Maybe Miss Peregrine had gotten trapped upstairs with no one at home to help her. I ran up the steps. On the fourth floor, I heard her calling from a room at the end of a long hallway. It was a section of the house I had not seen. The clanging began again. In a second I was down the hall.

"*It's me, Miss Peregrine*," I shouted. The clanging stopped.

"Get in here, child," I heard her call from a closed door to my left. I reached out timidly, turned the knob, and pushed open the door. I was shocked by her disheveled appearance. She lay against several pillows in a four-poster bed. The bedclothes were a tumble. Two dented silver trays, the obvious source of the clanging, lay on the floor by the bed.

"Is everyone dead?" she said, looking at me from glazed eyes. "Where is Tycie? I've been buzzing all morning. The confounded buzzer must be broken."

"I don't know, Miss Peregrine. I don't know where anyone is. Are you ill? Do you want me to call a doctor?"

"No, no, I want you to call Grayson Pinckney's office. Tell his secretary I can't make my appointment today and will call back later to reschedule."

I stood by the bed and made no move. The strangeness of the situation had overwhelmed me. "What is the matter?" she said. "There's the phone. Hurry up and make the call. I have other things I need you to do."

I obeyed, then waited for my next orders. There was a long list. Open the shutters; straighten the bedclothes; bring in wet wash cloths; find a hairbrush; fetch orange juice and the medicine bag from the kitchen. A busy hour passed before I was allowed to sit and rest.

"Where is Tycie?" I asked when I'd caught my breath. "Is she sick?"

Miss Peregrine didn't respond right away. She was sipping juice from a water goblet I'd brought up from the kitchen. "That darky has never been sick a day in her life. Lazy as hell maybe, but never sick."

I squirmed at the offensive remark, but did not challenge it.

"What about you, Miss Peregrine? Are you all right?"

"No, groggy from too much medication. I was having leg pains about four this morning. Louisa heard me groaning and talked me into taking an extra pill to finish out the night. Damn stupid thing, taking sleeping pills at that hour. I should never have let her convince me, not when I knew I had an appointment with Grayson. Now I'm too weak to go."

"But *we* had an appointment," I said, "you and I. Did you ask Louisa to call me to cancel? She did, you know."

"Of course not. I wanted you to come as usual. I thought I was going to need you to drive me to Grayson's office, but that was before the pill. I didn't want Louisa to know I was going. She pesters me so with questions. If there's anything I hate, it's pestering."

"Yes," I said, but she didn't hear me. Her attention had fastened on something across the room. I turned to see Louisa Hill standing in the bedroom doorway. Her lips were set in a thin tight line; she was looking straight at me.

"What are you doing here?" she said.

I stood, intending to answer, but Miss Peregrine cut me off. "She is here for our regular session," she said. "Your phone call fell on deaf ears, Louisa, as you can see. I suppose you called Tycie, too. Did you think I wouldn't figure that out, either?"

"Don't be peevish," Louisa said to her mistress without taking her eyes off me. "You've been so weary lately, you needed a day of rest."

"And you made sure I'd get it with those evil pills. Well, I'm rested now, and hungry. You'll have to take over Tycie's kitchen duties for the day. Too bad you didn't speak to me before calling her. You will never again take it upon yourself to do such a thing without consulting me first. There now, I'm ready for my breakfast. Please do the honors, Louisa. And prepare a tray for Mrs. Prince. I'm sure she's as famished as I."

Red streaks appeared on Louisa's pallid throat. I watched as they crept upward to her cheek bones and forehead, yet still she did not look at Miss Peregrine. Her eyes, yellow as saffron and glowing hot with fury, remained fixed on me. My muscles trembled as I looked into those animal eyes. Louisa did not move. I stared, fascinated, as she fought to control her temper. I watched as she curled her bony fingers into small knobby fists. Now I had done it. I had turned Louisa Hill into something far worse than a simple adversary. I had made her a raging enemy.

"I've been meaning to talk to you about her," Miss Peregrine said after Louisa had stomped out of the room, and I had collapsed into a chair. "She isn't nearly as bad as she makes out. That attitude of hers comes from sadness, really. Poor thing had a tragic early life, and lately...well, I have to admit that lately her mood swings have become unbearable. But I always forgive her. She has nowhere else to go, no family, no friends. I try to be firm without chasing her away. If I made her leave Peregrine House, she'd lose her mind—what with all those horrendous emotional ups and downs."

"Miss Peregrine, you don't have to ..."

"Hush up. I want you to know why Louisa behaves the way she does. I met her thirty years ago, in Schenectady, New York ..." My mind jumped to the entry in the Peregrine family Bible. Miss Peregrine droned on in her gravelly voice. "... when I took a trip there just after Father died. I went to present his bequest to Union College in person. That's where he got his Bachelor of Arts when he was young. It probably seems strange to you for Southerners to go north to be educated, but in Father's day there was a reason for it. A year or two after the War of Northern Aggression, a guilt-stricken Yankee woman traveled south and was heartbroken by the devastation of the war. I suppose she was discomfited by the atrocities committed by her fellow countrymen. At any rate, the experience moved her deeply. She felt compelled to make some sort of gesture to help us rebuild. Her family set up an ongoing scholarship fund at Union College and reserved it for Southern boys. She must have realized our only hope for recovery was through the education of our young people. Father's family was destitute for generations from the losses they sustained at the hands of those irascible Yankees. He was more than eligible for a scholarship. Then, later in life, when he became financially able, he began donating money to Union. I think he felt beholden, especially after making such a fortune over the course of his career factoring phosphate to the North. He married after he became financially secure, but his wife, my mother, became tubercular while still in her twenties. She died when I was seven years old. After that, I was expected to take her place representing the family. Father dragged me to all sorts of affairs having to do with Peregrine interests. I think he was on the board of every non-profit in the state of South Carolina, and a fair number of states beyond. We traveled to Schenectady countless times to attend special ceremonies at Union—building dedications, alumni gatherings, functions like that."

Abruptly she stopped talking and gave me a hard look. "Bored?" she said.

"No, Miss Peregrine, but you don't have to go into all this. I understand about Louisa."

"Don't tell me what to do. I'll go into whatever I like. Now then, that visit to Union after Father died was my last trip to Schenectady. I decided that as long as I was there, I ought to call on Our Lady of Grace Foundling Home, another of Father's philanthropic interests. He'd become attached to the little orphanage while a student at Union. His fraternity maintained a tradition of doing for the needy, and the children at Our Lady of Grace became the beneficiaries of their social responsibility—Christmas parties, new winter coats, toys, fruit baskets. After college and Father's unexpected financial success, he continued to remember the little orphanage. He was a stern, unfeeling man, my father. No one knows that better than I. But he could also be warm and generous. The foundling home had a wonderful benefactor in Smythe Hampton Peregrine."

Miss Peregrine stopped to rearrange her coverlet. I wondered...was she getting ready to tell me about baby Constantia?

"When I went to the foundling home on that last visit," she went on, "to see about any financial needs they might have, Louisa was working there as Assistant Director. We talked. I discovered she had grown up an orphan right there at Our Lady of Grace. The poor stunted thing had spent only one year of her life outside the walls of the orphanage, and that was when she hired out at age thirty as a companion to a wealthy spinster lady who wished to travel abroad. After a number of tours, the woman tired of Louisa and terminated their relationship. Louisa had nowhere to go, so she packed up and went back to her old job at Our Lady of Grace. She had no choice. It was the only home she'd ever known, the only place she'd ever lived or worked. When I met her there, she was forty-six years old, totally bereft of family or friends, bitter, alone, growing old prematurely. I showed her a bit of attention and she stuck to me like pitch on a bateau in the harbor. Nearly bored me senseless with sad, sad stories about her past, which I'm sure became more and more heart-wrenching every time she told them. Louisa had learned early the art of inducing pity. I think she confused it with love. Father having just died, I needed someone to keep me company—I was still traveling a great deal in those days—and I also needed help managing Peregrine House. Louisa leaped at the opportunity and we've been together ever since. Her darker side didn't emerge until later, unfortunately, though I'm sure she'd say the same about me. We've grown old together, Louisa and I, a couple of old dowdies, eccentric as hell."

I sighed audibly and shifted in the chair. "I still don't see why she's so mean," I said. "If nothing else, it looks like she'd be grateful to have this lovely house to live in. I wouldn't think many orphans end up in mansions."

"True, but you and I mustn't judge her, Arlena. We don't know what sorts of demons torment Louisa. She lived out her whole childhood without parents to love her. Children who grow up like that often develop problems."

"I know—what I *don't* know is why you feel you have to tell me all these details."

"Because that lovely cinnamon skin of yours turns white as raw milk every time Louisa appears. I'm trying to ease your anxiety. Tycie lives in fear of Louisa, which I regret, though there's nothing I can say or do to change it. I love Tycie dearly, as primitive as she is, but in her mind, Louisa will never be anything but an ogre. With you, I felt there was hope. Educated people have certain advantages over poor ignorant blacks."

"I don't agree with you on that point, Miss Peregrine. Tycie has more common sense than the two of us put together. But thanks anyway for your confidence. I'll try not to react so strongly next time Louisa makes a scene."

"Oh, you don't have to take any of her nonsense. Not at all. I simply wanted you to know what the matter was. Sh-h-h, here she comes now with our breakfast trays. Pretend we've been talking about something else."

Louisa opened the bedroom door and rolled in a cart bearing two, perfectly appointed trays. She wheeled the cart next to the bed and pulled a large folding tray from it's bottom shelf. Then, with a deftness that comes from performing a task dozens of times, she unfolded the legs of the bed tray and placed it across Miss Peregrine's middle. My smaller tray remained on the cart. Miss Peregrine examined her breakfast and nodded approval. Louisa poured coffee and left the room without speaking.

Miss Peregrine insisted I pull my chair closer to the bed to eat. Poached eggs, Tycie's warmed-over butter-biscuits, glazed figs, and cups and cups of steaming black coffee. For once, my attitude toward Louisa softened. After breakfast Miss Peregrine asked me to pour her a glass of the forbidden homemade peach brandy. She said Tycie had hidden it from Louisa, along with a crystal glass, in the bottom of the antique highboy that stood opposite her bed. Tycie had gone to the trouble of transferring the brandy from it's kitchen fruit jar to an old Jack Daniels bottle. I smiled at her notion of an innocent container. Miss Peregrine proposed a toast to *Tarnished Honor*. There was one glass, so I drank out of my coffee cup. After the brandy, she told me I should leave so she could sleep off the medication. I was to come back at my usual time on Tuesday the following week. She assured me she would be recovered by then and ready to get back to work. I helped her to the bathroom and back into bed, then tiptoed out of the room to the stairs. I made it to the stairwell between the first and second floors before being accosted by Louisa. She appeared like a ghost on the stairs below. There was no escape. I gripped the bannister as I struggled to remain poised.

"Thank you for the breakfast, Louisa," I said, my voice trembly. "It was delicious."

"Don't talk down to me," she said. "I'm not stupid. I know when people are talking down. Now look here—I have something important to tell you. I have to warn you." She looked all around to make sure we were alone before going on. "It's Miss Peregrine, she's crazy. She'll turn on you in a second."

I didn't move. I stood still and looked at her as if she'd grown two heads. She blinked alarmingly and said, "The things she's been telling you aren't true. She's the one who's crazy, not me. I know things about her." Louisa shook her head and wrung her hands as if the things she knew were too horrible to say aloud. Then she stretched her eyes and looked around again. Satisfied we were still alone, she whispered in a voice that was grainy with agitation, "You'd better not tell anyone we talked like this. If you do, we'll both be punished. Miss Peregrine likes to punish people, especially outsiders, like us."

"She does nothing of the kind," I said, "and you have no business talking about her behind her back."

I had spoken sharply to cover my fear. Until that moment, I hadn't realized how truly disturbed Louisa was. I felt certain Miss Peregrine had grossly underestimated the profundity of her madness.

"Miss Peregrine cares about you," I went on. "She doesn't want to punish you."

"Yes, she does. And she'll punish you, too, if you aren't careful. She'll fire you and stop your paychecks. I have to make sure she doesn't fire me. Every day, I have to make sure."

"She'd never fire you. She loves you."

"No, no, she hates me. I don't really belong here, you know. I wasn't born here. But she can't hurt me now—I know too many things."

"What things?"

"*Things.* Things you won't find out unless I decide to tell you. That's how I keep her from getting rid of me. She's afraid I'll tell her secrets."

"Stop talking like that, Louisa. It's crude. Miss Peregrine would be furious."

Fear appeared in her yellow eyes. "You won't tell her, will you?" she said.

"No, it would hurt her feelings too much. Why, this very morning she was telling me how much she cares about you."

"But she was angry. She threatened me."

"She did *not* threaten you. She was mad because you called Tycie and me and told us not to come to work. Anyone would have gotten mad about that. Now get hold of yourself. Tycie didn't come in today, and you'll have to carry on alone. Miss Peregrine is your friend. Have you forgotten that?"

"I don't know," she said, her eyelids fluttering. "Maybe I should make a pot of tea."

"That's a wonderful idea. Make tea for yourself and Miss Peregrine. And promise me you'll take care of her."

"I promise," she said, though her eyes showed no life and her face was ghostly pale.

"I'm counting on you, Louisa. You have to be strong. Are you feeling better now?"

She nodded. I eased past her down the steps and toward the front door, still unsure of my control of the situation. She followed me with slow wooden movements. I opened the door, hesitated, then stepped out on the piazza before turning to speak a last time.

"Good-bye, Louisa," I said, shocked by the greenish pallor of her cheeks in the unforgiving outdoor light. "And don't worry so much. It's bad for your nerves."

"Good-bye," she said tonelessly, and closed the door, this time without slamming it.

Chapter Eleven

The next day everything in my schedule was upside down by nine a.m. My original intention had been to spend the morning in the College of Charleston Library writing Chapter Eight of Mr. Pinckney's reminiscences, but Clifton Stanlock, headmaster of Southern Prep, and Raven FitzSimons, reluctant student, worked simultaneously to get me off track. With a minimum of effort, they succeeded in destroying my morning.

The day began easily enough: coffee on the porch with Stuart, kisses instead of arguments, an ocean view to knock your eyes out. Beyond the beach an iridescent Atlantic gleamed in airy morning light. Sea birds flew in concentric circles around shrimp boats anchored in the distance. I counted six white boats, each with butterfly arms lowered to let heavy nets drag bottom. Around the boats, gulls dove for chum and rotten bait. Stuart and I watched as they hovered, clipped, soared, and screamed—until the telephone rang in a disconcerting jangle, and Stuart had to leave the porch to answer it.

"For you," he called from the sitting room. "It's Raven FitzSimons. She's *whispering*, for chrissake."

"This will be grief," I said in a groan as I stood and moved toward the door. "No one calls at this hour unless it's grief."

Stuart squinted in agreement. "Want me to tell her you're still sleeping?"

"No, it's okay. She probably just wants to waste my time with a visit this afternoon."

I took the phone and pressed it to my chest to work up the courage to speak. "Hi, Rav," I said perkily. "What's new?"

"I'm scared, Mrs. Prince. Croom's father is going to school

with him this morning. They have an appointment with the head-master. I think they're going to talk about you."

"An appointment? With Cliff Stanlock?"

"Yes, and it's trouble. I'm sure of it. Can you meet me in a few minutes in the gazebo at White Point? I want to tell you what's going on in case Dr. Stanlock calls you in. Hurry and tell me if you can come. I have to get off the phone before Mother gets out of the shower."

"This is crazy, Raven. You're getting yourself all worked up over nothing. Stop being so dramatic."

"Listen to me, Mrs. Prince. I'll be at the gazebo in fifteen minutes. If you show up, I'll help you. If you don't—well, too bad."

She hung up without saying good-bye. I hung up with an angry crash of the receiver. But before I could take my hand away, the phone rang again. *"Raven,"* I said, jerking the receiver back to my ear, *"I'm going to wring your neck when I get my hands on you."*

At first there was silence, then a snigger. "Cliffton Stanlock here," a tenor voice said. "I assume you were expecting someone else. This *is* Mrs. Prince, isn't it?"

"Oh, no, excuse me, Dr. Stanlock. I thought it was...I thought you were ...."

"Never mind," he said. "I'm just glad I caught you at home. There's a problem we have to straighten out. Late yesterday I got a call from Dr. Croomer Calhoun. He requested a conference with you, immediately. He wants me to sit in on it. I know you don't have classes on Fridays, but I thought you'd like to come in and get whatever this is cleared up before the weekend."

"Do you know what the problem is?"

"I can't imagine. I was hoping you could fill me in."

"No, sir. I can't think of a thing. Maybe it's about my class. His son is in it ...."

"Perhaps—can you be here by eleven? I took the liberty of setting that time with Dr. Calhoun."

"Yes, I can, maybe a little earlier."

"Good, see you then. Good-bye."

I hung up again and looked at Stuart. He put his arms around me and patted my back. "Must be the morning for bad phone calls," he said. "Anything I can do to help?"

"Play chauffeur, I guess. Looks like I have to fight the dragon one more time." Then I slipped out of his grasp and moved to the bathroom. At times like these, Percodan tablets were more comforting than Stuart's arms.

"Who are you looking for, Rav? The enemy?" I asked. She jumped at the sound of my voice. She had been leaning over the railing of the gazebo.

"God Almighty, you scared me half to death," she spluttered. "I was just about to leave. What took you so long?"

"Stuart broke every speed limit in Mount Pleasant and Charleston, and you ask what took me so long. This better be good, *sweetheart.*"

"Please don't be mean, Mrs. Prince. I can't stand it. It's too much like Mother."

"Sorry, I don't have time for niceties today. I'm supposed to be working. And I don't like being in a public park at this hour. We're the only ones here except for those runners over there, the fools."

"A bum was sleeping in the gazebo when I got here," Raven said. "Can you believe it?" She stretched her neck and looked all around to make sure we were not being watched. I decided against mentioning the call from Cliff Stanlock. Raven's imagination needed no more fuel.

"Okay, this is it," she said, "the other day when Croom tried to get at you in class, he had already made bets with some of the kids in the hall on whether you'd recognize that passage. And when you did, he lost $47.00 I didn't tell you before—it was such a rotten thing for him to do. I try hard to love Croom, Mrs. Prince, but it isn't easy when he pulls stunts like that."

"And what else?" I said.

She shook her head and blinked, thoroughly surprised I would think there might be more. "Nothing else," she said. "I thought you needed to know what the story was, so you could defend yourself in case Dr. Stanlock tries to fire you."

"That's *all*?" I said, incredulous. "Stuart and I risked our lives coming across the Cooper River Bridge at eighty miles an hour for you to tell me Croom Calhoun Jr. lost a bet?"

"You're being mean again," she said, her face primped to cry. "Here I am trying to keep you from getting fired, and you're being mean. Dr. Calhoun and Croom want to get rid of you—God only knows why—and they'll go to any length to do it. If you don't believe me, you're crazy, crazier than Mother."

"We're talking about a part-time job here, Raven, less than a part-time job. It isn't that much to lose. And really, I hardly think a grown man would try to get me fired over an insignificant incident in one of his son's high school classes."

"He would, he would, I know he would," she wailed.

"All right, I believe you. Now be quiet. That policeman over there is looking at us." She hushed, but continued sniveling. "Listen, Rav, I want you to go to school and forget about all this. I can handle it from here. You're a dear sweet friend to warn me. I'm grateful, and I promise not to use your name if any of this comes up. Now let's get out of here. I'll give you a head start."

She gathered her books and moped toward the King Street boundary of White Point. The gray dew took her footprints in the grass. They showed up clearly in black-green parallel rows that stretched the full length of the lawn. Raven kept her head down, turning only once to wave. This girl could make a blue mood seem fatal.

I watched her disappear around the corner of King and South Battery, then turned my attention to the mansions across the street. Peregrine House stood directly in front of me, Pinckney House was farther down, closer to the corner of East Battery. I felt squeamish about the occupants of those houses observing me in White Point at such an hour. I sat for a long time in the gazebo, feeling miserable and out of place, trying in vain to sort out the morning's events. It was hopeless. My fate lay in the hands of Cliffton Stanlock, a wimp who considered me a smart-mouthed Yankee feminist. He wouldn't help me if he could. He had asked me idly once, when I first started teaching at Southern Prep, why I didn't consider going back to school and getting a Ph.D. in administration—like *he* had done. I told him I objected to the required frontal lobotomy. He didn't like me anymore after that.

The longer I sat thinking, the more depressed I became. After fifteen minutes of inertia, I watched dejectedly as an old green Ford scraped to a stop in front of Peregrine House. The driver was a young black man. He pulled up the emergency brake, slid from under the wheel, and walked around to help an old black woman from the passenger side of the car.

"*Tycie,*" I whispered when she turned her face toward me after kissing the young man on the cheek. A motherly gesture, perhaps grandmotherly. It was clear the man was family. I stared in surprise. I had never thought of Tycie having a life apart from Peregrine House. That was what happened to people when Miss Peregrine got hold of them. She swallowed them up and digested them like so many tea-time hors d'oeuvres. Tycie, Louisa, Jeannette, Dr. Calhoun. All had succumbed to her insatiable appetite for attention. In my own way, so had I. So had anyone interested in her fortune. And as much as I hated to admit it, I was interested. Somehow it got to it every month. I would find myself doing gymnastics for a fifteen-hundred-dollar check. Even Cliff Stanlock had to dance to her tune. Miss Peregrine was Southern Prep's biggest donor, and Stanlock was obligated to please her. The board would expect him to run naked down Broad Street if it would make Miss Peregrine happy. Suddenly something clicked in my brain, the self-evident simplicity of a solution. Miss Peregrine would take care of Cliff Stanlock for me. All I had to do was ask her. Dr. Calhoun might prove more difficult to handle, but Stanlock could definitely be squelched.

"*Tycie, wait,*" I called out. By this time the Ford had pulled away, and Tycie was hobbling up the long walk-way. She stopped when she heard my voice and turned stiffly.

"Lord in His Heaven. What're you doing here, Missy Arlena? The birds ain't hardly up yet."

"Just happened to be in the neighborhood," I said, moving swiftly across the street. "Thought I'd stop in for a visit. Do you think Miss Peregrine will mind?"

"She probably ain't awake yet," Tycie said with foreboding. "She sleeps too much now-a-days. But come on in, anyhow. You always make her feel better. I thank sweet Jesus you don't get her going like that trouble-making Louisa. She's meaner than our diamond-backs out on Edisto."

"I didn't know you lived on Edisto, Tycie. Isn't that where the

Pinckney family's old homeplace is—Planter's Hall Plantation? Do you know it?"

"Yes ma'am, I do. I was born on it, but the Pinckneys all live in town now, right here on South Battery. See that big brick house down the way? That's the Pinckney mansion."

"Yes, I went there once for two o'clock dinner. Come on, let's go inside now. I need to talk to Miss Peregrine. Hope she doesn't get mad at me for not calling before I came."

"She be mad *all* the time, 'bout everything, but she don't mean nothing by it. It's her rheumatism that makes her so ornery."

Tycie opened the front door with a large brass key strung on a chain around her neck. I suspected it never left the safety of her bosom except to lock and unlock Peregrine House front door. We went inside quietly. Neither of us wanted to alert Louisa. Tycie led me to the elevator and we rode to the fourth floor. I followed her to Miss Peregrine's bedroom.

"Come in," Miss Peregrine called in a drug-weakened voice. Tycie opened the door and stood politely to the side. *White folk* still entered rooms first in some pockets of the South. I despised those pockets.

"Good morning, Miss Peregrine. It's me again," I said.

"As I live and breathe. Come here. Sit with me while Tycie brings my pill bag and juice. And good morning to you, too, Tycie, you lazy h'ant. Did you enjoy your day off?"

"Your cousin told me to stay home yesterday, Missy Peregrine. That's why I did it." Tycie blamed everything blamable on Louisa. Most was deserved, some convenient.

"Quiet, Tycie," said Miss Peregrine. "I don't want to hear your prattle this morning. Get my pills and juice, and make my breakfast. I must keep up my strength."

Tycie hobbled out. I moved closer to Miss Peregrine so I could tell her my story. Her eyebrows knitted into a deep scowl as she listened to my convoluted tale. For a long time she did not speak. At first I thought she was angry, until she began issuing orders.

"I understand perfectly well," she said. "You need not fret another minute. Just listen to me carefully and do everything I say. Go to your meeting with Croomer and that worm, Cliff Stanlock, but be there at ten-thirty instead of eleven. I suspect the good headmaster will want to speak with you alone a few minutes before Croomer and the boy arrive. Now run downstairs and help Tycie with my breakfast. I must make a few phone calls."

I blushed and smiled and left the room quickly before she had a chance to change her mind. When I returned with her breakfast tray, she detained me another half hour, then sent me on my way on foot. I strode the six blocks to Southern Prep at a moderate pace to keep from straining my side. It was ten twenty-five when I arrived, thirty-five minutes early. I entered the administration building and walked smartly toward Cliff Stanlock's office. When the secretary saw me, her eyes grew wide, then Stanlock himself burst through his office door and charged at me across the reception area. He had a sick look on his face, ghost-white around the eyes and nose, greenish around the mouth. I took two steps backward.

"What have you been up to?" he said. "I've had calls from three senior board members this morning, including Grayson Pinckney. He spent fifteen minutes telling me how thrilled he is that you're teaching here again this year. He suggested we give you a raise for heaven's sake."

Bless Miss Peregrine's sweet alligator hide, I thought. A smile played around my lips before I could contain it. Stanlock became incensed.

"What do you have to say for yourself?" he said.

"I don't understand, Dr. Stanlock. Didn't you say I just got a rash of good reports?"

"Don't be cute, you devious little piece of trash." I was certain he was speaking with more emotion than he'd ever emitted all at one time in his whole impotent life. "You'd better understand this, Miss Smart-girl-from-the-North. Croomer Calhoun is on his way over here right now, and the only thing in the world that would satisfy that man this morning is seeing your ass fired."

"That's not what you said on the phone. You said you didn't know what he wanted."

"Never mind. Leave the building. Let me handle this alone. Maybe I can smooth it over without it getting to the board."

"You mean you can't fire me without board approval?" I was grinning.

"No, and I don't want it to get that far. There's enough to deal with around here without a fracus over a part-time teacher."

I laughed aloud. "Let me get this straight. You *can't* fire me;

you *don't* want me to stay for the conference; you *do* want me to leave before Dr. Calhoun gets here."

"Yes, yes, now get out of here. Oh God, look there, out the window. Here comes Calhoun now, thirty minutes early, and Croom Jr. is with him."

I glanced around for a place to hide. Stanlock appeared to be in danger of a cardiac arrest if I did not find a hole to drop into. I scuttled into a janitor's closet and slammed the door behind me. It seemed to be my lot lately to end up hiding in storage rooms. In the darkness I smelled sour mops and musty buckets of dust-down. All this *and* a college preparatory education. I hated Southern Prep.

Terry Ward Tucker

Chapter Twelve

I lay in bed and watched the blades of the ceiling fan make thirty-seven revolutions before my eyes blurred and I could no longer count. All night the bed had rolled in the syncopated rhythm of my dreams. I was exhausted. Dreams had been my private affliction as long as I could remember. They came to me in shapes and colors that did not exist in daylight. As I lay there, entranced by the fan, I became aware of Stuart's voice thrumming in the sitting room. It irritated me. Everything irritated me. I sat up on the side of the bed, wincing at the feel of sand when my feet touched the bare floor. Where were my slippers? My robe? I gave up the hope of comfort and shuffled into the sitting room as Stuart was hanging up the phone.

"Who were you talking to?" I said dully.

"A friend. Can't I talk to a friend without being interrogated?"

I raised an eyebrow. "Depends on who it was. But don't flatter yourself, big guy. I wasn't trying to check up on you. I thought it might be Cliff Stanlock again."

I gazed at the ocean through the bank of windows that separated the sitting room from the porch. They were coated with salt residue, opaque. The Atlantic appeared very far away through their smudgy, smeary panes. An impressionistic water color, blue on blue.

"We're out of money again," Stuart said. "I didn't want to tell you. I hated to tell you ..." He paused and dragged a hand over his face. "I've had to take steps to get us through. I've had to do some more borrowing."

Then big strong Stuart began to cry. Any warm feeling I had left for him disappeared in a tiny hiss. I was betrayed, let down. Here was the man who had spent every day of our courtship promising to take care of me. How could he stand before me like this, a sniveling idiot, whining that we had no money? I thought about Roz Pinckney and Caroline Priolieu and felt intensely jealous of their security. I gazed upon Stuart with disgust. He was a mess, crying at my breast like a baby. My emotions whirled in a jumble. I hated him; I felt sorry for him. One part of me wanted to attack him; another to take him in my arms. Why, I thought bitterly, is it always left to women to make men feel better?

"You have to stop that," I said with no feeling. My words were a recorded script: "It isn't your fault, Stuart; something is bound to turn up, Stuart; rest while I make you some lunch, Stuart."

Slowly he moved to the Boston rocker on the porch to rock away his depression. I padded to the kitchen to get some food. When I came back with coffee and stale pasta, he looked at me adoringly, as though I had acquired wings and a halo. He thought I was playing the part of good little wife who holds up bravely in a crisis. He should never have assigned me such saintliness. There are times when women have excessive dominance over men. Stuart was measuring his own self-worth in direct proportion to my approval, or disapproval if I so chose. I was bemused by his willingness to subject himself to my thoroughly female temperament. Could it be he really loved me? I did not know, but in case he did, I granted him a small measure of peace.

"Now, let's think things through rationally," I said, my emotions under control. "What, exactly, are the facts?"

"It boils down to this," he lisped through a mouthful of last week's linguini. "We have to survive somehow until Tuesday."

"What's magic about Tuesday?"

"Jim Rhiner is sending us a check. He said he'd put it in the mail today. If it comes by Tuesday, we can puddle-jump to Friday. That's when Bill Greene is due to pay me for the work I've done on Sea Bird."

"Was that Rhiner on the phone?"

"Yes."

"But why would he send us money? We hardly know him."

"I know him. I loaned him dough all the way through college. Now I'm calling in the favor. He's doing well these days—married a rich babe from Philly."

"This is borrowed money, right?"

"Yes, and I don't want to hear any self-righteous lectures about the pitfalls of borrowing. We need money, now."

I was quiet. I was thinking about the three hundred dollars in cash in the zipper pocket of my purse, the last of Mr. Pinckney's August tip. "But what about today?" I said. "And tomorrow?"

"We'll skinny by on nothing today. Tomorrow I'll go to the grocery store and write a check for twenty bucks or so over the amount of purchase. That'll get us food and a quarter tank of gas. Then, if Jim's check comes on Tuesday, like it's supposed to, we'll slide through okay. Hopefully the grocery check won't have bounced by then."

"But what if it doesn't come on time? You know how the mail can be."

"Then the grocery check will bounce, and we'll have to let it hang out there until Wednesday or Thursday, or whatever day Jim's money shows up. It isn't pretty, but it's the best I can come up with for now. The main thing is that we stick together. Things won't always be like this. They'll get better eventually."

I stroked Stuart's hair and told him I loved him, but did not mention my three hundred dollars. Something inside my chest kept me from it, something oddly familiar, yet until that moment, I had not been fully aware of its presence. It had kept itself hidden, silent, waiting for the right time to emerge. It was an animal, a beast, a being with definition and will. It told me what to say—what *not* to say. It drummed its evil sermon into my ears: "*Don't tell Stuart about the Pinckney money; don't tell him you've never really loved him; or that you're sick with pains in your belly and cannot survive without pills.*"

The spirit of the beast quickened within me and assumed a position of power. It pressed against my throat. I couldn't breathe. I broke into a coughing spell, and Stuart became distraught. "I'm okay," I said when the coughing subsided. "Let me go to the bathroom. I'll throw some water on my face."

I did not say I was going for Percodan. I did not say a beast was crawling on the underside of my skin. My hands trembled as I twisted the cap off the medicine bottle and shook out two tablets. I shivered as they slipped down my throat, then I leaned on the sink and forced myself to look into the mirror. It was at that moment I realized the magnitude of my problem—I knew I had lost control.

In a short half-hour a synthetic serenity had put the beast at bay. I was calm and beautiful. Nothing could touch me. I settled myself on the porch swing and listened to Stuart dictating into the

Dictaphone. He was composing pages for Mr. Pinckney's Chapter Eight, the one I had been unable to write. I should have been grateful for the help, but since I knew he was doing it to make dead sure I'd get my paycheck on time, I did not say thank you. An undisturbed hour passed before a car noise broke the peace. I moved across the sitting room to the window overlooking the street. Through my private haze, I saw Raven and Croom Jr. standing in the driveway. They were leaning against Raven's MG. I opened the back door and called down:

"Hi, Raven. Where have you been? Haven't heard from you in a while."

She wouldn't look at me, just stared straight ahead as if concentrating on something interesting down the street.

"Are you all right, Rav?" I asked. "You look like you just lost your best friend."

She glanced up, then cut her eyes away again. "I'm okay," she said. "Mad at Mother, that's all. When Croom brought me home last night, she was waiting up. I guess we were a little late. Anyway, she was drunk, and she got so mad she almost killed me."

"What time did you get in?"

"Four."

"Can't say as I blame her. She was probably worried sick."

Raven shrugged; I sighed. "Wish you'd phoned before you came out," I said. "Stuart and I have work to do. We can't entertain you."

"That's okay," she said, staring farther down the road. Croom remained silent. I studied Raven's perfect profile, and realized with a pang that something more was wrong. I took a step down the stairway.

"What's the matter, sweetie? You seem ...."

She didn't let me finish. She lurched forward and began shouting. "I'm losing my mind. *That's* what's the matter. My mother is the biggest bitch in Charleston. I hate her so much I can't stand it. I want to vomit I hate her so much."

I hurried down the rest of the steps. "Please don't talk like that, Raven. Your mother wouldn't want you to ..."

"My *mother*?" she said, lifting her head so her face caught full sunlight. I stared in disbelief. Her right jaw was swollen and bluish. An angry abrasion shone on her cheekbone. I looked into her eyes and was moved by their sorrow. Raven was an abused little animal whose spirit had folded in upon itself.

"You think I shouldn't hate my mother?" she said, her chin quivering like a child's. "Fine—then give me one good reason why not."

Chapter Thirteen

On Wednesday morning winds from the ocean gusted cool and clean over Sullivan's Island. When I woke up, I decided to spend the day on the beach letting autumn-freshened breezes blow away my worries, particularly those about Raven. But Miss Peregrine had a different agenda in mind. She called early to say she needed me at Peregrine House, though it was not our regular day, that there was something she wanted me to help her take care of, something important. I hesitated, then she told me Louisa would be away with her church cronies delivering charity goods to the poor on Daufuski Island. This changed things. I actually began to look forward to an hour or two alone with Miss Peregrine. Most of the time I enjoyed her company, despite her abrasiveness. And minus the specter of Louisa Hill, Peregrine House was a lovely place to visit.

When I told Stuart Miss Peregrine had called, he insisted on driving me into town. At five of ten, he dropped me off on the corner of King and South Battery. I carried a manila folder in one hand, a bunch of daisies in the other. I'd purchased them from a flower vendor on Church Street as an offering to the queen. Unfortunately, the joker answered the door.

"*Mrs. FitzSimons*," I said in unconcealed shock when the Raven-like frump appeared before me. My voice went up an octave. "*What are you doing here?*"

Jeannette FitzSimons was amused by my surprise. It almost helped her sour attitude. "I am sure it is none of your business, Mrs...Mrs...what was your name again?"

"Prince. Arlena Prince."

"Yes, Mrs. Prince. Sorry to have forgotten. But your name isn't important to some of us. The fact is, a number of people in

Charleston wish they'd never heard of you. Cliffton Stanlock is surely one."

Before I had a chance to collect myself, a loud crack came from the parlor. FitzSimons jumped. "It's Miss Peregrine," she said less confidently, "banging that infernal cane." She pushed open the door and yanked me inside. I dropped the daisies on the floor. "Leave them," she said. "Tycie will clean them up later. Hurry, get to the parlor."

I walked like a robot, through the foyer, under the archway, into the gloomy parlor. Miss Peregrine sat next to the fireplace in a large antique chair. She was a queen on her throne, complete with scepter and robe—her gold-knobbed walking cane and satin dressing gown. If I had not just endured a harangue from Jeannette FitzSimons, I'd have been overjoyed to see her looking so rested.

"You're late," said the queen. "You have no time to be lollygagging about on the piazza. Such ninnies you and Jeannette are, flapping your tongues like magpies with no thought at all about my air conditioning. Now go over by the mantel and stand quietly. I will deal with you later, after I'm finished with Jeannette."

I slunk to a corner and tried to make myself small.

"As for you, Jeannette," she said, "I have had my fill of advice on what property I should and should not sell. Don't ever again bring rubbish like this into my house. Do you understand?" Then she picked up a folder from the tea table and gave it an angry toss. Papers fanned out on the hearth tiles. FitzSimons stooped to gather them up while Miss Peregrine raved on.

"I will *never* sell my island property to developers," she said, "not one square inch. You know how I feel about that, yet every few weeks you skulk in here with more of your harebrained schemes. The people submitting these bids are carpetbaggers, do you hear? They'll steal your underwear if you blink once. Come to think of it, maybe that's what you'd like."

FitzSimons did not speak; her face had gone purple. She coughed once, buying time to compose herself. "They aren't developers," she said shakily. "They're part of a land-holding company, a group of wealthy businessmen interested in long term investments ...."

"Don't tell me any more," Miss Peregrine roared. "You don't know what these people are like. In five years they'd have Sullivan's Island looking like Myrtle Beach, or Florida, or worse."

"No, Fanny ..."

"Shut-up and get that garbage out of my house. I swear by Jehovah Himself, I will not let that island be ravished."

I watched Jeannette FitzSimons disappear. She faded from the room like an apparition. Miss Peregrine's rage had burned through her body until there was nothing left but vapor.

I did not move. I did not want to be dematerialized like FitzSimons. Slowly Miss Peregrine reorganized her attention, shifting me to its forefront. "As for you, little missy," she said in my direction a shade less acidly, "I expect you to behave today. May I have your full attention this morning, or must I hire someone else to assist me?"

She paused a moment, waiting for me to speak. *"Answer me,"* she said, again cracking the cane.

"Yes," I squeaked.

"You'll follow instructions with no back-talk, correct?"

"Yes." I had regressed to a one-word vocabulary.

"Good. Now then, look in the top drawer of the secretary there, where you find those early checks you need so regularly. My car keys are in the top drawer, in the back left corner."

I walked mechanically to the desk. The keys required a search. This was good. It gave me something to do with my hands. When I found the keys, I turned to face Miss Peregrine again, and received another shock. She had risen from her chair and was standing now, straight and tall, by the pink marble fireplace. Her robe was in a heap on the floor. In its place was a lovely blue dress with white lace cuffs and collar. There were pearls at her neck, a diamond watch on her wrist, and a polished wooden walking cane in her hand.

"How do I look?" she said, smiling as if she had pulled off some great trick. Somehow her face seemed less wrinkled.

"Beautiful—you look beautiful," I said.

"Rubbish, though I love the flattery. Tycie helped me dress this morning, then that worrisome Jeannette popped in here like a blue-jay and got in the way of my plans. I'll be damned if I'm going to let everyone in Charleston be privy to my business. Tycie had to move fast—what a joke *that* was, Tycie trying to move fast—to get this robe down here so Jeannette wouldn't know I was going out. I'd already had trouble enough getting rid of Louisa."

"Where are you going?" I asked. I sounded like someone speaking lines in a play.

"No more questions. I think there's a conspiracy in this town to keep me from going anywhere undetected. Tycie has worried me silly all morning, fussing about, acting flustered. I've been planning this outing a long time, but things have kept getting in my way. Have you forgotten about making that call to Grayson Pinckney's office the other morning? The one canceling my appointment? If you have, you've a decided lack of intellect. Well, I called him back yesterday and rescheduled for today, and you are going to drive me."

"*Me*? I can't, I don't have a car. Stuart dropped me off this morning."

"We shan't need your car. We'll take mine. Those are the keys in your hand."

"But I've never driven your car. What if I can't ...."

"*Hush.* You have three things to do: drive me to Broad Street; drive me home; and keep your mouth shut in between. For the amount of money I pay you every month, it isn't much to ask."

"I want to help you, Miss Peregrine. Really, I do ..." I looked down at my hands. They were trembling. "Maybe if I had a drink of water."

"*Tycie*," the old woman screeched, punishing my eardrums, "*fetch Mrs. Prince a glass of water.*"

Carefully, very carefully, I backed the Cadillac out of the carriage-house. Tycie stood to the side and smiled as if she'd been party to a miracle. She probably had. Miss Peregrine settled herself in the passenger seat and commanded that our journey commence. I drove to Pinckney Building on Broad Street. Parking did not present its usual problem, not when Fanny Peregrine was along. She told me to pull into the back lot, and pointed a crooked finger to a space marked in bold letters, JONATHAN PRIOLIEU. I gave her an unsure look; she pointed again; we parked. I was helping her out of the car when Priolieu himself pulled in behind us and began tapping his horn. I glanced at him and pretended not to know what he wanted. Miss Peregrine ignored him. He stuck his head out of his car window and called to me by name.

"Mrs. Prince, is that your car? You'll have to move it. This space is reserved."

I didn't answer. Aggravated, he got out of his car and approached the Cadillac to investigate this unacceptable situation.

"I said you can't park there," he began again, then stopped to stare at Miss Peregrine. She held her head far back and looked down her nose at him.

"It is *my* car, sir," she said, "and as you can see, there is no other place to put it."

"But this lot belongs to the Pinckney firm, madam. It isn't open to the public."

I realized Jonathan Priolieu didn't know who Miss Peregrine was. All that provocative talk over dinner at Pinckney House, and he did not know her on sight. I grabbed the opportunity to stick him.

"Mr. Priolieu, you've arrived at the perfect moment. Miss *Peregrine* and I are in desperate need of a big strong man like you. I'm sure you have the keys to the back door of the building. Miss *Peregrine* has an appointment with Mr. Pinckney in three little baby minutes—" I looked at my watch with a hugely exaggerated arm movement, "—and if we don't move along, I'm afraid we shall be late. You wouldn't want to make dear sweet Miss *Peregrine* late, now would you? Not after all the wonderful things you were saying about her at dinner the other day."

Miss Peregrine looked at me askance. I winked at her, then turned back to Priolieu and batted my eyelashes. He had not yet realized he was being made a fool of.

"Peregrine?" he said.

Miss Peregrine spoke sourly. "I am Fanny Hampton Peregrine, come to call on Grayson Lockwood Pinckney, IV. And who, pray tell, are you?"

"Jonathan Priolieu, ma'am—Mr. Pinckney's son-in-law."

"Do tell," Miss Peregrine said and sniffed loudly.

"Oh dear," I said, "please forgive me for not introducing you, Jonathan. I thought you and Miss Peregrine were old friends, the way you were going on about her the other day. Oh Miss Peregrine, you'd be so pleased by the kind remarks Mr. Priolieu was making about you and your family, especially your dear departed father."

"*Do tell,*" Miss Peregrine said again and looked Jonathan Priolieu up and down. He suffered under her gaze. For a moment he appeared to be shrinking.

"Please, let me help you ladies inside," he said in a burst of Southern courtesy. "You'll wilt like cut gardenias in this sun."

"Do tell," I said in a perfect mimic of Miss Peregrine. She cast me a withering look. I decided to back off. Priolieu stumbled all over himself trying to help us into the building. When we stepped off the elevator on the second floor, he announced our arrival to Mr. Pinckney's secretary as if we were visiting dignitaries. Mr. Pinckney was mortified by the folderol and took control of the situation with dispatch. Miss Peregrine was given the seat of honor across from his desk. I was told to wait in Lillian's reception area as she was out for the day. Son-in-law was dismissed. But the instant Mr. Pinckney closed his office door, Priolieu reappeared, angry enough to kill. I gave him a superior look and turned away, which infuriated him even more. He caught me by my arm and pulled me to his chest. I felt his breath on my face.

"You think you're so smart," he growled. "Well, you contemptuous little bitch, you're going to have to get a lot smarter if you want to survive in Charleston. This town is shark infested, or haven't you figured that out yet? By the way, the invitation to my office is still open. I like the way you smell today."

I jerked away and slapped him full across the face. A drop of blood formed at the corner of his mouth. "*Bitch*," he said again, then goose-marched out of the reception area and down the carpeted hallway. When he was out of sight and hearing, I sank gratefully into a chair to wait. An hour later I was still there. Two hours later I was asleep, in the same chair, in the same room. Miss Peregrine and Mr. Pinckney had forgotten me.

Chapter Fourteen

"Wake up, Arlena," Miss Peregrine said from an echo chamber deep in my brain. "Wake up, child. Don't you know sloth is the handmaiden of ruination."

Miss Peregrine and Grayson Pinckney had finished their meeting and come looking for me in the hallway. Mr. Pinckney laughed as I blinked and tried to focus.

"A marvelous way to earn the minimum wage," he said. "Are you working by the hour or the day?"

My head was swimming; I had trouble understanding what he'd said. I stood, got dizzy, and had to sit again. "I'm sorry, Miss Peregrine. I waited and waited...I must have fallen asleep."

"Stop apologizing and get yourself up," she said. "Grayson, fetch the girl some water. Can't you see her brain is fogged?"

I stood again, this time more slowly. Miss Peregrine frowned. "Ready to go?" I said cheerily in a failed effort to redeem myself.

"Yes, but not home. If you can manage to regain consciousness, I want you to drive me to Sullivan's. Haven't seen that old sand dune for a year or more. It's time I paid her a call."

"Sullivan's? But what about two o'clock dinner? Won't Tycie be expecting you?"

"I've already taken care of that. Grayson called and told her I'd be late. And Louisa won't be back until evening. I can gad about all afternoon if I want. Tycie has instructions to tell callers I'm not well and have taken to my bed. For one afternoon I'm going to do precisely what I please without it being broadcast about."

I nodded while sipping from the paper cup Mr. Pinckney had brought from his office. He took it from my hand when I finished drinking and asked if I were ready to go. I said yes, and he escorted us to the car, strolling along politely at Miss Peregrine's side as if her snail-like pace were normal. As we made our way to the parking lot, the two old aristocrats traded memories about people who had died long before I was born. It made me glad I'd spent the last two hours napping instead of being bored by go-ings-on behind closed doors. Mr. Pinckney took his time helping Miss Peregrine into the car. I was thankful. It gave me another minute to shake the cobwebs from my brain before I had to start driving. They said their good-byes and promised to stay in touch. He thanked her, then stood back and directed me out of the park-ing lot. The appointment was officially over.

At Miss Peregrine's insistence, I headed toward Mount Pleas-ant and Sullivan's Island. As we approached the Cooper River Bridge, she smiled and patted my leg. I was surprised. It was a tender gesture, almost loving. I smiled back and took a cleansing breath, allowing myself a softer mood. Miss Peregrine's new and pleasant attitude, uncharacteristic though it was, was taking away some of my tension.

"Miss Peregrine," I said, enjoying the easy feeling, "did you ever cross the harbor on *The Sappho*?"

She laughed. "About a million times. Where in the world did you hear about that creaky old ferry?"

"I specialize in memoirs, remember? Things like that come up."

"*The Sappho* was a far sight safer than this monster of a bridge," she said, craning her neck upward to see the steelwork of the sec-ond span. Her eyes moved slowly down to the roadway. "Great Scott, look at that multitude of automobiles. I remember the day when only two or three cars could be found in all of Charleston."

I held the wheel steady as we joined the river of cars descend-ing into Mount Pleasant. We took the main road to the right, Coleman Boulevard. It would bypass the crooked streets of Old Town, and eventually become a straight shot to the Ben Sawyer Swivel Bridge that traversed the Intracoastal. Miss Peregrine con-tinued her observations while I negotiated light traffic.

"And none of these roadside businesses were here," she said. "Would you look at that? Restaurants have closed off every inch of Shem Creek, all the way to the waterway. Used to be nothing along there but shrimp boat docks."

"They're still there," I said, "just hard to see because of the restaurants."

I kept my eyes on Coleman. Soon we saw the mile-long causeway that led to the Ben Sawyer Bridge. The marsh road along its middle, from Mount Pleasant to Sullivan's Island, had been built in the early thirties from spoil dredged from the Intracoastal. I loved the expanse of sawgrass and mud flats that spread out from it in serene acreage along both its banks. On the right, an asphalt bicycle path formed a narrow ribbon between the roadway and a row of oleanders. I reveled in their pink and white. As the black Caddy transported us over the causeway, I glanced across the salt marsh to check the direction of the tide. There was nothing more renewing to my soul than sea water rushing through sawgrass on indrawn evening tides. The ruts and gullies would fill and overflow until every inch of satiny pluffmud would disappear beneath the surface of the water to be washed and fed by the tide.

Miss Peregrine became wistful as we turned right onto Middle Street and headed toward the lighthouse, but when she spied the walls of Fort Moultrie, her spirits lifted again. A mood to talk came upon her.

"My ancestors had a summer home on this island," she said, "not too long after that maniac Edgar Allan Poe was stationed at the fort. What a pitiful excuse for a soldier he was. Can't imagine why they named the library after him."

"But Miss Peregrine, I love Sullivan's old library. It's wonderful the way they built it into the dungeon. It's like a cave in there."

Miss Peregrine paid no attention to what I was saying. She was engrossed in her own musings. "Who'd ever have thought Fort Moultrie would become defunct," she said and clucked her tongue softly. "It used to be critical to defending the harbor, but that was before we had sonar and nuclear this-and-that. Those battlements up there may as well be torn down. They never did that much good in the first place, not even in the big war."

Miss Peregrine was not talking about World War I or II. To her, there was only one "big war," the War Between the States. After surveying the fort, she asked me to drive north to Harbor Point. She wanted to watch the ships going in and out of the harbor, and enjoy the ocean breeze.

The harbor view stirred her memory. She spoke of her childhood when whole summers were spent swimming, marooning, playing whist (cards), sleeping outdoors in hammocks, feasting on shrimp, playing in the sand, flying kites, sailing, hiking. She laughed when she remembered her knee-length bathing suits and matching ruffled caps. Memories of old times made her think of her mother, a rare occurrence, for her mother had died so young. I told her what had happened to my own mother, which made her sad.

When we left the point, she insisted we drive from one end of the island to the other, up and down every street and lane, by each landmark and house, alongside every body of water. We traveled south on Ion Avenue until it converged with Middle Street, then turned west on Bayonne and headed toward the marsh. There we explored the crisscrossing back streets that had been named in honor of the mad poet: Goldbug, Raven, Poe. For two hours and a tank of gas, we rode the streets and byways. Miss Peregrine would not let me stop until every palmetto had been inspected, and every oleander examined. When she finally grew tired, she instructed me to park in the public lot overlooking Breach Inlet for one last look at the ocean. She asked if I were in a hurry. No, I was not. The afternoon had become a nostalgic trip back in time. I wished it did not have to end.

"This may be the last time I see this place," she said as we watched the roiling waters of the inlet.

"Don't say that, Miss Peregrine. You'll see it again," I said. "But if you decide to come back any time soon, you may have to find another driver. You've worn your old one out."

My effort to save her from her sinking mood failed, which saddened me. She had been so young and lighthearted the last few hours. I hated to see her lose the feeling.

"Arlena," she said without changing expressions or taking her gaze off the water. "I have not often spoken to you of serious matters. Today I wish to do so. Are you listening?"

I straightened in my seat and became attentive. I was a child preparing to be lectured. "Yes," I said, remaining perfectly still.

She turned and looked into my face. "You have to understand that you and yours must protect places like Sullivan's," she said. "If you don't, they will vanish from the face of the earth forever. If your generation doesn't do its part to preserve what little we have left of natural beauty, there will soon be nothing left. No beaches, no oceans, nothing. What a sad, sad eventuality that would be."

I did not speak. Saving the oceans and beaches of the world was too big a concept to assimilate. Miss Peregrine continued. "I am informing you of your duty, lamb. I hope you and that citified husband of yours have developed a sense of responsibility some-where along the line."

"What do you mean, Miss Peregrine?"

"Just say that given the opportunity you'd do the right thing by Sullivan's Island—no more, no less."

"I will, I'll try. But I don't know what you're talking about ...."

"Trying will be quite enough," she said. "I thank you for that much. Now let's not discuss it further today. It's time for me to go home."

Part Two
The Beast

Chapter Fifteen

"How could you forget, Arlena? I've been talking about the oyster roast for weeks. It's Southern Prep's biggest fall fund-raiser."

Stuart kicked a deck chair out of the way and paced the length of the porch. But in spite of his show of temper, and intimidating scowl, he looked better than I'd seen him in weeks. White duck pants and brown leather loafers—leftovers from more affluent times—with a classic navy v-neck, sleeves pushed up to the elbows oh-so-casually, to show off a Sullivan's Island tan. And under the sweater, a white knit polo, two buttons undone at the neck to reveal a section of male chest. Stuart was all bronze skin, damp brown-blond curls, and straight white teeth. He had stepped straight out of *Gatsby*.

"I'll hurry," I said, contrite and bedraggled upon entering the presence of this clean and perfumed Stuart, this disarmingly stylish, good-looking Stuart. "Give me fifteen minutes and I'll be ready. I promise."

I had abandoned my shell bucket outside by the door, along with any hope that a simple walk on the beach could calm my jangled nerves. I now had to begin a frantic rush to shower and get dressed. My hands shook as I went through the routine. "Are white slacks okay for me, too?" I shouted from the bedroom. "We don't want to look like cheerleaders."

"No, wear the white dress, the cotton sleeveless that comes down to your ankles. Your black espadrilles will be good with that, and your long black cardigan. Drape the sleeves over your shoulders and loop them in front. And clean that seashell crud out from under your fingernails."

With the exception of my favorite hoop earrings, I dressed exactly as Stuart had instructed. But since he forgot to mention hair, I decided to get extravagant. I brushed out all the tangles, swept my whole mass of heavy dark hair to one side, and secured it in a large silver clamp. Several snaky tendrils escaped and wrapped themselves around my throat. I leaned over and gave my head a shake to get everything properly tousled, then stepped back from the mirror to evaluate. A thick rope of blue-black hair hung from the top of my left ear, over my breast, almost to my waist. It was bohemian, gypsy-like, *not* to be mistaken for the locks of a blunt-cut Southern honey. I hoped Stuart wouldn't notice. He was always afraid some prospective Southern client would be offended by my slightly ethnic look and his own Boston accent. And without clients, he reminded me daily, we would have to give up paradise and move back north.

"Arlena, I will never understand you," he said when I joined him on the porch. "Why would you want to go to a business function looking like that. We've both worked on projects at Southern Prep, and any idiot could figure out that the board members could be good references. That's how we're supposed to get new work, word-of-mouth. We've been over that a thousand times, but you never seem to get it. You act like you don't give a rip if we ever get a referral. There are times I think you do things deliberately to be offensive, or at least, different. And I have no idea why. You took as many psych courses as I did. You *know* that people who take pains to be different are usually just insecure, or have you forgotten everything you learned?"

God, how insulting Stuart could be, all under the guise of learn-ed discourse. I extended my claws for battle. "I know one thing I haven't forgotten," I said, chin thrust forward. "I haven't forgotten you close off everything you ever say to me with some condescending remark like *have you forgotten?* I haven't forgotten *that, Stuart.*" His name came out nastily, a lot of hissing on the "s."

"Don't start," he said. "I want to get through the evening without an argument. This is an important event, a chance to meet people. Are you ready now, or do you have to primp for another hour?"

"Why don't you stop blaming everything on me, *Stuart.*" More hissing. Then cold war. Stuart drove in silence the six miles to Charleston. Half-way there I wanted to tell him I was sorry for being so mean, but the words would not come out. After a while, I gave up trying and concentrated on a new pain that radiated from my forehead down the bridge of my nose.

"Stuart *and* a headache," I thought. "Well, maybe they'll serve drinks at the oyster roast, something to help this head. A bar. Yes. There's definitely hope for a bar at the fund-raising soiree. After all, the address is Old Charleston."

Autumn in the South Carolina lowcountry is a carnage of roasting oysters, with Southern Prep a leader in the glorious tradition. As Stuart and I got out of the Romeo and trudged across the manicured athletic field, beach music blared at us from all sides from six sets of speakers. A healing surge of blood squeezed through my veins. I sneaked a glance at Stuart and wished he weren't still angry. Surely he wouldn't pout all evening. I tried to match his long strides, but when I couldn't, he grabbed my arm and pulled me through the crowd. Together we moved toward a makeshift bar at the far end of the field. I stumbled twice; he didn't notice. I wheezed with every step; he didn't care. By the time we reached the bar, I was perspiring and out of breath, but when I got a look at how it was set up, I felt an infusion of strength. Well, well, well...an *open* bar, we have. How nice.

Stuart ordered beer for himself and white wine for me. The black bartender handed him the drinks in two plastic go-cups that looked as if they might have come from a cheap motel room. It made no difference. You could get just as drunk. He wouldn't give me my cup until I looked him in the eye and pretended to listen to orders.

"You're on your own now," he said coldly. "Mingle, try to drum up some business. We'll leave around eleven. Be ready. And, Arlena, don't drink more than one of these."

He walked away and left me standing by myself, but I didn't feel alone—I had my booze to keep me company. It took seconds to finish off that first cup of wine, minutes to order another and another. The fourth I asked for over ice. *No more headache.* The fifth in a larger cup. *Euphoria.* It was then I noticed how warm the night had become. *(Oh, those balmy Southern nights. Velvety, starry, intoxicating. My soul feeds on moonlight, sweet Southern moonlight.)* I do not think in all my thirty years I had ever gotten quite that drunk quite that quickly. I sighed, peeled off my sweater, and laid it across the end of the bar. The black bartender frowned. I smiled at him brilliantly and the ice cube I had been sucking fell out of my mouth. He widened his eyes, then scanned the area to see who was supposed to be minding me. No one looked promising. When his gaze circled back around, I smiled again, waved cutely with my fingertips, and glided away from the bar. I had decided to go exploring.

Little knots of people carried on animated conversations as I slipped and slid between them. I glided like a serpent through the territory of the party until I'd seen everything worth seeing. This did not take long. Across the field, opposite the bar, a sweating cadre of black men manned three long rows of oyster grills, those menacing contraptions specifically designed to roast defenseless animals alive. The grills were homemade devices, metal drums cut lengthwise and welded, curved sides down, to lengths of pipe that served as legs. Piles of red coals lined the bottoms of the drum halves; gigantic metal racks lay across their tops. On the tops of the racks, dozens upon dozens of unshucked oysters steamed and cracked under wet burlap sacks. When the oysters were ready, about half-cooked, the black men would shovel them into tin buckets and distribute them among the groups of tables set up near the dance floor. They would dump them on the table-tops upon week-old editions of *The Charleston News and Courier*, traditional table covering at all lowcountry oyster roasts.

Each time a new bucket of oysters appeared, barbarous shrieks arose from the crowd. Guests flew to tables, pulled on garden gloves, grabbed chisels and screwdrivers, and resumed shucking and splitting the gritty gray shells. They ate the oysters off knife blades and dripping from tips of screwdrivers. The women dipped them in hot sauce, or squeezed lemon juice on them, or slid them onto saltine crackers. Between the orgies of oysters, other delicacies were devoured. Several grills held vats of water for boiling corn on the cob, shrimp, and sausages. Red peppers and jalepenos were used as seasonings, and when I moved too close to the vats, the spiced steam burned my eyes and throat. In the center of every table was a large platter of sausages, shrimp, and corn, and beside every plate, a malodorous pile of shrimp peelings, corn cobs, and oyster shells. There looked to be more left over than eaten. I watched the worst of it from a distance, then glided back to the bar and ordered myself another wine. The bartender was

Terry Ward Tucker

very black and very polite and very very sorry to see me.

"What's your name?" I said.

"Isaac, ma'am."

"Well, Isaac, I used to teach school up north, but we never had parties like this, no sirree, and we dang sure never had a bar. Guess that's the South for ya, huh?"

The man looked at me as if I'd grown two heads, then glanced around for rescue from a white woman dumb enough to talk to hired help.

"Oh, you don't have to be nervous, Isaac. I'm not a parent. I work here same as you. I teach, part-time."

"Yes'm," he said while making someone else a drink. His effort to remain cool was failing. He could not get away from me. When I realized I had him trapped behind the bar, the sheer power of it went to my head.

"Isaac, Isaac, Isaac," I said. "Don't look so desperate, Isaac. I'm not going to bite you. All I want is to talk to you. Can't you see how lonely I am?"

Isaac examined his fingernails, scratched his temple, and polished a spot on the bar that did not need polishing. He appeared to have gone deaf.

"Isaac, have a heart. Here I am alone, haven't talked to a soul all night, and you're playing hard-to-get. Isaac, Isaac, let's run away together, Isaac. I'm begging you, please."

Poor Isaac set his jaw and would not speak. I was just getting ready to torment him more when someone tapped me on the shoulder. "Let's not be too forward, Mrs. Prince," a man said. "One of the guests might hear."

I turned to see Jonathan Priolieu grinning a crooked grin. Isaac looked hopeful and began rearranging his liquor bottles.

"Well, well, well," I said. "If it isn't the lecher of Pinckney House. Belly up to the bar, Jonathan. Talk to Isaac and me. We're discussing the curious Southern tradition of setting up open bars at school functions, or maybe it isn't Southern at all. Maybe it's just Cha-a-hl-ston. What do *you* think, Isaac?"

The bartender was now approaching panic. Jonathan rescued him. "It's quite Cha-a-hl-ston," he said, "and exceedingly civilized. Ours is a culture rich in tradition, Mrs. Prince. We brought our customs to the New World from the royal courts of Europe."

Priolieu was drunker than I, but we were running neck and

126

Elegant Sinners

neck on obnoxious. I laughed in his face, then insulted him out-right. "You're an overweight, garlic-breathed fool, Jon Priolieu. You give new meaning to the term 'royal ass.' Now go away and leave Isaac and me alone. We have private matters to discuss. We're running away together. Actually, Isaac is thinking of going to graduate school up north to become a lawyer, then maybe a federal judge or a Justice of the Supreme Court. He may even become the first black President of the United States, at which point all you whitebreads from South Carolina will probably se-cede from the Union again and have to have your asses whipped worse than last time. Isn't that right, Isaac?"

This time Isaac backed away in sheer terror and disappeared into the night. Jonathan Priolieu laughed until his side ached, then draped his arm around my shoulders in a style that reeked of familiarity. I did not resist. "Let's dance," he said thickly. I did not say no.

He pulled me toward the temporary parquet dance floor that had been laid out next to the tables. It did not surprise me he was a dance king. Smooth as silk. Cut a rug. He definitely grew up in Charleston. For over an hour we shagged and dipped and swayed, and had just gotten down to some serious cheek-to-cheek when Stuart materialized at my side.

"Time to go," he said and jerked me out of Priolieu's arms.

"No, go away, I'm having fun."

"Arlena, it's late. We have to leave. Pull yourself together."

"Let go of my arm, Stuart. You're hurting me."

"Hey, buddy," Priolieu said in a slur. "Leave the little gal alone. You're not jealous, are you? Why won't you let her have a little fun?" He put his hand on Stuart's shoulder and leaned on him for support. Stuart did not acknowledge him. He pulled away with a sharp jerk, then focused again on me.

"We're going home," he said, "*now.*"

His fingers tightened around my wrist. I struggled to break free. He squeezed my hand until I gave in, then dragged me to-ward the edge of the dance floor. Then, in total drunken idiocy, Priolieu initiated events that would end the night in disaster. He caught up with Stuart and me in the middle of the dance floor and stepped directly into our path. Stuart tried to get around him, but Priolieu was too drunk to be reasonable. He took a wild punch at Stuart's face, his fist making contact with the bone just above the left eye. There was a thud. Stuart let go of my hand. He lurched sideways and fell across two couples shagging to "Sixty-Minute Man." I scrambled after him and heard myself screaming his name. The dance floor cleared instantly except for two gallant preps who helped Stuart to his feet.

I became immediately hysterical. There was a cut through Stuart's eyebrow that had not yet begun to bleed. The blood vessels were squashed flat. Stuart said nothing. He touched the cut in his eyebrow and gazed vacantly at the people nearby. I thought he might fall or faint. Then slowly, intently, he surveyed the crowd. His eyes went past Jon Priolieu, stopped, and came back. Priolieu, who swayed drunkenly near a tall speaker, did not realize what was happening. It was my turn to beg to go home. Stuart wouldn't listen. He approached Priolieu and glared into his face. Priolieu smiled stupidly and continued to sway. Stuart stood still another second, then shoved Priolieu backward. A rather gentle shove, really. Quite controlled. Clearly not intended to make a man fall. Priolieu staggered. Stuart shoved him again, this time a little harder. He kept at it, harder and harder, forcing Priolieu in the direction of the tables. Priolieu asked him to stop several times. Stuart either did not hear or did not care. Then again Priolieu's temper got ahead of his good sense. He took another swipe at Stuart's face. Stuart stopped his arm in mid-air, and swung from the right to deliver a stunning blow to the mouth. He pumped two fists into Priolieu's gut and finished with an upper-cut to his chin. Priolieu fell on a picnic table, sprawling spread-eagle across a pile of new-lain garbage. Looking like a fallen street bum, he rolled slowly onto his side and spit blood on *The Charleston News and Courier*.

I ran to Stuart and tried to pull him away. I pleaded with him to take me home. He would not move. He would not listen. He would not take his eyes off Priolieu. I hoped to God that Priolieu would not get up from the table. He lay still, then moaned like a child and vomited into a bucket of oyster shells. But that was not the worst. The worst was when he put his hand to his mouth and spit out three broken teeth. The men who had helped Stuart were now helping Priolieu. They glanced in Stuart's direction several times to make sure he was not planning to move in again. I stood at his side, crying into his sweater sleeve, begging him to take me home. Then I was aware of someone else close by, someone trying to get Stuart to move. Grayson Pinckney had come to our rescue.

"Come on, son," Mr. Pinckney said. "You just meant to conk him, not kill him. That's the thing you can't afford to forget when you find yourself in a throw-down. Damn...Jon just spit out half his front teeth. Probably cost his mama and daddy two or three thousand dollars to have them straightened. Time to quit now, son. Come on, take your lady home. No sense hanging around until the last dog is hung, especially if it might be you."

Stuart's muscles yielded. He allowed himself to be led away. The crowd opened and we moved through unchallenged.

"Thank you, Mr. Pinckney," I mumbled between sobs. "We can handle it from here. Thank you."

Grayson Pinckney chuckled. "Don't thank me," he said. "Just get this brute husband of yours home before he whips anyone else, though I will say it did my heart good to see Jon's ass splattered through those oyster shells."

"Stuart's sorry, sir. I know he is."

Mr. Pinckney shook his head. "Done and over now. Can't undo it, can't fix it. Best to go on home to bed. I did learn one useful thing tonight, though. The next time we want to liven up one of our oyster roasts, we'll just invite a couple of damn Yankees."

Chapter Sixteen

My shoulder banged against the car door as the Alfa-Romeo lurched off the curb of Southern Prep's athletic field onto the asphalt of Philip's Street. Stuart pushed the accelerator to the floor and I realized the night's events were just beginning. I blew my nose into a tissue and wished for Darvon or Percodan, anything to deaden the pounding in my head. I'd thought Stuart was going to kill Jonathan Priolieu with his bare fists.

"We should have left sooner," I said between snubs. "You've never been that mad...it was awful...you might have been hurt...oh."

"Stop your bawling," Stuart shouted as we swerved around the corner of Meeting Street. Again my shoulder into the door. Same door, same bruise, only worse.

"Stuart, what're you doing? Slow down."

"Shut-up telling me what to do, shut-up bawling, shut-up all your bullshit. I'm not just leaving the party, Arlena. I'm leaving *you.*"

"Please slow down," I said. "We're coming to the bridge." I stared in alarm at the bleached concrete roadway to the great Cooper River Bridge. Its north ramp loomed before us like some magical pathway to the sky. I tried to fasten my seat belt. The lock wouldn't catch. We roared up the ramp at sixty miles an hour, then seventy, then eighty. The Romeo's engine strained.

"You're a *bitch*," Stuart said, forcing car after car to let him pass. "I'm not going to put up with it, anymore."

"*Let me out*," I screamed. "*I want out. Stop the car.*" I grabbed Stuart's wrist and yanked his hand from the steering wheel. He looked at me with angry eyes and held up a bloody fist. For a second I thought he would strike me. I shrank back and waited for a blow that did not come. Then the bright lights of the bridge shone through the windshield, and for the first time I had a clear look at Stuart's injuries. His knuckles were purple and bloody from their encounter with Jon Priolieu's teeth, his face was streaked with dried blood. There was more blood on his sweater, collar, pants, and shoes. The gore added mightily to the impact of his rage. A stranger would have thought him crazy. Perhaps he was temporarily, and I was the culprit who had driven him to it.

I pressed myself against the passenger door. Sea air rushed into the car as we flew over the bridge. I shivered from cold and shock, remembering mournfully my warm black sweater lying limp and forgotten on Isaac's bar. Stuart would not look at me. He stared straight ahead and drove as fast as the Romeo would allow. We catapulted from the Mount Pleasant incline onto Coleman Boulevard, completely air-borne the first twenty feet. Not a policeman was in sight. Blurred streetlights and stoplights came whizzing toward us as cars veered right and left. There was a terrifying rush as the causeway to the swivel bridge appeared out of the night. In the tunneled glow of our headlights, the marsh road became a gray-white ribbon floating in silky darkness. It flagellated gently above the enormous expanse of colorless autumn sawgrass. Ben Sawyer's warning lights blinked red, yet we raced forward without caution. Stuart judged his timing to a divided half-second, then jerked the car onto the bridge at the exact moment the guard bar started down. We slipped under untouched. The Atlantic Ocean was now two blocks away, and Stuart had taken dead aim on it. I braced myself and closed my eyes as our tires thudded into the dunes. The Romeo lost momentum immediately. Her engine sputtered once, then died.

I opened my eyes. Somehow the car had spun around. I was now looking up the same road we had just roared down. I stared at it dumbly while my brain tried to process what had happened, where we were, why. Bit by bit I recognized familiar sounds—wind blowing in from the ocean, waves slapping the beach, a freighter's horn warning small craft of its approach. I looked at Stuart. He was leaning on the steering wheel breathing in short gasps. I wanted to get away from him, but my attempt was aborted when a tiny click alerted him that my fingertips had touched the door handle. He snapped his head around.

"Don't move," he said. "You're going to sit here and listen while I tell you what I think of a woman who'd dance with a weasel like Jonathan Priolieu. A woman like that is trash, *that's* what I think, and so does everyone else. I should have decked you instead of him. I know what you did. You drank two dozen cups of that cheap-ass wine, and didn't eat anything, and your idiot brain went numb. But that's nothing new. You've been screwed up in the head for months."

Stuart's fury made me afraid but not smart. I insulted him one more time. "Funny thing, you don't call me an idiot when you're depositing all the checks I bring in."

"I'm sick of hearing that," he said. "I've brought in twice the money you have in the last six months, but you don't pay any attention to that. You're too busy waving your piddly little client checks under my nose. It's driving me nuts. Lately I catch myself trying to think of ways to avoid you, so I don't have to hear you complain. That's stupid. I'm supposed to be trying to build a business, for us, together...developing a stable of clients, making new contacts, not wasting my time and energy coddling a neurotic wife."

"What am I supposed to do, Stuart? Live on the bark of trees? You want me to starve supporting your stupid dreams?"

"*My* dreams. I'm not sure their mine at all. Sometimes I think they're yours, *all* yours, *always* all yours. I wish your demented aunt were still alive. I'd like to ask her a few questions about that family thing you blame everything on. Maybe she could tell me why you're such a lunatic. You are, you know. And it isn't covered up, anymore. It's right out in the open, or you wouldn't go out and put on a show with a maggot like Jonathan Priolieu, for all the town to see."

"You're *jealous*," I screeched. "That's what this is about. You're jealous because I got sloshed and danced with the town lecher. Hell's bells...I wish the town fool had been there, *and* the pervert *and* the murderer *and* the rapist. I'd have danced with all of them. There surely wasn't anything else to do. Who *knows* where you were."

"Oh, I was just mingling, like a regular Southern good old boy, so maybe we could keep our jobs. Could have saved myself the trouble if I'd known you were working the crowd on the other side of the field to get us fired. And it's not just the part-time jobs that'll go down with this. It's the connections, names, referrals. It's *everything*."

"If this rotten place is everything, we should have thrown in the towel a long time ago. I hope you didn't seriously think we could have gotten a real business going in this backward little time capsule."

"Oh my God, you're just like every other woman I've ever known. No sense of process. No sense of interrelationships. No sense of *anything*. No, I never thought we could establish a business here. Most of the things we've done were to buy time, get experience, earn a few credentials that we might be able to parlay into bigger projects in bigger towns somewhere down the road. But that's over now, and it's all your fault."

"I don't have to listen to this. I'm getting out of the car."

"Oh no you're not."

"You're crazy, you can't stop me." I dodged his grasp and opened the door. He jumped out of the car and ran around to my side. There was no struggle. He pushed me back into the car and told me he'd break my arm if I tried to get out again.

"You're going to listen to me," he said. "For once in your life you're going to listen."

I struggled one more time. He dropped to his knees by the car and clamped my wrists in his hands. "Look at my face," he growled, then jerked me again to get my full attention. Our eyes were on an even plane. "That business at the oyster roast means we'll both be thrown out of Southern Prep. Do you understand that? Do you understand what your arrogance has caused now?"

"Stop squeezing my arms, Stuart. *You're* the one who started the brawl."

"No, *I* finished it. *You* started it. Everyone was raising their eyebrows at you, rubbing yourself all over that sleazy creep."

I pulled my hand away and tried to slap him. He stopped my arm in mid-air, the same way he had stopped John Priolieu's.

"Oh no, precious-darling-girl. Old Stuart's tired of being slugged. And he's more tired of schitzoid women like you dumping their problems all over him. You've dumped every off-the-wall thing that ever happened to you on me, especially that mishmash about your long-lost mother and father, most of which I don't even believe."

"Stop it, Stuart. You said you were leaving. *Go*."

"And when I do, who'll be your goat then? It won't be me. It won't be your aunt. You finished her off years ago. Probably wore her out and left her in a ditch somewhere. I'm almost worn out myself. And another thing, I can't help wondering why I have to worry myself sick about coming up with rent and grocery money every month when you have three hundred dollars stashed in your purse. I found it yesterday by accident. How much more do you have squirreled away? And where are you getting it? Dumbass Stuart would like to know."

I looked into his eyes. They were shining with the hard glitter of hatred. So, I was not the only one who had been visited by the beast. "Do you hear me, you little liar?" Stuart yelled. *"Where did you get that money?"*

I did not speak. He twisted my wrist. *"Where,"* he said again.

"Stop, please," I cried out. "It was Mr. Pinckney. Mr. Pinckney gave it to me."

"What are you talking about? Mr. Pinckney pays you in checks."

"Tips...sometimes he gives me tips. I would have told you, but I wanted to surprise you. I was saving it, in case we had an emergency."

"You *liar*. You've been hoarding it, while you watched me scrounge for rent. Cripes, you let me bounce a check to the grocery store last month."

"I would have given it to you—I would have. But you're always so good at figuring things out. I knew you'd get us through."

"Maybe you were stockpiling it for a bail-out. Maybe you're planning to leave me."

"No, no," I said. "I was afraid of running out of cash. We've been through that so many times, I didn't think I could stand it again."

He looked at me in a strange way, as if he were not sure who I was. I thought he was going to ask about the pills, that he'd found my hiding place in the storeroom under the porch and was about to confront my habit.

"Why would Pinckney give you extra cash like that?" he said more calmly. "Is something going on I don't know about?"

"No, nothing. I've never done anything for Mr. Pinckney except work my butt off. I'm sorry about the money. Really, I am. If I ever get another dime, you can have it. You can have everything. I mean it."

"You don't have to share money or anything else with me ever again," he said in a voice that was unnaturally soft. It frightened me more than the shouting. He let go of my wrists and stood up. There was a sense of finality in his movements. So, here at last was the end, the extinguishing of the flame, the death of the relationship. My emotions marshaled to save it, though instinct told me it was too late.

"It's over," he said, then fumbled in his pants pocket and pulled out a thin roll of folding money. "Here...here's a little more cash to go with your fat tips from Pinckney. I'll keep fifty to get by on, and you'll still have Peregrine and Pinckney checks to count on for a while. Maybe you can get a real job by the time their projects run out. If you can't, I'll help you until you do. The keys are in the ignition. Take it easy when you pull out of this sand."

"Please, Stuart ..." I could not go on. Tears had choked off my voice. Stuart remained unmoved. He leaned over and brushed away the sand that clung in wet clumps to his pants.

"I'm going to the cottage to pack a bag," he said. "Give me a few minutes. Don't come in there raising sand. I'll be back tomorrow to pick up the rest of my stuff. And Arlena, I want you to know, it wasn't the Pinckney thing that killed it for me, or the money, or that absurd business with Priolieu. It was the hatefulness, the pure and simple hatefulness that you carry around in your insides. You went too far, too many times. I'll be at the cottage. Don't come in on me."

"But I want to go with you. I *need* to go with you."

"It's too late. I'll walk home on the beach. I don't want anyone to see me with this blood on my clothes. Twenty minutes, that's all I'm asking."

He turned and walked away. When I could no longer see his form in the darkness, I panicked and ran after him.

"*Stuart, wait,*" I shouted, using up the last of my strength.

He didn't wait or come back. He was too far away to hear. Once more I tried calling out, but the words caught like thorns in my throat. My body stiffened as a white hot pain tore through my insides. It stopped all conscious thought. I gagged and fell to my knees.

"*Someone...please...help me,*" I sobbed to the moonless night. Then I looked down the beach one last time before pitching forward into darkness.

Chapter Seventeen

I had never fainted before and did not know to stay prone after waking up. Twice I came to and tried to stand. Twice I passed out again. The third time there was no more getting up. I was unable to move. Pain rolled in and out of my abdomen on measured waves of nausea. But somehow it didn't matter. I was detached, separated from my own agony by an interruption of brain function. After a time I felt myself being pulled and lifted by hands I did not recognize. Faintly, beyond a great buzzing sound that roared in my ears like insects, I heard unintelligible voices, deep and low one second, high-pitched and fast the next. I could not tell if they were inside or outside of my skull. Were they talking to me? Or just yammering among themselves? Once I heard my name called distinctly. I opened my eyes a milli-second and saw a man's face an inch from my own.

"Don't go out again, Arlena," he said in overlapping metallic syllables. "Tell me where you hurt. I'm a doctor, I'm here to help you."

I closed my eyes to block out the spotlight shining behind his head. Its glare pierced my eyeballs in painful darting arcs. I could not focus.

"*Hurt*," I heard myself say in reverberating tones.

"Where?" the man asked, his words repeating over and over in a hollow space in my head.

"*My side*," I said. The man patted my hand and tried to get me to say more. Then he was gone and I was gone and there was nothing.

Deep in blackness I slept a dreamless sleep, unencumbered by the processes of life. I existed nowhere and felt nothing. Infinity had rescued me. I wanted to float forever in that secure black vacuum. But life was not through with me. It forced its way back into my consciousness, reminding me who I was. Awareness returned in threads and wisps over hours of altered time. Millions of electrical impulses jumped back and forth across the neurons of my brain, stimulating my mind with impulses of fear. I did not want to remember. I only wanted to drift.

Voices and visions called to me from the darkness. I fought their intrusion. For a while I was able to resist. But soon my own brain betrayed me, swelling and bulging with familiar dreams that raged out of control. Then I saw it. The beast. It came at me with a jeweled ax and split open my skull, the two halves flying off into oblivion. One eye saw mile-high waterfalls, the other a solid wall of fire. There were two of me, eight of me, eight hundred of me, racing through space like eyeless zombies rushing to join ceremonies far more wicked than the desecration of one human soul. The sounds and colors and tastes of these visions flooded my body with pain. I am certain that if my skin were peeled back, even today, its inside flaps would reveal enormous tattoos of other-world images permanently inked into the remotest corners of my body.

For hours, days, I drifted back and forth between hallucination and reality. Nurses spoke to me in soothing tones, but I was not comforted. I forced my eyes open and realized I was bound to a white metal bed. I fought the restraints until the sheet under my back was wet with sweat and blood. With strength born of fear, I pulled and tugged until my body would no longer respond. Exhausted, I lay still and prayed that the beast would not return. Then something touched my hand. I jerked away. Perhaps if I did not move, it would seek livelier game. Again, my hand. This time I made a fist and pounded the bed. A voice called to me softly and begged me to keep still. It was a male voice—sweet and musical. Somehow Stuart had penetrated my terror.

"Can you hear me?" he said. I opened my eyes but could not answer. Pain radiated from every pore of my body.

"Hurt," I whispered.

"It'll pass. The doctor said it would pass."

"I need medicine."

This time Stuart was silent, afraid of my rage. He was now the enemy, the object of my anger. I hurled threats at him for withholding my pills. I screamed and begged to die. He stood beside me and absorbed it all. Time and more time crawled by, dissipating my strength and will. Then, in an unexpected moment, I awoke from a dream to a world that slid miraculously into place. I looked around a clean white room and focused on a curtainless window. Flowers and potted plants sat crowded on its sill. I continued my surveillance until my eyes met Stuart's. At first he didn't speak, just stared. But after a moment he leaned closer and whispered, with great apprehension, "Ready for another round, tiger?"

"I'm hungry," I said. He looked at me a second longer, then laid his head on the bed and cried.

My hunger created a stir among the nurses. They examined me in turns, probed here and there, and asked questions I could not answer. But Stuart did not push. He came to my bedside like a winged angel and fed me salted broth from a stone-white bowl. I was able to swallow several ounces before drowsiness overcame me and I fell into an untroubled sleep.

When next I awoke, the wrist and ankle restraints were gone. I was overjoyed to be free, though still too weak to move. Stuart returned with more broth, which I drank greedily through a straw. He grinned and said I looked like hell. I dozed off in the middle of an effort to defend myself.

Sleep and broth became my life. But the pain was not done with me. The soreness in my abdomen and chest made me cry out at the slightest wrong move. It was worse when the dreams returned. There was nothing I could do upon rousing from the dreams but lie still and concentrate on breathing. Gradually, after a time of sleeping and waking without the aid of pills, the good times outnumbered the bad. I knew where I was, but not why or how I got there. And Stuart, my only source of information, sidestepped every question.

"Let's take a walk," he said when he came to see me the third evening I'd been awake. Together we spent ten minutes figuring out how to maneuver my legs over the side of the bed without disturbing the six-inch incision directly below my navel. Stuart was more compassionate than the nurses. He helped me to the bathroom and back to bed without hurting me once.

"Enough, I'm finished," I said, sinking back into the pillow.

"Today the bathroom, tomorrow High Battery," he quipped. "In a week, California. So how's the big cut tonight?"

"A tyrant, won't let me move."

"Have you talked to the doctor yet?"

"No. He came in and looked at me earlier, but wouldn't say a word. Guess that means you have to tell me."

"Tell you what?"

"*Tell* me, Stuart."

"Okay. This is the way it is. You had a cyst on your right ovary; it ruptured and bled into your abdominal cavity; there was poison and puss, and they had a heck of a time cleaning it up; you now have one ovary, one fallopian tube, and one uterus left; the infection is clearing up faster than they expected; the worst, I guess, is that you lost so much weight, but that's what cheeseburgers are for."

"Cheeseburgers? You have a cheeseburger?"

"Maybe," he said.

"Please, please, give it to me."

He disappeared into the hall and came back with a warm burger wrapped in foil. I moaned in ecstasy over the taste of broiled beef.

"Oh, I love you so much."

"The nurses were against it," he said. "Didn't think you could handle junk food yet. Looks to me like you could handle a live steer. I think you should eat slower."

"I'm *hungry*. Dinner was hours ago. It must be eight or nine by now."

"Eight-thirty to be exact, almost bedtime. Do you know what day it is?"

"I don't know what *month* it is."

"It's Tuesday...Tuesday night."

"When am I going home?"

"In a week or so, maybe."

"How long have I been here?"

"Four weeks."

I stretched my eyes wide. "*Four weeks?* My aunt had a full hysterectomy—I remember the whole ordeal—and she was in the hospital five days. What do you mean, four weeks?"

"I don't know why it was so hard on you, Arly. A ruptured cyst must be bad. And then it got worse when you ripped your stitches open somehow and had to go back to surgery. That was a real mess."

For a moment neither of us spoke, and Stuart avoided my

eyes. After an awkward silence, he said, "But I guess it was the other thing that stretched it out so long." He was still unable to look at me directly.

"What other thing?"

"The drug thing, all those pills you'd been taking. It took a while to get your body cleaned out—detoxed, they called it."

Again I was speechless. Stuart tried to explain, nervously. "Everything went haywire after your surgery. Nothing helped. The nurses said you looked like you were going through some sort of withdrawal. They kept asking me what medication you were on. I brought some of your pill bottles from home. They sent me back to see if there were more. That's when I started finding them, everywhere, all over the cottage. Darvon, Valium, Percodan. There must have been twenty or thirty bottles. When I brought them to the hospital, everyone freaked. Some of the bottles were dated as far back as a year. They had doctors' names on them I'd never even heard of. It took a day or two to figure it all out. By then you were already in la-la-land, coming off the stuff cold turkey. I never saw anyone get that sick. It was awful. There were times I thought you might ...."

His voice broke on the last few words. He quickly wiped away a tear.

"I'm sorry," I said, groggy now. "I'm so very sorry."

"It's over now, Arlena. Go back to sleep. We'll talk again in the morning."

The dreams continued to haunt me. Three times that night I awoke terrified and exhausted. Three times the nurses brought in cold packs for the back of my neck, and fruit juice over ice to drink. They said not to worry, that I was doing great considering all I'd been through. I asked for something to kill the pain in my muscles, but Tylenol was the best they could do. No one mentioned the pill bottles Stuart had found; no one mentioned addiction. I gave up trying to communicate with the nurses and concentrated on eating. Had I realized how emaciated I'd become, I would have understood my preoccupation with food. I would also have known that my loss of strength was not from the surgery, but from starving almost a month.

"I look anorexic," I said to Stuart the next morning.

"Let's just say it's a good thing I like my women skinny. Come on, Dr. Merritt says you have to walk."

"Who is Dr. Merritt?" I asked as we crept down the corridor.

"The guy who writes hieroglyphics on your chart every day. He's the one who figured out you were hooked on Percodan, right after he figured out you were hooked on Valium and Darvon. He began to suspect something the day after your second surgery. You didn't come out of the anesthesia right. Fought everyone. The nurses couldn't do a thing with you. They panicked and called Dr. Merritt in from his golf game. When he tried to examine you, you snatched his glasses off and gave him a black eye. And I don't mean a little one. I mean one that made his eye swell shut. It took three stitches to sew his eyebrow back together. That's when they tied you down and told me not to get close enough to get bitten."

"I can't listen to this, anymore. I have to go back to bed."

"Want me to carry you?"

"No, it'll hurt too much."

We turned and shuffled back to 205 where my beautiful bed awaited. "I'm amazed at how weak you are," he said. "Four days ago you were threatening the lives of the whole hospital staff."

"Don't tell me anymore," I said, eyes closed, aware again of the hunger. "Do you think you could get some crackers from a machine somewhere? My stomach is growling."

"Hey, I forgot. I brought you a Butterfinger."

My sleepy eyes became alert. I grabbed the candy bar from his outstretched hand and unwrapped it tenderly. "Oh, Stuart. It's gorgeous. I love you."

"Funny thing how you love me best when you're stuffing your face with goodies. So, right after you slugged Dr. Merritt, they strapped you to the bed. But you were still floundering around so much, you pulled out some more of your stitches and everyone went crazy again. The nurses said you could hemorrhage if you kept tearing your incision open. They strapped you even tighter. The only thing they didn't do was gag you, which probably would have been a good idea. You were wild, yelling and screaming like a banshee. Didn't even look like yourself. I can't believe you went through all that and don't remember it."

"I remember the dreams."

"What dreams?"

"Bad dreams. Sometimes I still have them."

Stuart looked disturbed. "The doctor said Percodan was dangerous. You could have those dreams for years, the rest of your life, maybe. Are they getting any better?"

"When I'm eating."

"We do have a one track mind, don't we? Why were you taking all that stuff, anyway, Arly? Dr. Merritt was amazed you could still function."

"My side hurt...I was nervous."

"Okay, your side is fixed and you're off all the crap. Everything is great. The doctor says people who get hooked on pain killers because of physical problems aren't the same breed as the ones who use them for joyrides. He thinks you'll be all right now the bad ovary is out."

"Stuart, you were going to leave me. Why didn't you?"

"I don't know. Probably should have, you've caused me so much trouble. Guess I forgot about it when you ended up in the hospital. Maybe I still love you. Maybe I can't live without you."

"I still feel sick, Stu."

"I know, but you're getting better every day. I can see it in your eyes."

The work of healing was difficult. I ate and slept like I might never get the opportunity to do either again, and walked the drab hospital halls a dozen times a day. Stuart came to see me morning and night. He encouraged, helped, cajoled, negotiated, and teased me into staying focused.

"I've never known anyone like you," he said the fifth morning I'd been up. "You're the Madonna herself, so frail and thin and pale, but you eat like a great white shark."

"I'm hungry," I said for the two-hundredth time.

Stuart feigned nervousness. "Anymore, I'm afraid to come in here without food or drink in my hand. Some days I've considered tossing in a piece of raw meat and running for my life."

"Stop harassing me. Talk about something else."

"Okay, your highness. You will be gratified to learn the time has come for the presentation of the flowers and cards. Please hold your applause."

"Forget the cards. I've already read them. Bring on the flowers. Bring up the music."

"Certainly, madam. We have here a begonia from the grandame of Charleston, Miss Fanny Peregrine. And here, a sensible potted plant from my concerned parents. That about does it for tasteful remembrances. The rest of these gaudy things arrived day by day from Grayson Lockwood Pinckney, IV. Six gargantuan baskets, all equal in ostentation. I think he's trying to express his gratitude to you for inciting your husband to riot. I separated Jonathan Priolieu from his front teeth, you may recall, on the night of the fateful oyster roast. If we are to believe Mr. Pinckney, he has been longing to do just that for many a frustrated year. Even as I speak, he is nullifying a lawsuit filed against me by Jon Priolieu. He accused me of assault, the cad, the infamous cad. What vindictiveness. I am outraged."

Stuart placed a hand over his heart and bowed. I clapped. "Thespis himself," I said. "But what do you mean, a lawsuit? Are we in some kind of trouble?"

"Not anymore, thanks to Mr. Pinckney. But for a while there, Priolieu wanted to wade into me in court the same way he waded into me on the dance floor. He isn't very graceful, I've noticed. I think he should consider lessons."

"Yeah, maybe the two of you could get in the same class. How did Mr. Pinckney stop him?"

"Don't know. He called me at home a week after our night-of-nights and told me to be careful, that son-in-law was on the war path. But you were still so sick, I didn't care what son-in-law did. The next day a guy brought some of those long blue papers out to the beach cottage, and it looked like old Stuart was going up the road. Then Mr. Pinckney called again and said he'd see to it I wouldn't be charged. He told me to keep my mouth shut and forget it ever happened. I didn't know the old guy had so much power."

"Mr. Pinckney has the power to make Jon Priolieu kiss a cobra," I said. "He probably makes him do it every morning."

Chapter Eighteen

It soon became apparent that docility in a recently reformed addict is interpreted as great progress. I became exceedingly docile. I applied pink blush to sallow cheeks and saffron neck, massaged glycerin into peeling hands and lips, worked conditioner into brittle hair. The nurses said I was beginning to look almost normal. Stuart asked for one thing—cooperation. I gave him slavish subjugation. Unaccustomed to power, he became an absolute dictator. If I would follow his every order, I'd be well in a few weeks, or so he said. I had a thought or two of my own on the subject, but decided to keep them to myself until the timing was right. Declarations of independence could wait.

The night terrors did not go away. They continued to appear without warning or identifiable cause. The beast had been forced beneath the surface, and I could no longer hear him distinctly, yet he still came to me in the night. I began to realize I would never be totally free, that my personality would have macabre overtones in harmony with the voice of the beast all the days of my life. Stuart was my only sanity. Dear Stuart, who lived in light and mingled with light and was part of light. The purity of his soul was my lifeline to light, my clean, generative lifeline. I chose not to tell him the story of the beast. I did not wish to compromise the loveliness of his spirit.

The day before I was to go home, if by a stretch one could call a rented beach cottage a home, a promise was breached. It happened early in the afternoon, a time when doctors were absent, nurses distracted, and ordinary visitors elsewhere. It was the time chosen by Raven FitzSimons to slip into my room.

"How'd you get in here?" I said, amused by her guile. I was aware Stuart had told her I was not ready to have visitors.

"*Sneaked in,*" she whispered.

"It's two thirty, Raven. Aren't you supposed to be in school?"

"Not today. I'm cutting. And you can't say a thing about it. You're supposed to be in school, too, teaching our writing class."

"I'm sick, you know. And stop whispering. No one cares if you come in here as long as I don't get upset."

"My God, Mrs. Prince, you look like hell."

"Oh, thanks. I just spent fifteen minutes putting on make-up and brushing my hair, and you say I look like hell. You and Stuart ought to get together, work on some new lines."

"How much do you weigh?"

"I don't know. This place isn't exactly a health spa. You don't weigh in every day."

"I think you're anorexic."

"Cripes, Raven. No wonder Stuart wouldn't let you visit me. He was afraid you might cheer me up too much. Now sit down on my bed and talk to me. You look like you're bracing for a quick get-away."

"What's maudlin?"

"I don't know...sappy, sad. Why?"

"Stuart said you couldn't have visitors yet. He said I could see you in a few days, and when I did, I shouldn't be maudlin. I didn't know what he meant. But now I think I'm going to be maudlin anyway."

"You mean you're going to cry?"

"Yes."

"Well, come over here and bawl your eyes out. Stuart doesn't know females are born maudlin and can't help themselves."

Raven ran to the bed and hugged me until my incision rebelled. I yelped. She jumped back, put both hands over her mouth, and dissolved into sobs again. I motioned for her to come close so I could hold her while she cried.

"There's some tissue," I said after a minute, pointing to the medical clutter on the bedside table. "Stuart says I've been through four dozen boxes of it. One more won't hurt. Let me see your face. Oh, terrific. Now we both look like hell. I think you should drink some water."

"I didn't mean to cry," she said. "I've just needed someone to talk to so badly, and you've been sick forever, and they wouldn't let me see you. I heard you screaming a couple of times when I sneaked down the hall. It was awful."

"So everyone tells me. I'll be glad to get out of here so I can forget all this ever happened."

"Oh, Mrs. Prince, I wish Stuart had let me talk to you sooner. It might be too late now."

"Too late for what?"

"To keep Dr. Calhoun from stirring up more trouble about your job at Southern Prep. I heard Mother on the phone with him last night. She told him to call Stanlock and have you fired. She was going to try to get Stuart fired, too, but he'd already quit. Guess he had to, after starting that fight at the oyster roast."

"Stuart did *not* start that fight."

"Mother says he did, because he was humiliated by the way you were acting with Jon Priolieu's dad."

My hands drew into small white fists. I closed my eyes and breathed slowly, trying to stave off nausea. Raven stopped talking. After a few seconds, I relaxed my fingers and asked for a sip of water. At that precise moment, Stuart opened the door.

"What are you doing in here?" he said to Raven. "I told you Arlena couldn't have visitors yet."

Raven's eyes became saucers. She ran across the room and flattened herself against the wall next to the window. *"I'm sorry,"* she said, her voice a piccato violin. *"Please don't be mad at me. I'll leave."*

Stuart looked at me and did not like what he saw. He turned back to Raven. "What do you plan to do? Jump out the window? I think the door would be more appropriate."

He followed Raven into the hallway and closed the door quietly. But when he returned, the flush on his face and neck belied his mild manner. The perspiration that had gathered at my temples belied my own. We carried on a conversation about nothing for ten minutes, and I began to feel better. I was supposed to be getting out of the hospital the next day. It was obvious Stuart was worried about the prospect. I assured him everything would be all right, that *I* would be all right. Twice he told me he had cleaned the cottage, washed the sheets, and stocked the refrigerator. The third time I stopped him.

"I promise you, I won't be any trouble," I said. "I'm afraid to cause trouble. I'm afraid you'll leave me to croak by myself right there in the cottage. Besides, Dr. Merritt says I'll be as good as new in three or four weeks."

"He doesn't know for sure."

"Stuart, I can feel myself getting stronger."

"Yeah, well, we'll see how it goes when you get home."

"Okay, but now you have to talk to me. You can't put me off any longer."

"Talk about what?"

"Things...things you've been avoiding."

"I don't know what you mean."

"Lord, I hate it when you act dumb. I feel like slugging you."

"Have you forgotten what happened to the last dude who tried that? The newly gap-toothed Jon Priolieu?"

"Good, let's start there. Did you quit Southern Prep because of the fight?"

"How did you know I quit?"

"Raven told me."

"Damn, Arlena. For a woman who's been stuck in the hospital for a month, you know an awful lot."

"No thanks to you. But for your information, I remember most of what you told me the night I got sick. You said we were through in Charleston, that we were both going to be fired from Southern Prep and lose all our connections."

"I was furious; I could've said anything. The truth is we were finished here months ago, way before that sorry little oyster roast, and sorrier little fight. I don't know where I got the idea we could establish a client base in a small town like this. We never got to the point of making ends meet month to month, much less a profit."

"You sound like it's all over."

"Not really, but we do need a paradigm shift. That's what they used to talk about in all those English departmental meetings I slept through at Boston U....*paradigm shifts.*"

"Does that include quitting your job?"

"First of all, we mustn't dignify the grunt work I was doing at Southern Prep by calling it a job. It was a half-baked, part-time consulting stint. All I did was write a few lousy brochures and dream up two or three fund-raising schemes. Second, I had no choice but to quit. Those people can't afford a consultant, anyway. Half the board was against hiring me in the first place. Then I had to go and clobber a board member. This was not helpful."

"I didn't know Jonathan Priolieu was on the board."

"Oh yes, as of this fall. It seems you don't have to be competent to serve in certain, let us say *positions* here. Being associated with the right family is enough."

"So you quit before they got organized enough to fire you."

"I had to. Actually, the proper word is resigned. And I must say I did it with class. My letter to Grayson Pinckney reeked. I told him I was sincerely grateful just to have had the opportunity to kiss the board members' behinds. It's probably one of the reasons he saved me from Priolieu's lawsuit, that and the fact that you've become—what is it he calls you—his 'sweet summer rose'? The man is suffering from delusions about you, I'm sure of it."

"And did you write a letter of resignation for me?"

"What?"

"Did you tell Mr. Pinckney I wouldn't be back to teach my class?"

"No, I talked to Cliffton Stanlock. He excused you from your duties for the rest of the semester, because of illness, officially. But believe me, it's understood you won't be coming back. It's just as well, though. You weren't doing it for the money so much as to please Miss Peregrine, and the hope of meeting new clients."

"Miss Peregrine will be disappointed."

"She'll get over it. Southern Prep is history."

"You talk as if everything were history."

"Not everything, not yet. I've still got a pile of stuff to write for Bill Greene. He's planning a spring promotion for his condo development on Kiawah. Thank God he's not from Old Charleston. He grew up next to Hell Hole Swamp over in Berkeley County. Doesn't give a damn what people south of Broad think. All he wants to do is sell condos to poor schmucks who come down from the frozen North and become enamored of springtime on Kiawah. He doesn't tell them they'll die of a combination of mosquito bites and heatstroke come summertime."

"But what're we going to do, Stuart?"

"*We* aren't going to do anything. *You* are going to park your beautiful fanny on Lucretia Middleton's screened porch and concentrate on getting your strength back. *I'm* going out to forage for grubs and berries."

"What about money? Doctor bills? The hospital? We haven't had health insurance in years."

"And what about the meaning of life and religion and philosophy? Why don't we settle it all right now, right here in room 205 of smelly old Roper Hospital?"

"All right. I get the message. I'll leave it alone another day or two, until I get a little stronger. But then you're going to have to spill the whole story. Just one last question for now. Does Mr. Pinckney want to finish his memoirs?"

"Sure, though he did mention he thought it would be ever so much nicer if you came back on your feet instead of a stretcher. The man wants you to get well, Arly—all the way well."

"Okay, what about Miss Peregrine?"

Stuart didn't answer. "*Tell* me," I said. "I hate it when you hold things back."

"Did Raven mention Miss Peregrine to you?"

"Yes," I lied.

"I intend to break that girl's upper-class neck. I'm sure Miss Peregrine will be all right."

"Has she been ill?"

Stuart looked pained. "She was, but I think she's better now. Mr. Pinckney told me she got sick about the same time you did."

"I'll call her tomorrow."

"Not yet, Arly. It might cause more trouble. There's a letter waiting for you back at the cottage. Its return address is Jeannette FitzSimons's office. You were out of your head when it arrived a couple weeks ago. I thought I should go ahead and open it to see if there was some problem. It's signed by Miss Peregrine, but I'm sure FitzSimons wrote it. Miss Peregrine was too ill at the time to write anything. At any rate, it says she no longer needs your services; her health is getting worse; she can't go on with her memoirs; she's tired and ill."

"I don't believe Miss Peregrine told Jeannette FitzSimons to write anything of the kind."

"It doesn't make a damn who wrote it. Face it, dollface, you've been canned."

Chapter Nineteen

I had forgotten autumn. I had forgotten its annual taming of the brilliant light of summer, its sure focus of September's shimmering whiteness into the un-muted hues of October. This was the light that clarified lowcountry air the day Stuart drove me home from the hospital. It sharpened the outline of every cloud and leaf and blade of grass. It tempered autumn's chill with its soft solar heat. I was intoxicated by its purity. There was nothing suggestive about this light, no blurred edges nor auras nor insinuations of dimensions unseen, no queer movements nor shadows nor flickerings. As I absorbed its immaculate beauty, my spirit began to heal in the same rhythm as my body.

Stuart arranged everything to make my homecoming easy. I looked at the expanse of harbor waters as we drove over the Cooper River Bridge, and thought of the reckless crossing we had made the night of the oyster roast. Today Stuart drove slowly, taking care not to jar my incision as he maneuvered through traffic. I held a pillow against my abdomen for security.

On the marsh road, just before the swivel bridge, I picked up the odor of pluffmud. Low tide. Waves of sawgrass, newly tannic, rippled in a cold sea breeze. A flock of blackbirds moved south over the marsh, so low I thought I heard wingbeats. Their flight had a special urgency, for even the semi-tropical winter of Sullivan's Island would not be warm enough to sustain them until spring. From the crest of the Ben Sawyer bridge, I gazed down the alley of the Intracoastal Waterway. Sea birds and white sailboats were superimposed on the horizon. My eyes filled with tears. Stuart became alarmed when he saw me crying. I reassured him with emotional little phrases—I'm all right; the tears are for happiness; I'm grateful to be getting well.

Reluctantly, he turned his attention back to driving. I talked him into a swing around Harbor Point and begged to watch the fifteen-minute approach of a Caribbean cruise vessel. It reminded me of my and Miss Peregrine's nostalgic afternoon on the island. Stuart then exercised his hard-won position as "commander-in-chief" by denying my request to visit Breach Inlet. I did not argue. I was too tired. On arriving at the cottage, he carried me like a bride up the back stairs to the porch. The slat swing and flower pots welcomed me. Stuart had promised I could relax on the porch for as many weeks as I needed, like a cloistered nun praying in the holy presence of ocean, beach, and dunes. That quiet time of healing will stand apart in my memory always, like a scene embroidered in vivid colors on a length of watered silk. It is a sweetly lush memory in which Stuart is always young and handsome, and I am always blooming with the delicate colors of renewed health. It was a time of falling in love with my husband again, of noticing and appreciating his patience, his thoughtfulness, his willingness to lay bare his heart with ardent declarations of love. I rewarded him by gobbling up his attention like a hungry little caterpillar preparing for its own natural miracle. It took but a few weeks for my metamorphosis to become complete. Then, a lowly creature once confined to crawling on its belly suddenly attained the ability to fly.

As he settled me into a cushioned porch chair, Stuart said, "That, my waif, was the first time you ever entered the doors of this cottage without testing the strength of the pilings." He observed my stiff posture and decided I was uncomfortable.

"I must fetch the royal footstool," he said. "The queen needs to put her feet up." He disappeared into the living room and brought out a wobbly coffee table.

"Lucretia Middleton would die if she saw how we abuse her furniture," I said. "She told me when we moved in here that this table is over fifty years old, practically a sacred relic."

"And looks every day of it. Here, let me put a pillow under your legs. Oh no, it's been an hour since you last ate. I have to prepare something fast."

"Stop making fun of me. I'm tired of it."

"How about homemade chicken pie from Mama Chloe's and sliced tomatoes from Charlie Black's vegetable truck? He stopped by yesterday and said he was getting ready to close down for the winter, maybe for good. Guess vegetable peddling isn't as profitable as it used to be."

Stuart bustled into the kitchen while I savored the view. It had not changed. Equal parts of sky and ocean accentuated the fluffy whiteness of drifting cumulus clouds and crashing breakers. Foam-fringed waves flattened over tawny sand, paused, then slid back—gliding silk—into a cerulean sea. I thought about the rust stain of autumn in the sawgrass on Sullivan's back beach. Was the Atlantic taking on autumn colors, as well? I had spent whole days in the summer months watching it turn every shade in the spectrum, from sultry lavender to simmering vermilion, depending on the time of day or position of the sun or amount of moisture in the air. I dreaded the approach of its winter gray dress.

Stuart fed me lunch, then reminded me he had an appointment with Bill Greene in Mount Pleasant. I said I would be fine, that I'd take a nap while he was gone. He settled me in bed and opened the windows. No more canned air blown through hospital vents. I tilted my head back and inhaled as far as my incision would allow, then exhaled slowly and fell asleep. No dreams disturbed me. In two hours I woke up, refreshed and calm, to the peace of a beach cottage in autumn. The house was silent. Stuart had not come home. Disconnected thoughts formed and dissolved lazily in my mind. They drifted one to another and did not become disturbing until I came to the thought of money, or lack thereof. It was then I remembered Stuart telling me about the letter from Jeannette FitzSimons. It revived the old anger that had lain dormant during the weeks of my illness. After stewing about it another five minutes, I did something incredibly stupid, something that would have made Stuart furious.

I picked up the phone from the night table and balanced it on a pillow. *Miss Peregrine's number*, I thought. *I've forgotten it.* I called information and remembered the number as soon as the computer voice repeated it. My nerves fluttered as I punched it in. One ring, two, three, four, five...too many for politeness. I did not hang up. Six, seven, eight. Finally, on the ninth ring, Tycie answered.

"Peregrine residence," she said, her accent thickly black.

"Hello, Tycie. This is Arlena. How have you been?"

"Lord have mercy, Missy Arlena, you'd better get off this phone. Missy Peregrine is bad off sick, and the folks who mind her business are swarming 'round her like bees."

"May I speak to her, Tycie?"

"No, she's too weak. One day she feels good, the next, I think she might go on to heaven. That's the way things have been going lately. Never know what to expect."

I bit my lip. "Is Louisa there?"

"Yes'm, but you can't talk to her, neither. You can't talk to nobody. They don't want to hear from you no more. Been running you down something awful."

"But why? I don't understand."

"Missy FitzSimons says you're on dope; Missy Louisa calls you white trash."

"And what do you think, Tycie?"

"It don't matter what Tycie thinks. I got to hang up now. And don't you call back here. Missy Jeannette comes snooping around every day, answering the phone, plundering, ordering me about. She's meaner than that ugly cousin, Louisa."

"I'll figure something out, Tycie. In the mean time, take care of Miss Peregrine, and yourself."

"Yes'm. I'll do that, and I'm gonna start by hanging up this phone."

I closed my eyes in frustration when I heard Tycie's click. It was final. There was no use in calling her back. I was still turning the conversation over in my mind when something bumped on the porch. Shoving the phone quickly to the night table, I lay back in bed like a good sick person. Another bump. I held my breath. It was difficult to see into the sitting room. Stuart had closed the blinds to darken the house, "...so you can rest," he had said. Only one small corner of the room was visible from the bed. I peered at it intently and saw a figure move in the dim.

"Raven, I could strangle you," I gasped when I realized who it was. "You scared me half to death. Why are you sneaking around like that?"

The startled girl darted into the bedroom and closed the door behind her. "I'm hiding from Stuart," she said, taking a last peek into the sitting room. "He isn't here, is he? I figured he must be gone since the car isn't downstairs. I wanted to see you, but he got so mad at me at the hospital, I was almost afraid to come out here."

"But not *too* afraid," I said. "Stop acting like Mata Hari. Sometimes you're so immature I can't stand it."

Now she was grinning like an imp, already tired of her own

game. "I'm not immature," she said with a toss of her head. "I'm all grown up. Croom thinks so, if you know what I mean. And I never listen to adults, especially bossy ones like Stuart."

"That's great, Raven. Attack my husband now. Ignore all convention. Pretty soon you'll have the whole world against you."

"Yep, I'll probably grow up to be like you. Mother says everyone in Charleston detests Arlena Prince."

A twitch took control of my cheek. I had to lie back and breathe slowly to keep from losing my temper. Raven became aware of my struggle. "God, Mrs. Prince, you *still* look like hell. Think you'll ever get over this?"

My eyes snapped open. I stared into her perfect face and felt old and wasted. "Yes, I will," I said evenly, "and when I do, I intend to drag you down to the blackest, greasiest pluffmud flat I can find and rub your beautiful face in it. *Then* we shall see who looks like hell." I lay back again to breathe.

"You won't be able to," she said. "By the time you get strong enough to do that, I'll be too fat."

"What?"

"I think I'm pregnant."

I rolled my eyes and wished I were back in the hospital where this sort of thing didn't happen. Again, I looked at the girl before me. She was no longer smiling.

"Why do you say things like that, Raven? It isn't funny. It's crazy."

"Not when my period is a week late. I don't know what to do. I'm scared."

"Have you seen a doctor? Had a test?"

"Don't have to. I already know. I'm psychic, remember?" Her voice broke and she began crying a disturbed little cry. I felt very much like joining her.

"You have to tell your mother," I said nervously. "You have to, so she can help you. I'll tell her myself if you don't."

Raven's body locked in the middle of a sob. "*No, you can't, please.*"

I was about to try logic again, but my words were cut short by a familiar rumble. The Romeo was coming up the drive.

"It's Stuart," Raven said. "I have to go. And don't you dare tell him I was here. He'll strangle me if he finds out."

"Call me," I said to her slender back as she ran through the sitting room toward the porch. "Call me...tomorrow."

At the same moment that she faded into the shadows of the sitting room, Stuart began his climb up the street-side stairs. I counted off the seconds in my head. At thirteen, he entered the kitchen door. At seventeen, he poked his head into the bedroom.

"Hi," I said sweetly.

"Hello there, my baby. How're things in sick bay?"

"Fine," I said, smiling an artificial smile. "Things couldn't be better."

Chapter Twenty

On Thursday, at ten a.m., two days after Raven announced she might be pregnant, she returned to the cottage to confound me again.

"Hey, guess what," she said, climbing the back steps to the porch nonchalantly, as if she might have been gone on a ten-minute errand instead of two whole days. "I'm not preggie after all. Grandma Moses finally arrived, a week and a half late. Wow, you look great today, Mrs. Prince. Stuart must be a good nurse."

I unlatched the screened door and yanked her inside. "How could you do this to me, Raven? Why didn't you stay in touch? I called your house six or seven times, scared to death every time that your mother might pick up. I'm so mad at you I could scream."

"Isn't life stupid?" she said, flopping gracelessly into a misshapen wicker chair. "You can't call me because of Mother; I can't call you because of Stuart. How long will he be gone, anyway? I saw him leave a few minutes ago?"

"You were spying?"

"Why shouldn't I? He's horrible to me. You saw how he treated me the day I sneaked into your room at the hospital. He said he'd call my mother if I bothered you again."

"He didn't mean it. He was just trying to protect me. But now that I'm better, he'd like you to come visit me once in a while...*after* school, not during. You have to stop cutting classes, Raven. Tell you what, if you'll promise to stop cutting, I'll help you make peace with Stuart."

"Yeah, sure, and I'll help you make peace with Mother, which we both know will never happen. If she had her way, I'd never see you again."

"Maybe she's right, Rav. No sense borrowing trouble."

"If I gave in to her on every little thing, she'd turn me over to a psychiatrist and let him pick my brain like seagulls pick blue crabs. Then she'd try to force me to become a proper virgin debutante, as if it weren't a bit late for that, the virgin part, I mean. She thinks my attitude toward the season stinks."

"Season?"

"The winter social season. She's getting a real bang out of my being a deb. I'm her ticket back into society. Isn't that a hoot? She bought five new ball gowns for me last week. She won't buy a cheap pair of shoes for herself, but I can have five expensive gowns. And that's not all. She's going around apologizing to everyone because they aren't handmade. I hate it. It's like she's getting me ready for sacrifice or something. That's what they did with virgins a long time ago, you know. Mother is trying to attract some well-off law school grad to support my young ass. Only it won't work. I ain't no virgin no more. Wouldn't she just die if she knew I almost got myself pregnant?"

She put her hands up to muffle her giggles. I laughed with her, though it was a sick joke and I was uncomfortable with it. Raven was too young to be so cynical.

"You're mixed up on one point, sweetie. The most dangerous person in your life right now is Croom Jr., not your mother. From what you've said, he wouldn't help you with anything, particularly not something serious, like figuring out what to do about a baby. He doesn't care if you get hurt. He's too young to care."

"I'll get birth control pills," she said. "That'll fix everything."

"I don't know. Maybe I'm old fashioned, Rav, but somehow I don't think you're ready for all that. Please talk to your mother. I know she'd tell you the same thing. These are decisions that could affect the rest of your life, not simple things, like what dress to wear to what party, or how you're going to do your hair. Your mother would be frantic if she knew you were taking chances with Croom. What did he say when you thought you were in trouble? Did he try to help you?"

"I never told him."

"Yes, and I know why. You were afraid he'd run out on you."

"Yep, old Croom would sprint all right. He couldn't handle a knocked-up girlfriend."

"He's only a boy, Raven. You can't expect him to know how to deal with something like that. Now stop being a smart alec. There comes a time in every girl's life when she has to start taking responsibility for herself."

"Oh, no...not the when-are-you-going-to-grow-up lecture. I refuse to discuss this one more minute. If we can't talk about something else, I'm going to leave."

"You just got here, silly. And anyway, I'm ready to drop that subject. There's something else I want to ask about. Tell me what's going on with Miss Peregrine. Tycie says she's sick."

"I don't know much about it, only that Mother goes over there a bunch. She says Miss Peregrine has gotten old and sick. I guess her body is wearing out."

"I've called Peregrine House every day since I got home from the hospital," I said, "and every time I call, Tycie answers and says Miss Peregrine might die any minute. She never lets me talk to her."

"You could try the other housekeeper, that crazy one, but it probably wouldn't do any good. Mother says she's wacko. Maybe if you wrote a private note...I could deliver it to Miss Peregrine on the sneak."

"And why would I want you to do that?"

"Because those buzzards hovering over Peregrine House are complete and total snots who hate your complete and total guts. That's why."

It was the wrong thing to do. I knew it was, even as I reached for a pen. I wrote the note and handed it to Raven, who read it aloud like she was auditioning for a part in a bad movie:

Dear Miss Peregrine,

Thank you for the beautiful potted plant you sent to me at the hospital. It made me feel so much better. I plan to visit you as soon as I'm strong enough, maybe in a couple of weeks. My surgery went well. The doctor says I'll be working again by Christmas. Hope you're feeling better, too. Tycie told me you've been ill. Thanks again for the plant. I love you and miss you.

—*Arlena*

Raven laughed and clapped her hands, then folded the note four times to make it small. This was the kind of game she loved.

"Don't bother Miss Peregrine if she's too sick," I said. "I don't want to do anything to upset her."

"I'm not stupid," she said. "I know more than you think. I know you and Stuart can't pay your hospital bill, and you won't be coming back to Southern Prep this semester, and...."

A male voice cut her off. Stuart had come in without either of us hearing him. "Well, well, well," he said. "If it isn't Raven FitzSimons, mouth-of-the-South." I was startled; Raven was terrified. Her face went white. She rushed toward the door. Stuart took two long strides and blocked her. He stared coldly into her eyes.

"Don't be in such a rush, Raven. I'm interested in where you get your information. And what's that piece of paper wadded up in your hand? Writing your news down now? So you can get it all straight when you blab it elsewhere?"

"Stuart, don't," I said. "Raven didn't mean anything. We were just talking."

But he would not let her move. "She isn't supposed to be here," he said, still staring. "I told her to leave you alone until you had a chance to get better."

"But I am better. Look at me. I'm dressed and walking all over. I couldn't wait for you to get home so we could go for a walk on the beach. Please don't be mad at Raven. I told her you wouldn't mind if she came."

"I don't like the way she talks. Dr. Merritt said you shouldn't get upset, and here I come home and find the queenlet prep running off at the mouth about things that are none of her business."

"Let it go, Stu. It was nice to have someone to talk to. I get lonely here by myself."

I touched him on the arm. He stiffened, then relaxed and dropped his head. The confrontation was over. "Hell," he said. "Who cares? I'm too beat to care."

He turned abruptly and walked into the sitting room. I motioned for Raven to leave. "You can come back whenever you want," I said. "Stuart isn't really that mad, just exhausted from overwork."

Raven ran to me and gave me a hug, then left without another word. I tried to regulate my breathing before calling to Stuart. When calm, I shouted into the sitting room, *"Hey, handsome. I'm out here by myself. Where did you go? To China?"*

"The kitchen," he called back, his voice a fraction brighter than I expected it to be. I was thankful for the improvement. *"Want a pretend wine spritzer?"*

"No, bring me the real thing."

He returned to the porch with a Bud for himself and a club soda over ice for me. "Use your imagination," he said, then, "thanks for sending brat-face home. I need your undivided attention a few minutes to talk something over. I've been looking at that manuscript you helped Miss Peregrine write last year. How many publishers did you send it to?"

"Twenty."

"Twenty?"

"Maybe it was only ten. I've forgotten, what with going to the hospital and being sick ...."

Stuart looked at me until I blinked. I knew he did not believe me. "You didn't send it to anyone, did you? Miss Peregrine gave you money for copying and postage, and you used it for pills, instead. Isn't that right?"

"Yes, but I was in pain all the time."

"I know you were—let's not get into that again. Let's talk about the manuscript. Yesterday, while you were sleeping, I took a second look at it. It's pretty good. The problem is you never spent any serious time polishing it."

"So?"

"So now's the time. You're stuck here on the porch indefinitely. You say you feel better. Why don't you shape it up. Maybe you could sell it."

"I don't own but half of it, Stu. Miss Peregrine owns the other half."

"Half is better than nothing, and didn't you tell me Miss Peregrine is dying to see it in print?"

"Sure, but even if I whipped it into perfect shape, we don't have enough money to have rewrites typed, or copying or postage or all the other hidden junk it takes to promote a writing project. *Tarnished Honor* is four hundred pages long. That's twenty-five dollars per clean copy. And there's no telling what it would cost to have corrections typed."

"Don't worry about money. Just do the initial work. I've already put things into motion to get myself a regular job. But there's no reason both of us have to give up freelancing. You can work on creative things right now. Let me bring in the bread and butter. I don't see that we have a choice, anyway. You're too weak to do much else."

"You're going back to teaching?"

"Sure, why not?"

"But you've tried so hard to build a consulting practice. It isn't fair for you to have to give up now."

"I'll get over it. Besides, self-actualization is way down on my Maslow right now. The main priority is scrounging up money to get us out of the current financial mess. Rent is the immediate concern. Mrs. Middleton told me this morning she wants us out of here by the weekend if we don't come up with a few hundred to go against our arrearage. She's been a real bitch the last few days. I haven't mentioned it—I didn't want to worry you. She says she doesn't want slow-paying druggies living in her cottage, as if her husband wasn't the biggest drunk in Charleston. What I don't understand is how people in this town know every damn detail of our lives."

"I can't leave, Stuart. I can't go anywhere. I'm not well enough"

"Don't worry, I'll take care of Lucretia. I just couldn't risk your staying in the cottage alone anymore, not without knowing she's on the warpath. She could come out here any day demanding money."

"I can't stand it. It's terrible," I said.

"Don't worry, Arly. You can count on me to get us through."

"I'm not trying to be mean, Stuart, but I don't know any such thing."

It wasn't easy staying angry at Stuart, not after all he had done for me, but somehow I managed for the next two hours. Then, just as I was about to forgive him, Raven complicated the moment by pushing open the screen door and accidentally thwacking Stuart on the back. She was so excited, she forgot she was supposed to be avoiding him.

"Don't you have anything better to do than harass the innocent?" he said when she shoved him aside to get to me.

"You can stop trying to intimidate me," she said haughtily. "I've decided it's stupid to let myself be jerked around by a jackass like you. Now get away from me. I have to give this envelope to Mrs. Prince. It's full of money, lots of money. Miss Peregrine asked me to deliver it, right after she read the note."

"What note?" Stuart said, red blotches appearing on his face and neck.

"Nothing," I broke in. "It's nothing. Raven just ran a little errand for me. She took a get-well message to Miss Peregrine. I couldn't go out to buy a card, so I wrote a note instead."

"But why did you send it by *her*? I could have taken it." More red blotches.

"No reason. You've been too busy. Good grief, look at all this money. The envelope is stuffed."

"Fifteen hundred dollars," Raven said. "I counted it out of a money pouch Miss Peregrine keeps under her mattress. She must have five or six thousand dollars under there. She told me not to tell anyone."

I handed the cash to Stuart and watched him finger it lovingly. He counted it hand to hand, fifteen one-hundred-dollar bills. The blotches were still apparent. The reason for them had changed.

"I have a letter, too," Raven said, "from Miss Peregrine." Then she paraphrased its contents in one, long run-on sentence while Stuart stood by dumbstruck.

"Arlena, darling, you missed your paycheck last month, here it is in cash, sorry it's so late, can't wait to see you, call soon. Love, Miss Peregrine."

"Is there anything you don't pry into?" Stuart said.

"You'd better be nice to me, creep. I brought the money. I noticed Miss Peregrine didn't put your name on the envelope. It's only for Mrs. ...."

I stopped her. I did not want to see Stuart strangle a young girl. "That's enough, Rav. Look here, there's something not right about this note. This can't be Miss Peregrine's handwriting. It's too steady."

"It's mine," she said with a self-satisfied smile. "Miss Peregrine dictated the note to me. She was too tired to write."

Stuart had finally had enough. "Look, Arlena and I appreciate all your help, but don't you think you should be going home now? We'll try to think of something nice to do for you later, to repay you for all the trouble you've gone to."

"I know when people are trying to get rid of me," she said.

"No, no, no—don't take it like that. You can come back tomorrow after school. Arlena needs help with a project she's going to be working on. Maybe we can pay you a little something."

Raven looked pleased. For some reason—she couldn't imagine

what—Stuart had actually had to lower himself to asking for her help. She milked the moment.

"I don't know. I might be too busy. I'll try though, maybe, since it's for Mrs. Prince."

"Thanks," Stuart said without sincerity. "Now run along. Mother-dear will be wondering where you are."

Raven made a face and took her leave slowly. Stuart came close to losing his new-found patience. If she had stayed one more second, he would have barked at her again. When she was finally gone, he sat down next to me to go over a new plan.

"This is great," he said. "I can't believe Miss Peregrine did this. Gives us all kinds of wiggle room. We'll pay Lucretia five hundred to take care of the rent a few weeks—money always makes her feel better. And you can have five to finance rewriting *Tarnished Honor*. I'll use the rest for expenses and getting out job applications. I'll also keep plugging away on Bill Greene's condo promotion and finish up my other small projects. Even so, I'll still have to beat the bushes for a loan. Those medical bills aren't going away."

"Who in the world would lend us money?"

"Don't know yet. My dad, maybe."

"How much do we owe?"

"Thousands. The worst screw-up of my life was letting our medical insurance lapse. I know that's why you didn't tell me how sick you were. If we'd had decent insurance, you wouldn't have let it go that far."

"I don't want to talk about it."

"Okay, we won't. Now what about *Tarnished Honor*? When can you start on it?"

"I hate this, Stuart. It isn't fair—you giving up your dream of owning your own business while I piddle around with a so-so writing project."

"I'm not giving up anything but heartache. There'll be plenty of chances for me to do wonderful things in the English department of some grade-B college."

"All right, but reworking a manuscript is no guarantee of selling it."

"I know, but there's always a chance. Write some letters. Find an agent. Have Raven run errands and help you proofread. Didn't you say she's a pretty good writer herself?"

"Yes."

"Then she ought to be able to help you. But right now you have to call Miss Peregrine, to thank her for sending you this cash. She didn't have to do that, you know. It's not as though you were on salary."

"It's no use. Tycie'll just answer and say Miss Peregrine is still sick. I don't want to call again. I want to go see her in person."

"I don't think you should go back to Peregrine House. That letter from FitzSimons's office sounded final."

"More guerrilla warfare in the ongoing campaign to sack the Yankee ghostwriter. Jeannette FitzSimons has been trying to get rid of me for months. Imagine her consternation when I lived through major surgery. She must've been devastated. And it's all about money. Money, money, money. She's terrified Miss Peregrine might pay out one thin dime to someone other than herself. It's no wonder Raven hates her. But then Raven is indiscriminate—she hates everyone equally."

"That girl has the soul of a boa constrictor."

Chapter Twenty-One

I finished editing *Tarnished Honor* in less than three weeks. This was possible because Raven helped me every afternoon. Stuart almost regretted calling her a boa. The typing bill alone came to fifteen hundred dollars, three times the amount we had budgeted. I negotiated with the typist, and she agreed to forgive the bill and take ten percent of the advance if I were able to sell the manuscript. If I couldn't move it in a year, I'd pay her the full fifteen-fifty, plus twenty percent interest. Stuart and I were grateful for this breathing space. It freed up the whole five hundred for copying, postage, letters, and miscellaneous. Raven worked for nothing. On the Friday that she delivered the thrice-corrected manuscript to the beach cottage, I made a speech about appreciation and gave her my copy of *The Collected Poems of Sylvia Plath.*

"How long have you had this book?" she gushed.

"Years. For a long time I thought I *was* Plath."

"And you're giving it to me? And you don't want it back? It's mine to keep forever?"

"Sure, why shouldn't I give you something personal? As sick as I've been, I may never have children of my own to save things for. But don't make me out a saint. I can always scare up other copies of Plath. My friends up north all read her."

"But not this copy. This is the one you read when you were a kid, like me. Look, there're margin notes on every page."

"Maybe a little older. I'm thirty now, remember?"

"Thank you, Mrs. Prince. I'll keep it forever."

"You can give it to your own daughter if you ever have one."

Raven became suddenly silent. She dropped her head and clutched the book to her chest. At first I thought she was ill. I didn't realize she was crying.

"What's wrong, Rav? Are you sick?"

"Yes, I'm dying. I don't know what to do."

"What is it? What's the matter?"

"I lied about starting my period. I'm pregnant. I took a home pregnancy test this morning."

My skin turned to goose flesh under my clothes. "But Raven, you said ...."

"Don't you understand? I *lied*."

"But that was three weeks ago. You were almost two weeks late then. Three plus two, plus two more...you could be seven or eight weeks by now. Why haven't you told anyone? Why haven't you gotten help?"

"I don't know. I guess I thought it would go away. And now I wish I hadn't said anything to you. You'll probably just call my mother. That's what you threatened to do last time."

"Hush, Raven. I can't think. I can't think what to do." I stared at the stack of manuscript pages in my lap. I was waiting, hoping, for some sensible idea to formulate in my brain. When none came, I plowed forward without a plan. "Get the phone book," I said. "We have to look up a clinic, some sort of women's medical office. Do you have any money?"

"Seventy-three dollars. Is that enough for an abortion?"

"I don't know. We're not talking abortion yet. We have to find out if you're really pregnant."

I looked in the Yellow Pages and found five clinics, all with large ads: pregnancy testing, abortions, family planning, pregnancy counseling, prevention of sexually transmitted diseases.

"Don't you have a family doctor, Rav? These ads are scary."

"Are you crazy? Croom's father is our doctor. He'd have Mother on the phone before I got my panties off."

"This is serious, Raven. It's asinine to make jokes."

"I didn't mean to, I'm just scared."

"Okay, hand me the phone." I punched in the number of the first clinic, FEMMES CLINIQUE. The conversation was brief. How much for a test? What does it involve? When can it be done? The woman said she was a nurse. She answered my questions clearly and concisely. I was satisfied. When I hung up, I tore off the top sheet of the note pad and handed it to Raven.

"I think this is all you need," I said. "The nurse says you can take a urine specimen in tomorrow morning. They open at seven.

You won't have to miss school. She said they'd do the test immediately, and you can wait to get the results then or call back later. And you don't have to give your name."

"Then what?"

"I don't know. Maybe that will be the end of it. Maybe the test will come back negative. Let's pray the home test was wrong."

Raven left the cottage clutching *Sylvia Plath* in one hand and the note with the clinic information in the other. I tried to put the situation out of my mind by busying myself with assembling mailing packages for *Tarnished Honor*. The week before, I had gone through my two-year-old copy of *Literary Market Place* and picked out names of ten literary agents. On checking them out with phone calls, I discovered one was no longer working, three nowhere to be found, and one dead of wounds from a subway mugging (Oh, Jesus!). That left five. I knew I should have contacted them one at a time, but I ignored good form and prepared five large envelopes. After sealing and stamping, I said two *Hail Mary's* and three *Our Father's*, then slid the envelopes into a large plastic bag to protect them from seaside dampness. My hope was that one reputable agent would see marketability in the sample chapter and ask to see more. One encouraging word, and the other chapters could be mailed immediately.

When I finished taping up the packages, I went out to the porch to sit in the swing and worry about Raven. When Stuart came home, he mixed two cocktails and joined me.

"What's this?" I asked. "An inch? A half inch?"

"A mini-liqueur," he said. "We don't want nightmares sneaking up on us again."

"The dreams have been gone for weeks, Stu. I haven't had one in ..."

"Yeah, sure, that's why you only cry out in your sleep two or three times a night now." Stuart fixed a cool gaze on my face. I stared back without blinking.

"I want to propose a toast," I said, changing the subject. "To—" Stuart raised his glass ceremoniously and waited for me to finish, "—the mailing of *Tarnished Honor*," I said.

"Salute," he responded and clinked my glass.

I sipped at my short drink, savoring the taste of amaretto, wondering if I should mention Raven's latest travail, hating to spoil the moment, deciding finally against it.

"I got five packages ready to mail today," I said. "Will you have time to drop them off at the post office in the morning?"

"A labor of love," he said. "I'll send them off with my twenty-two job applications. You're not the only one giving the typist work."

I cringed when he mentioned the typist. "I hope you paid her more than I did."

"And how much was that?"

"Not a cent. Not for the manuscript, anyway. There were a couple of odds and ends I had to spring for."

"How did you get away with that, Arly? You must have given her something. You should have given her something."

"Who are you kidding? The next thing you'll want to know is how much I have left out of the five hundred we budgeted. You're delighted I avoided that bill."

Stuart looked uncomfortable, but asked the question anyway. "How much?"

I smiled an I-told-you-so. "Three hundred," I said. "I gave Raven a hundred and fifty for copying and this-and-that, and the other fifty went for the synopsis and cover letters. Please tell me we aren't out of money already. I'm not up to that again so soon."

"What can I say? Cash runs through our fingers like water. And now the car is making funny noises. Cold weather doesn't agree with it. Any chance Miss Peregrine might kick in a few more bucks?"

"I don't think so. Tycie is the one life-form I can get hold of over there. And all she does is discourage me."

"I know, I know. I'm groping, trying to think of every angle. Let's see, we have your three hundred, five due from Bill Greene, a couple hundred in cash. Who should we pay? The hospital? Lucretia? The doctor?"

"Shouldn't we get the car fixed?"

"Your guess is as good as mine. I don't know what to do. At this point every financial decision is a judgment call."

I pulled my eyebrows together and thought. "Fix the car," I said. "The other things can wait."

"Sounds good to me. I'll take care of it tomorrow. Hey, look outside. The wind is dying down. Let's go for a walk."

Stuart bundled me into two sweat shirts to brave the November air. As we trudged along the beach path, a cold wet wind pushed us along. It was definitely not dying down. As always on blustery days, I found the wildness of the ocean overwhelming. It rolled and thrashed about like an enraged animal. Stuart led me in the direction of the lighthouse. We had just found our pace when the wind shifted and began blowing directly into our faces.

"We're the only people on the beach," I said.

"The only ones crazy enough," he answered. "Want to take a break, sit for a while in the dunes?"

"No, I'll freeze. Let's keep moving."

We pushed ahead. Once or twice I jogged a step or two and made Stuart laugh. "Come on," he said. "Let's get out of this wind. We can sit down and rest behind the sea oats." He moved his eyebrows up and down lasciviously.

"I'm well, Stu, but not *that* well."

"Come on," he said. "I'll behave."

Among the dunes he pulled me down in the sand and wrapped his arms around my shoulders. "This is romantic," he said.

"This is uncomfortable," I complained. He shifted his position and patted me on the back. "Better now?"

"A little, but stop wiggling so much. We need to talk something over. I want you to repeat after me: *Arlena is doing great.*"

"Arlena is doing great."

"She is totally recovered."

"She is totally recovered—except for having sex—she hasn't had sex yet."

"Stop that and listen: *Arlena can go out tomorrow and visit Miss Peregrine...and Mr. Pinckney.*"

"Nope. Arlena is not that well."

"Oh, you make me furious. You thought I was well enough to work on that manuscript three whole ...."

"Hush, I hear someone talking."

Angry voices, borne on the wind, clacked erratically from the dunes to our left. I listened a few seconds, then jerked my head in recognition. "It's Raven, and Croom Jr.," I said softly.

Stuart put a hand to his forehead. He knew the scene would be one more display of adolescent histrionics. "Quiet, maybe they'll go away," he said. "I don't want to be bothered with them today."

I nodded and sat still. The voices were muffled, blown about by the wind. Only a few clear sentences came through. Raven screamed them hysterically. *"I'm pregnant, Croom. Don't you understand? Pregnant!"* Then she disintegrated into sobs.

Stuart stared at me. "Do you think she's serious?" he said, then looked deeper into my black eyes and picked up a signal I did not mean to send out. "Good God, of course she's serious...and you already knew. Just like always, you knew."

Chapter Twenty-Two

I refused to talk to Stuart about Raven, and after a question or two he stopped pressing. In his own words, he "really didn't give a rip about the problems of a teenage floozy." Two more days passed before she came back to the cottage to tell me what had happened at the clinic.

"Raven," I said, holding open the screened door for a pale green girl to drag herself onto the porch. "You promised to call me as soon as you got the test results. First you drive me crazy telling me a bunch of junk, then you won't call to let me know what's happening."

She sprawled the length of the porch swing and moaned like she was dying. This enraged me even more. *"Dammit, Raven. Why didn't you call?"*

"I had the stinking test at the stinking clinic two stinking days ago," she whined, "which took some doing, with Mother in my face every minute. I finally had to tell her there was a seven a.m. emergency rehearsal for the drama club production, and I absolutely had to go. I didn't make it to the clinic until seven-thirty. A million girls were already there, waiting at the door like criminals sentenced to the gas chamber. A nurse came out and gave us numbers and told us to line up in order in the reception area. Can you believe it? I had to take a number. We all got positives. Everyone came out bawling. I only saw one girl get a negative. She was bawling, too, but laughing at the same time. I figured she had to be a negative. My test showed up positive so fast the nurse looked at me like she thought I might start having labor pains any second. I cried like everyone else, then went straight to the drugstore and bought another home test kit to make sure the nurse wasn't wrong. She didn't look too smart to me. It made a perfect little doughnut hole right in the middle of a test tube full of my wee-wee. No hope now. I'm done for."

"Are you sure?" I asked stupidly.

Raven didn't answer. She looked at me as if I were a dolt.

"I'm sorry, Raven. There's only one thing left to do."

"I know, an abortion. You can get them at the clinic for two hundred and seventy-five dollars. The nurse said they do them on Thursdays. They call them procedures. I wonder if you have to take a number?"

"That's not what I meant," I said quickly. "I meant you have to tell your mother. You shouldn't do anything drastic until you talk it over with her."

"I can't. She'd kill me. But you don't have to worry about it, anymore. It isn't your problem. I've decided to stop coming out here bothering you all the time. But there's one really important thing I have to tell you, and I mean it more than I ever meant anything in my whole rotten life. If you call my mother and tell her about this, I'll run away and never come back. No one will ever know what happened to me. And it'll all be your fault."

"I don't know, Raven ...."

"You'd better think it over before you go blabbing, Mrs. Prince. I don't have much to lose. It won't be long before they expel me from school for good. Yesterday Croom told me he doesn't love me and never did, and now you might rat on me to Mother."

"Okay, I won't say anything, not unless you tell me it's all right. Only don't cut yourself off from me. The last thing you need right now is to feel alone. I want you to call me every day until you decide what you're going to do."

"I will...promise. But I have to go now. I'm on my way to school. How's that for total insanity?"

"Call me, Raven."

"Sure, every day."

I checked my watch as her red MG sputtered out of the cottage drive. Quarter of ten. Stuart was due back in fifteen minutes. I walked into the sitting room to call Peregrine House. I was determined not to let Raven's never-ending problems dominate another of my mornings. Earlier I had decided to put a small plan into action, and I meant to see it through. And Stuart, though he didn't yet know it, was going to be my accomplice. As soon as he came in from his appointment with Bill Greene, I intended to wheedle him into driving me to see Miss Peregrine. That part of the plan I knew I could pull off. Getting Tycie's help wouldn't be so easy.

She answered the phone on the third ring and again tried to get rid of me. But this time, to my everlasting surprise and relief, Miss Peregrine came on the line, shouting above Tycie, telling her to "get off the phone." It was the first time I'd heard her voice since our respective illnesses. It had not changed an inflection.

"Hang up, Tycie," she commanded again. "I want to talk to Miss Arlena in private."

"Miss Peregrine, is it really you?" I said.

"Of course it's me, you ninny. Where in thunder have you been? I've not heard a word from you in weeks."

"On Sullivan's, recuperating. But I'm much stronger now. Stuart may drive me into town this afternoon. Is it all right if I visit you?"

"Yes, they've left me to myself for a change. I told them all to get out, I needed room to breathe."

"Does it matter what time?"

"As early as you can get here. I want to see you. I've missed you frightfully."

"Me too you, Miss Per..." But my words died away. She had already hung up.

Stuart was back by five of ten. I met him at the end of the driveway. "How long have you been standing out here?" he said. "Don't you know you could get chilled?"

"Stop fussing over me, Stu. You said you'd be home by ten, and since you've never been late for anything in your entire life, I knew you'd get here at exactly this moment. Now hurry. Miss Peregrine said I could see her today."

"You're not well enough. We already discussed it."

"No, *you* discussed it, over a week ago. Come on, look at me. You can see how much better I am."

He put the Romeo into first gear and lurched down Atlantic Avenue. He pouted the whole way into the city, but I didn't care. I was out of the cottage, off the island, zinging along in an automobile. It was wonderful, until we came upon the formidable mansions of South Battery Street. They stood like a row of giant chess pieces poised to crush an opponent.

"Oh, help," I said, staring up. "The houses have grown taller."

"The nature of affluence, my dear. It compounds upon itself. The same principle operates with poverty," I understand."

"Are you planning to be snotty with everyone today, Stuart? Or just me? It's time I got out and about."

"No, it isn't, but I'm tired of trying to stop you. Get out of the car. You're not the only one with things to do. I'll pick you up at High Battery in an hour."

I watched him round the corner of King Street, and wished I hadn't been so mean. I sighed and turned back toward the mansions. I'd have to face Peregrine House alone. A small cramp of fear entered my lower stomach when I thought of Louisa Hill. It took effort to make myself go to the door and rap with its shiny knocker. Maybe Stuart is right, I thought. Maybe I'm not ready for combat.

Fearfully I waited for someone to answer the door. Tycie was the most likely candidate. "I told you not to come here," she said, cracking the door an inch.

"It's good to see you, too, Tycie...and you're going to have to let me in whether you want to or not. Miss Peregrine is expecting me."

She stared at me sullenly, lips poked out, facial lines drawn into a frown. "Well?" I said. "Are you going to leave me standing out here all morning?"

She harumped loudly, swung open the door, and told me again, with great emphasis, exactly what she thought: "Come on in and join the troubles, Missy. May as well. Everybody else has. But don't come crying to old Tycie when you get hurt. Tycie's done told you to mind your own business. Ain't nothing going on in Peregrine House except moaning and groaning. Missy Peregrine is doing all the moaning, and those other two white women, they're doing all the groaning...flying around here like two wasps trying to sting each other in the throat."

"Who are you talking about, Tycie?"

"That 'tetched' cousin, Missy Louisa. She's one, and Missy Jeannette is the other. All the time squabbling about who takes care of Missy Peregrine the most, sometimes squabbling about you, saying you ain't nothing but white trash what's hooked on dope, then coming back around to Missy Peregrine. And the whole time, I be walking around the house thinking to myself, *Tycie is the over-*

worked mule who takes care of Missy Peregrine. Been taking care of her fifty years, same like always, same like a lifetime—not those two puffed up blow-fish."

She punctuated her last remark with an eloquent snort. I hoped the tirade was over. "I'm sorry you've had so much trouble, Tycie. I'll try to stay out of your way. Is Louisa here now?"

"No ma'am. She's still at her church meeting, the old hypocrite."

"May I go upstairs to see Miss Peregrine then?"

"Do what you please. Tycie ain't going to stop you. She ain't going to stop nobody."

She turned her back on me and hobbled away. I decided to go upstairs by way of the elevator. No use testing my incision on four flights of stairs. I stepped off on the fourth level and started down the hall, calling out hesitantly. *"Are you awake, Miss Peregrine? It's me, Arlena."*

"Get yourself in here, you errant child. I'm starved for the company of a sane human being."

I ran down the hall to her room and flew to her bedside. She held out two grotesquely thin arms. I sat on the edge of the bed and held her hands in mine. A rattly chuckle came from deep within her chest. "You look terrible," she said.

"Everyone tells me that. I'm used to it," I said back, squeezing her hand and patting it. "But *you* don't. You look beautiful."

"Lying is a mortal sin, girl. I look dreadful and you know it. I'm in my dotage now, not long for this world."

"No, no, you're fine. I'm the one who almost died."

"Yes, I understand you had a little of that 'female trouble' folks used to hush-hush."

"Yes, I did."

"And what else was wrong?"

"Not anything."

"Arlena, I've already told you, you'll go straight to hell for lying. Now tell me about the other problem, the *drug* problem. Lord knows, I've heard enough about it from Jeannette."

"I...I was...well, I guess my body was dependent on some medicine I'd been taking. I was having a lot of pain and—"

"That's an interesting way of saying you were addicted. Sounds so benign when you put it like that."

"I'm sorry, Miss Peregrine. I didn't do it on purpose, but the pain was awful. I suppose I should have been seeing a better doctor."

"Is it over now?"

"Yes, they took out my ovary."

"I wasn't talking about that part. I was talking about the dependency."

"Yes, I haven't needed medication since the pain went away."

"I knew Jeannette was lying, that it was something like that."

"But how did she know about it?"

"The same way people know everything in Charleston...raw juicy gossip. There's a never-ending supply of it in this town."

"Are you angry with me, Miss Peregrine?"

"No, it makes you seem a tad less goody-good. Nothing more boring than perfection."

"But what about you?" I said. "Tycie told me you've been ill, terribly ill."

"I did have a little trouble getting my prescriptions regulated, but I think I've got them straightened out now, for a while, anyway."

"Good, we're recovering at the same time. I'm so glad you're better."

"You will visit me often now that you're well, I trust?"

"Yes, as often as ..." But my thought was stopped by a horrendous crash. I turned to see Louisa standing in the bedroom doorway, shards of glass at her feet.

"What are you doing here?" she said to me, her voice crackling as if electrified.

"Visiting Miss Peregrine. We were talking ...."

Miss Peregrine interrupted. "How could you be so clumsy, Louisa? For heaven's sake, clean up that mess."

Louisa vanished immediately. I moved closer to Miss Peregrine. "Sorry, dear," she said to me soothingly. "Louisa has been on a tear since I got sick, ranting and raving like a mad woman."

At that moment Louisa came sweeping back in like a hawk diving for prey. In one motion she flew across the room and shoved a tattered folder into my hands. Then she turned to confront Miss Peregrine.

"Now you've done it," she said. "You've finally done it. I've tried and tried to make you listen, but you have steadfastly refused. You've kept right on disobeying."

Miss Peregrine ignored Louisa's outburst and focused her attention on me. She spoke quietly, her tone calm and even. "We'll have to finish our conversation later, Arlena. As you can see, I must deal with Louisa now. Thank you for coming to see me this morning. We'll plan another visit soon, tomorrow perhaps. Now go home and rest. You'll need it for when we start back to work."

"But, Miss Peregrine, I ...."

"Arlena, *please leave*."

Chapter Twenty-Three

I left Peregrine House angry. So angry I could not recall how I made my way back to the battery. My incision must be healed, I thought, as I looked out over the harbor, to have walked that fast without feeling it. The yellowed folder Louisa had thrust at me was still in my hands. It felt suddenly heavy, a cream-colored albatross, a trove of dark secrets meant to expose Miss Peregrine. What was I supposed to do with the thing? Read it? Toss it? Who did Louisa possibly think could be interested in an old woman's past?

I snapped open the folder, eager to prove Louisa's stupidity. I was already aware of the information on the first few pages, the part about the baby. But the name was different from the one in the family *Bible*. Somehow *Jane Smith* did not sound as refined as *Constantia Elizabeth Peregrine*. The details, however, were new to me.

Constantia Elizabeth had grown up to marry a man from New York, a Thomas Wendell Stafford. They'd had one daughter, Louisa Jane. I read the name over several times as the fact of the matter jelled in my brain. Louisa...Louisa Stafford...Miss Peregrine's granddaughter. I lifted my eyes and watched the small white triangles that were sailboats navigating the harbor. By quirk of circumstance, Louisa Jane Stafford had also been reared at Our Lady of Grace, like her mother, Constantia Elizabeth. Jane Smith Stafford (Miss Peregrine's secret child, whose real name was Constantia), and Thomas Stafford, her husband, had both died of polio in 1946. The foundling home had taken little Louisa in, and there she'd remained for all intents and purposes until Miss Peregrine invited her to live at Peregrine House forty years later.

Now I understood Miss Peregrine's interest in Louisa. She must have known about her all along, since her birth, but could

do nothing to help her until old Mr. Peregrine died. I also understood that her position as a spinster in Old Charleston society
prevented her from acknowledging Louisa publicly. Such a thing
would not have been acceptable, dead father or no.

I was so engrossed in the contents of the folder that I didn't
see the Romeo roll up. "Pick you up, baby?" Stuart called out.

I jumped; he laughed. "I asked if I could pick you up," he
said, "the way little boys pick up little girls?"

"Sorry, Stu. I was thinking too hard. Louisa came after me
again today. Now she's claiming to be Miss Peregrine's... Oh,
never mind. It's all too ridiculous to tell."

Still smiling, he got out of the car and joined me on the bench.
In his hands was a small box gift-wrapped in silver paper. This
was a different Stuart from the one who had dropped me off earlier, a more relaxed Stuart. Something had happened.

"What's this?" I asked.

"Oh, something I picked up off the ground."

"Stop teasing. What is it?" I reached for the box. He held it
an arms-length away, elongating his moment of power.

"Not so fast, my greedy little pet. Promises first."

"What promises?" Another grab.

"You must love me forever."

"I promise, I promise."

"You must be faithful and loyal and true, forever and ever and
ever."

"I promise."

"You must obey me, always."

"Not a chance." I lunged for the box again. This time he let
me grab it.

"Stop, don't rip it open yet. I want to tell you something first."

"Tell me quick, I can't wait."

"I love you more than anything in the world," he said, "the
galaxy, the universe."

I looked at his face and was envious. Why couldn't I be an
open book like Stuart? Why was I splintered and layered? "I love
you too, Stewy," I said simply. It was the best I could do.

"Open it, then. It's yours."

Inside the box was a thin bangle bracelet that matched my
silver hoops. "Oh, it's beautiful," I said, "but why did you spend
money like this?"

"The worm turned today. We can breathe a little easier." He took a pale blue check from the inside pocket of his sportcoat and placed it reverently in my hands. I felt my eyeballs swell.

"Five thousand dollars," I read aloud from the check. "Signed by Grayson Pinckney? What does this mean, Stuart?"

"Just a small loan from a friend, my dear."

"A what?"

"A loan, or sort of a loan. Mr. Pinckney said to think of it as fair compensation for knocking Jon Priolieu's teeth out."

"But how did he know we needed it?"

"Well, after trying everyone else on the American continent, I decided to call your Mr. Pinckney. I figured there was nothing to lose, maybe he'd feel sorry for us, give us a break. I was in his office just now while you were playing patty-cake with Miss Peregrine. I told him my whole life story. Yours, too. But it turned out he already knew we were in trouble. Our good friend Dr. Calhoun has been spreading the news. He must have followed your case minute-to-minute the whole time you were in the hospital."

"That guy is a first-class jerk. He'd love to pull me down."

"Seems he wasted his breath on Grayson Pinckney."

"Five thousand dollars," I said, still staring at the small blue rectangle of paper that trembled in my hands.

"It's nowhere near enough to pay everything we owe," Stuart said bluntly, "but it'll keep us on solid footing while I interview for jobs. We'll be chipping away at that hospital bill for years. But this little baby—"he tapped the check with his forefinger,"—will help us keep our heads up in the mean time."

"We have to pay it back, though, right?"

"That's the deal loosely, though forbearance is the key word, I suspect. There's something else Mr. Pinckney wants more than money—a firm commitment from you to help him finish his reminiscences. He's worried you might give up on them, considering all you've been through. He's going to draw up a simple contract to keep it all legal."

"For five thousand dollars, I'd sign a contract with Jack the Ripper."

Stuart laughed again. Had a miracle occurred? Had he somehow become ten years younger? "Come on, Margaret Mitchell," he said. "Let's go home. We have reason to celebrate."

"An understatement," I said, finally able to smile, "but first I need to go back by Peregrine House. I have to return something. It won't take a minute, honest." I held up the folder and watched the smile slide off his face.

"Good grief, Arlena. You'll be begging St. Peter at the pearly gates for an extra half hour to deal with one more piece of paperwork."

"And he'll give it to me to shut me up. Now on to South Battery, Julius Caesar."

Louisa opened the front door before I had a chance to knock. I tried not to wilt under her stare. *Where are Tycie and Jeannette? I thought irritably. How could they leave Miss Peregrine at home alone with a maniac?*

"Did you bring it back?" Louisa said curtly.

"If you mean the folder, yes, not that you deserve the courtesy."

"Give it to me then," she said.

I hesitated a second too long; she snatched it from my hands. Frantically, she flipped it open and began to examine its contents. I watched her for a moment before speaking.

"I didn't tamper with your precious papers if that's what you're worried about," I said, "but I'm going to tell Miss Peregrine you showed them to me."

"Get out of here and don't come back," she said. "I've taken care of Fanny Peregrine half my life, and I'm sick and tired of people like you and Jeannette FitzSimons trying to take all the credit. I just wish I hadn't lost my temper and shown you this folder. You'll probably tell everyone in town what's in it."

"You weren't that angry, Louisa. You showed it to me on purpose. Any excuse would have been good enough to let me know you're blood kin to Miss Peregrine. You'd like everyone to know, wouldn't you? It's been eating at you for years. Just think—to be Fanny Peregrine's only granddaughter and forbidden to reveal it."

This time she did slam the door.

A five-thousand-dollar check from Grayson Pinckney and two

confrontations with Louisa were enough to exhaust anyone, particularly someone who'd been ill eight weeks. I slept on the drive back to Sullivan's , through dinner, to the next morning when the phone rang at eight. So much for our celebration. Stuart jumped out of bed on the first ring and ran into the sitting room to answer it. In two seconds he was shouting for me to come there.

"It's an *agent*," he yelled, "from New York, calling about *Tarnished Honor*. Hurry up—she wants to talk."

My heart began pounding. I couldn't get my body organized to move. "Come on," he yelled louder. I ignored the frantic thumping in my chest cavity and made my way rockily to the sitting room. It was a brief conversation: Sarah Goldstein introduced herself; I remembered having spoken to her when researching the agent listings; she did not remember our conversation, but had received my material and liked my synopsis; liked the chapter; wanted to see more. Yes, I'd send the complete manuscript right away. No, it had not been passed around among publishing houses. Yes, she could have an exclusive contract to represent the work.

I hung up and stared at the wall. Stuart shook my arm to bring me to my senses. I was too deep in shock to notice. I stood by dumbly while he located, sorted, stacked, and boxed the remaining chapters for mailing. When done, he raced away, package in tow, to try to make the nine o'clock mail drop in Mount Pleasant. In his hurry he forgot to give me instructions on how to spend the rest of the morning, which, as it turned out, was a very big mistake.

I considered calling Miss Peregrine to tell her an agent had contacted me. No—no use in getting her hopes up without a contract in hand. Then I spent ten uneasy minutes wondering if I should let her know I'd returned her folder and had no intention of divulging her secrets. No, not that, either. That particular situation needed to cool down a while. Then, out of nowhere, Raven popped into my mind. Was she okay? Should I risk calling her at home? I could always hang up if her mother answered. But before I could decide which pot to stir, the phone rang again. I picked up and said hello, irritation apparent in my voice.

"Hi, Mrs. Prince. What's wrong?" Raven said. "You sound like you swallowed a pickle."

"*Raven*. Where are you? I was about to call your house. Have you told your mother about the baby?"

"Don't need to. Croom already helped me work things out. We scraped up enough money for an abortion. We're going to the clinic tomorrow."

"Don't do it, Rav, not yet."

"There's no other way. I'm glad it's almost over." Then another goodbyeless click.

I stared at the clock next to the phone and tried to think what to do next. Eight forty-five; no idea what time Stuart would be back; no idea how to help my young friend. My mind skipped back and forth between Raven and her mother. I wavered one more anxious moment, then went to the closet to find some clothes. Informing a mother that her daughter was about to have an abortion was not something one could do by phone. I dressed hurriedly, then rummaged through my purse and found twenty-seven dollars, enough to take the bus into the city with plenty left over for a cab ride from the bus stop to FitzSimons's office. I put on a heavy pea jacket over my sweater and jeans, stuffed the twenty-seven dollars deep into my pants pocket, and walked purposefully to the kitchen door. For a second I reconsidered. I had not gone anywhere alone since my surgery. Stuart would be livid. But there was no alternative. Someone had to tell Raven's mother.

Slowly, timidly, I made my way down the stairs, to the end of the drive, to the bus stop a block down the street. The sea breeze blew away a little of my fear, yet I dreaded with every fiber of my being having to face FitzSimons. Why hadn't I called to make sure she was in? What was I going to say to her when I got there? When the cabby pulled in front of her office, I would have told him to keep driving had the image of Raven's childlike face not been hovering the last hour in a surreal hologram just behind my eyes. Seventeen-year-old, fresh-faced Raven, going to an abortion mill alone with no one to help her but Croom Calhoun, Jr. Boldly, I walked into FitzSimons's office.

The receptionist was not happy to see me. "Good morning," I said, trying to make myself official. "Is Mrs. FitzSimons in?"

"Yes, but she's tied up. Do you have an appointment?"

"No, I'm here to see her about a personal matter. It's important, extremely important. I need to talk to her now."

My urgency did not impress this woman. She put on her most bored expression, sighed heavily, and slid her chair back from her desk. "I didn't get your name," she said.

"Prince. Arlena Prince."

She walked into FitzSimons's private office and closed the door behind her. In seconds she reappeared. "Mrs. FitzSimons will give you five minutes, no more. She says its imperative that you be brief."

I stepped into the inner office to a hyper Jeannette FitzSimons. She was sitting behind a disorganized desk, rifling through papers, carrying on a disjointed telephone conversation.

"May I call you back in five minutes?" she said abruptly into the phone. "Good...five minutes...certainly." She hung up with no good-bye.

On shifting her attention to me, she looked as if she suddenly got a bad taste in her mouth. "You're here then," she said, "and high time. You have some explaining to do. What is the meaning of *this*?"

Turning to the credenza behind her, she picked up a copyshop box and heaved it on top of her trash-pile-of-a-desk. The title, *Tarnished Honor*, was scrawled on the lid.

"Where did you get that?" I said. "No one is supposed to ...."

"Never mind where I got it. What are you planning to do with it?"

"I...I don't see that it's any of your business."

"This material is derogatory. Surely you don't intend to publish it. If you do, you're worse than I thought."

"It's just a story," I said, tight-lipped with anger, "and it isn't even mine. It's Miss Peregrine's. Where did you get it? Miss Peregrine didn't keep a copy at her house."

"I found it, in my daughter's room, which brings me to another issue. I've told Raven repeatedly that she isn't to associate with you, yet I find this pile of feces, with your name plastered all over it, hidden under her bed."

"I don't know how she got it," I said.

"You're lying."

"Why don't you ask Raven about it? She obviously stole it from my house."

"Lucretia Middleton's house, not yours. And Raven doesn't steal, certainly not from the likes of you. Besides, she's a child. She doesn't understand the importance of certain things."

"May I have the manuscript back, please?"

"You may not. You may take nothing from this office. And,

since you're here, let me inform you of something else. Miss Peregrine's family and friends have met together and decided she's too weak to continue her memoirs. Do not harass her about it one minute more."

"I agree with you on that point," I said. "Miss Peregrine isn't well enough to work, but you can't stop me from visiting her."

"I most certainly can. Louisa told me how badly you upset her yesterday. I'll stop you from seeing her by court order if I have to."

"Louisa is deranged. You know that. She's the one who caused the trouble."

"Poor Louisa suffers from an emotional disorder. She's a bit confused at times. But I assure you, no matter what her mental state, she is always protective of Fanny. I suppose a peasant like you wouldn't understand that sort of thing. Some people are hopelessly vulgar, barging in where they aren't wanted."

"I didn't come here to discuss Louisa," I said, fighting to hang onto my composure.

"What *did* you come for then?"

I couldn't answer. There were no right words.

"Speak, or get out. I'm too busy for drama."

"Mrs. FitzSimons, I'm sorry ..." I could not go on.

"My God, what's wrong with you, woman?"

"It's Raven, Mrs. FitzSimons. She's in trouble. She needs help, but she's afraid to tell you."

"I thought I made it clear—stay out of my daughter's affairs."

A glint appeared in her angry eyes. I now felt more afraid than angry. "She came to me for help," I said, "but the problem was too big. I couldn't do anything about it behind your back. Mrs. FitzSimons, Raven is pregnant, eight weeks. She's planning to go to North Charleston in the morning, to get an abortion. Croom Calhoun, Jr. is going with her. It's his baby. I couldn't let them go without your knowing about it. Raven needs your help desperately."

Jeannette FitzSimons's face turned red, then purple, then almost black. Very slowly she rose from her chair and leaned upon her desk. The pile of papers slid this way and that.

"Have you lost your mind?" she said in a throaty whisper. "Raven is only seventeen years old. She's a debutante, for Christ's sake."

"I know that, and I also know she's probably going to need an abortion, anyway. I just didn't want her to go through it without family to help her. She's too young."

"*Get out. Get out of my office,*" FitzSimons screamed, the veins in her temples bulging into pulsing ridges. Then she stepped from behind her desk and came at me. Fearing an actual physical attack, I backed away clumsily and fled.

Chapter Twenty-Four

"Have you lost your mind? You went into the city alone?"

Stuart was furious. He stamped the length of the porch and back again, kicking at a wicker footstool as he went. For once, I was not the one shaking pilings.

"Maybe I have," I said. "You're the second person to ask me that today."

"Yeah, and the first was probably Jeannette FitzSimons. I don't see why you had to go sticking your nose into other people's business. I knew this thing with Raven would be trouble."

"Someone had to tell her mother. What else could I do? Send her an anonymous note?"

"You could've stayed out of it altogether. Everything was going so great, Arly. Mr. Pinckney's check, the call from Goldstein. Why couldn't you have just left this alone? Why do I have to come home and find out you've been agitating a rattle snake? There's no telling what that woman will do to Raven *or* to Croom. I just hope she'll be so busy working them over, she'll forget about coming after you. One thing I know for sure. Raven FitzSimons is going to hate your guts when she finds out what you've done."

"Maybe she'll thank me later."

Stuart looked at me with withering disdain. I considered that he might be right. Maybe I should have stayed out of it, let Raven get the abortion without her mother's knowledge. But whether he was right or wrong no longer mattered. I had already broken Raven's confidence.

Later that afternoon, while Stuart was in the shower, I made a secret phone call. I could have saved myself the trouble; no one was picking up at Raven's house. I gave up trying when the shower water stopped and Stuart's whistling grew louder. He makes me sick, I thought. An hour ago he was mad enough to kill me. Now he's whistling Gershwin. I stalked into the bathroom with the intention of starting a fight.

"Hey," Stuart yelled from the shower stall. "You must be getting well. The whole house shook when you walked in here, just like the old days."

"I don't know how you can be so insensitive," I said to the steamy shower curtain.

"Don't be so touchy, Arly. I was only teasing." He pushed open the door and showed himself all wet and curly-headed. I handed him a towel, then re-positioned myself. One look and he knew he was in for trouble. "Raven FitzSimons is scheduled to have an abortion tomorrow," I said, "and you don't care if she lives or dies. You're doing absolutely nothing to help her, and you won't let me do anything, either."

"I'd say you've done enough. Thanks to you, I'd bet my life there won't be a simple abortion. Jeannette FitzSimons will put poor Raven through far worse than that."

"Can't we do something?"

"No, leave it alone. For once in your life, leave something alone."

I turned around in anger and slammed out of the bathroom. I went out to the porch and pranced up and down until Stuart appeared before me and lifted me by my bony shoulders completely off my feet. He held me up two inches above the floor, and glared into my eyes. I was frightened, though not enough to stop me from glaring back.

"Put me down," I said.

"Shut-up and listen," he demanded. "I've put up with all manner of crap from you, and my patience has run out. It's time you started behaving yourself. If you can't—or won't—you can go it alone from now on. I need help, not resistance. So what's it going to be? How do you intend to play it?"

He shook me a little. "Go ahead," he said. "Burn holes in me with those black eyes. I'm used to it. But don't forget, I have limits. Maybe you should think that over."

He lowered me gently to the floor and took his hands away to tighten the towel around his middle. He looked so vulnerable standing there, half naked, still wet. I felt a rush of remorse.

"I'm sorry," I said. "You really have been good to me. I shouldn't...I shouldn't ...."

He looked at me coolly while I stuttered over my words, then he shuddered a nervous sigh and met me halfway. "Okay, I'm sorry, too. I admit I behaved badly about Raven and the abortion. But you've done all you can do for now. It's time to let it go."

"I will, if you say so."

"Good. Now get undressed already. You need your rest. Tomorrow you have to talk Miss Peregrine into signing with Sarah Goldstein, which will be no insignificant task."

My old friend was happy to see me the next morning, until I brought up the subject of the contract. Then she turned up her nose in aristocratic frigidity and proceeded to wreck my life.

"I don't see why you're so excited," she said. "This woman is an agent, not a publisher."

"No, but there won't *be* a publisher without an agent. It's the first step. Don't you see?"

"No, I don't, not that it makes any difference. We must decline her offer at this time. There'll be other opportunities." Then she blew her nose with a honk.

I was astonished that she could be so stupid. Anger overtook me entirely. I trembled all over. Tears spurted from my eyes. Words spurted from my mouth. "You mean selfish old woman," I cried. "How dare you deny me a chance like this? How *dare* you?"

"Arlena, calm yourself. Such displays are unbecoming. Ladies don't speak that way. Think how horrified you were when Louisa ...."

"I'm not a lady. I'm just a poor schmuck who has to work for a living."

"Now, now, I didn't say we would turn down every contract, just this one."

"But you don't understand. There may not *be* another."

I buried my face in her lace coverlet and cried out of sheer frustration. "There, there, darling,", she said, "other agents will come along. This Goldstar person isn't the only fish in the sea."

"Gold*stein*," I said, and burst into a new round of sobs. It was hopeless, utterly hopeless. I wanted to shoot myself, or Miss Peregrine, or both.

"You mustn't be so emotional," she said. "All I want is to make a few changes in the ending. Then we can sign the little contract, and there'll be no more tears."

"Miss Peregrine," I snubbed. "I'm begging you to listen to me. There is no way I can explain something like that to Sarah Goldstein. She won't understand. She'll tell me to drop off the planet and take *Tarnished Honor* with me."

"Let her then. You and I will not be led about by the likes of common pushy New Yorkers. Here, wipe your nose. I'm beginning to think you're still sick."

"Ha," someone said from the other side of the room. "People who take drugs are always sick."

Not Louisa, I thought in panic. Oh, please, not her, not now.

"Hush, Louisa." Miss Peregrine said. "Can't you see Mrs. Prince is upset?"

"I hope you don't think I care. And what's this business about a manuscript. Surely you aren't calling your memoirs *Tarnished Honor*. Wouldn't that be too close to the truth?"

"Don't be cheeky, Louisa. None of this concerns you. Dismiss it from your mind."

"Whatever you say, Fanny, though it doesn't matter anymore that you hide things from me. I can just ask Jeannette what you're up to. We talk things over now, you know."

"Do what you will, but surely you've realized by now I am not moved by threats. I've been more than patient with you, Louisa. Don't test me further. Go on about your business."

Louisa lifted her upper lip as if nauseated, then huffed out the door. Her chill remained in the room. Miss Peregrine sank back into her pillow and put a hand to her forehead. She looked at me with sad wet eyes and spoke with a tremor. "I'm sorry you had to witness that, dearest, and on top of a crying spell. I think you should go home and rest now. We'll talk more in the morning, perhaps by phone. Call me when you wake up. I'll not change my decision about signing, mind you, but I will give you a chance to apologize for resorting to such rudeness."

"Yes, Miss Peregrine," I said without an argument. I was her servant, her wooden puppet, beaten into submission. I turned and left the bedroom, left the house, and began a slow walk toward High Battery. I remembered Louisa's current mood and picked up my pace. I was sure I could feel her eyes burning into my back from some darkened window of one of the upper stories. Faster and faster I walked until I found myself running. Stuart saw me coming and called to me to slow down.

"What's wrong?" he said and reached out to help me as I climbed, panting, into the car. I lay my head back and closed my eyes. "Breathe slowly, Arlena. You're pale as death. I don't want you to have a convulsion right here on the street."

I flashed open my eyes and hit the dashboard with my fist. "I *hate* Louisa Hill; I *hate* Miss Peregrine; I *hate* this whole miserable town." My jagged breathing gave my words an odd husky sound. I felt dizzy. My chest ached. Odd little pinpoints of light jumped about in front of my eyes.

"What are you talking about? What happened in there?" Stuart was ready to panic.

"*She wouldn't sign the contract*. Can you believe it?

"But why not? It doesn't make any sense."

"She refused, plain and simple. She wants to change the ending. And you can forget trying to argue with her. She's adamant."

"No reason? Just muleheadedness?"

"I *told* you. She wants a new ending."

"But we already mailed it. Goldstein will think we're crazy."

"*I* know that, *you* know that, *Goldstein* knows that. But I'm telling you, Miss Peregrine doesn't care."

"She'll change her mind."

"Don't count on it."

"Then you'll have to sign without her."

"Impossible. She owns half the copyright. If I did that, without telling Ms. Goldstein, and it all came out later—I may as well blow my brains out."

"I swear, Arlena, between Raven and Miss Peregrine, I don't know who's more crackers."

"What are you talking about? When did you see Raven? *Look at me, Stuart.*"

"All right, all right," he said, regretting his slip. "She left a long-assed note in our mailbox this morning. I didn't give it to you because you already had so much other stuff going down. I didn't think you could handle anything else."

"Where is it?" I barked. Stuart's eyes glazed over. He dug into his jacket pocket and produced a tightly-folded, badly-mutilated note. I grabbed it, singed him with another fiery look, then turned my back to him to read:

Dear Mrs. Prince,
At first I was mad that you ratted on me, but it wore off after a while and I felt better. Mother was furious. She went a little crazy, I think. First I thought she was going to kill Croom, then his father. There were a couple of bad arguments. She didn't let me go for the abortion like I'd planned, but after a while she thought it over and decided I really did need one, only not at the clinic. Yesterday she drove me to a hospital in Columbia. I guess she thought a two-hour drive was far enough away to keep anyone from finding out about my, you know, problem. Croom and his father won't blab. That's for sure. Mother said the only person we had to worry about gossiping was a certain Yankee hussy. That's you, Mrs. Prince. I told her you'd never tell a secret. Only you did tell one. You told mine. The nurses in Columbia said I didn't have to go through with the abortion if I didn't want to. They said it was my own personal decision. I didn't know that before. I thought if you were seventeen, you had to do what your mother said. When I found out I didn't have to, I told Mother I'd changed my mind and wanted to keep the baby. She went crazy again and the hospital people threatened to call the police. After a zillion God-awful arguments, we drove back home. It was terrible. We didn't get in until after midnight. Now Mother is begging me every minute to let her make another appointment for me. I've really got her going this time. I told her this morning if she didn't leave me alone, I'd cut my wrists.
—Love, Raven

P.S. I wrote this letter instead of coming to see you in person so I wouldn't have to listen to you tell me not to fight with my mother. Anyway, you said not to get an abortion without her knowing about it, so now I'm not getting one at all. One thing I've found out, adults change their minds a lot.
—Rav

P.P.S. I'm still planning to run away as soon as I've saved up enough money. Why don't you go ahead and tell that to Mother so she can freak out worse? Adults are all weird.

Chapter Twenty-Five

The next morning I woke up determined to take control of the shambles that had become my life. This was determining a great deal. Though Stuart counseled against it, my first move was to call Miss Peregrine and inform her of my suspicions about Louisa.

"Arlena, dearest," she said when she finally came on the line, "if you're calling to discuss that tiresome contract again ...."

"No, Miss Peregrine. I've given up on that. I want to talk to you about Louisa. You know what's in that folder she threw at me yesterday—I know you do—and honestly, the information is safe with me, but have you considered some of those things might not be true? Louisa may have ...."

"Oh, Arlena, you're fretting about nothing. Louisa isn't my granddaughter. She couldn't be. The material in that dreadful folder is all wrong. My Constantia died when she was a baby, nine months old, so long ago. Louisa lives in a fantasy world, always has. Nonetheless, I cannot put her out. She's totally dependent, has no place else to go. The poor thing tried to dupe me years ago with those preposterous false documents, but she couldn't fool me then, and she's certainly not fooling me now. She's a sick woman. You have to take that into account. She can't believe anyone could care for her just for herself. That's why she pretends to be family. Are you listening to me, dear? Are you there?"

"I'm here Miss Peregrine, but I don't understand."

"What is so difficult? I took Louisa in because I was lonely, not because I thought she was of Peregrine blood. I needed companionship, and so did she. But she was always afraid I'd ask her to leave. She thought she had to trick me into keeping her on. I should have straightened it out at the very beginning. I should never have let her go on pretending. But the years slipped away somehow, and before I realized what was happening, her emotional condition had deteriorated. She doesn't even respond to firmness, anymore. I may have to seek professional help for her soon. But I don't mind; I love Louisa. She has been a good and faithful friend, and now that she's in a confused state, I shall not desert her. Understand me on that point, at least. I will not desert my Louisa."

"But why do you let her get away with threatening you with that folder? She must know you don't believe ...."

"I told you, she is beyond rational thought. She can no longer separate fact from fiction. That worn out old story about being my granddaughter is all she has left to hold on to."

"I don't know, Miss Peregrine. It sounds so—bizarre."

"It is bizarre, lamb. Louisa herself is bizarre, but then aren't we all?"

"Miss Peregrine, I have something else to tell you. A few weeks ago I found your family *Bible* at the fireproof building. I saw the entry you made about Constantia Elizabeth. If she died at nine months like you said, why didn't you record her death date?"

The old woman was silent a long moment, then chuckled as she spoke. "Of all the nosy...you unearthed that moldy old *Bible*? Oh well, I knew someone would come across it sooner or later, though I hoped it would be after I was dead and gone. I trust you didn't say anything to Grayson. His father would turn over in his grave if he knew I let that secret out. Death date, death date. I don't know. I guess I forgot to set it down. Perhaps you can help me attend to it sometime. In fact, I need your help with several things. Can you come by to see me today to talk them over? Tycie has to go to the doctor around five, and I'd be grateful if you'd come sit with me while she's gone. Oh, I almost forgot, I must speak with you again about that business matter you threw such a tantrum over yesterday, the contract with that literary agent. Perhaps I'll reconsider signing. I don't have the strength to tackle changes in the manuscript just now."

"Reconsider? But ...."

"Now, now, you mustn't pester. I may recant if you do. Come at five and don't be late."

Stuart questioned me with his eyes when I hung up. I stared past him without responding. He gave up after a short moment and went out to the kitchen to make coffee, grumbling under his breath that if I planned on calling up anyone else to make trouble, he didn't want to be around to witness it. Somehow I didn't think he would have been so disagreeable if he'd known Miss Peregrine had changed her mind about the contract.

Not a second after he'd left the room, someone tapped tentatively on the outside porch door, someone who didn't want Stuart to know she had come for a visit.

"Raven," I said and ran to let her in. "You're pale as death. Did you have the abortion? Did your mother go with you?"

She threw her arms around my neck and sobbed into the collar of my robe. *"My whole life is ruined,"* she wailed in a little-girl voice. *"I can't do anything right, not even get an abortion."*

"Okay, okay. Come sit down and warm up. Stuart is making coffee. You look like you could use some."

She wiped her runny nose on her jacket sleeve and stumbled into the sitting room. Stuart brought in the coffee and handed me a mug. I offered it immediately to Raven; she took it with shaking hands and pretended to take a sip.

"Getting an early start this morning, Raven?" Stuart asked. I frowned at him. He held up a hand in retreat. Raven did not acknowledge him. She spoke only to me.

"Oh, Mrs. Prince, you still look like ...."

"Don't say it. I already know, and you look pretty rough yourself."

"That's because Mother has been so mean."

"From the things you wrote in the note you left me, I'd say you've been pretty mean yourself. Did you let your mother make another appointment?"

"No, and I'm not going to. But I didn't come here to argue about that. I came to warn you."

Stuart grunted sarcastically and looked bored. I hoped Raven wouldn't irritate him further.

"Thanks, Rav," I said, "but you have to stop worrying about me. Stuart and I are big people. We can handle whatever comes. You need to focus on yourself right now, your own problems. I'm sorry you think I tattled on you to your mom, but there was nothing else I could do. And I still think you should listen to her. This is no time to do things out of spite."

"I don't want to be lectured," she said, the tremor in her voice worsening as she spoke. She put down the coffee mug and worked her hands nervously in her lap. Aristocratic hands, small and delicate, bluish, untouched by physical labor, fingers barely visible inside the huge cuffs of a black wool athletic jacket that probably belonged to Croom Jr. She was about to cry again. A bright red spot appeared in the middle of each cheek.

"Listen, sweetie," I began, "Stuart and I care about you. That's why we want you to listen to your mother. You need to let her help you with this problem, so you can get on with your life."

"*You're* the one with the problem," she said. "People are out to get you."

Stuart could control himself no longer. "Cut the crap and say whatever it is you came here to say, Raven. All this build-up is horse-shit."

Raven moved closer to me and grabbed my hand. "See there. I told you he doesn't like me."

"Come on now, don't be a baby. Stuart is just trying to get to the bottom of things."

"No, he isn't. He's *mean* like *Mother*. She hates everyone, but she hates you worst of all, Mrs. Prince."

"Not really," I said, trying to keep my voice calm in spite of the chill that had begun its stealthy crawl up my backbone. "Your mom is upset, Raven, over your...condition."

"What's wrong? Can't you say it? I'm *pregnant*, and everyone wants me to get an *abortion*. Why do those words make adults act so stupid?" Raven paused. I didn't answer her question. "Screw it", she said. "I don't care, anymore. I only came out here to warn you to stay away from Peregrine House. It's dangerous for you there."

"Why?" Stuart said angrily.

"You don't need to know why, mister. Just *do* it, that's all."

"I'm tired of your stupid games," he said, giving in now to his temper. "This kind of bullshit may get past your mother, maybe even Arlena. But with me, it *stops*. Did you hear that? I said it stops. If you have anything else to say, say it and get out of here."

Raven jumped to her feet and clamped her hands over her ears. She squeezed her eyes shut and screamed a long, piercing scream. Stuart and I sat frozen as she jerked off her jacket and pushed up the sleeves of her sweater. Two stark white bandages encircled her wrists. With jerky movements she ripped them off to expose several ugly gashes stitched with black surgical thread.

"You think these are bullshit?" she screeched. "Look at them. You think my mother listens to me when I say something now? You bet your life she does, you son-of-a-bitch. And you'd better start listening, too."

I felt nauseous. The scene with Raven had taken the last of my strength. Stuart paced while I lay on the sofa and wept. Though she had been gone over an hour, her presence still hung in the air like thick, oppressive fog. The cottage, which on most days exuded airiness and light, was now shrouded in gloom.

"*Damn* Jeannette FitzSimons," Stuart said. "*Damn* Raven. They're both full of bull."

"I'm so sorry you've had to...put up with all this," I said with a little hiccup. "It's too much. I know it is. And now you're going to have to drive me back into town. Miss Peregrine said she might reconsider signing Sarah Goldstein's contract. I didn't get a chance to tell you before. Then Raven came in and I forgot."

"Miss *Peregrine* is as bad as FitzSimons," he said. "Nope, I'm going for a run. Raven really got to me this time. What a waste that girl is."

"But you have to. Miss Peregrine ...."

"That old woman will do anything for attention. I'd lay down a hundred dollars she has no intention of signing. And you don't need to go running over there blowing sunshine up her butt. You can't. Look at yourself. You can barely sit up. And aren't you just a little concerned about what Raven just said? According to her, everyone at Peregrine House is out to get you, whatever *that* means. Doesn't anything scare you off?"

"Raven exaggerates everything. She just went too far this time. Sometimes I think she needs help worse than Louisa."

"I'm gone," he said, zipping his jacket. "Try to sleep for a while. Maybe we'll both feel better in a couple of hours."

I looked at my watch. Eleven a.m. Maybe if I closed my eyes for five minutes ....

I woke up three hours later, at two, and spent another hour

trying to clear my head. Coffee and aspirin helped. A shower helped more. I dressed in black jeans and a black sweater, and plaited my hair into one long black braid. It hung down my back like a rope. I went out on the porch and stood self-consciously while Stuart looked me up and down and suggested I write black poetry to round out the effect. He also wanted to know if I had stopped wearing makeup to support my literary image or out of plain laziness. I sighed and went into the bedroom to smear on lip gloss and blush. This changed nothing. I was still somber and dark. I went back to the porch to be evaluated again. Stuart pronounced me hopeless, then disappeared into the kitchen. When he came back, he had a huge bottle of wine in one hand and two of Lucretia's tenant-grade wine glasses in the other. "For our nerves," he said. "We need it."

"But I've only had a few drops of alcohol since ...."

"Yeah, since your surgery. Maybe it's time you loosened up."

Suddenly I realized that half an hour into a wine bottle, Stuart would do anything I wanted. And what I wanted was to go to Peregrine House. I had to drink far too much to accomplish my goal, but by five minutes of four, Stuart had put up a white flag and agreed to chauffeur me into town. Gratitude made me behave myself most of the way in, but by the time we reached the row of storefronts along King Street, the red wine had successfully dissolved the last of my good judgment. I demanded, and haughtily, to be taken to Church Street where the flower ladies set up shop every day to peddle their wares to tourists. I wanted to take Miss Peregrine an evergreen wreath. Stuart, drunker and more unreasonable than I, responded by giving me a you-must-be-crazy look. We argued about it for a block and a half, then he cursed inventively, screeched to a stop at the corner of King and Broad, and told me to get out of the car, that I'd have to walk wherever else I wanted to go. So I did, not thinking for a moment that the trek to Church Street to buy the wreath, and then the longer trek to Peregrine House on South Battery, might be too much for me.

And it was. I had to move at a much slower pace than everyone else on the sidewalks, creeping along, trying not to draw attention to myself, resting at every corner. Twice I had to stop and take fifteen-minute breaks on park benches that were chained to wrought iron fences outside private residences. The whole journey, from the time Stuart put me out on the corner, until I reached

Miss Peregrine's front door, took an hour and five minutes.

By the time I reached her walkway, I was exhausted, and feeling the effects of the wine even more. I sat down wearily on the piazza steps to rest before entering a different brand of tumult. Without meaning to, I found myself scanning High Battery across White Point garden to see if I could spot the Romeo. As mad at Stuart as I was, and he at me, I knew he wouldn't leave me stranded. I covered the area twice with my eyes, but saw nothing of Stuart or the car. He'd better show up, I thought angrily. When I come back out on this porch, he'd better be here to pick me up.

I got up slowly, turned to the door, and knocked a bit harder than necessary. No one answered. Hurry up, Louisa, I said to the door, or I may punch your face in. False courage, this was, a dangerous side effect of wine. I rapped harder. Still nothing. I gave up any pretense of delicacy then, and banged bare wood with my fist. As a last resort, I kicked several dents in the ostentatious kickplate. I was on the verge of another display when something peculiar happened. The lock clicked and the door swung back with a horror-movie creak. I waited for some deformed face to appear.

"Louisa, it that you?" I said, my anger replaced by uneasiness. "Answer me, Louisa, or I'll tell Miss Peregrine you've been acting out again." The tiny muscles around my eyes twitched; my scalp tingled with electricity.

"*Louisa—*" I was shouting now, "*—I'm not afraid of you.*" Still no response. Muttering in disgust, I pushed open the door. The dusky outdoor light of late afternoon did not penetrate the darkness of the foyer. I had become accustomed to the pleasance of daylight on other visits to Peregrine House. These long shadows of evening waxed forbidding. My uneasiness turned into fear.

"Louisa, I'm here, I'm coming in," I said, then stepped inside without giving myself time for second thoughts. I walked briskly up the first flight of stairs, then stopped on the stairwell to catch my breath. "Louisa, I know you're there," I said to the empty staircase. "Miss Peregrine is going to be furious when she finds out you've been causing more trouble."

From somewhere below, a voice crackled a message. "I doubt that, Mrs. Prince. I seriously doubt that."

"You're crazy, Louisa. I don't see how Miss Peregrine tolerates you."

"She tolerates all manner of stray dogs and cats, including white trash like you." I was still not dead certain it was Louisa. The voice sounded alien.

"Go upstairs and see the old lady," it said next. She's waiting for you. Pity you didn't come sooner."

"You'll be sorry for this, Louisa. I'm going to tell Miss Peregrine everything."

"Go ahead. It won't change a thing. Fanny will protect me. I am blood of her blood."

"You are not. You're a cheap impostor. All you want is to take advantage of her. She'll listen to me this time. I'll make her."

I ignored the tenderness in my still-testy incision and ran up the last three flights of stairs. Cackling obscenely, the voice followed me flight after flight. The pain in my abdomen almost doubled me over, but fear forced me to keep going. Then, on the last step of the last flight, I heard a peculiar sound. A wail, muffled and sorrowful, rose and fell behind the door to Miss Peregrine's private bedroom. When I stopped to listen, Louisa plowed directly into my back.

"What's that?" she said, her voice a scrape. I did not respond. I was too shocked by her sudden appearance. She ignored me and concentrated on the sound. It stopped, then began again. She walked past me toward the bedroom door. I could have been another piece of antique furniture for all the attention she paid me.

"Who's there?" she shouted as she moved down the hall. Though still lightheaded from my dash up the stairs, I forced myself to follow her. I had no choice. What if Miss Peregrine were ill? What if she needed help?

Louisa spoke louder. "*Tycie, is that you?*"

The moaning ceased. I heard a scuffling sound, but Louisa had gotten ahead of me in the dark hallway. I couldn't tell what had caused the commotion. Another scuffle and a bump.

"You liar," Louisa shrieked "I thought you were at the doctor's. What are you doing here?" Then a loud slap and a yelp.

"*Tycie,*" I called out. "*Is that you?*"

"Here, Missy Arlena. I'm here." Another slap.

"*Take your hands off her, Louisa,*" I screamed as I ran toward the voices. Surprised by my appearance, Louisa released Tycie and let her tumble to the floor.

"Oh, Tycie, are you all right?" I said, trying in vain to help her up.

"Yes'm...you go see about Missy Peregrine. I'm afraid she's dying."

I let go of Tycie and pushed past Louisa. The bedroom was dark. I fumbled for the switch on the bedside lamp, turning over a drinking glass in the process. At last I touched the switch, wincing in pain as the light came on in blinding brilliance. Through throbbing eyeballs I found myself looking into the face of Miss Peregrine. It was blue and immobile.

"*Miss Peregrine*," I cried out, and shook her by her shoulders. Her head fell backward revealing unseeing eyeballs that rolled back in her head. I let go of her and put both hands over my mouth. My body jerked in a nervous chill. Louisa came to my side and stood silently. I could hear myself whimpering into my own cupped hands.

"Now you've done it," Louisa said, her voice strangely calm. "You've killed her. Miss Peregrine is finally dead."

I looked at Louisa in astonishment, but was rendered speechless by the racking chill. She turned and walked slowly into the hallway. I had never seen her so composed. In less than a second she reappeared in the doorway half-carrying the sobbing Tycie. She dragged her to my side and dropped her cruelly to the floor. I was able to break her fall only slightly. Look at your Missy Peregrine now," she said as Tycie scrabbled crab-like up my leg. She was sobbing so loudly that my chill ceased. I felt oddly flushed. With no warning, my knees buckled beneath me and I crumpled to the floor. Tycie grabbed me around my neck and clung to me, while crying for the soul of her dead friend.

Part Three
The Will

Chapter Twenty-Six

Confusion swept through Peregrine House. One moment I was weeping with Tycie, the next surrounded by people I didn't know. Police officers swarmed in rooms and hallways, and though I realized Louisa had summoned them, I did not understand why. Stuart was there, and Jeannette FitzSimons, Dr. Calhoun, other medical people, neighbors, curiosity hounds off the street. Tycie's grandson rushed in at the height of the confusion, eyes enormous at the sight of his distraught grandmother. Without a word he picked her up bodily and carried her out of the house. Stuart and I followed as far as the foyer, where Dr. Calhoun rudely stopped us.

"What's all this business Louisa is carrying on about?" he said.

Stuart tried unsuccessfully to dodge him. "I don't know," he said. "Would you mind stepping aside? I'm trying to get my wife out of here."

"Oh no, not until she has talked to the police. Louisa claims she had something to do with Miss Peregrine's death."

"Louisa Hill is an idiot," Stuart said. "Surely you know that. Now get out of my way. My wife is ill." Then he gave the haughty aristocrat a beefy left shoulder. I gasped as Calhoun went sprawling across the bottom three steps of the staircase. At the same moment a brawny policeman stepped through the doors to the parlor.

"What's going on out here, boys?" he said.

Stuart answered, "Nothing, officer. I'm just trying to get my wife home. She's sick. I'm afraid she's going to faint."

Stuart kept his eyes riveted on Calhoun even as he was speaking to the policeman. I started to cry again, whimpering softly. The policeman watched Calhoun flounder about on the floor a few seconds, then adjusted his holstered firearm, walked to where the doctor lay struggling, and hauled him to his feet.

"And I suppose the good doctor here happened to trip over his own shoelaces. Is that right, sir?"

Croomer Calhoun was thoroughly flustered. "This goon struck me," he said, "He *struck* me. I shall press charges."

Stuart spoke calmly, but with obvious disdain. "He was harassing my wife, accusing her of God-knows-what. Look at her; she's spent. She's been extremely ill recently. I have to take her home."

"Ill?" Calhoun shouted, red-faced with anger. "Is that what you call it? In Charleston we call it drug addiction, a damned expensive habit from what I understand."

Stuart lunged for Calhoun again, but this time the burly police officer blocked him, almost without effort. Stuart looked surprised. He gave in to the man's strength, but the officer took no chances. One huge hand remained firmly gripped about Stuart's upper arm.

"You're not from around here are you, boy? I can tell by that Yankee accent." Stuart tried to pull away, the officer held him fast. Calhoun took advantage of the moment to jump in with more accusations.

"That's correct, officer. He isn't. Nor is his wife." He gestured toward me. "They're troublemakers. Ought to be tarred and feathered, run out of...."

"...*town on a rail*," the policeman intoned, and winked at Stuart and me. "Good thing ya'll ain't black," he said. "You'd probably be strung up to the nearest oak tree by now. I'm assuming you're Mrs. Prince, young lady...and this here brawler your husband?"

"That's right," Calhoun said. "You will arrest them both this instant."

The officer was not pleased. "Dr. Calhoun," he said, "there are several hysterical ladies in the parlor. One of them looked to me like she might swoon any minute. Do you suppose you could amble on back to see if there's anything you could do to help out? I have to ask Mr. and Mrs. Prince here a few sensitive questions."

Calhoun narrowed his eyes and lifted his chin. He fixed a cool gaze on the policeman. "You'd do well to be cautious about whom you insult in this town," he said. "You might have regrets later."

"Yes, sir," the officer answered subserviently, though his eyes met Calhoun's in an unwavering stare. "I try to be cautious about everything. Thank you just the same, though, for reminding me."

Calhoun took a spotless white handkerchief from the inside pocket of his coat jacket and blotted his perspiring forehead. His poise had suffered. He did not look at Stuart or me again, just dipped his chin slightly and walked away. The policeman waited until he was out of earshot before resuming conversation.

"Okay, folks," he said when he thought it safe. "Let's sit a spell in these straight chairs and talk things over a bit. By the way, I'm Sergeant Ray Bob Hanahan."

"Stuart Prince," Stuart said, nodding. He could not shake hands. He was having too much trouble getting me into a chair. I was too dizzy to walk without help.

"I'll try not to keep you, Mrs. Prince," Hanahan said to me politely, despite the fact that my eyes were closed. "I know all this has been tough on you. Are you aware of the fact that Louisa Hill is in there screeching like some wild woman that you killed Miss Peregrine? She says you were mad at her about some paper you wanted her to sign, a contract or copyright...some damn thing like that."

I opened my eyes and started to speak; Stuart cut in. "Louisa Hill is a certified nut, man. Didn't you catch that when you talked to her?"

"Matter of fact, I did notice that something about her was a hair off, but people do have a tendency to get excited when death comes knocking, especially if they think foul play was involved."

"Fanny Peregrine was pushing ninety, Sergeant. She just died, that's all. She's been dying for months."

"Mind telling me what a copyright is, Mr. Prince?"

"As a matter of fact I do. My wife is sick, and I have to get her home before she falls on her face. Come on, Arlena, let's go."

With no warning he jerked me out of the chair and pulled me across the foyer toward the door. I tripped. The officer reached out to catch me. "Whoa, boy," he said. "This little gal is wobbly. You're gonna have to take it easy on the git-go for a spell."

Stuart turned to steady me. I mumbled that I needed to sit down. "Please, Arlena. We have to go," he said. "Louisa is trying to make trouble."

"I know, but I can't walk any farther. I'm sick, nauseous."

Stuart gave up on getting me to walk. He leaned over, picked me up, and carried me outside. The policeman followed and watched with interest as I threw up a pint of red wine on Miss Peregrine's prized azaleas.

"Whew-ee," he said. "Smells like this little lady's been hitting the bottle this evening. No wonder she's a mite staggery."

"No, that's not it, she's ill," Stuart insisted. "She's been ill a long time."

I coughed and gagged disgustingly. "I'll get her a wet towel," Hanahan said. "Must be towels around here someplace."

"No, no, she's all right. I'll make her spit. Do it, Arlena. Spit it out."

I spat and cried, then begged for a towel. The policeman handed me his neatly folded handkerchief. I thought through my tears that every man in Charleston must carry the things, every man except Stuart.

"I'm better now," I said, snuffling. "I need to go home."

Stuart put his face close to mine and spoke as if trying to communicate with a mental patient. "Arlena, listen to me," he said. "You have to pull yourself together. You *have* to. The car is parked on High Battery. Can you make it?"

"Why is it way over there?" I whined. "I can't walk that far. I can't."

"I always wait for you there. But I got scared when police cars started showing up all over, and ran over here to get you. I don't know how Louisa rounded up all these cops so fast. She must have told 911 an ax murderer was on the loose."

"Yep," said the sergeant. "Miss Hill is the one who called in all right. Reported Miss Peregrine dead and her killer about to get away. But when the first two officers got here, she changed her story. Said she was confused, didn't remember exactly what had happened. A woman was with her, trying to keep her from falling apart. The FitzSimons woman, I think. Miss Hill must have called her first, then us. Anyhow, by the time I made it to the house, she was going around and around. First she'd say Miss Peregrine died in her sleep. Then she'd start up again about somebody murdering her. That was when she was throwing your name around, Mrs. Prince. Said you as good as killed the old woman, getting her so upset over that copyright business. Yessir, I'd say Miss Hill is powerful wound up...in shock, maybe. It probably wouldn't be

207
Terry Ward Tucker

too smart to put much stock in anything she said tonight."

I began to weep again. "We have to go," Stuart said to the officer. "My wife is on the verge of collapse."

"Where do you stay?" the sergeant asked as Stuart led me down the front walk.

"Sullivan's Island, front beach, the Middleton cottage," Stuart said.

"Thank you, Mr. Prince. I'll try to get by there tomorrow morning, to straighten some of this out. Ya'll be careful going home now, you hear? Those bridges can be the pure devil."

The rest of the night was difficult. I was jarred awake again and again by familiar frightening dreams. And every time I opened my eyes, trembling and perspiring, sick to my stomach with fear, Stuart was gone from the bed. Twice I found him pacing the porch in the dark, once dozing on the sofa in the sitting room, and once just standing in the bedroom doorway. As dawn broke over the ocean, I pleaded with him to come back to bed to try to get one more hour's sleep. He refused. At eight-thirty, I stopped begging, took a shower, and dressed for warmth in sweats and wool socks. When I emerged from the bedroom, I was met with smells of toasted bread and brewed coffee drifting in from the kitchen. After a time Stuart brought out a plate of buttered English muffins and two smoking coffee mugs. He set them on the rickety coffee table, then relocated his brooding spot to the sitting room sofa. Just as I sank down beside him, a car engine coughed outside. He got up to check the window.

"A cop," he said, squinting. "*Damn*, it's that police officer from last night...Hanahan."

My stomach fluttered as I watched him walk toward the door and open it to our uninvited guest. "Morning, Mr. Prince," Hanahan drawled. "I need to talk to you and the missus a few minutes. Nothing serious, mind you...just want to let you know what's going on in town."

"Come in," Stuart said.

Hanahan stepped inside and took off his hat. He was a hulk of a man, filling the narrow doorway as he passed through. "Morning ma'am," he said in my direction. "Hope you're feeling better today."

I nodded and lowered my eyes.

"Sit here," Stuart said to him and pulled up a chair. "Would you like a cup of coffee? I just made some."

"No, thanks. I don't want to put you out none. I know you're both tired...I'll get right to the point. I came to tell you about Miss Hill. That little woman has been doing a heap of talking these last few hours. Says she wants me to arrest you, Mrs. Prince."

I looked at Stuart. His face reddened. My own became stiff with fear. The sergeant held up both hands to reassure us. "Now don't go getting yourselves all worked up," he said. "Ain't nobody paying her no mind. Mrs. FitzSimons is doing the best she can to get her under control. Dr. Calhoun—you remember him—well, he says old Miss Peregrine just up and died, that's all. Sounds reasonable to me, a woman her age."

"Can't you stop Louisa Hill from saying those things?" Stuart said. "Surely it's against the law to go around calling someone a murderer."

"Best thing is to ignore her, Mr. Prince. I mean...you could go to the trouble of getting a restraining order and all, but frankly I think you were right when you said Miss Hill's a little off her rocker."

"Anyone could've told you that," Stuart said.

Hanahan nodded assent. "With that in mind, I think the two of you ought to lay low for a while. Miss Hill will get tired of running off at the mouth when she finds out ain't nobody listening."

"What exactly is she saying?" I asked. The sergeant looked at me in surprise. It was the first time I had been coherent in his presence.

"Well, ma'am, I reckon the gist of it is that she thinks you've been tormenting Miss Peregrine about some sort of business paper. A copyright, I think she said. Plus squeezing money out of her to support some kind of drug habit. But every now and then she just goes slam out of her mind and says you killed the poor woman outright. It doesn't matter, though. Nobody else seems to think you've done anything out of the way, including Tycie Roosevelt."

"You've talked to Tycie?"

"Yes'm. Drove out to Edisto last night. That was one scared little blue-gum. Blacks sure don't like nothing to do with dead folk...scared of h'ants, you know."

"What did she say? Did she know anything?"

"Said she ain't talking to no whitebread policeman. But when I told her about Louisa Hill badmouthing you...well, old Tycie came to life when she heard that. Decided to talk to whitebread, after all. She thinks highly of you, Mrs. Prince. Don't get me wrong, though. She didn't make the mistake of going off on Miss Hill. Island people are known for their horse sense. They know who and who not to rile."

Chapter Twenty-Seven

Hanahan had just driven away when the phone began to ring.
Stuart picked up to an overwrought Grayson Pinckney demanding in his courtroom voice that we come to his office immediately.
Stuart agreed, I balked until he reminded me that Mr. Pinckney
was quite probably the only friend I had left in Charleston. We
walked into Pinckney Building at five of ten. Mr. Pinckney was in
a state.

"Ah, you're here early," he said briskly, his face flushed from
activity. "That's good, good. I need to speak with you privately,
before the others arrive."

"Others?" Stuart said as Lillian hustled us to a row of chairs
set up in Mr. Pinckney's private office.

"Don't waste time with questions, boy. We can talk at length
later. Right now I have to brief you on a few details. We have a bit
of a crisis here."

I looked at Stuart. His eyes had grown dark with anxiety.
Alarmed, I turned back to Mr. Pinckney in the hopes he would
offer some shred of reassurance. He persisted in his uncharacteristic jumpiness, hardly noticing when I asked a simple question.

"What crisis, sir?" I said. "Stuart and I have had enough crises
for one week."

"Yes, well, the week isn't over yet, is it? The reason I was so
willing to make you that substantial loan the other day is about to
be made clear. I'm going to have to break some news this morning, in regard to the demise of Fanny Peregrine—God rest her soul—
news that's bound to upset a few people. The two of you could
become the target of a host of ill feelings."

"Briefly, the story is this," he went on. "Fanny changed her
will a few weeks ago, in secret. You accompanied her here the day
she started the process, Arlena. Do you recall?"

I searched my brain, then nodded. "I think so. Was it the day I fell asleep in Lillian's office?"

"Yes, and after, Fanny asked you to drive her out to Sullivan's Island. The poor thing had become nostalgic during our meeting—too much talk about the past, I suppose. Dwelling on memories has a way of making one want to visit the old places. She was having a difficult time with her personal life just then; suffering from the common pettiness of certain loved ones—I think that's how she put it. She told me she still cared about them, always would, but no longer had confidence in their judgment, particularly when it came to managing her estate, her *considerable* estate.

"It isn't all that unusual a phenomenon, you know—people becoming disenchanted with their heirs. Fanny felt she needed to make some adjustments to her will. She wanted to make sure the bulk of her father's fortune would go directly to philanthropic interests instead of a few individuals. Before, she had been comfortable with quite a simple will, really—everything divided among her closest friends, her family as she was fond of referring to them. She did not include me in this elite group at the time, though these things have a way of changing. We all know the members of her so-called family: Jeannette FitzSimons, Croomer Calhoun, Louisa, Tycie.

"Originally, Fanny expected Jeannette and Croomer to provide for Louisa and Tycie out of their own portions of the estate. Also, to assume the responsibilities associated with her various causes. But she had begun to fear this would not happen, which was the crux of her problem, a basic loss of faith. For any number of reasons, she had become convinced her heirs weren't interested in things charitable, cultural, environmental, or any of the other of her lofty concerns.

"Thus, we have a new will this morning, one that is going to cause an uproar. Arlena, don't be shocked, but you and I are included in this revised document. Fanny has made some interesting provisions for the two of us. We are to be employed by her estate, if we so choose, to serve as co-directors of a foundation that will exist for the sole purpose of lending support to Fanny's favorite philanthropies. One of these is the sponsorship of several environmental protection projects to be implemented on Sullivan's Island. She wants you to manage those efforts personally. In return, you will be paid handsomely, in addition to having the option of living rent-free in one of the island cottages owned by the estate.

"For our activities relative to the foundation, we will each be paid one hundred thousand dollars per annum, though I'll do the bulk of the work, even as I pray to God that my health holds out long enough for my grandson to grow up and take over my duties. We, you and I, will also manage a large block of investments—stocks and securities and such—from which we will receive a percentage of annual profits. This is where the real money will come to us. Now then, it is important for you to know that I have already signed on contractually to do my part of all this work. You, however, still have a few days to think it over before committing, seven to be exact. Basically, your choices are these: buy into the arrangement I've just outlined, the whole kit and kaboodle, or take a one-time, one-hundred-thousand-dollar payment from the estate and be on your merry way. Fanny wanted you to have some say in the matter. It was not her purpose to imprison you, not at your tender age. On the contrary, she wanted to help you. And she definitely meant for you to have control of your own future, something she never had. In short, you are looking at the difference between a lifelong commitment, and a once-in-a-lifetime windfall of cash. The choice is yours."

I stared at Grayson Pinckney through unblinking eyes. His words had not penetrated my understanding. They banged around inside my head like steel balls in a tilt machine. "My one regret," he continued, oblivious to my dazed condition, "is that Fanny did not explain all this to you herself. I know she meant to, planned to. But the grim reaper came around unexpectedly. Perhaps that's the way it always happens. At any rate, the morning you drove her here, she retained me to work out the details of this rather complicated new document. We started the process that day. And no, she didn't cut her other friends out entirely. She simply changed things around a bit. The new will still provides for the continued care and sustenance of Tycie and Louisa, plus modest lump sums for Jeannette and Croomer, and trust funds for each of their children's educations. She has even taken care of Tycie's grandson in this way. But the millions are now earmarked for specific philanthropies, which is not going to set well with the *family*."

"But why, Mr. Pinckney?" I said, finding my voice. "Why me?"

"Why, indeed? There's no one answer, my dear, but I think the trifle that turned her decision was your attitude toward Sullivan's Island. Fanny told me you and she participated in many a spirited discussion about that old sandpile—you defending its virtues faithfully, she playing devil's advocate. She said Jeannette and Croomer wanted to sell all Peregrine coastal property to investors, whose plan it was to develop it commercially. This thoroughly offended Fanny's sensibilities. Her concern was for the environment, not the bottom line. She had a deep and abiding love for the coastline of South Carolina, gave millions every year to help protect it. And now she wants the two of us to continue that noble effort. Southerners are always carrying some banner or another. This one happened to be Fanny's. She hoped you'd be proud to be a part of her vision...you and your husband."

My vocal chords went rigid again. Stuart was forced to speak for me. "If it's all so wonderful, sir, why does it feel like we've been handed a hot coal? What about it, Arly? Does any of this make sense to you?"

Confused, I stared down at my hands. "I can't fathom it," I said shakily, "but you know how Miss Peregrine was. In a way, it's exactly the kind of thing she would do. Only there must be a catch somewhere? What is it, Mr. Pinckney? What's the catch?"

Grayson Pinckney frowned and stroked his chin. "To be honest, I've been wondering the same thing. Then, when I heard by the grapevine how Louisa Hill was carrying on last night, I realized I had my answer. She is most probably the 'catch' we both fear. Not to mention Ray Bob Hanahan, a known pot-stirrer. I admit, I wouldn't be nearly as nervous if that mongrel hadn't come along and started sniffing about."

"What do you mean?" Stuart said, the skip in his voice matching the one in my heart.

"Think, boy. The ravings of a mad woman can generally be discounted if they don't fit in with the other facts. After all, Louisa's accusations toward Arlena, even if they were all true, aren't bad enough to implicate her in murder. Ray Bob would have to figure against it. The only motive he might be able to come up with would be that business about the copyright. But he must not think it's important enough, or else he'd already have done something about it."

My heart began to beat in quivering thumps when I realized

what Mr. Pinckney was getting at. "But when he finds out I'm included in her will," I said, "I'll have an instant motive."

Mr. Pinckney saw I was on the verge of panic and spoke to me in quieter tones. "He may not jump to that conclusion immediately, Arlena, though we need to be prepared in case. Ray Bob Hanahan is an ignorant man who considers himself cunning. A most dangerous combination."

"But Miss Peregrine didn't tell me she was going to do this," I said. "How could anyone say it was a motive when I didn't know?"

"There's no way you can prove that. It could get to the point where it would be your word against Louisa's."

"But Louisa is crazy. She's sick," I said too loudly.

"Stop shouting," Stuart said. "None of this is Mr. Pinckney's fault. He's doing the best he can to help you."

I spoke no more. I couldn't. The iron band of pressure that had closed off my throat was now crushing my skull. My eyes felt too large for their sockets. I grabbed Stuart's hand and held onto it tightly when Lillian's voice rattled through the intercom that "the others" had arrived.

"Thank you, Lil," Mr. Pinckney said directly into the speaker. "Send them in, and get my son-in-law up here. I need him to sit in as a witness."

Mr. Pinckney looked hard at Stuart and me and warned us one last time. "You must present an unflappable image," he said. "It is imperative."

Lillian led Jeannette FitzSimons and Croomer Calhoun into the office. "Jeannette...Croomer," Mr. Pinckney said. "You've already met Mr. and Mrs. Prince, I presume. Please, have a seat. Make yourselves comfortable."

Stuart rose, nodded, then sat again. We both remained silent. Mr. Pinckney did battle alone, his usual aplomb suffering no discernible strain. Stuart and I were grateful for his presence, especially upon observing the furtive glances between FitzSimons and Calhoun.

"Where is Miss Hill?" Mr. Pinckney said abruptly. "I asked that everyone be on time."

"At Peregrine House," FitzSimons answered. "I'm afraid last night finished her. Croomer had to give her a sedative to get her to sleep. She'll be down for hours yet."

"And Tycie?"

Jeannette answered again. "She won't be coming, either. We couldn't get in touch with her this morning. She has no phone. What is this all about, Grayson? Frankly, Croomer and I are exhausted. We've both endured hell ...."

"I'm sure that's true, Jeannette. Please forgive me for having to infringe upon your time of grief. Truly, I had no alternative."

"No alternative about what?" said Calhoun. "Get to the point, man. I'm supposed to be making rounds at the hospital. Life goes on."

Just as Mr. Pinckney was about to respond, Jonathan Priolieu stepped into the room and took a seat next to Stuart. The memory of their fight at the oyster roast sprang into my mind. I felt as if the oxygen supply in the crowded office had dwindled to a perilous proportion. Mr. Pinckney picked up a blank legal pad from his massive desk, tossed it to his son-in-law with a tad too much force, and instructed him to take notes. Without speaking, Priolieu took a pen from his breast pocket and readied the yellow pad. He allowed himself one visual survey of the room to identify everyone present. It was clear he had no knowledge of the subject of the meeting.

Mr. Pinckney let it be known he was ready to begin. Everyone waited expectantly. First he handed out copies of the will to everyone present, with the exceptions of Stuart and Jon Priolieu, both of whom stretched their necks to see mine. "You don't have to read this now," he said, "but as you can see, it is Fanny Lockwood Peregrine's last will and testament. You three individuals—not you, Jonathan, nor you, Stuart ... I'm speaking to the others now—plus Louisa and Tycie, have been remembered by the kind lady. I'm sure you'll be pleased with how. Jeannette and Croomer, you will receive lump sums of one hundred thousand dollars each. You may collect your checks within the week. In addition, Raven and Croom, Jr. have been provided trust funds which will cover the entirety of their educational expenses. Abe Roosevelt, Tycie's grandson, will enjoy the same consideration. Personally, I think helping these young people finance their educations was an exceptionally thoughtful gesture on Fanny's part...damned generous. I don't know why she didn't think of our Jon, Jr."

He coughed once, then plunged ahead before anyone could interrupt with questions. "Louisa is to live in the South Battery house as long as she wishes, though she will not actually own it. The house will remain part of the estate. Nevertheless, she may occupy it indefinitely. Her other financial needs will be managed in trust. The exact same arrangement has been made for Tycie, although Fanny understood Tycie would probably elect to stay on at Edisto rather than move in with Louisa.

"As for you, Mrs. Prince, yours is a different situation. In a sense you will remain an employee, but of the estate rather than any one person, if you feel so inclined, that is. I have the same opportunity. Fanny...Miss Peregrine...made special provisions to this effect that are detailed in our personal copies of the will. They have to do with what we discussed in private earlier. The balance of the estate will remain intact. Proceeds from investments are to go in a systematic manner to help the many organizations and institutions Fanny has supported over the years, which makes for a long list, I must say. Well, ladies and gentlemen, that covers it, in a cursory sort of way. We can hammer out details later. Croomer, my man, if you hurry you can still make rounds."

I looked at Calhoun and FitzSimons. They were chalk-white with shock. FitzSimons's gaze roamed the room, stopping first on Stuart's face, then on my own. I lowered my eyes to avoid her disdain. Suddenly she lost interest in me and confronted Mr. Pinckney.

"You know this isn't a legitimate will, Grayson," she said. "It can't be. *I* have Fanny's will. I helped her make it out years ago."

Calhoun kept silent, his eyes trained on Grayson Pinckney.

"It isn't that difficult to understand," said Mr. Pinckney. "She decided on a new will a few weeks ago. Had a change of heart so to speak. You're a lawyer, Jeannette. You've seen this sort of thing happen. I sincerely hope, out of respect for Fanny, you'll be gracious about honoring her last wishes."

Croomer Calhoun was now standing. "*This*," he said, shaking the blue folder in Mr. Pinckney's face, "is *not* what she wished. It is outrageous. I won't allow you to give credence to such an obvious pack of lies."

Calhoun's entire body was trembling with fury. Stuart and I stopped breathing simultaneously. There was a single second's vacuum of silence before Jeannette FitzSimons got to her feet and leaned far across Mr. Pinckney's desk. Her nostrils were flared out like two small red wings.

"Grayson," she said hoarsely. "I have had to endure every kind of abuse imaginable at the hands of this *woman*—" she pointed a finger at me—"and now I am called here to be insulted with a bogus will I am certain is somehow of her making. I assure you, I will not let her get away with this. I will see her rot in hell first."

Chapter Twenty-Eight

Stuart led me out of Mr. Pinckney's office while the arguing was at a pitch. We moved silently down the carpeted hallway, agreeing with nods of our heads to pass up the elevator and take the seldom-used stairs. I gave no thought to where we were going, I only wanted to escape. But stairs, even descending stairs, are cruel to recent surgical patients. I was winded by the second-story landing, in pain and seeing spots by the first. Stuart saw I was in trouble, but didn't seem to care. He was intent on getting out of the building. Holding me fast by my hand, he pulled me through the hallway of the street-floor, through the ornate reception area, and out its walnut door to freedom.

Here I thought we would rest, Stuart thought to go faster. He walked briskly across Broad Street—traffic bearing down on us from both directions—and ignored my pleadings to stop.

"Why...are...we running?" I said, my words coming in spurts and starts as he hurried me toward the Romeo. "I have to stop...please."

"Get in the car," he said. "We're going to look for Tycie." He shoved me into the passenger seat, then ran around and climbed in on the other side. "Didn't you tell me she lives on Edisto?" he said as he coaxed the engine to life.

"Yes," I said, "but I don't know exactly where. And what's the point of talking to her, anyway? What can she do?"

"We have to find her. Jeannette FitzSimons was dead serious back there, and Tycie is the only person alive who can say for certain that you never did anything out of the way to Miss Peregrine. Louisa is crazy, hardcore. No one will listen to her. But FitzSimons and Calhoun are professional people, both of whom hate your guts. That leaves Tycie, no one else. We have to find her and let her know what's going on. Let's just hope she'll back you if it comes to it. She has to know those other three are damned dangerous."

On Highway 17, traveling south toward the Edisto turn-off, Stuart pushed the Romeo to eighty while I braced my hands on the dashboard. "You're crazy", I said, tears flowing freely now. "Everyone I know has gone crazy. Please, Stuart, let's leave here. I'm scared of these people. Let's leave now."

"And you think the police won't come after us? Things are looking bad for you, Arly. FitzSimons and Calhoun could have you thrown in jail any minute. You saw how nervous Mr. Pinckney was. He's more afraid of them than we are."

I put my face in my hands and sobbed. Stuart made no effort to console me. At the turn-off he took a hard left and put his concentration into driving. At eleven thirty-five exactly, we crossed the narrow Dawhoo Bridge and rolled onto Edisto Island. Stuart pulled to a stop before a dilapidated country gas station and put the Romeo in neutral. "That guy, Hanahan," he said. "I think he mentioned Tycie's last name. Can you remember it?"

I stopped snubbing and tried to think. Somehow, from a cloudy abyss in the farthest corner of my brain, the name floated forward. "Roosevelt...Tycie Roosevelt," I said.

Stuart's eyes flashed recognition. He got out of the car and strode toward the store. Two untidy black men sat precariously on upturned orange crates on either side of the door. They remained motionless as Stuart approached. I strained to hear their answers to his questions, but the distance was too great. Stuart gestured toward the road a few times, then there was much head-nodding and finger-pointing in the same direction we'd just come from. The black men jabbered knowledgeably as Stuart frowned and peered down the road. When he came back and got into the car, I forced myself not to question him. For several minutes we proceeded slowly, looking for some landmark, I assumed. Then a sand road appeared on the right and Stuart turned into it carefully. The white sand looked smooth on the surface, but the Romeo began jouncing and lurching immediately upon contact. I could keep quiet no longer.

"Did they say Tycie lives on this road?" I said.

"Yes, at a place called Freedmen's Village, whatever that is."

"Look, there." I said, pointing toward a cluster of box houses in the clearing just ahead.

"A bit remote for my taste," Stuart said. "Wonder how long it's been since anyone from above the Mason-Dixon line ventured back here? Is that marsh grass behind the houses?"

I squinted. "Yes, looks like a tidal creek. Are you sure this is the right place?"

"I think so. Those old codgers said Tycie's house was brown with blue shutters. They didn't mention there'd be ten more just like it. Do you see anyone outside?"

Toward the little village of houses, the road diminished to a trail. Stuart scoped the area and decided if we ever wanted to get the car out, we'd have to park it at the end of the road and walk the rest of the way in. I was afraid to go any closer, but more afraid to stay alone in the car. When we stepped into the clearing, a slender black man appeared in the doorway of the first house.

"Hello," Stuart said, smiling, nodding, reaching too hard for friendliness. "Excuse me, sir, do you know Tycie Roosevelt? We're looking for her."

The man did not speak. He picked up a shaved stick that was propped next to the doorway and aimed it at the house opposite his own.

"Thanks," Stuart said. More smiling. More nodding. The man remained unimpressed. He faded back into his blue-trimmed dwelling, a shadow melting into darkness. Stuart and I adjusted our course and moved toward the house the man had pointed out. As we approached, I observed the arrangement of the structures in the clearing. Nothing could happen in the common area without every person in every house knowing about it instantly. Another man stepped forward, this time from Tycie's front door. He was old and hoary-headed.

"Do you think he's her husband?" I whispered. "She never said a word about being married."

"Maybe," Stuart said softly, then, loud enough for the old man to hear, "Excuse us, sir. We're looking for Tycie Roosevelt. Is this where she lives?"

The man dipped his chin. "Tycie is at church," he said, "funeralizing Sister Washington. That makes two old women she'll bury this week. The other one is that white woman in town, Missy Peregrine."

"Where is the church? Maybe we can speak to her after."

"Up the road. You can hear the singing before you get there."

"The hard-top road?" Stuart said. "The one we turned off to get here?"

"That's right. Go back to the hard-top and turn left. You can't miss it. It's the only church on the road."

Stuart kept talking as we backed away to leave. "Thank you for your help, sir. We have to talk to Tycie about Miss Peregrine. My wife worked for her, too."

The old man's eyes grew wide. His thin body stiffened. "What's your name, man?" he said.

"Stuart Prince, and this is my wife, Arlena. She and Tycie are friends."

"Best you leave my Tycie alone. Missy Peregrine is dead and gone. Tycie can't do nothing about that now."

"She doesn't have to. We want to talk to her, not harass her."

"Git on back to Charleston, boy. White folk don't belong in Freedmen's Village. Ain't you paid no mind to these blue markings? People here are protected by the voodoo."

"We're going...right now. Sorry to have disturbed you. Thanks again for the help."

Stuart clamped a hand on my arm and guided me toward the path. I did not fully comprehend what had taken place. "Don't talk," he said. "The last thing we need is to antagonize a crowd of degenerates who practice voodoo. Walk faster."

"Now what?" I asked once we were in the car and Stuart was forcing the gears into reverse.

"We intercept Tycie at the church and try to get some sense out of her. Then we *git on back to town* like we've been told."

The abused little Romeo bumped onto the highway with a shudder. Stuart shifted into second and began searching for the church. It turned out to be a small white picturesque building, set neatly in the center of a leaf-strewn lot close beside the road, just as the black man had said it would be. A giant live oak dominated its sloping front lawn. The somber old tree appeared to have somehow escaped the dark wood that edged its grounds all around. Stuart pulled into the sand drive that led to the building and parked in the shade of the tree.

"Want to get out and walk around?" he said. "Looks safe enough, and there's no telling how long it takes to *funeralize* somebody."

"I don't know. Maybe we ought to leave."

"No. I'm talking to Tycie if I have to kidnap her. You saw that old man's reaction when I mentioned Miss Peregrine's name. He knows something...something Tycie told him. People don't try to spook you with voodoo unless they're scared to death themselves. Come on, let's walk, I'm jumpy."

We got out of the car and picked our way through a maze of twigs and limbs that had fallen from the huge tree. An acre of lawn that was also littered with debris spread out behind the church. Its autumn-brown grass was wiry and thick. We stood looking at it a few minutes in full sunlight before moving into the shadow of the structure.

The music beating inside the church was rich with complicated rhythms and counter melodies, African in origin, yet with curiously English lyrics. I had heard spirituals before, even sung them, but this pulsing syncopated music made the white man's imitations seem lifeless. It was loud and primitive, like the spirit choirs in my dreams. I moved closer to Stuart for comfort, though he seemed to have forgotten I was there. The wood at the edge of the churchyard had captured his attention.

Silent shadowy movements floated in and out among the black-green tangles of vines. At first I thought I was imagining things. Then I realized this was no illusion. A human form stepped soundlessly from among the trees. It was black, wholly a part of the forest, a wild thing belonging to shadows. Surely if Stuart and I kept quiet, kept still, it would return to its murky home. We waited; it did not retreat. It stood at the edge of the lawn, stalwart and still. I could not see its eyes, I could feel them. They were focused on Stuart and me.

In a haze of time impossible to measure, the shadow was joined by another and another, until thirty or more men formed a rough half-circle at the back edge of the clearing. One by one they emerged from the wood and formed an arc of strength. There was no escape. We were blocked all around. Stuart stepped in front of me to shield my body from view. I held my breath and waited for the unfolding.

A strident male voice rang out. It sounded like Tycie's husband. "I told you to leave this island, white boy. Why did you come here to scare old Tycie? As if she ain't scared enough. Now you're in sorry shape. The conjure woman has spoken. She means to put a hex on you, a hex that will keep you from harming my

223

Terry Ward
Tucker

Tycie. You're going through the rite. You're going to spit out your poison so Tycie can be free at last from you and that witch woman in town."

"We're not here to cause trouble," Stuart said. "We want to talk to Tycie. You're right, there's a woman in town who is bad, who hurts people. Her name is Louisa Hill. We think Tycie can help us stop her from hurting anyone else."

"She's the one who threatened to cast a spell on my Tycie. Touched in the head, she is. Bad to the bone. But the brass-ankle conjure woman who lives on Snake Island has promised to take away her power. She is the Queen Mammaloi. I won't let my wife die of a witch spell, not if I can help it. If white folk come to Edisto and meddle in our business, they have to pay the price. It'll be dark soon. That's when the conjure woman takes out the poison."

Stuart said more shakily, "We don't want trouble." Then he gripped my hand and pulled me rapidly along the back wall of the church. We headed in the direction of the car, but the black men closed ranks and stopped us at the corner of the building. Stuart panicked. His body went rigid. Then, with no warning, he slid his grip upward from my hand to my wrist, tightened it like a vice, and plowed headlong into the line of men. We crashed into the wall of muscle, bounced back, and landed on the grass like two ragdolls. I lay stunned. Stuart scrambled to his feet and attacked the first man in his path. He struck one ineffective blow before the man knocked him out cold. I clambered to his side and screamed his name, but he did not move again.

It was then I became aware of the men closing in. I looked up in terror, but could scream no more. Rough hands overpowered me. One man dropped to his knees. I looked into his face and knew I had seen him before. He was Tycie's grandson, the one who had taken her from Peregrine House the night Miss Peregrine died. I opened my mouth to speak, to beg mercy, but he held my temples in both his hands and forced me to tilt back my head. At the same moment, another man held a small bottle to my lips and poured a bitter liquid into my mouth. I gagged as a thick syrup slipped down my throat in hot, oily strings. It slid over my chin and cheeks, one stream defying gravity and running upward into my eyes. I closed them against the burning. After a brief moment of struggling against the mental fog that was released by the drug, the dream beast sprang forth in my head, incarnate, grotesque,

224

Elegant Sinners

hammering out his satanic rhythms upon other-world drums. His barbarous moans mingled with the funeral choir still keening within the church. My last thought was of Tycie's heartbreaking cries on the night of Miss Peregrine's death. Tycie on her knees, crying for the soul of her dead friend. I choked on the last drops of the vile liquid and went limp in the arms of the grandson.

Terry Ward
Tucker

Chapter Twenty-Nine

When I came to, my perceptions were still clouded by the drug, yet somehow I sensed it was nighttime. Strange rhythms beaten out on hollow drums pounded inside my skull. Rattles vibrated all around me. Then, from some lightless, airless metaphysical dimension, a choir of male voices hummed a funeral dirge in low sorrowful dissonance. I opened my eyes to a blur of motion. Slowly I focused on a great pit alive with leaping flames. Uneven firelight danced in the air.

I was too frightened to move. I scanned the scene with my eyes, but was afraid to turn my head. Stuart lay on his back beside me, still as death, eyes closed. I watched his chest rise and fall in shallow, jagged breaths. At least he was alive. We were strapped down beside each other flat on a wooden incline that was slanted slightly upward at our heads. I whispered Stuart's name, but he remained immobile. Before I could say anything else, a solo animal scream went up and was answered by an explosion of drums. An obsidian hand shook a rattle two inches from my face.

"She sees," a female voice croaked from somewhere behind me. I strained my neck, but could not see who had spoken. Then a rough hand covered my face with a thin, gauzy cloth. I could barely see through the filminess. Vaguely, I was aware of another hand adjusting the incline. With one quick jerk, mine and Stuart's heads were raised a foot higher. At the same moment, there appeared before us a roundish woman with a face a wash of blue. As if in fear of her presence, the music died away and an uneasy hush settled over the proceedings. The woman snatched the gauze from my face and I saw her clearly for the first time. She was obese, with wild orange hair and mulatto flesh that hung loosely from her throat and arms. I could tell nothing of her face. It was painted all blue, except for her eyelids, which were red and outlined in white.

"I am the Mammaloi," she said, then held up a human skull inches from my eyes. I opened my mouth to scream, but only a whimper emerged.

"Come, Damballah," the woman cried out, and raised the skull high above her head. Her hands and arms jerked in spasms. A clamor of music went up, then stopped abruptly when she lowered the skull. The woman stared at me with glowing eyes.

"I am the Mammaloi of Snake Island. I am the conjure woman who casts out evil spirits. Tonight I will take out your poison as you go through the rite. You bring evil-evil to our islands. I beg Damballah to protect us from you. I beg him to bring the white fire. *Come, Damballah, come.*"

Again she held the skull aloft. Her swag-bellied body shook grotesquely as the drums and voices roared. I looked beyond her into the center of the room and saw more dancers, men and women, naked from the waist up. They took turns cavorting around the pit. The woman who called herself Mammaloi danced separately, closest to the fire. Finally her legs folded beneath her and she sank into a shapeless heap on the ground. Two young men picked her up and carried her to a throne-like chair a few feet away from the incline. There she drank from a tin dipper and leaned back to rest.

The drums and rattles grew louder and more frantic. Voices, low and mournful at first, now rose to a roar. Blue-faced dancers took the floor spontaneously, writhing and shaking, working themselves into a frenzy. They formed a circle around the pit and clapped out complicated rhythms, bodies swaying in perfect time. Then the orange-haired woman rose from her throne and waddled to the edge of the pit. She tossed in a handful of pebbles. Flames shot to the rafters; black smoke poured through a gigantic hole in the ceiling. The dancers leaned backward in unison, widening their circle around the fire. Something was about to happen. A young man stepped into the circle and bowed low before the Mammaloi. He handed her a gleaming machete. She smiled wickedly as the drums speeded up, then she lifted the great knife and shook it menacingly at the dancers. They cowered before her as she leaped about on small bare feet, brandishing the cruel weapon. With every sweep of the blade, the dancers fell away in fear. I was terrified to think what she might do next.

I looked at Stuart. He was still unconscious. Then, slowly, his head rolled to the side. I prayed our captors wouldn't notice. Stuart's eyelids fluttered. He opened his eyes too quickly and blinked in confusion. I called his name, but he could not hear me above the din. He tried to get up before realizing he was tied, then looked down at himself and at me. His eyes stretched to abnormal proportions. I mouthed his name, but could not help him. The machete sliced the air directly above our heads. We forgot each other and stared at the Mammaloi. She swung the machete over our bodies, lower and lower, closer and closer. The dancers' bodies vibrated out of control. Damballah, Damballah, they screamed. I was certain we were about to be killed, dismembered, never to be found. I prayed with all my might that I would go first. I did not want to watch Stuart die.

But with perfect timing the oddly graceful Mammaloi glided back to the fire. The man who had produced the machete now handed her a live rooster. She shook the writhing animal and threatened it with the knife. Her eyes glistened. Her mouth dropped open in triumph. The twitching dancers leaned forward in one motion, screaming for the kill. Mammaloi held the rooster up, and with one stroke of the machete, cut off it's head. Blood spurted from the arteries in the protruding stump. The conjure woman put it to her mouth and drank the blood, the excess running down her chin and throat in black-red streams. The dancers surged forward and held out their fingers to catch a bit of sacrificial blood. Everyone licked themselves in blind ecstasy.

When the climax was over, Mammaloi dropped to her knees. She tossed the slain rooster to the side and wiped sloppily at her face with the hem of her tent-like gown. Then slowly and ponderously she pulled herself to her feet and struggled to where Stuart and I lay bound. She leaned over me and breathed into my face. Her stench was nauseating. I cried helplessly as she smeared blood over my face and arms. Stuart struggled in his restraints. He was in anguish at not being able to help me. Then he, too, was smeared with blood, and slapped to subdue his anger. I closed my eyes in a faint. When I opened them—after how long a time I don't know—the Mammaloi was gone and someone was pushing back a pair of tall plank doors at the far end of the enclosure. A section of sky, deep purple and glimmering with stars, appeared beyond.

Someone else, male from the feel of the hands, cut mine and

Stuart's bindings and forced us to our feet. Stuart said my name and reached out to help me. The man struck him and told him not to touch me. He shoved us toward the door and out into the night. Gratefully, I filled my lungs with cold air. In the distance, across a broad stretch of sawgrass, the pale light of a gibbous moon outlined a row of palmettos. They stood, silent as sentries, at the edge of a vast marsh, their long fronds rattling like unearthly musical instruments in the chilly night wind. To their left, as far as the eye could see, pearl-lucent water shimmered in the Canaan of Southern moonlight.

"White folk aren't supposed to know about Snake Island" our guard said. His voice had the resonance of an adult male Negro. "I'm going to bind up your eyes. Be still."

"Aren't we on Edisto?" Stuart asked. I wished he had kept quiet.

"Shut your mouth," the man said, then tied strips of burlap around both our heads and pushed us forward into darkness. I fell to my knees in the sand. He jerked me up by a handful of hair, which caused me to cry out. Stuart pushed him aside and tried to help me. We took a few more unsuccessful steps, after which the man swore impatiently and ripped off our blindfolds.

"Get in the boat," he said. I looked around once more and concluded that the location of Snake Island was forever secure, blindfolds or not.

"Are we going to Edisto now?"

"I told you to shut your mouth, man. Yes, we're going to Edisto, but I'll have to row with the tide. Ain't got no motor."

After an interminable time of pitching about and rolling over waves, the boat mercifully struck bottom. Our rower clattered his oars together and dropped them in the bottom of the boat. Stuart helped me over the side into knee-deep water and dragged me to a muddy bank. The water was icy. A steely sheen reflected eerily from its dawn-pinkened surface. I looked at Stuart and gasped, then realized he could look no worse than I. We dipped our hands into the water and tried to wash our faces. It was useless. The blood of the rooster had dried and caked. Cold water would not wash it away. I shivered from humiliation and cold. Stuart moved closer to me and put his arms around my shoulders. He looked about, trying to get his bearings. The man in the boat had already pushed off and was floating away on the tide. Stuart took my hand tightly in his and helped me along the only path he could pick out along the wooded bank. We had gone but a few yards when we came to the clearing of familiar blue-trimmed houses.

Every shutter and door was closed. We avoided the open space in the middle of the clearing, slinking in and out among narrow-trunked pines until we reached the sand road where we had parked the Romeo so many hours before. We made a short and futile search for the car before remembering we had moved it to the churchyard. Stuart cursed under his breath as we crept up the road toward the highway. Once on the hard-top, we broke into a jog. No one got in our way; no one pursued us. Twice I had to stop and rest in spite of Stuart's angry protests. Somehow we made it to the church without being seen, at least we hoped we had not. At times the trees along the road seemed to burn with pairs of eyes. When we turned into the church driveway, Stuart sprinted forward, overjoyed to have spotted the car.

"It's here," he breathed. "Thank God, it's still here."

He jerked open the door. "No key," he said, striking his thigh with his palm. "They must have taken the key."

"Are you sure?" I said. "Maybe we lost it in all the craziness." Suddenly Stuart had a flash of memory. He thrust his hand into his shirt pocket and pulled out the precious key. In minutes we were racing for the Dawhoo River. As we neared the bridge, a faded green Ford came speeding toward us head-on. It was grandson. I looked over my shoulder as the car whizzed by. Tycie was in the passenger seat. "Wait, Stuart. It's Tycie, and the boy is driving. Look, he's turning around. He's coming back this way."

"Are you crazy? We're not waiting for that pervert. We're getting out of here."

"But you said we had to talk to Tycie. You said it was life or death."

"That's her *grandson*, Arlena, the one who helped kidnap us last night. We have to get off this island."

Suddenly I remembered the evil syrup sliding down my throat. "Oh, Stuart...he was in the churchyard. I remember now."

"The guy is definitely a bad-ass, Arly. We'll have to find another way to talk to Tycie. Hold on, we're coming to the bridge."

I watched the Ford fall farther and farther behind. Then it stopped, turned, and headed back toward the interior of Edisto. At the same moment, the Alfa Romeo rolled across Dawhoo Bridge.

The little car lurched forward upon reaching the opposite bank, as if loosed from some invisible bond. The spell of Snake Island was finally broken, or so Stuart and I prayed.

Terry Ward
Tucker

Chapter Thirty

It was four in the afternoon by the time we got back to the island. We had been gone seven hours although it felt like seven days. Stuart informed me that I looked like death and would end up back in the hospital if I didn't get some rest. Exhausted, we lay down together on our unmade bed and fell dead asleep. I opened my eyes at half past six, instantly alert, instantly afraid. Stuart had left the bedroom.

I got up and checked the house, then peered with binoculars through the porch screening to see if I could spot him on the beach. Maybe he'd gone jogging to clear his head. I focused on a silver ocean whose modest breakers flashed platinum and gold, and whose moving surface sparkled with phosphorous on the crest of every wave. It rocked gently beneath a sky preparing for darkness behind a veil of translucent mist. I stared, entranced.

"Hypnotized?" Stuart said from somewhere at my back. I jerked my whole body around. He was standing in the doorway between the sitting room and the porch.

"Don't startle me like that," I said. "My nerves are shot. I didn't know you were anywhere around."

"Hope you're rested," he said. "It's time to take another shot at finding Tycie."

"Huh-uh, not if it means going back to Edisto."

He didn't have a chance to rebut. From the shadows of the sitting room, a female voice stopped him. "You won't have to go all the way to Edisto to see Tycie," Raven said nonchalantly, as if unaware her presence had the power to send Stuart into orbit.

He whirled around to face the invisible girl. She chose that instant to step forward into the light. *"Raven, have you lost your mind?"* he shouted. One of these days you're gonna sneak up on somebody and get your head bashed in. I don't know who's worse, you or your mother."

The pale girl moved past him into the half-light of the porch, acknowledging me only with her eyes. I started to speak but she held up a hand to stop me. Then, slowly, she turned back toward Stuart and stared at him with contempt. Without flinching, he stared back, though what he saw was terrible. Her face was chalk white, her eyes sunken and red. Yet, from some inner fire, they blazed with hatred. She tightened her lips into a thin blue line and brushed back a lock of hair.

"You're a jerk, Stuart," she said. "If it weren't for you, Mrs. Prince wouldn't be in the mess she's in. You've never taken care of her, not the way a real man is supposed to take care of a woman."

"Don't, Raven," I said. "You shouldn't ...."

"Shouldn't what?" she said, turning on me like a cat. "I guess you don't want to face the truth about your husband, Mrs. Prince. He's a bigger waste than Croom. At least Croom admits he doesn't love me. But Stuart here goes around pretending. If he cared a dip about you, he wouldn't make you sell your soul to creeps like Grayson Pinckney and Fanny Peregrine. Men are all jerks."

Stuart was seething. I moved to his side and took a firm hold on his arm. I feared what he might do.

"Raven," I said sharply. "I don't want you talking to Stuart like that. It isn't fair to take it out on others every time you get mad at Croom. Behave yourself or you'll have to leave."

"Don't worry, I don't plan to stay long. I came to tell you Mother's been beside herself ever since she heard about that new will. If I were you, I'd leave Charleston. It's dangerous for you here. But if you're serious about seeing Tycie before you go—I heard you talking about her just then—I might know where she'll be tonight."

"This is too important for cuteness," Stuart said. "If you have something to say, say it, but leave out the 'cute'."

Raven cut her eyes at him. They were enormous cracked marbles set deep in a porcelain face. "I won't tell *you* a damn thing, scumbag. I wouldn't give *you* a drink of water if you were dying."

"Raven, please," I said. "Stuart is trying to ...."

"Shut-up," she cried out. "You can't tell me what to do, either. You're not my mother. I came out here to try to help you, and now I don't know why. It was a dumb, stupid idea. Hells bells, you never helped me. All you did was rat on me. You didn't even pay me when I worked on your stinking manuscript."

"Raven, I ...."

"Raven, Raven, Raven," she repeated in staccato. "All I ever hear is 'Raven, do this; Raven, do that; Raven...drop dead.'"

When certain her tirade had played itself out, I went to her and pulled her close. She wept in my arms like a child while I stroked her tousled hair.

"Don't cry, Rav," I said. "No one is mad at you. Stuart and I appreciate your trying to help us." I cast Stuart a withering look to make sure he kept his mouth shut. He looked as if he might throw up.

"No one loves me," she said, a vibrato on every syllable. "I might as well run away. I came here to tell you about Mother. But if I'd known you were going to be mean again...oh, who cares? All anyone ever wants is to use me. Even you, Mrs. Prince. You're not thinking about anything right now except how much information about Tycie you can squeeze out of me. Well, she's supposed to be at Peregrine House tonight. That's all I know."

Stuart's expression became hopeful. I pressed Raven for facts. "But why would she go back there?" I said. "Louisa was horrible to her the night Miss Peregrine died."

"I was eavesdropping on Mother and heard her talking to Louisa about the memorial service they're planning for Miss Peregrine. Then they got talking about her belongings. Mother said she thought they should give some of them to Tycie. Later, she called Tycie's grandson on the telephone—at his dormitory, I think. He's a student at the College of Charleston—and told him to bring her to Peregrine House this afternoon to pick up a few things. He said he couldn't leave town to go get her until after his last class, at five-thirty or so. Which means he and Tycie won't make it back to Peregrine House until late—seven or seven-thirty."

"Are you sure about that, Raven? It'll be dark by then. Seems to me Tycie would rather come in daylight, if at all."

"She doesn't have a choice, not if she wants anything of Miss Peregrine's. Mother and Louisa are so greedy about her things. Tycie has to do whatever they say, or they won't give her a scrap. She's lucky they called her at all. Mother has already moved a ton of silver and cut glass to our house. She packed it up and hauled it away while Louisa was sleeping off those pills Dr. Calhoun gave her."

"But Louisa is supposed to have those things. She's supposed to have use of Peregrine House and everything in it. It says so in the will."

"Mother claims she's clearing things out to keep certain people—you and Mr. Pinckney—from getting their hands on them. But I know that isn't true. She's bringing the stuff home for me. She told me this morning that everything she's ever done was for me. I felt like a worm. Maybe I ought to stop being such a brat. Maybe I ought to start helping her more."

"I'd like to agree, Raven, but your mother is so awful. I can't think of one kind word to say about her. And from what you just said, she's taking criminal advantage of Louisa and Tycie."

"Don't say bad things about my mother," she said, changing her tone with no warning. Her voice was on the fringe of hysteria now. "You're the one who said to let her help me. You went to her office and told her about the abortion, for God's sake. Don't you say bad things about her ever again. I feel so guilty. Just think of how I've treated her. And she's had such a terrible life. She told me all about it this morning. From now on I'm going to do everything she says."

"I understand, Raven. Really, I do."

"Leave me alone. I know you never liked my mother."

"Me? But you've said more mean things about her...."

"I didn't mean them, though. I love my mother."

I turned to Stuart for help. His face was stone. He stared at Raven with unfeeling eyes while I tried again to reason with her. She refused to listen, lurching clumsily toward the porch door even as I spoke. The last we saw of her, she was running down the beach, blond hair streaming in the wind like the wings of a fleeing angel.

"Good riddance," Stuart said. "Maybe she'll go somewhere and finish what she started the other day...do the world a favor."

"I can't stand anymore of this, Stuart. Everyone has gone nuts. I'm going to call Mr. Pinckney and tell him I don't want any part of the will. He can tear it up for all I care."

"You can't. It's the only card we have left to play. And let's say you did throw it in, FitzSimons and Calhoun may not be satisfied with just that. They may want a piece of your hide. No, you have to choose a path and stick to it."

"But I'm scared. Those Edisto crazies...Louisa...Raven. And

now you're going to try to drag me to Peregrine House, in the dark, to look for Tycie, who probably won't even be there. You know you can't depend on anything Raven says."

"Maybe not, but driving into Charleston beats heck out of going back to Edisto. Now go find your black pullover and jeans. The last thing we need is for some blue-blood to spot us prowling around the battery at night."

Chapter Thirty-One

We talked very little on the trip into town, less after we arrived
south of Broad. Six blocks above the battery, we turned off East
Bay onto a narrow side-street and parked among the lesser mansions of Tradd and Church. From there we walked to White Point
Garden along tree-darkened sidewalks to avoid being seen. No
one was in view as we crossed the width of the lawn and stationed
ourselves in the gazebo.

"Look there," Stuart said after fifteen minutes of waiting. "A
car is stopping in front of the house. Is it a Ford? Is it green?"

I studied the vehicle and decided it was a Chevy, not a
Ford...black instead of green.

"Look at that," he said more urgently not half a minute later.

I peered into the darkness. "I can't see a thing," I said. "What?
Where?"

"The front door," he said softly. A catch had come into his
voice. "Someone is coming out of the house."

I focused on the door and strained my ears to pick up the
sound of a voice. But it was impossible to hear anything above
the everpresent wind. It whispered nastily in the oak branches
that swayed above our heads. I squinted, watching and waiting
anxiously for some movement.

"It's Tycie," I said at last. "I can see her blue bandanna. Look,
Jeannette is behind her. She's handing Tycie two grocery bags. If
that's all they gave her, they're lower than I thought."

"Where do you suppose grandson is?" Stuart said. "He should
be here by now. And what if Grandpa Voodoo comes with him? I
wish we'd hidden closer to the house. If we try to make a move
from way over here, someone could see us and set up a ruckus.
Where the devil is that boy?"

"Watch the direction Tycie walks in," I said. "She'll probably head straight for his car."

Tycie finished her good-byes, then turned and doddered across the piazza and down the front steps. She pulled her coat closer about her as she started down the walk-way toward the street.

I bristled in anger. "Do you suppose Jeannette FitzSimons would be mean enough to make her wait out in the cold for her ride?"

Stuart didn't answer. His eyes darted here and there looking for the grandson's car. My own zeroed in on Tycie. At the end of the walk, she turned right and shuffled in the direction of King Street. "Maybe she's supposed to meet him on the corner," I said, "or a block or two down."

"Yeah, and maybe if we follow her, the boy will see us and blow our frigging brains out. Come on. Let's sneak up to King. Try to stay out of the light."

We walked fast but noiselessly along the left side of South Battery while Tycie continued on the right. When she reached the corner, Stuart lost patience and urged me to call out.

"Tycie," I said weakly. "It's Arlena."

No response.

"*Tycie*," I called louder.

This time she heard, and, after a brief visual search for the source of the voice, walked bravely toward us. Then she was no longer walking, she was running. The grocery bags dropped to the pavement as she jogged lightly across the street. My mind could not make sense of it. Feeble old Tycie, moving so fast. But when she snatched off her blue headcloth, the mystery was no longer. The woman before us was not Tycie. It was Louisa—face blackened, hair slicked back, eyes wild. In her hand was a silver revolver, its slender barrel pointed toward me.

She grinned and held the gun higher. Stuart and I stood perfectly still, the sense of the situation exploding in our heads. This woman was not of the same ilk as superstitious blacks of Edisto Island. This woman was a psychotic who would as soon kill us as look at us. We did not move. Puffed up by the power of a gun, Louisa's usual rudeness changed to outright aggression.

"Well, if it isn't Sullivan's Island's resident junky and her poverty-stricken husband. Turn around, the both of you. Walk to the house at a normal rate and don't give me a reason to shoot you. I suppose you've noticed this gun has a silencer."

We walked several paces in front of her, eyes straight ahead. "Guess this explains the missing car," Stuart said.

"Shut your mouth," Louisa said. "Keep quiet until we get inside. I'm sick of having the two of you stuck in my craw."

We followed orders. We had no choice. Stuart used the excuse of my faltering a step to move closer to me. *"Do everything she says,"* he whispered. *"Don't cross her. And watch out for Jeannette FitzSimons. She's around here somewhere. I saw her in the doorway earlier."*

Louisa pushed us through the front door and shouted at Stuart to be quiet. With my eyes I begged him to obey. Then she slammed the door with the heel of her shoe and reached back to turn the lock. I shivered when the grandfather clock next to the door made soft ringing sounds.

"Get to the parlor," Louisa said. "We're going to have a little chat."

She prodded Stuart with the barrel of the gun and we moved quickly left. The parlor was dark except for a fire hissing in the fireplace grate. A large impressive fire, it was, though it gave off no comfort or warmth. Louisa went over and inspected it, then stepped into the shadows on the far side of the room and disappeared in the dim. We heard a fumbling noise, a click, then squinted against the glare of an old fashioned table lamp complete with silk fringe. The harsh light shone beneath Louisa's chin distorting her blackened face.

"Sit," she said to Stuart and me, "over there on the settee. And don't try anything. Jeannette told me to be careful about tricks. She had a feeling you might be sneaking around here tonight, especially after Raven paid you that 'spontaneous' visit earlier. She helped us set this little trap, you know. Maybe I should call Ray Bob Hanahan and tell him where you are right now. He'd be interested to know why you were roaming around our genteel neighborhood at night."

Stuart and I lowered ourselves onto the settee, trying not to antagonize our captor. Louisa swaggered over and waved the gun in our faces, then strode back to the fire. She switched the gun to her left hand to accommodate a poker with her right, then leaned forward and stirred the coals carelessly. Stuart tensed, a tiger ready to pounce.

"First fire of the season," she said. "Fanny didn't like fires. Wouldn't let me have them. She said the chimney was old and might have cracks—a spark could escape and start a fire between the walls. She was a mean stubborn old woman, Fanny. Sometimes I had to punish her, like I'm going to punish you."

I watched in terror as she drew circles in the air with the end of the gun barrel. Had she somehow forgotten we were there? Had she slipped so deeply into her own private hell that she was fading in and out of reality? Stuart sat on the edge of the settee, sizing up every opportunity to grab for the gun.

"I've been thinking it over," Louisa said. "Maybe there're other people around here who need punishing. Maybe Jeannette and Croomer. I don't trust them, anymore. First they tell me not to say you killed Fanny. Then they say you've cheated us out of millions and I can say anything I want. By the way, have you heard that Croomer wants to do an autopsy? Disgusting, isn't it? He's determined to prove to the world that foul play was involved in her death. Funny—he wasn't interested in an autopsy until he found out about the new will. But I don't care if he cuts her up. I never touched those pill bottles without gloves on my hands. You did, though, Arlena Prince...many times. Croomer thinks he can prove Fanny died of an overdose of her own medication, and that you're the one who administered it."

"Louisa, please ..." I said.

"That's good. I like to be spoken to politely. Fanny never did that. She treated me like a servant. I'm really her granddaughter, you know. What a big secret *that* was, almost as big as the one about my own dear mother, who, believe it or not, was your high-and-mighty Miss Peregrine's illegitimate daughter. The pretentious old battle-ax never acknowledged either of us. Well, it isn't important now, I suppose. She did leave me the house, or the use of it, and wheelbarrows full of money. Jeannette showed me the will this morning, the real will, not that fake one you and Grayson Pinckney cooked up. She said the two of you tried to cut me out completely."

"No, she's lying. The new will says you can live right here in Peregrine House the rest of your life if you want, and have all the money you need. Ask Mr. Pinckney if you don't believe me."

"Pinckney wouldn't tell me the truth. He's a liar like all the rest of you. Look at this room. Jeannette has taken every single thing of value out of here...crystal, china, silver, even the paintings. The whole ground floor is stripped; the other floors are worse. Jeannette is the biggest liar of all, and a coward. She wanted me to scare you tonight, so you'd destroy the new will and leave town. She said she'd go after you herself, but couldn't handle any more problems right now, not with Raven in the fix she's in. Innocent little Raven needs her *mama*. Her *mama* can't risk going to jail. Have you ever heard anything more nauseating? Jeannette must think I'm the biggest fool in Charleston. She wants me to do her dirty work, as usual. The only reason I believe what she says about the original will is I read it with my own eyes. But now she's gone too far, stealing Fanny's things. I have to stop her."

"You're right," I said. "She isn't to be trusted."

"You're one to talk. You convinced Fanny to turn her back on me altogether. You're jealous of me. That's why you talked her into cutting me out of her will. But I'm going to make you fix things back like they were. If you don't, I'll tell that idiot sherriff I saw you kill her. And this time Jeannette and Croomer won't stop me. They'll produce evidence. Croomer is already working on it."

Stuart held his hands up, palms out. "We apologize, Miss Hill," he said. "We never meant to cause you trouble. Arlena and I will destroy the new will and leave town—tonight, if you want. You'll never hear from us again. I give you my word."

"Well, well, well. Hubby has seen the light. But I don't trust hubby, either. Let me show him how I'm going to help him re-member his promises."

With that she jerked Miss Peregrine's afghan off two card-board boxes that were sitting too near the fire. "Look," she said, lifting a five-gallon gas can out of one of them. A gun in her right hand, a gas can in her left. Stuart was having difficulty containing himself. Louisa, pleased by his reaction, became bolder. "If you don't leave me alone," she said, "I'll soak the house in gasoline and burn the damn thing down. Maybe I'll do it tonight."

"But why?" Stuart said frantically. "You're right about every-thing. You've been right all along. Arlena should never have been included in the will. Everything should have been left to you. We'll explain that to Mr. Pinckney...we'll call him, now."

Louisa sneered at his words and brandished the gun about carelessly, until a voice from the foyer arrested her.

"You'll do nothing of the kind, Mr. Prince," Jeannette FitzSimons said. There was no mistaking her nasal tone. She strode confi-dently to the middle of the room and addressed the crazed house-keeper.

"What are you doing with that gun?" she said. And where did you get gas cans? For pity's sake, move them away from the fire."

"Don't come any closer," Louisa said, now pointing the gun at FitzSimons instead of us. "And don't think you're going to waltz in here and start giving orders. *I'm* giving the orders tonight."

A surprised FitzSimons sidled closer to Stuart and me. It was clear she did not expect hostility directed toward herself. Louisa sucked in a long breath and exhaled in irregular puffs. "You've got some nerve," she said to FitzSimons. "You're the one who gave me the gun in the first place, helped me with the disguise, told me what to say. What are you trying to do now, keep these two out-of-towners from figuring out how you use people?"

FitzSimons cleared her throat, trying to buy time to regain her composure. "You've done well, Louisa" she said. "But enough is enough. Everything is going to be all right now. You don't have to carry this any further. The gas cans were an unnecessary...."

"Oh, I see. A gun was necessary, but gas cans weren't. Why, Jeannette? Why was it so important for me to have a gun tonight?"

"For protection, of course, in case these two criminals tried to harm you when they found out you'd fooled them."

"*Ha*...what you wanted was for me to use it, kill them, maybe. Well, all your worries are over now. Hubby here says they're leaving town. No more new will, Jeannette. Your plan worked. They're leaving."

"Good, and right they should. They aren't part of us. Fanny would have realized that if she'd lived a little longer. So, now we can put the gun away. Give it to me without a fuss and no one will ever know you had it. If the Princes say anything to the police, I'll swear they're lying. I'll say they're trying to make you look unstable so they can cheat you out of your house, the way they tried to cheat you out of your money."

Louisa shifted her weight from left to right but did not lower the gun. "Obviously you haven't been listening," she said. "I've stopped taking orders from you. Besides, it's the gas cans you should be worried about, not the gun. You see, my dear backstabbing friend, the gun was for the Princes; the gas cans are for you. Take a good look. They're common old gas cans. You can buy them at any hardware store...much easier to come by than guns. What I'm saying is this: I will burn this place to cinders if you don't stop walking off with Fanny's things. Do you hear me, Jeannette? I will *burn* Peregrine House."

"How can you talk like that, Louisa? Fanny would turn over in her grave if she heard. She *wanted* you to live here. We all do."

"I don't believe you. Next thing, you'll try to commit me to some asylum so you and that whore daughter of yours can slide in here and take over."

Jeannette shook her head violently. "No, no, you're wrong," she said. "There's nothing Raven and I want more than for you to have the security of this house. Croomer feels the same way. It's your home. You've lived here twenty years."

"But can I *sell* it?" she said, thrusting the gun forward.

"No, Fanny didn't want that, but you can stay here indefinitely. Isn't that enough?"

FitzSimons's tone was slippery. Stuart and I glanced at each other. It was clear the old will gave control of Peregrine House to someone other than Louisa. The most likely candidate was FitzSimons herself.

"There you are," Louisa said. "I can live here, but I own nothing. Not a damn thing. Miss Peregrine didn't trust my judgment. I have to accept that since I have no choice. But what I *don't* have to accept is you and Croomer and Raven conspiring to take even the privilege of living here away from me. Why can't the three of you back off and let me enjoy my inheritance, conditional though it is."

She waved the gas can about without regard for the fire. Gasoline splashed to the rug. "All right, all right," FitzSimons said. "We will. The house is yours. That's final. Now put down that can and help me get these two trouble-makers out of here."

FitzSimons then took one foolish step forward, whereupon Louisa panicked and threw the gas can directly into the fire. Stuart grabbed FitzSimons and me by our forearms and flung us backward over the settee. He tumbled over on top of us just as the gasoline ignited. An explosion blasted the room. After the initial shock, Stuart roused FitzSimons and pushed her through a doorway behind the settee. He and I followed, and the three of us found ourselves in a cold hallway. Stuart yelled at us to get out of the house, then turned to go back for Louisa.

"No," I screamed. *"The other can hasn't blown yet."*

He pulled away and ran back into the smoke-filled parlor, returning in seconds with Louisa draped over his shoulder. Jeannette FitzSimons led us through a maze of corridors that meandered through the heart of the mansion. After traversing the complicated warren of halls and rooms, we escaped to the coolness of the garden. There, beneath the branches of Miss Peregrine's graceful dogwoods, we heard the other gas can explode.

Chapter Thirty-Two

Stuart knelt on the grass and let Louisa slide from his shoulder. "Is she dead?" FitzSimons asked, dropping to her knees beside the still form.

"Unconscious," Stuart answered. "We'll watch her while you go next door to call an ambulance and the fire department. Hurry, the whole house could go up."

"Shouldn't I go with her?" I said.

"No, she can do it better alone. She knows everyone. They'll listen to her."

"But someone is already coming...the sirens."

Stuart ignored me and concentrated on FitzSimons. "You can't wait any longer," he said to her. "If they catch it now, they can contain it."

Jeannette FitzSimons nodded, got up, and disappeared into the night. Stuart straightened out Louisa's arms and legs and covered her with his sweater. Although nothing of the fire was visible from the garden, acrid smoke wafted through the trees like ghosts of ancient aristocrats.

"Let's go," he said when he finished with Louisa.

"We can't," I said, surprised he would leave anyone who was incapacitated on the lawn of a burning building. "The fire is spreading too fast."

"She'll be okay until FitzSimons gets back? Are you hurt?"

"I don't think so."

"Then stop arguing and move it. We can't be anywhere near here when the cops descend."

Stuart took my hand and led me to the side of the house. People were already gathering in the street out front. We turned back and stole to the rear of the garden, slinking behind the carriage house like thieves. I followed close behind as he looked for an opening in the high brick wall. There was none. After a quick search, he motioned that we'd have to climb over, then showed me how to use inset bricks as footholds. He went up first, dropping silently to the ground on the other side. I followed. We found ourselves in the garden of the house next door.

"But why do we have to hide?" I whispered in irregular puffs. "We didn't do anything."

"Maybe you'd like to spend the rest of the evening talking to Ray Bob Hanahan, or better yet, explaining all this to Mr. Pinckney."

There was nothing left to say. Running seemed the only alternative. We hunched low and moved quietly through several unwalled gardens, though we could have marched through with a drum and bugle corps for all the attention anyone paid us. Everything important was happening on South Battery. A squadron of fire trucks and police cars had gathered, their blue and red lights flashing.

We came to another wall. Stuart found a tiny gate and we slipped through to a side street. People were milling about as if it were broad day. A shout arose now and then. Once I heard a male voice call out in loud clear tones, *"It's the Peregrine mansion on South Battery, some sort of explosion."*

We hurried north on King Street against a crowd hurrying south, and except for being jostled by a few fire voyeurs, we made it to the car without incident. The sight of the Romeo shocked me. Every window had been smashed. Stuart cursed under his breath as he brushed away slivers of glass and hustled me into the car. After getting in himself, he drove up the peninsula, working his way along one-way streets and alleyways toward East Bay and the Cooper River Bridge. He had a single destination in mind, the Middleton cottage on Sullivan's.

"The *windows*," I said in a whine as he drove in silence. "What do you think happened?"

"How should I know?" he said. "The whole town is one big nut farm. Nothing would surprise me."

"Can't we go any faster?"

"No, I don't want to risk getting pulled over for something stupid like speeding. Jeannette FitzSimons is probably blaring our names up and down South Battery right now. We need to get through Mount Pleasant without tangling with the police."

"But what are we going to do?"

"There's one thing I'm sure of. We can't admit to being at Peregrine House tonight. If we make it home without getting stopped, it's FitzSimons's word against ours."

"But the car, the windows ...."

"I wish I could believe it was vandalism—a kid with a tire iron and nothing to do—but I'm afraid it was more than that."

"These people are going to accuse me of murder, Stuart. We have to call Mr. Pinckney and tell him to destroy the new will."

"Good, and right after that, we can take out an ad in *The News and Courier* saying you've turned Peregrine estate over to its rightful heirs and should now and forevermore be considered innocent of any wrongdoing, particularly of murder. Somehow I don't think it's going to be that simple."

"I don't care. I'm going to get my name out of it somehow. I can't risk going to jail. Who knows? They might try to kill *me* next."

"No, FitzSimons knows better than that. If you were to die, your part of any money would go straight to your heirs, not anyone in Charleston. They're trying to scare you now. It's turned into a game of nerve."

"Stop it. You sound like we're playing Russian roulette. Are you sure you're as concerned about me as you are about the will?"

"Come on, Arlena. You can't keep getting hysterical like this. Stay in control."

I began crying again and did not stop until we reached the cottage. Stuart parked the car between the pilings under the house, covered the broken windows, and helped me up the stairs.

"Let's get you into bed," he said, "before you end up in the emergency room again. We were lucky to make it back without being spotted. I was afraid one of those cops at Peregrine House would radio ahead to the Mount Pleasant Police Department. Guess I gave them too much credit for brain power."

When we reached the top step, Stuart uttered a frightened oath and jerked me behind his back. The kitchen door was dripping with bright blue paint. I put my face in my hands and begged him not to go inside. He wouldn't listen. He left me crying at the top of the stairs and went through the house alone. Nothing else was out of order, though the paint itself was more than enough to finish off my nerves.

"It had to be those Edisto jerkweeds," Stuart said when he

came back to the door. "Probably the same ones who broke the car windows, as if last night wasn't enough to do us in. What they don't know is I'd rather take my chances with twenty Mammalois than one Louisa Hill. Come on, let's get out of these sooty clothes. If Hanahan comes out here snooping around, we don't want him smelling smoke."

A police car rolled up before my hair had dried from the shower. It was greeted by darkness. Our plan was to claim we had been home all evening and could certainly know nothing of a fire. Stuart lifted a blind slat an inch to see what new demon had come to visit.

"It's Hanahan," he said, "with the biggest damn flashlight I've ever seen. He's going under the house...to check the car, I guess."

"What if he sees the windows?" I said.

"Broken windows don't have anything to do with fires, but I agree, it looks bad. Maybe he won't pull the tarp up high enough. He's coming up the stairs now. Go to the bedroom. Let me handle this alone. I'll pretend we were sleeping."

I tiptoed to the bedroom and hid in a dark corner. In a second, Hanahan was pounding on the outside door. Stuart let him bang away a good long time before switching on a light. "Who is it?" he called out. "People are trying to sleep in here."

"Sorry, Mr. Prince. It's Ray Bob Hanahan. We had some more problems in town tonight. I hate to tell you this, but your wife's name came up again."

Stuart muttered convincingly as he unlocked the door. Suddenly the two men's voices grew louder. I shrank farther from the bedroom door.

"There was a fire," Hanahan said. "The whole left front of Peregrine House got burnt out. Part of the old staircase went—a real shame. It was one of them rare kinds, you know, sort of spiraled and carved-like. Gonna take a pretty penny to fix it...oh my God, I didn't see this here paint. What in tarnation? All kinds of crazy things going on tonight."

"Vandals," Stuart said curtly. "And how did the fire start?"

"Don't know exactly. Louisa Hill was alone in the house, then Mrs. FitzSimons showed up about the time it started. Damn good thing. She had to pull Miss Hill out. Unconscious, she was. Had to take her to the hospital. Last I heard, she hadn't come around enough to say much. But Mrs. FitzSimons— well, that's a different story. She's said a whole heap. Claims you and your wife were the ones started the fire, with gasoline of all things. Looked to me like she was talking out of her head, about like Miss Hill was the night old Miss Peregrine got murdered. On, excuse me, I meant to say died, not murdered. Nobody's saying anything else yet. Frankly, I wouldn't worry about it much. What she was saying don't make sense no way, seeing as how you're probably about to tell me you've been at home all evening."

"We have," Stuart said. "And we're getting tired of people in town accusing us of crimes. Maybe we need a lawyer ...."

"No, no. I don't think that's necessary. Miss Hill and Mrs. FitzSimons seem like the kind of women who like to tell their tales, same as I like to sit on my own. One thing for sure, though—all anybody around here wants to talk about is the fortune Miss Peregrine left your wife."

"Is the house still standing?" Stuart said, ignoring the leading remark.

"Yep, but she looks mighty pitiful. I knew you and Mrs. Prince would want to know about it, the house being part of the estate and all. Shoot, you two might find yourselves living in that castle some time or another."

Stuart couldn't help responding to this last jab. "Sergeant Hanahan," he said. "The way things were explained to us is that Peregrine House belongs to Louisa Hill for all intents and purposes, and since Jeannette FitzSimons appears to have taken charge of Miss Hill's other affairs, I'm sure she'll manage the house for her, as well. Now if you don't mind, I'd like to get back to bed."

"Sorry, Mr. Prince, but you can't blame a fellow for wondering why she's over there telling anyone who'll listen that you and Mrs. Prince torched the place. You folks have had more bad luck the last day or two than anybody I've ever come across. And now your car windows, too. I saw them when I drove up. The wind must have blown the tarp off. I tried to put it back on for you. What happened to them windows, anyhow?"

"Vandals," Stuart said again dryly, "the same ones with the paint, we think. Did you get the tarp back on securely? We're trying to keep the dampness out."

"Sure did. Good idea, that tarp. It'll keep your interior from ruining. Look here, Mr. Prince...I'd like to ride back out here tomorrow if it's all right with you, to talk to your wife. Those ladies over at Peregrine House are working overtime stirring up trouble. It's getting harder and harder to keep things straight. Oh yeah—and I saw Dr. Calhoun again last night. He does love to carry on, don't he? Seems to be the only male animal trying to help out with this mess, except for you and me, of course."

"If that's all, Sergeant ...."

"Yessir, that's all—for now, anyway. But you never did say about tomorrow. Can I come back to talk to your wife?"

"Certainly, but call first. We may go out."

"I'll do that, sir, and thanks a heap for speaking with me tonight. Some folks might not have done that. Goodnight now. See you."

The outside door opened and closed. Hanahan clomped noisily down the wooden steps. Stuart came into the bedroom and flopped down on the bed.

"It's worse," he said. "It keeps getting worse. Tycie is the only chance we have."

"You can forget about Tycie. She's terrified of Louisa and Jeannette. She wouldn't tell us even if she knew anything. The only real chance I have is doing away with the will. I'm going to Mr. Pinckney's office tomorrow morning and tear it up myself. It's the one thing I can think of that would make me feel safe."

"For an intelligent woman, you can be a real pighead sometimes, Arlena. I get so sick of trying to reason with ...."

There was another car noise. "Damn," Stuart said, and again hurried to the window. "It's a Cadillac. Grayson Pinckney is getting out of it. I guess we'll have Queen Elizabeth next." He adjusted the blinds and walked quickly to the same door he had just closed on Hanahan. Now he opened it for Mr. Pinckney.

"Evening, boy," Mr. Pinckney said. "Kind of dark in here, don't you think? How about turning on some lights for an old man. Don't see as well as I used to, though I did see that snake Ray Bob Hanahan crawl down Atlantic Avenue a minute ago. Hope you didn't tell him anything."

"No, sir," Stuart said as he switched on a table lamp, "but he's coming back tomorrow."

I crashed into Stuart's shoulder blade as I flew past him to Grayson Pinckney and threw myself into his arms. "Oh, Mr. Pinckney," I cried. "I'm so glad to see you. I was planning to come to your office in the morning to tell you to get rid of the will. Stuart and I want you to destroy it the first possible minute."

Grayson Pinckney looked me in the face, but did not respond. He turned and addressed Stuart as if I hadn't spoken at all. "Get your car keys, boy. We have to hide that clunker of yours under my cottage down the way. Then no one can tell if you're home or not. I want you two to lay low a few days, especially while Ray Bob's sniffing under every bush. Looks like we're officially under siege. Someone threw blue paint on Pinckney House tonight, too...the same kind as on Lucretia's door out there. Looks like we've got ourselves a bonafide voodoo warning. I wouldn't want to know from whom, although I'm certain it's somehow linked to the fire at Peregrine House."

"Arlena and I didn't have anything to do with that fire, Mr. Pinckney. We haven't been in town since ...."

"Stop lying to me, boy. Get your keys and be quick about it."

Stuart picked up the keys from the coffee table and held them out to the old gentleman. "No," Mr. Pinckney said. "Go downstairs and give them to Julius Caesar. He'll drive your car to my cottage; I'll follow him in mine. That way he won't have to walk back. Caesar ain't no young buck, you know."

Stuart did as he was told. Mr. Pinckney turned to me. "There's something you need to understand," he said to me soberly. "You're going to be charged with murder whether you destroy the will or not. I will represent you gratis, if you like. I'd do it for any one of my employees. As for right now, all we're doing is stalling for time. I'd let you stay at my cottage a few days, but the water and electricity have been turned off for the winter. Plus, I don't think it would do you any good for your lawyer to be discovered harboring a suspect. Just remember, the only thing you have to do at the moment is remain calm. Don't get emotional like some other women I could name. In the morning early, I'll send Caesar out to fetch you and Stuart to my office. We'll all be more rested then. Maybe we can map out a strategy. I promise to do everything I can to help you, Arlena, but you have to face reality—the lid on this thing is about to blow."

Chapter Thirty-Three

Stuart and I huddled together in the bedroom the rest of the night, sleeping off and on, imagining noises, expecting far worse than fires and voodoo warnings. When dawn finally broke over the ocean, we dressed and waited for Caesar. He arrived at five of seven, and since there was little traffic on the bridge at that hour, we made it to Pinckney Building by seven-twenty. We walked up the stairs to Mr. Pinckney's office and found him staring out his corner window at Broad Street below. He did not turn around.

"Will wonders never cease," he said, then checked his watch. "It's not seven-thirty yet, and Jonathan is coming in. The man hasn't shown up before nine in a decade. Something must be up."

At the mention of Priolieu's name, Stuart shot out of the office and ran down the hall. I stared after him in stunned silence. Mr. Pinckney turned around to see what the commotion was. "Damn, must be a fire under that boy. Where's he off to?"

"*Priolieu,*" I breathed.

Mr. Pinckney and I tripped over each other getting to the stairs. On the street floor we found Stuart holding Priolieu in a headlock. Mr. Pinckney bellowed for him to let go. Stuart wouldn't listen— he was too angry. He forced Priolieu to his knees, grabbed a handful of hair, and whipped back his head.

"Talk, you dirtbag," he growled through clenched teeth, "or you might find yourself going to the dentist again."

"I don't know anything...I don't," Priolieu squeaked.

Stuart gave him a knee in the back and yanked his hair again. "You knew we were at this office. Who told you?" he shouted. Another knee. Another yank. I screamed for him to stop.

"No, please," Priolieu said. "All I did was take the money."

At that, Mr. Pinckney stepped forward. He leaned over until

the tip of his long Roman nose came within inches of Priolieu's pug. "What money, you low-down scoundrel?" he said.

"From Croomer Calhoun, sir. He's been paying me to feed him information. He said he'd pay me thousands if I'd help him get rid of the will."

"Turn him loose, Stuart," Mr. Pinckney said. "He's in a talking mood now." Stuart released the panting Priolieu and propped him against the wall. Mr. Pinckney breathed into his face. "Tell me everything, you weasel, or I'll inform Caroline you're after every secretary in this office."

"There isn't anything else. I swear it."

"Then why are you here so early? I'm no fool, man. Talk."

"Calhoun called me at home last night, while you were outside looking at the fire at Peregrine House. He said if I wanted more cash, I should get over here early this morning and keep tabs on what's going on."

"And how did you know the Princes would be here?"

"I didn't, sir. It was a coincidence. I couldn't believe it when I saw Prince."

Mr. Pinckney frowned and turned to Stuart. "Croomer Calhoun is more involved in this than I thought," he said. "I assumed it was mostly Jeannette and Louisa. But now I have to think the good doctor has his own designs on Fanny's fortune. He sent a message to me by courier yesterday. Said there's evidence Miss Peregrine was murdered, an overdose of pills or some damn thing. He threatened to tell the police about it unless something fair was done about the will."

"He's right about her being murdered," Stuart said. "Louisa as much as admitted to it last night."

Mr. Pinckney looked pained. "I won't embarrass you, Mr. Prince, by asking what in the name of God you were doing in the company of Louisa Hill last evening, or why you felt the need to visit Peregrine House. Suffice it to say I already knew you had been there. Jeannette was broadcasting it up and down South Battery even as the old mansion burned."

"I'll say she was lying," Stuart said lamely.

"Don't be an ass, man. And believe me, the fire is the least of your worries. Arlena is about to be arrested for murder. Everything else pales next to that."

I let out a cry at the word *murder*. "Please, Mr. Pinckney. Please tear up the will."

"No," he said, and turned away. His coldness infuriated me. I grabbed his arm and pulled him back around.

"Pay attention to me," I said angrily. "You, too, Stuart. And you, Jonathan. As of this minute, the new will is null and void. I reject it out of hand."

"No, Arlena," Stuart said. "Listen to Mr. Pinckney. Things have gotten crazy. Louisa can't let herself be incriminated any further. Jeannette FitzSimons is desperate; so is Calhoun. You're becoming a more convenient scapegoat by the minute."

"No," I said, my voice even louder. "Jonathan, call Calhoun. Tell him he can have the money, all of it. I never wanted it in the first place. Tell him I'm leaving town."

I looked into the faces of the men standing before me and realized they thought my mind had snapped. "Stop staring at me," I demanded, then ran back up the stairs to Mr. Pinckney's office and began shuffling through the papers on his desk. Just as I found what I was looking for, the three men—Stuart, Jonathan and Mr. Pinckney—stepped into the room.

"Look," I said, and shook the blue folder in their faces. "It's the *thing*...the thing that's caused all the trouble." Then, two and three pages at a time, I ripped the will into shreds. The men watched as strips of blue and white paper fluttered to the floor.

"Don't do this," Mr. Pinckney said.

"It's too late. I've already done it. Now, Jonathan, make your call."

"No," Mr. Pinckney said. "It's a mistake."

He reached out to take hold of my arm as Stuart came at me from the other side. I eluded them both and rushed down the hallway. My heart was beating against the walls of my chest like a trapped bird struggling to escape. Fear fed my strength as I raced down the stairs with the three men charging after me. I strained to run faster—out the front door, across the street, down a narrow alleyway. I ran until my lungs almost burst. At the end of the alley, an opening appeared. When I reached it, I found myself on the other side of the block, cars whizzing up and down as if nothing in the world was more important than beating the next red light. There I stopped to catch my breath and wait for my heart to stop pounding. The bus, I thought in panic. I'll ride the bus back to Sullivan's and hide at the cottage. No, that's the first place they'll look. Where then? The Pinckney cottage? Yes, they won't think of looking there for hours.

I brushed myself off, smoothed back my hair, and stepped into open sunlight. The bus stop was a four-block walk. Several times I ducked into doorways and alleys in case Stuart and Mr. Pinckney, maybe even Jon Priolieu, were still around. From one hiding place I saw a taxi cruise by, with a man who looked like Stuart sitting in the back seat. I waited until it turned the corner before scurrying the rest of the way to the bus stop. But not until I had already boarded the bus did I realize I had no money. The driver recognized me from other trips and said I could pay later. I was on my way toward a seat at the back when Stuart and Mr. Pinckney began shouting my name from the other end of the block. The driver twisted his body around and stared back at me. His eyes were all questions. I shook my head— he slammed the door and sped away.

I fell onto the bench seat at the back of the bus and looked out the rear window. Stuart and Mr. Pinckney were running after the bus. The driver turned left on Meeting Street and headed for the bridge to Mount Pleasant. As my pursuers receded in the distance, possibilities whirled in my mind. If I could stay out of sight a few hours, maybe even the whole night, then everyone would have time to get word that I had destroyed the will with my own hands. All my problems would be solved.

The driver let me off at the Middle Street stop on Sullivan's. As I ran up the block and dashed between two houses, I hoped against hope he wouldn't tell anyone where he last saw me. I walked briskly in and out of yards, around garbage cans, behind fences, and up and down sand dunes—gratefully reaching the Pinckney cottage just before exhaustion overtook me. The Romeo was still parked under the house, hidden from view by the palings of a tall wooden gate. I opened it just enough to squeeze through the crack, collapsed in the sand next to the Romeo, and cried myself to sleep. I did not wake up until I heard Stuart calling out my name from somewhere deep in my subconscious. His voice intermingled with my dreams.

"Arlena, sweetheart," he said in a voice with a weird Doppler effect. When I realized he was kneeling beside me, I opened my eyes and smiled at him before realizing where I was. But in an instant, the morning came rushing back, and I began struggling to escape again. I fought like a cornered animal and would not give in until I saw Mr. Pinckney, feet planted wide apart, standing over us.

"I'm sorry, Arlena," he said. "You've been through hellfire these last few days at the hands of Charleston arses, and I'm afraid I've been the biggest arse of all. Can you ever forgive me?"

"I'm tired, and confused," I whimpered. "I don't know what's happening, anymore. Did Jon Priolieu call Dr. Calhoun, like I asked?"

"I don't know," Stuart said. "Mr. Pinckney and I have spent the last two hours looking for you. Priolieu stayed behind. Listen to me, Arly. I think you need to see a doctor. Sometimes people break down under stress ...."

"No. I'm hiding here until everyone gets word about the will. Now go away and leave me alone."

"Come on, baby. Let's get some coffee at Mama Chloe's. Mr. Pinckney has a taxi waiting."

"Go without me. Take the taxi with you. I don't want to take a chance on being seen."

"Don't be ridiculous. I can't leave you here alone." Stuart looked over his shoulder at Mr. Pinckney. "Maybe you should go on without us, sir. She seems set on hiding out a few hours. I'll have to stay here with her."

"Not a chance. Neither of you is staying. This little lady is going to get up off her back-side and go to Mama Chloe's with us if I have to haul her like a sack of grits. I'm starving. Haven't raced around this much in twenty years. I think my sacroiliac has slipped."

"What do you say, Arly?" Stuart said softly. "We could all use something to eat. I'll tell the driver to park the cab behind the building."

"Check outside," I said. "If no one's there, I'll go. But I'm not talking to anyone."

"No one ever comes this far down the beach in November," Mr. Pinckney said, peering through a space between the palings of the gate. "Not even a stray dog out there. Get yourselves up, you two. Let's get some food at Chloe's. Old men have to eat."

Chapter Thirty-Four

"I've made a decision," Stuart said when we were seated at the back of the restaurant, "and I don't want either of you to try to talk me out of it. I'm going back to Edisto. Arlena, you'll have to stay with Mr. Pinckney."

"No," I said, close to bolting again. "Mr. Pinckney, please. Tell him he can't go there, it's too dangerous."

But Grayson Pinckney didn't hear a word I was saying. His attention was arrested by something at the front of the restaurant. I turned to see what he was looking at and recoiled at the sight. Ray Bob Hanahan stood motionless in the doorway, his snake eyes trained on me.

I stood up on reflex. Mr. Pinckney and Stuart each grabbed an arm and pulled me back into my chair. "Stay calm," Stuart said in a low voice. "Don't say a word. Let Mr. Pinckney handle this."

Grayson Pinckney rose to his full height before speaking. "Morning, Ray Bob," he said as the officer approached our table. The two men shook hands perfunctorily. "Have you had the pleasure of meeting Mr. and Mrs. Prin...."

"Yessir, Mr. Pinckney. The Princes and I met at the Peregrine mansion a few days ago. Funny—for some reason I thought you would have known that. I hated to have to come out here today and ruin a perfectly good afternoon."

"And how might you do that?"

"By delivering bad news, sir. Dr. Croomer Calhoun found out this morning that Miss Peregrine died of an overdose of pills. He thinks it wasn't accidental. Fact is, we have an eye witness who'll swear to the fact that Mrs. Prince is the one who gave them to her."

"*You're crazy*," I blurted out, and stood again in spite of Stuart's efforts to restrain me. I would no longer be silenced. "If anyone killed Miss Peregrine, it was Louisa Hill," I said, all the while struggling with Stuart. "She as good as confessed last night. Tell him, Stuart. Tell him what she said."

"Arlena, let Mr. Pinckney do this his way...please."

Hanahan scratched his head. "Damnedest thing, Mrs. Prince. Louisa Hill is singing the same tune about you. Seems like the two of you keep going around and around. Weren't for some of them other things, I wouldn't know *who* to arrest."

"What other things?" Mr. Pinckney said coolly.

"Oh...fires, copyrights, fingerprints on pill bottles, little things like that. We lifted a perfect set of Mrs. Prince's prints off a barbiturate bottle that was right there in Miss Peregrine's bedroom."

"And how did you know they were hers? You had nothing with which to compare them."

"Sure I did, Mr. Pinckney. You talk like I'm ignorant or something. I got a clean set of your lady's prints the same night Miss Peregrine died. Louisa Hill gave me a brandy snifter Mrs. Prince had been holding earlier. Still had the smell of peach brandy in it. Guess you could say I was already a little suspicious of her, or else I wouldn't have been nosing out fingerprints. Anyhow, it ain't no never mind. It's the kind of thing that's easy enough to check. You know that, sir."

"But I'd never hurt Miss Peregrine," I said tearfully. "She was my friend. She was ..."

"I don't know, Mrs. Prince. It's hard to imagine a lady like you getting involved in a thing like this. Guess drugs do funny things to people. Why, Miss Hill says you're an out-an-out drug addict ...."

"You can't take the word of a psychotic," I said, "not about something as important as this."

"Arlena, stop," Stuart pleaded.

"Leave me alone. Someone has to tell him ...."

Mr. Pinckney squeezed my arm, forcing me into silence. Then to Hanahan he said, "Who's been telling you this nonsense about drugs, Ray Bob? Mrs. Prince doesn't have a drug problem."

"Maybe not now, sir, but she did a few weeks ago. Dr. Calhoun and Mrs. FitzSimons told me all about it. You know how this town is—ain't nobody got no secrets."

"Indeed," Mr. Pinckney said, then paused before adding, "Ray

Bob, the time has come for me to inform you that Mrs. Prince is my client. I intend to do the best I can to help her with this matter, and you, sir, will cease your threatening remarks unless you can produce a paper with teeth in it."

"If you mean a warrant for her arrest, sir, I wouldn't have come out here without that." He reached into his breast pocket and brought out a folded document. Grayson Pinckney jerked it out of his hand and flipped it open. "Are you daft, man? This is a first degree murder charge."

"That's right, sir. And now I guess I ought to read Mrs. Prince her rights."

I was stricken dumb. Hanahan rattled off the Miranda rights and told me to follow him to his car. From the corner of my eye I saw Mama Chloe wringing her hands and weeping. Stuart lost control and grabbed for Hanahan. Only through the efforts of Grayson Pinckney and two bystanders did he avoid being arrested with me. I was informed by Hanahan I'd have to ride to Charleston in the squad car. "Rules," he said. Again Stuart made advances.

"I'm all right," I told him calmly, though I was clearly in an unnatural state. "Really, I am. It'll all be over soon. Croomer Calhoun and Jeannette FitzSimons will straighten everything out as soon as they find out I've destroyed the will. I just wish I'd done it sooner."

"Oh, the will," Hanahan said. "I meant to mention that earlier. Dr. Calhoun says it ain't no good, that Mrs. FitzSimons could prove Miss Peregrine wasn't of sound mind and body when she wrote it. I reckon she could, being a lawyer and all."

"You don't know anything about it," I said to him in my newly steady voice. I stared into his face fearlessly. He felt my contempt, faltered slightly, then discovered there was a speck of lint on his sleeve.

"Let's go, Mrs. Prince," he said. "I got no choice but to take you in. Please don't give me no trouble. I don't want to hurt you none."

Mr. Pinckney held Stuart by the arm as Hanahan guided me to the squad car. He helped me in and was about to close the door when someone called out my name from a distance. I turned to see Raven running across the street. Her MG was parked on the curb opposite the restaurant, engine running, door standing open.

"Mrs. Prince, Mrs. Prince—wait," she shouted. "Where are you going? What are they doing to you?"

She pushed by Stuart and Mr. Pinckney, her eyes darting from Hanahan to Stuart to me.

"Aren't you Mrs. FitzSimons's daughter?" Hanahan said.

"Yes, now tell me why you're bothering Mrs. Prince, or I'll kick your redneck balls in."

"Hold on there, missy. Ain't no call to go talking trash. Mrs. Prince is going downtown to answer a few questions, that's all, and it's no concern of yours. Now run along and stay out of trouble. Aren't you supposed to be in school this time of day?"

Raven raised her hand and slapped him across the face. "I'll scratch your eyes out, you son-of-a-bitch," she said, and Stuart and Mr. Pinckney grabbed her arms to keep her from doing worse. Hanahan's composure was destroyed. His face went crimson; he trembled as he spoke. "This woman has been charged with murder, young lady, and you're going to be charged with assault on a law officer if you raise a hand to me again."

"But she didn't murder anyone," Raven screamed at him, thrashing about between Stuart and Mr. Pinckney.

"Stop it, Raven. You can't help me," I said.

But my words went unheeded. Raven leaned over almost double and bit Mr. Pinckney on his hand. He swore from the pain as she jerked away and ran back to her car. No one tried to stop her as she whipped the MG around in the middle of the street and sped toward the Ben Sawyer Bridge.

"God bless America," Mr. Pinckney said as he wrapped his bleeding hand in his handkerchief. "I'll spit to Georgia if females aren't the most vicious devils on this planet."

Hanahan immediately closed me into the police car and prepared to depart. As he pulled away from the restaurant, Mr. Pinckney and Stuart rushed to find the parked cab. The cabby succeeded in catching up with the squad car at the base of the Ben Sawyer bridge, and stayed close behind through Mount Pleasant. It wasn't until I saw the steelwork of the Cooper River Bridge that I realized traffic had come to a complete stop along its great left span. Hanahan put on brakes and cursed. "Damn—what's the problem now? If it ain't one thing, it's another."

Traffic was backed up to the foot of the bridge; people were getting out of their cars and running up both sides of the incline like a pack of wolves to a kill. For a moment I thought a section of the bridge had collapsed. Then Hanahan clicked on his blue light and forced the squad car forward. We inched between several cars, but soon could go no farther. I strained my eyes to see what the problem was. People on the bridge were pointing upward. I lifted my eyes to the high suspension work, and what I saw there chilled my blood. A girl stood balanced on a connecting length of steel that towered above the left span of the bridge. She was far away, but her long blond hair whipping in the wind made her identity unmistakable. It was Raven...Raven FitzSimons.

"Lord," Hanahan said. "There's a jumper up there."

I banged my fists on the squad car window and begged Hanahan to let me out. For security reasons, there was no inside door handle in the back part of the car. Otherwise, I'd have already escaped.

"What's the matter with you?" Hanahan said. "No way I'm letting you out of this car."

"But I *know* her," I said. "It's Raven FitzSimons, the girl from back at the restaurant. For God's sake, don't you recognize her?"

"Damned if it ain't," Hanahan said, staring up.

"Please, let me out. Maybe I can get her to come down."

Hanahan looked back at me and made a quick decision. He got out of the car and opened the door that was holding me captive. "Get her talking if you can," he shouted as I dashed away. "Sometimes if they talk, they don't jump."

I raced up the incline, shoving people aside as I went. Raven stood perfectly still on the beam. The only thing that moved was her hair. It blew wildly about her face and shoulders as if anxious to be free of the gravity of manmade structures called bridges. She had chosen the highest climbable point on the steelwork from which to jump. Her back was to the roadway, her eyes on the water.

"Raven," I shouted, but my voice was drowned out by the power of the wind. "*It's Arly, Raven. Look at me.*"

She started, then turned her face to an angle that would allow her to scan the bridge. When she spotted me, waving below her like a mad woman, she leaned farther out over the water, her free hand covering her face.

"Keep your eyes open, Raven. You'll get dizzy," I said.

"Go away," she cried out. "My life is garbage. I'm pregnant, my boyfriend is a jerk, my mother is a bitch. And now I've started hearing voices. They scream inside my head. Everything will be all right, they say, if I can get up the courage to kill myself."

"What voices, Raven?"

"Scary voices. I'm afraid of them, but I know they're telling me the truth."

"No, no, they're lying. Don't listen to them, Raven. I know about them, I've heard them, too."

"But they won't stop talking about the bad things I've done, things I can't live with. Mother said you cheated us out of Miss Peregrine's estate. She wanted me to help her scare you into getting rid of the will. *I'm* the one who set you up the night of the fire. I lied when I said Tycie was coming to Peregrine House. Mother told me to. But she didn't tell me she was going to accuse you of murder. She hates you, Mrs. Prince. But she hates me worse. She hates me for getting pregnant and ruining all her plans."

"Everything is going to be okay, Raven. I don't want any of Miss Peregrine's money. I never did. I destroyed the will this morning. It's gone. When your mother finds out, she'll leave me alone. She'll leave *you* alone. Please come down. We can talk this out. I know we can...please."

For a second she looked as if she might give in, then stiffened suddenly and leaned farther out. I looked around to see what had frightened her. Croom Calhoun Jr. was running up the ramp. The look on his face was pure terror. I knew instantly he was going to do something stupid. I called to him to stop. He ignored me and ran to the base of the steelwork. He pulled himself up to the first set of connectors and began a swift climb. Raven shrieked for him to stay back. He would not. He reached out for her in the middle of a scream, his fingertips brushing her hair. This was the moment she vaulted over the edge and fell straight down. She looked like a white-throated sparrow, shot out of the sky on the wing. I did not see her hit the water. All I saw was Stuart standing over me, trying to get me to move.

"Come on, we have to run," he said.

"Did you see?" I cried. "Raven jumped. I'm going to the river bank. I have to help her."

"It's too late, Arly. You have to help yourself now. Come on. We have to get out of here."

"No, I'm going to find her. She could drown."

"Arlena, there's *no hope*. Now come with me without a hassle, for once."

"Get away from me. I'm going to Raven. *Get away.*"

He gave up arguing and forced me in the opposite direction of the swiftly moving crowd. "No, no," I cried out. "Raven is hurt. Hanahan will be looking for me. Mr. Pinckney will be looking for me ...."

"Hang them all," Stuart said, slowing down not at all. "I'm taking you somewhere safe, somewhere no one can find you." He clasped my hand tighter in his own and plowed headlong through the throng. We did not stop until Mr. Pinckney and the cab driver miraculously appeared before us.

"Don't get in our way," Stuart said to the men, his free hand clenched in a fist. "Arlena is right about one thing. We have to hide until this thing blows over. Let us go before Hanahan shows up."

"You shouldn't," Mr. Pinckney said. "It'll only make things worse."

"Step aside, sir."

"All right then. I won't try to stop you. God be with you, son. I'll tell Hanahan I saw you going the other way. Now take the taxi and git. I already gave the driver here a hundred dollars. There'll be more for him waiting at my office if he can get you out of here safely." The cabby nodded. "*Git*," Mr. Pinckney said again.

The three of us—Stuart, the cabby, and myself—hurried down the Mount Pleasant ramp. Our progress was retarded by the crowd moving against us. Then, without warning, Stuart dropped my hand and rushed back to Mr. Pinckney. I watched as he leaned close and said something into his ear. Mr. Pinckney frowned and gesticulated sharply. Stuart shrugged, then shook Mr. Pinckney's reluctant hand, and returned to the cabby and me. We picked up our pace when we caught sight of the yellow taxi parked on the shoulder of the road. I was grateful that traffic was moving toward the bridge instead of away from it. All lanes into Mount Pleasant were clear. The cabby made a U-turn and screeched his tires as we fled.

"Where to?" he said to Stuart, his voice as excited as fearful.

"The Isle of Palms," Stuart said. "We have to find a boat to get to Edisto."

"I won't...I can't go back there," I said. "I already told you that."

"The hell you can't. If I can do what I just did, you can go with me to talk to Tycie."

"What? What did you do?"

"I told Mr. Pinckney to send word to everyone that you've rescinded any claim to Miss Peregrine's estate and have decided to move back north. You're no a longer part of this mess."

"I haven't been since early this morning. I was serious when I tore up those papers at Mr. Pinckney's office."

"Fine, now he's convinced. But we still have to find Tycie, to make sure she'll take your part if you need her. Throwing in the will may not be enough for FitzSimons and Calhoun. They may want blood."

Chapter Thirty-Five

"Did you hear? Some society girl jumped off the bridge," a clerk said when we rushed into Two Brothers Marina on the Isle of Palms. "A FitzSimons girl. It's all over the radio. Broke right in to tell it. They're trying to find the body now. Next they'll be using them grappling hooks."

I closed my eyes against a wave of nausea and leaned against the wall. The cabby stood close by me while Stuart took care of business.

"Where's the manager?" he said to the clerk. "We need a boat. We need to rent one right now."

"Down at the dock, gassing up his dinghy, I think. He's going to the harbor to see what he can see when they pull that girl up."

I winced again and wrapped my arms tightly around my body. Stuart raced outside and down the back stairs to the dock. The cab driver rummaged through the store and found a crate for me to sit on, then took his hat off and stood next to me like a guard. The clerk prattled on about the drowning of Raven FitzSimons, debutante of Old Charleston.

In a few minutes Stuart came blowing back in and began giving orders. The taxi was to be kept on the Isle of Palms overnight. Stuart had given one of the marina owner's cronies twenty dollars to hide it. Another had agreed to drive the cabby back to Charleston by way of Georgetown to avoid the police. Bubber Hampton, the owner himself, would take us to Edisto by boat. There was no time to lose. Hanahan had probably already radioed an all-points bulletin about the disappearance of a dangerous murderess. The clerk produced jackets, toboggans, and mittens for the boat trip.

We never thought once about anyone from the marina calling in our whereabouts. The patrons and staff of Two Brothers were experienced at circumventing the law.

"Did you tell Mr. Pinckney where we were going?" I said to Stuart as he helped Bubber shove off from the dock.

"No, only that I wanted to hide you long enough for everyone to find out what we've done about the will. I'm sure he knows where we'll be. He wouldn't forget what I said in the restaurant about trying again to get to Tycie. He just won't have to come right out and lie about it to Hanahan."

The trip was slow, over an hour. I buried my face in Stuart's shoulder to block out the wind. We were too cold and miserable to talk. Finally, the dinghy bumped into a rotten dock off Edisto's Intracoastal bank. Bubber stayed in the boat while Stuart and I climbed the rickety ladder to the dock. Stuart asked Bubber how long he could wait. The old man studied a sky of yellowy clouds and said we'd have to leave two hours before nightfall to make it back in daylight. Otherwise, night would catch us with no lights or radio. It was already four p.m. Stuart thought a moment while Bubber fidgeted. Then, suddenly decisive, he told the old man to go home alone, we'd call him later if we needed him. I felt a terrible sense of desolation as the boat motored away from the dock. Stuart and I watched as it rounded a curve in the shoreline and disappeared from sight.

"There's no marina here," Stuart said, "but Bubber mentioned there used to be an old fishing store up the way. Let's try it. Maybe we can get directions."

We trudged along a path perpendicular to the Intracoastal to a shack of a store fronting a dirt road. Stuart tried the front door, which opened with a jingling of bells. We stepped inside. A half-dozen black men turned to look at us from a circle of straight chairs arranged carelessly around a free-standing stove. They stared without expression from indolent black eyes. I shrank back in fear. The memory of Snake Island made their faces dark and evil, though no particular one was familiar. The men did not appear to recognize us. Yet I was certain that somehow they all knew we were the same ignorant white people who had visited their island earlier.

"We're lost," Stuart said to the gathering. "We're looking for a church on the road to Dawhoo Bridge."

"What for?" asked one of the men.

"We're supposed to...tune the piano."

"Ain't got no piano. Somebody told you wrong. How did you get on this side of the island? Dawhoo Bridge is on the other side."

"By boat. We live near Ashpooh Cut."

The black men exchanged looks. Stuart had obviously said something stupid. He tried to recover. "We won't be long. All we need to do is take a look. We'll bring our tools back later."

"I told you, white man. We ain't got no piano. Who would ask you to fix a piano that everybody knows we ain't got?"

Stuart hesitated. "The preacher," he said. "He called us yesterday. I can't remember his name."

A murmur of laughter rippled over the group. One man resumed whittling as though bored by the lies of white people.

"Preacher be dead," said the spokesman. "Dead of the gravel."

"Gravel?"

"Yep, kidney gravel."

Stuart refused to give up. "Got any coffee in that pot? We sure could use some."

This time his question was answered by a basso somewhere in the back. "No coffee," he said. "We ain't open to the public today, especially white public."

Suddenly Stuart was brave. "I don't know who you are, mister," he said, "but I'd recognize that voice anywhere. You're one of the jerkweeds who took us to Snake Island. But today you may as well back off. We're not afraid of that crap, anymore."

I stared at Stuart. Obviously he had taken leave of his senses. *He* might not be afraid. *I* was terrified.

"Stuart, don't," I said. Then basso stepped into the light.

"Ain't no such place as Snake Island, man, unless you've been clear to Haiti."

"Look," Stuart said, changing his tone, holding up his hands in surrender. "We never should have bothered you ...."

"Shut-up, man. You never should have bothered old Tycie, neither. I got a notion to throw you in a gator hole for scaring that poor old woman."

"But we didn't scare her," Stuart said, his voice an unattractive tenor in contrast to the black man's rich bass. "We haven't been able to find her. Look, my wife has been accused of murder. Tycie could help her out of it. What's it to you if ...."

But his sentence was cut short by a jingling of the bells. Everyone looked toward the door. Tycie's grandson stepped inside, the same boy who had held me down in the churchyard while someone poured the evil syrup down my throat. He turned to leave when he saw Stuart and me, but the voice of basso stopped him.

"Stay where you are, boy. White folk are looking for trouble today. We're going to need your help."

"Mama Tycie said to leave them alone."

"Your grandmama is an old woman, boy. She don't know good from bad no more. We gotta protect our own. Now go get some rope out of the storeroom."

"Mama Tycie told me not to be taking part in anymore voo-doo rites. She said the devil is in that brass ankle, Mammaloi."

"I told you, Tycie is *old*, man. Done lost her reasoning. Any-how, ain't no voodoo nowhere strong enough to hex lying white folk. We ain't gonna do nothing but take them up the crick a ways and dump them on the bank. Now get the rope, or I'm gonna stretch your neck like a chicken's. It ain't nothing for me to whip a boy's ass."

"Don't have any rope. Don't plan to find any. And you aren't my boss, William. I'm a free man from Edisto Island, a man who goes to college."

With that, he backed out the door and slammed it. The bells fell to the floor. Stuart and I made moves to follow him out, but the circle of men sprang into action. I struggled and cried as they overpowered us. Stuart's face went scarlet. Veins stood out on his neck as the men pinned back his arms and forced him to bend at the waist. Basso tied his hands and gagged him, then held him against a wall. Two others were in the process of binding me when grandson came back in. This in itself would have made no differ-ence, but this time Tycie was with him.

"I heard your tripas talk, William," she said, "and I mean for you to stop what you're doing and listen to your elder. There ain't gonna be no trouble with white folk today...nor with black folk. Now cut them lines off their hands, boy. A big man like you ought to be ashamed, trussing up a slip of a gal like that."

"Stay back, old woman. This be menfolk's business. We gotta protect our own."

"Tripas," Tycie muttered as she hobbled past him to get a bet-ter look at his captives. She flinched when she saw my face. "Great Lord, Missy Arlena," she said. "You're whiter than flounder meat, looking like a h'ant from the graveyard. William, I'm gonna beat you with a hickory stick if you don't untie that child's hands. Hurry up, boy."

Basso grumbled under his breath and took his time undoing the rope. I ran to Tycie when it fell off my hands. Stuart was not far behind. Grandson wasted no time hustling us outside and into his car. He raised a cloud of dust in front of the store as he whipped his Ford out of the parking area.

"Oh, Tycie, we've been looking for you everywhere." I babbled as we bounced down a road of potholes. "Everything is horrible in Charleston. People are saying Miss Peregrine was murdered. They think I'm the one who did it. We came to Edisto, to try to find you, but someone—" (the grandson stiffened) "—someone took us to a voodoo island and scared us out of our minds. That was before I was accused of murder, but now the police are after me because Louisa and Jeannette have told them so many lies. And Raven FitzSimons jumped off Cooper River Bridge this morning. She's dead, Tycie—dead."

The old woman stared at me from the front seat. "Sweet Jesus...not Missy Raven," she said. "Charleston has got a mantle of evil flying low over her crumbling walls. Wickedness is going to choke that city for sure."

"Where are we going?" Stuart said to the back of grandson's neck. Then to Tycie, "Arlena needs to talk to you calmly a few minutes, Mrs. Roosevelt. We don't care where, as long as it isn't Snake Island." Again grandson stiffened.

"We're going to my house," Tycie said, "so we can sit and talk in peace. I have to decide what to do. Missy Peregrine has been coming to me in my dreams, begging me to tell the truth."

"What truth?" Stuart said. "What do you know?"

"Hush-up, boy," Tycie said. "You can't trick no old black woman like me into saying what she don't want to say. That policeman, Ray Bob Hanahan...he already tried to fool me, and so did those devil-angels at Peregrine House, with their black wings flapping around South Battery Street like two blackbirds fresh out of hell."

"Louisa?" I said. "And Jeannette?"

"Yes, and Dr. Croomer Calhoun. They're greedy vultures, those three. Like Beelzebub and his hoards. Night rulers, fallen angels, whisperers of black lies."

Chapter Thirty-Six

Stuart leaned closer to Tycie. "Maybe we should go somewhere besides your house," he said. "William might call someone and tell them where we are. Arlena isn't exaggerating about the trouble we're in. Half the Charleston police force must be after us by now."

"William is more scared of the police than you are," Tycie said. "He won't call nobody."

"What about the other men?" Stuart said. "They could have heard something on the radio. Isn't there somewhere else we could go, somewhere safer?"

Tycie touched her grandson's arm. "Turn around, Abe. Take us to the chapel. We'll do our talking in the house of the Lord."

Grandson made a U-turn and headed back toward the church. Tycie spoke to him sternly. "Hide your automobile behind the building," she said, "then walk back to the store. Tell those trouble hounds they'll answer to me if they call the law on Missy Arlena. Liquor will be flowing like milk out of a pitcher before the moon comes up. That's when the witch Mammaloi will take over. Go on, boy. Hurry."

I glanced at the young man's ebony face and remembered his hands on my throat. Would Tycie believe me if I told her he had taken part in the rite at Snake Island? I decided against finding out.

Grandson gave Stuart and me a hard look before backing his Ford out of the driveway. Out of Tycie's earshot, Stuart said, "He could be trouble, that boy. I can't tell who he hates worse, us or big basso."

"Just be glad he loves his grandmother," I said. "That could be the only thing that saves us."

Inside the chapel, Tycie seated herself on the back pew and

folded her hands in prayer. Stuart and I sat down beside her.

"Amen," she said aloud, and opened her eyes. "I'm praying for the souls of dead folk—Missy Peregrine and Missy Raven. The Lord takes the young and the old." She bowed her head again and wiped her eyes sadly. "Sometimes I wish he'd take me."

I drew in a long breath and began my strange story. "We came here to ask you about Miss Peregrine," I said, then paused for a response that didn't come. Stuart urged me on. "I know you're afraid, Tycie, but so are we. A policeman, Ray Bob Hanahan, arrested me earlier today. He thinks I killed Miss Peregrine. Louisa and Jeannette have been lying to him. Dr. Calhoun, too. I don't know what to do."

"I'm scared," Tycie said. "Missy Louisa threatened to boil me in oil if I opened my mouth to anyone. I spat in her face and told her she had no hold on me. The good Lord watches over old black women. But she squinted up her witch eyes and said she'd kill my boy, my grandchild, if I didn't do as I was told. Daddy Abraham and me—we're the only family young Abe has got. But Daddy is a no-account drinker, all the time studying about voodoo. Abe depends on me. I can't do nothing that might hurt him."

Stuart could restrain himself no longer. "Did you see Louisa do anything to Miss Peregrine, Tycie?"

The old woman wouldn't answer. She stared at her hands, which rested primly in her lap. "For God's sake," Stuart said. "Don't you understand what's going on? Arlena has been accused of murder. You can't stand by and let this happen. You saw something. I know you did."

Tycie glared at him with angry eyes. "You make me sick," she said. "You aren't black. You don't live in fear."

"What do you think we're living in now?" he said. "Someone has to stop Louisa. Please, you can't let her hurt Arlena."

"It isn't just Missy Louisa," she said, her eyes rolled far to one side. "It's all of them. They all killed Missy Peregrine."

"What? What are you saying?" Stuart said.

The old woman rose from the pew and lifted her arms above her head. She rocked back on her heels and looked up at the ceiling. Her whole body trembled. "Dear Lord," she cried out, tears streaming now. "I saw them drug Missy Peregrine. And now they want to hurt my Abe."

"Tell us what you saw," Stuart said, reaching out to steady the small woman. She grabbed his hand and stared into his face with wet fearful eyes.

"I was standing in the bathroom," she said. "They didn't know I was anywhere around. Missy Louisa thought Abe had already come to take me to the doctor. But he was late, so late. He'd forgotten me—he admitted it later. I went up to Missy Peregrine's room to sit with her while I waited. She was asleep. She was always asleep because of the pills they gave her. I was afraid she would die, afraid of Missy Louisa, afraid of all the evil goings-on in Peregrine House.

"Then I heard them coming up the stairs—Missy Louisa, Missy Jeannette and Dr. Calhoun. *Oh Lord, save me*, I prayed to myself, and ran into the bathroom to hide. I watched them sneak into Missy Peregrine's room. They shook her to see if she'd wake up. But she didn't; she was too dead asleep. Then Dr. Calhoun got nervous and wanted to leave. He said what they were doing was bad business—that she'd die soon enough. But Missy Jeannette lost her temper at that. She said if he expected to take part in the inheritance, he had to take part in the killing. I saw when they gave her the pills, too many pills. Missy Louisa and Missy Jeannette held her head while Dr. Calhoun made her take them. I cried when I saw them do it.

"I was crying still when they rushed out of the room like fallen angels fleeing God. They left Missy Peregrine to die alone. But she wasn't as alone as they thought. *I* was close by, hiding in the bathroom, too scared to show my face, lest any one of them should come back in the room and find out I'd been there all the time. I stayed hidden a long time, praying and crying, crying and praying, not knowing what to do. Then, *you* came into the bedroom, Mr. Prince—big as life, an answer to my prayer. I didn't know what you had come for; I didn't care. I just thanked the Lord He'd taken pity on me and sent someone to save me.

"But the sight of you shocked me so, I couldn't speak a word. I knocked over a jar on the vanity table and made a terrible racket. It scared you, too. It must have, you ran back into the hallway before I could tell you it was just me. Everything happened so fast, for a moment I thought you hadn't been there at all, that my mind was playing tricks. But I couldn't have imagined it. I'd heard something fall to the floor when you ran out of the room, something smaller than the jar I'd just turned over. From the bathroom, I could see a brown prescription bottle lying on the rug near the bed. It must have popped open when it struck the floor and bounced onto the rug; pills were scattered all over. At first I thought they were Missy Peregrine's, until I saw they were the wrong color. I knew I should go pick them up, but I was too scared to leave my hiding place. Not until Missy Peregrine called out my name did I find the courage to leave the bathroom."

"*Tycie*," I heard her say. "*Help me.*"

"I forgot my fear and ran to her side. I held her while she took her last breaths. That was when Missy Louisa came barging back in—and you right behind her, Missy Arlena. But when I heard the two of you outside the door, I leaned down and grabbed up the pills and the pill bottle and hid them in my pocket. I didn't want anything that belonged to Mr. Prince to be left in the room. Three evil angels killed Missy Peregrine, not Mr. Prince. I didn't want him to be blamed.

"Then Louisa came flying back in like the demon crow she is. She slapped me to the floor, and would have done it again if you hadn't stopped her, Missy Arlena. How I despise that woman. Lord, forgive me for despising her so. But how can I stop when I saw her help those two other white devils kill my Missy Peregrine? *Oh, I hate them all.*"

Her testimony over, Tycie threw back her head, let out a piercing scream, and lurched forward into Stuart's arms. Her head rolled to one side as he eased her onto a pew.

"She's out," he said. "Hand me a stack of those books. We have to elevate her feet."

"But they're *Bibles*."

"I don't care. It's a good use."

He propped up her feet and patted her hands and cheeks. "Tycie, wake up," he said. Her eyes opened slowly. She looked old and wasted. Stuart spoke again. "Lie still, Tycie. Close your eyes and rest."

"I knew I was right," he said to me when Tycie appeared to have dozed off. "I knew she'd seen something incriminating."

"I don't understand, Stuart. She said *you* were in Miss Peregrine's room, before the police and everyone else got there, before *I* got there. How can that be?"

He put a finger to his lips and led me to the front of the church where we could talk without disturbing Tycie. "She's wrong," he said, a peculiar intensity in his voice. "No way I was in that room. She must have been hallucinating from stress. But you can bet money those other three were there. That's the important thing. I'll talk to her when she wakes up. I'll tell her to be careful what she says to people. The last thing we need is for us both to be accused."

"But the pills—she said you dropped a bottle of pills."

"Listen to yourself, Arlena. You're talking crazy again. Why would I have pills? You're the one into that. Give Tycie a break. She got a couple of details mixed up, that's all. Who wouldn't after witnessing a murder?"

I looked at Stuart with fierce bright eyes at the mention of the word *murder*. "Those people are monsters," I said. "No wonder Raven jumped."

Stuart kneaded his temples with his fingertips. "No one will believe a word of this," he said, "unless Tycie talks to the police herself."

"She'll have to," I said. "I'll make her."

"I don't know if you can. She's terrified ...."

"And rightly so," a voice cut in from the shadows behind Tycie's pew. "She should fear for her very life."

Stuart and I turned to see Dr. Croomer Calhoun standing behind the pew where Tycie lay in her faint. "Sounds as if you know everything now," he said with a sneer. "Tycie must have done some talking. It has always been my opinion that if women would keep their mouths shut, the world would be a better place. Louisa woke up from her concussion this morning, crazier than ever, raving about Tycie. She said she thought Tycie may have seen us in Fanny's bedroom. Jeannette and I were surprised to hear that. Louisa, you see, had neglected to tell us Tycie was in the house that evening. We thought she had left with her grandson. Poor Louisa has her lapses, as you know. I had no choice but to give her another sedative and put her back to sleep, along the same line I kept putting you back to sleep when you were in the hospital, Miss Prince—excuse me, *Mrs*. Prince. If I hadn't spiked your IV every night, you'd have been over your withdrawal symptoms in days instead of weeks. My mistake was in letting you come around at all. But I was soft. I thought discrediting you would be enough. I thought you'd get the message and leave town. How stupid that was. I never realized you had designs on the estate. Jeannette and

I were naive not to pick up on that. No matter, I'm getting rid of you and Tycie now, perhaps even Jeannette. She's distraught over Raven, could certainly be the next suicide, as early as tonight."

"You'll never get away with it," Stuart said. "It's too much. People will find out."

"People are stupid. It took an intellect like mine to figure out where the two of you went after Raven jumped. Hanahan surely didn't think of Edisto. If it hadn't been for me, he'd still be looking in Georgetown. I'm somebody. A medical doctor. My heritage is south of Broad. I'm a god to the lower classes ...."

That was all he had time to say. Abe, who had sneaked noiselessly into the front entrance of the church, cracked him over the head with a board.

"Are we glad to see *you*," Stuart said, hurrying toward the young black man.

"*Stop*," the boy yelled, grabbing Calhoun's gun and pointing it at Stuart's chest. "Where is Mama Tycie? What have you done with my grandmama?"

I looked at the pew where Tycie lay. Grandson's eyes doubled in size as her head rose slowly into view. "Hush, Abe," she said. "We're in the house of God. Nothing bad can happen to Tycie here. Now give that gun to Mr. Prince and come help your grandmama up. The night air has brought on her rheumatism."

"Look what I've done," Abe said. "I've knocked Dr. Calhoun senseless. I don't want to go to jail, mama."

"He'll be all right," she said, "soon as he wakes up. Stop fretting and help me to your automobile."

"Things were bad at the store," he said. "By the time I got there, Dr. Calhoun and Hanahan had already cornered William. He'd told them everything he knew. I hadn't been there a minute when Calhoun lit out for the church in his car. I couldn't catch him on foot. That's why he beat me back here."

"Hanahan and Calhoun?" Tycie said. "Carrying on with William?"

"Yes, ma'am. William told them you'd be at home or at the church. That's how Calhoun knew where to look for you."

"I said help me up, boy. We're going home. Missy Peregrine left something with me to give to Missy Arlena."

I moved closer to Stuart. Abe still clutched the gun. "You hear me, child?" said Tycie. "Give the gun to Mr. Prince. You're too young to be toting a weapon."

Reluctantly the boy held the butt end of the pistol toward Stuart, who wasted no time racing up the aisle to grab it. I went to Tycie to help her up. When Abe and I got her to her feet, we all walked in a wide half-circle around the body of Calhoun, and out the front door of the church. I took only one look back.

"You don't think he's dead, do you?" I said to Stuart. "Shouldn't we check?"

"No. Even if he is, we're never going to admit we saw the boy hit him. People around here would put a black man *under* the jail if they knew he put out an aristocrat's lights."

Stuart picked up the board Abe had used on Calhoun and heaved it into the woods. "Tycie," he said, "is there someplace we can hide until Hanahan leaves the island?"

"No, but we won't need to if we can get to the house quick enough. Hurry, Abe. Drive faster. I have something important to give to Missy Arlena. Then we're all going to Charleston in Daddy's boat."

"What is it?" I said. "Is it something of Miss Peregrine's?"

"It's two things," Tycie said. "One is a promise from me to you that I'm going to tell the police exactly how Missy Peregrine died."

"Oh, Tycie, thank you," I said. "I'll be grateful to you forever."

"That isn't all," she said. "Missy Peregrine wrote you a letter, only I've been too scared to give it to you. I've been hiding it all this time."

"What letter? What does it say?"

"I don't know. It's still sealed."

"Does it have my name on it?"

"Yes'm. Mine, too, but I didn't open it. No use to—can't read it no way."

"How long have you had it?"

"Since the day the mailman brought it to Edisto, the day after Missy Peregrine died. She knew the end was near. She wrote the letter a few hours before she went to sleep that last time, and told me to give it to the mailman in Charleston. It came to me at home the next day."

"I don't understand," Stuart said. "You mailed a letter to yourself?"

"Missy Peregrine told me to, that it was important to give it to Missy Arlena on the day Mr. Pinckney read her will. But no one has mentioned a will yet, and I've been too afraid to ask questions."

"There is a will," I said. "And you're in it, Tycie. Mr. Pinckney has the papers in his office." I forgot momentarily I'd destroyed them.

"Praise God," she said. "Maybe Missy Peregrine left me enough money to pay for the rest of Abe's schooling."

Everyone grew quiet when Abe drove into the settlement of blue-trimmed houses. He parked behind two pine trees at the edge of the clearing, and the four of us walked to the same house where Stuart and I had talked to Daddy Abraham the afternoon of Snake Island. I expected him to meet us at the door. He did not, and Tycie didn't comment on his absence. We went into the house and stood by silently as Tycie unlocked a wooden chest. Deep inside, under a stack of ancient patchwork quilts, was the unopened letter. It was addressed to Tycie and myself in Miss Peregrine's wobbly script, and postmarked the day of her death.

Tycie took the letter from the chest and handed it to me. Then, almost as an afterthought, she rummaged around among the quilts again and produced a small prescription bottle. "It's the one Mr. Prince dropped in Missy Peregrine's bedroom," she said, "the night she died."

I stared at its label when she handed it to me, shocked to see my own name typed neatly around the curve of the bottle. It was one of my old Darvon prescriptions, nearly full. I looked at Stuart with questioning eyes. He offered no explanation. I was about to press when grandson silenced me.

"Quiet," he said. "I hear a noise outside. We have to run and hide."

Tycie sighed heavily. "We run; we hide; we kiss the white man's foot," she said in a tired voice. "But no more after tonight. The Lord is going to protect us for telling the truth."

Chapter Thirty-Seven

Smelling of alcohol and the great salt marsh, Daddy Abraham staggered into the house just as Tycie was re-locking her trunk. We were grateful he was the source of young Abe's "noise." Stuart took this opportunity to seize the letter and prescription bottle and stuff them into his pants pocket. It was clear there would be no time to deal with either of them now, and I, their owner, was too stressed to keep up with them through more troubled waters.

"Are you liquored up, old man?" Tycie said to her husband.

"You best stop your complaining," he answered, "and listen to what I have to tell you. Bad William is drunker than ten of me, and meaner than a swamp moccasin. He and a policeman from town are packing guns and looking for these two whitebreads. They're on their way here now."

"Missy Peregrine left me some money when she died, old man, and Abe is going with me to get it. But if you tell William we took your boat, Tycie ain't going to give you one dime of that money. You hear me, old man?"

"Money? Your white lady left you money?"

"It's a fact, she did. And if you want some of it to buy yourself a truck, you'd best keep your lip tight."

Daddy Abraham was silent. I smelled his whiskey.

"Git," he said, when automobile engines and men's voices disturbed the silence outside. "William and the policeman are coming in a run."

Grandson turned to Stuart and spoke earnestly. "You have to carry Mama Tycie," he said. "I'm going to lead you to the boat. And I mean for you to watch your step, man. The vines will catch your legs."

We followed the boy in silent procession as he led us out the back door, across his grandmother's moon-shadowed yard and into the same desolate stand of trees that Stuart and I had passed through on the last leg of our terrifying journey back from Snake Island.

"A motor," Stuart breathed in elation when he saw Daddy Abraham's john boat.

"That's right," grandson said, "but we can't crank her yet. Here, take this oar. We're going to paddle up the creek a ways. The motor would make too much noise."

"Does William know where you keep your boat?"

"Probably, but it doesn't matter. Daddy Abe will put him on the wrong trail. By the time he figures it out, we'll be half-way to Charleston."

Stuart and the boy rowed in perfect tandem. The boat made measured whooshing sounds as it sliced through black water. I handed Tycie the knit hat the clerk from Two Brothers had given to me when we left the marina earlier. She pulled it on over her headcloth and hunched against my shoulder. Stuart and grandson rowed fifteen minutes before we sighted green and red channel lights blinking in the distance. Grandson cranked the motor with one yank of the rope. We had reached the great Intracoastal Waterway, and were out of the clutches of Edisto.

"We'll dock at Adger's Wharf," the boy said when harbor lights appeared an hour later. "No people come around Adger's at night—nobody to ask questions."

To my eye, no familiar landmark was visible, but Abe knew every dock and piling. He tied up at the end of a creosote wharf and began the delicate business of getting his grandmother ashore. Stuart and I helped him as best we could before disembarking ourselves.

"Are we going to Pinckney House now?" I said to Stuart as he struggled up the rough ladder to the dock. He was the last of us to leave the boat, the last to climb the ladder.

"Yes," he said. "We'll walk. The boy and I will have to make a basket seat for Tycie."

"You can't march along East Bay Street in the middle of the night carrying a little black woman on your arms. Someone is bound to notice."

"We'll cross East Bay and go the rest of the way on side streets. Isn't Tradd up the way?"

"I think so, but we can't waste time looking for particular streets. Hanahan might be around somewhere. He could've made it back faster by car."

"Hanahan isn't important, anymore. He's out of the picture now that Tycie is going to make a statement. We'll be home-free then."

"If that's true, why did we have to freeze our rear ends off sneaking away from Edisto by boat?"

"We were running from Bad What's-his-name, and Croomer Calhoun, assuming the boy didn't kill him with that board."

"I hope I never see him again as long as I live. All I want is to get to Pinckney House. You still have the letter, don't you? Shouldn't we read it now?"

"Too dark...no time. You can read it at Mr. Pinckney's."

Stuart and grandson faced each other and locked arms. Tycie sat across them daintily. I acted as look-out as we walked up the dock and stepped onto the cobblestones of Adger's. We scuttled across East Bay Street, and walked along the sidewalk a half a block before fading into the shadows of Tradd. At Pinckney House I led the group through a small wrought iron gate in the back wall of Miss Roz's garden. Tycie demanded to be allowed to walk once we were inside the gate. This made for slow-going across the mossy flagstones. Stuart had taken over the lead now, and was on his way to a shrubby corner he hoped would shield us from light. He left us there, hidden in shadows, then sneaked up to one of the three back doors of Pinckney House and rapped timidly with bare knuckles. A male voice rumbled from within.

"Who's there?" it said. "I'm gonna call the police if you splash this house with paint again." Though not positive, I thought the voice belonged to Peter.

"I'm Arlena Prince's husband," Stuart called out. "Tell Mr. Pinckney I'm here. He knows me."

There was a long silence, then lights flashed on. "Is that you, Prince?" Mr. Pinckney said, flinging open the back door. "Where have you been, man? The whole town is looking for your wife."

Stuart stepped into the light and raised an arm. The rest of us converged on the door. Mr. Pinckney held it open as we paraded inside.

"My God," he said. "You brought half of Edisto with you. Is there a Wadmalaw contingent?"

Miss Roz led us to the front parlor, where I sank gratefully onto a sofa near the fire. It was then I heard the voice of Croom Calhoun Jr. "Are these the cigars you wanted, Mr. Pinckney?" he said. "I found them upstairs in your study."

I looked toward the archway that separated the parlor from the foyer. Croom stood there, motionless, tensed. Instinctively, I rose to face him. It was clear he had not heard us come in and that our presence was an unwanted surprise.

"Yes, son," Mr. Pinckney said. "Those are the ones. Arlena, you may sit and relax. Croom has unburdened his soul to me tonight. The death of dear Raven has shaken some sense into his head. Stuart, sit down by your wife. And stop looking like a wildcat ready to pounce. Great Jehovah, man—you look worse every time I see you."

Stuart sat, but did not relax. He was ready to spring at any provocation. Tycie and grandson took twin chairs opposite Stuart and me. Croom balanced his own large frame upon a footstool at the end of the sofa. Mr. Pinckney stood before the fire.

"Good evening, Mrs. Roosevelt," Mr. Pinckney said to Tycie in a tone that was all respect. "To what do I owe this unexpected nocturnal visit?"

Tycie would not look at him. She cast a glance in my direction, then focused on the floor. I assumed she wanted me to speak for her.

"Tycie ..." I stopped and looked at her again to make sure I was doing the right thing. She nodded. "Tycie wants to tell you and the police what she saw the night Miss Peregrine died."

"Indeed," Mr. Pinckney said. "And what might that be, Mrs. Roosevelt?"

With facial expression alone she begged me to speak in her place again. "She saw," I said. "She was a witness to ..." I could not get it out. In the middle of my pause, Miss Roz flittered into the room and told Mr. Pinckney that a Sergeant Hanahan was at the door. Stuart stood, again, and Mr. Pinckney ordered him to sit.

"Hellfire, Prince," he said. "You're more nervous than a marsh tacky pony."

Stuart poised himself on the edge of the sofa. Mr. Pinckney left the room with Miss Roz. No one spoke while he was gone. I looked at Croom Jr. His face was red and swollen, as though he had been crying a very long time. Mr. Pinckney returned with Hanahan, who stopped under the archway and swept the parlor with his eyes. His gaze halted on me, then moved around the rest of the room in silent observation. Mr. Pinckney pointed to a chair well away from the inner circle. Hanahan sat and placed his hat on his knees. Mr. Pinckney crossed the room and reclaimed his position by the fireplace.

"All right," he said, "with Mr. Hanahan present, we have an excellent witness to whatever might be said here this evening. Soon we'll have a few others. Miss Roz is rousing my daughter and her husband, Mr. and Mrs. Jonathan Priolieu. Now, Ray Bob, to bring you up to date—Mrs. Prince was just telling me ..." He stopped in mid-sentence to wave Miss Roz, Caroline, and Jonathan to an out-of-the-way corner. "Where was I? Oh yes, Mrs. Prince was telling me that Tycie Roosevelt witnessed a crime. She was about to give us details. Go ahead, Mrs. Prince."

"It was the murder of Miss Fanny Peregrine," I said. A murmur went up from the corner where Miss Roz's party stood.

"Is that correct, Mrs. Roosevelt?" Mr. Pinckney said. Tycie nodded. "And who did you see kill Miss Peregrine? Can you name the name?"

"Not just one," she answered. "Three—Missy Jeannette, Missy Louisa, and Dr. Croomer Calhoun."

Mr. Pinckney turned his eyes toward Hanahan and spoke to him sharply. "Did you hear that, Ray Bob? This woman is an eyewitness. I'm sure she will give you a detailed statement before the evening is out."

"That's right," Tycie said, newly bold.

Mr. Pinckney leaned forward and patted her on the shoulder. "Fine, Tycie. That's fine. We all thank you. Now then, to move on, there's a young man among us who has told me a heartbreaking tale this evening. Croom, my boy, I know you've been through misery these last few days, but can you find the strength to tell your story one more time?"

"I guess so, sir, only it's hard, awfully hard."

"I know, son. Make it brief, as painless as you can."

"My father ..." Croom began, then cleared his throat and started over. "I heard my father on the phone with Mrs. FitzSimons, talking about doing away with Miss Peregrine. They were definitely in it together—with the housekeeper, Louisa Hill. Father said he needed money right away, he was in financial straights ...."

Croom could not go on. He dropped his eyes to the floor and wiped away a tear. "You'll be okay," Mr. Pinckney said. "Did your father realize you heard?"

"Yes, sir. It upset him badly. He almost went crazy. Said he needed my help."

"What kind of help?"

Croom looked at Stuart and me and winced. "He wanted me to scare Mr. and Mrs. Prince into leaving Charleston. I was the one who smashed their windshield and threw paint on Mrs. Middleton's cottage. I was downstairs hiding in the storeroom when they came home from Edisto one morning—a bunch of voodoo crazies had kept them out all night, scared them half to death. Father had told me to trash their stuff, that maybe it would frighten them into giving up their part of the estate and leaving town. I went out to the cottage to see what I could do. They weren't home when I first got there, but just as I was about to break in the screened porch, I heard their car in the drive. I barely had time to hide. I ran down the porch steps and slipped into the storeroom under the house. It was a miracle they didn't see me. Guess the voodoo thing had them distracted. I could hear everything they said after they went upstairs—their bedroom is right over the storeroom. They talked for an hour about voodoo rites and secret islands and people with blue faces. That's when I thought of throwing paint on the cottage.

"I sneaked away after they got quiet. Figured they'd gone to sleep. Later, sometime in the afternoon, Raven told me she and her mother were planning to set a trap for the Princes that night. I don't know everything, but somehow they lured them into town after dark, on the pretense that Tycie was going to be at Peregrine House, I think. I decided to go back to Sullivan's to keep an eye on them. It was late, almost dark when they left the cottage. I followed them to the peninsula, and when they parked their car on a side street off East Bay and started toward Peregrine House, I waited for them to get far enough away so they couldn't hear anything, then I broke their car's windshield and windows with my baseball bat. They made it easy for me, really...parking out of the way of streetlights like they did. Afterward, I doubled back to

Sullivan's and threw blue paint on the cottage. I did some driving that night."

"And you vandalized my house, also?"

"Yes, sir. I knew my father was angry at you because you helped Miss Peregrine write the new will. I decided on the spur of the moment to hit your house. Dumb, huh? I've done a boat-load of dumb things the past few weeks."

"How old are you, Croom?"

"Seventeen, sir."

"And what made you come forward today?"

At that, Croom put his head in his hands and sobbed. "There, there, boy," Mr. Pinckney said. "It's almost over. What was it that made you want to tell the truth?"

"I...I saw Raven die. She jumped off the bridge and killed herself. I can't believe she did it."

Again his voice broke with emotion. Tears glittered in his eyes. "It was all my fault," he said. "From the beginning, Raven wanted to tell the police the truth, what her mother and my father had done. But I talked her out of it, more than once. Then everything came crashing down on her, especially the part about the abortion. Her whole life was falling apart. And the worst was that she thought I didn't love her. But I did. I loved her more than anything. I just didn't know what to do about her being pregnant. I'm only seventeen. I don't know things. And now she's dead. I hate my father. I hate Mrs. FitzSimons. Oh God, I want to die like Raven. I never wanted any of Miss Peregrine's money. I was just trying to help my father."

"It's all over now, son," Mr. Pinckney said. "You've done the right thing by speaking out." Then he indicated with his eyes that Miss Roz should come over and comfort the grieving boy. Stuart and I looked at each other. I bit my lip to stay steady.

"Ray Bob," Mr. Pinckney said. "Would I be correct in assuming you will now destroy that dog-eared warrant for the arrest of one Arlena Prince?"

"Correct, sir."

"Good. Then there is nothing further to discuss ...."

"Mr. Pinckney," I said. "Stuart and I have something to show you. It's a letter from Miss Peregrine." I looked at Stuart, who had a stricken expression on his face.

"Are you sure you want to do this now?" he said. "Maybe we should wait."

"Yes, now," I answered. "Give the envelope to Mr. Pinckney." Reluctantly, he pulled the rumpled letter from his shirt pocket and handed it over. Its seal was still unbroken.

"Miss Peregrine had Tycie put this in the mail the afternoon she was killed," I said to Mr. Pinckney. "Look at the postmark, sir."

"And why have you not produced it before?"

"Tycie has been hiding it. It came to her in the mail at Edisto, the day after Miss Peregrine died. She was afraid to give it to me. Louisa had threatened to kill her grandson, Abe, if she talked to anyone."

Mr. Pinckney walked across the room in huge strides and presented the letter to Hanahan. "Examine this envelope, if you will," he said. "Make sure you can say in a court of law it was sealed with sealing wax when I showed it to you. Look there, that's the imprint of the Peregrine family crest."

Hanahan turned the letter over in his hands, then gave it back to Mr. Pinckney. "Yes, sir, it's sealed."

Mr. Pinckney then handed the letter to Jonathan Priolieu and issued the same instructions. When satisfied the envelope had been thoroughly inspected by more than one witness, he directed his gaze toward me. "Well, Arlena," he said. "Do you wish to share your letter with the group?"

"Yes," I said, my voice husky from exhaustion. "Will you read it for me, please?"

Grayson Pinckney picked up a silver letter opener from a writing table next to the archway and slit open the envelope. He put on his spectacles and read aloud:

Dearest Arlena,

I awakened early this morning and have spent some time gazing out my window at the harbor. It will not be long before my old Peregrine eyes will be closed to these sights forever. Even now I'm unable to see very far, though my memory still tells me what is there. In my mind I can picture blue water stretching toward Fort Sumter and Morris Island. Sullivan's Island is somewhere beyond. I see gulls flying into the wind. They look as if they hang suspended in the heavens. Oh look, sailboats are running before the wind. And clouds, stacks and stacks of beautiful white clouds are piled high against azure skies. They're racing faster than the sailboats. Now I see the smudge that is Sullivan's. It makes me think of my childhood, those carefree days when no monstrous bridge connected the island to Mount Pleasant. Lately, Arlena, I have pined for those times, those innocent times before my life stopped at age sixteen. To have a child out of wedlock in my day was a moral outrage in Charleston. Father never forgave me. He said I was a whore and a sinner, no matter being born to an elegant family. But I was neither of those things. I was a girl, a frightened girl who had nowhere to turn. And isn't it ironic that the child I bore lived only nine short months?

Please forgive me, dear. I know it is not logical that you should make me long for a daughter I never knew. All my life I have searched for her, though I know she lies dead in a northern grave. The search has been my life's heartache, especially considering the derangement of Louisa. I wanted so much to care for her, like a mother would care for a daughter, but she lives in a dark world of confusion. I no longer know how to reach her.

Then there was Jeannette. She could have been the one, but over the years, greed has crippled her into something unlovely. Perhaps I expected too much. Perhaps I assumed too much. You see, Arlena, I always thought Louisa and Jeannette loved me. I thought they cared enough about me to use my father's fortune to help preserve the natural treasures that belong to us all: the beauty of Charleston, the rarity of Sullivan's, the marshlands, beaches, islands, swamps, tidal creeks, rivers and inlets...even the grand old Atlantic. But I was wrong. They never loved me. It was my money they were after. Filthy lucre, Father would say.

And now I face something terrible enough to break an old woman's heart. For months I have lived with the knowledge that the people I care about most deeply are trying to shorten my life. With the exception of Tycie, I have lost faith in everyone around me. Louisa, Jeannette, and Croomer have been tampering with my medication. I am ill most of the time. For a long while I was able to monitor the medicine myself. But they've caught on to that now, and have become more clever at deceiving me. Perhaps I should save them the trouble and end my own life. Unfortunately, I was born a coward. By now you must know about the new will I drew up with the help of my old friend, Grayson Pinckney, and why I had to do it. Grayson is my last chance at trusting someone, someone like family. I hope you and he are over-joyed by the provisions I have made for each of you.

Now, about this long epistle, I hope it has not put you off. My intention was to discuss all this with you face to face, but I fear I will not have the opportunity. Things have been tense at Peregrine House of late, as you have observed. I am writing this letter in case anything happens to me. They think I don't hear them when they whisper, but I assure you, I do. Arlena, please be kind to my good and faithful Tycie. She is to give you this letter should anything unexpected befall me. You, in turn, deliver it to Grayson. He will know what to do legally.

One last thing, you must not fret over the general sorriness of one old woman's misfortunes. Life in its fullness was never meant to be soft. Not from the first. I believe this from the bottom of my heart. And if it is true, life in Old Charleston has had a glorious expression. Perhaps that is why I am not more shocked by the ruthlessness of my loved ones. Please give my love to that Lancelot of yours—I cannot recall his name. Allow him to heal the wounds of your childhood. He is the balm I never had. Let him make you whole before you turn into a wizened old woman like me. I suppose you have realized this letter, sadly, is my new ending to *Tarnished Honor*. Makes for a real stinger, don't you agree? Too bad it will never be published. Now I must close quickly, for Louisa is on the stair. Take care of yourself, my precious. I continue to think the best of you and everyone.

Forever,
Fanny Peregrine

A tear ran down Grayson Pinckney's face as he refolded the letter and laid it on the mantel. With great dignity he took off his glasses and dabbed at his eyes. Then he walked to where I was sitting. I stood to face him. "There's one last thing I have to tell you, sweet rose," he said, his aristocratic eyes, delphinium blue, locking with my own jet blacks. His voice quavered as he spoke. "After experiencing the heartfelt sincerity of Miss Peregrine's letter, I am relieved to have ignored yours and Stuart's requests to destroy the original of the new will. The copy you shredded was just that...a copy. Thanks to my good judgment, you are still an heiress."

Chapter Thirty-Eight

You are still an heiress ....

My story should have ended there, with those words of Mr. Pinckney, if ever there can be a final ending to a human story. Something in us longs for the satisfying conclusion—villains found out, questions answered, loose ends tied up. We dream of being rescued from the messiness of life by some gloriously happy Act IV. *You are an heiress*, indeed. In real life, there is always another road to go down, another treacherous journey to make. *You are an heiress*. Such lovely, comforting words. Words that ended one disturbing story, and promptly began another. But the unfolding of the latter was quite different from what anyone expected.

After our late-night at Mr. Pinckney's house—the night he read Miss Peregrine's letter to the group, and Tycie gave her statement to the police—Stuart took me back to the beach cottage, where I slept for two days straight, dreaming continuously of my father and his pretty lies. When I awoke, groggy and stiff from too many hours in bed, I walked out to the sun-warmed porch and found Stuart dressed in jeans and a plaid flannel shirt, reared back in a new lounge chair, sipping periodically from a bottle of beer. He was poring over one of those elaborate advertisement booklets of the sort you find in automobile showrooms.

"Well *hello*," he said when I stepped into the light. His face was open and relaxed. "How would you like a cold brewski to celebrate the beginning of our new life?"

I glanced at the plastic ice bucket, also new, that sat on the floor by the chair. Three sweating long-necked Budweisers stood at jaunty angles in the ice. Two empties sat to the side.

I re-fixed my gaze on Stuart's face, but did not return his smile, nor respond to his banter. He plunged forward undaunted, used to having to salvage the good out of my frequent difficult episodes.

"I thought you were going to sleep forever," he said. "Two days is a long time. Tell me when you feel hungry and I'll feed you. There's some bacon in the fridge, and eggs. Hey—come sit with me a minute, look at what money can buy." He held the slick booklet up next to his face and grinned like a little boy. "We're going to give the Romeo a decent burial," he said.

I remained unresponsive. His chatter struck me as banal. He dragged a hand down over his face when my silence had sufficiently chilled the encounter to destroy all pleasantness.

"What's wrong now?" he said. "I thought you'd feel better once you got some rest. Guess that was too much to expect from a chronic depressive."

I narrowed my eyes slightly and continued to stare. Irritated, he slapped the booklet shut and tossed it to the floor by the ice bucket.

"*What?*" he said, voice louder, deck shoes scraping the gritty floor as he struggled to get out of the chair. "What ax do you want to grind now? Nothing is ever enough for you, is it? Here we are, problems solved, money forthcoming ...."

"Why were you in Miss Peregrine's room the night she died?" I said without a trace of emotion. "And why did you have one of my prescription bottles with you?"

He glared at me, then turned and panned the spectacular seascape that was our backyard. Seagulls crisscrossed each others' flight paths high above the surf. Indifferent waves glinted silver.

"For the last time," he said, enunciating each word carefully, yet not turning to look me in the eye, "I was not in that room, not until I came to rescue you. And I don't know anything about a prescription bottle. Tycie said it had *your* name on it, not mine. You could have dropped it yourself. Did you ever think of that?"

My skin went clammy. After a moment I said, "Tycie can't read, Stuart. She never said whose name was on the bottle. Not once did she say it."

"Then *you* did," he said. "*Some*body did. No...I remember now. I saw it, on the bottle, just before I put it in my coat pocket when I took it from you at Tycie's. That's it. I *saw* it."

"Where is it now?" I said.

"I don't know. It must have fallen out of my pocket in all the confusion...Daddy Abraham, the rowboat, getting Tycie back to Charleston."

"It didn't fall out of your pocket," I said coldly.

He breathed deeply before restating his response. "I don't know where it is," he said, "and I'm not going to worry about it. It's lost, that's all. Gone forever. Which suits one or two players in this soap opera just fine. Tycie, for instance. It definitely suits her. She didn't want to leave anything lying around that might confuse the police about who killed Miss Peregrine. She knows who killed her. She saw them do it with her own eyes. And now she wants them put away so they can't get at her for speaking out."

He turned then and faced me, meeting my gaze directly for the first time. "I'm not the enemy," he said dispassionately, though I knew he was furious. "You're making a mistake to attack me like this. Look, I'm going for a run on the beach. I'll be back in a couple of hours. If I were you, I'd do some serious thinking before you carry this any further. Some things are best left alone."

I watched him cross the dunes in his graceful stride, as I had watched him do a hundred times before. He distanced himself from me as swiftly as my parents had done on the day they sailed out of Boston Harbor on *The Beautiful Ghost Dream*, with the same vast horizon as a backdrop. The difference, I understood all too well, was that Stuart would come back. Not necessarily because he wanted to, not after I had practically accused him of attempted murder. He'd come back because of the money, though I knew instinctively that from then on, I could expect little more from him than his physical presence. Emotionally and spiritually, he had departed forever, for trust within our relationship died that day. Stuart would never tell me his whole story, nor would I tell him mine. Our two hearts had separated as cleanly as if some wicked knight had galloped up and hacked them apart with his sword. All because of one question, one essential unanswered question.

When Stuart was no longer visible on the beach, I went to the telephone in the sitting room and called Grayson Pinckney's office. Heretofore, I had been put on hold for long periods while the receptionist and various secretaries of Pinckney Building conferred in whispers as to whether I was worthy of being put through to their boss, but today the waters parted instantly. I was thankful there was no change in Mr. Pinckney's behavior. He was his same old sweet polite self. I made an appointment with him for eleven the next day, then went back to bed and slept another sixteen hours.

I woke up at nine the following morning, eyelids no longer able to filter out the white sunlight that was streaming over my face. Headachy and hot from sleeping too much, I got up and trudged to the bathroom. There I found a note from Stuart taped to the mirror of the medicine cabinet. He had gone for another run and would see me later. But I didn't care to see *him* later. I didn't care to see him at all, not until I'd had a chance to talk to Mr. Pinckney alone. This was the day I intended to set in motion plans for my own liberation, and I didn't want Stuart interfering.

My purpose in scheduling an appointment with Mr. Pinckney was to ask for, beg for, help. I realized I had been under too much strain recently to make any sort of sound decision, particularly one involving Miss Peregrine's will. Of the two options she had written in for me, the job with the estate would be the more lucrative, *if* I could settle my nerves from the harrowing experiences of the last few days and give a job my full attention. But I couldn't, not for a good long while. I needed time...to rest, think, plan. And time was what I was banking on Mr. Pinckney being able to give me.

I dressed quickly, trying to make it out of the house before Stuart came back. It was an odd drive into town. Every few miles I had to remind myself to slow down, I was no longer being hunted like a wild animal, the murderers were all in custody. I felt so panicky at one point, I had to stop at a convenience store and drink a Coke to settle my sour stomach.

Mr. Pinckney was glad to see me when I walked into his office. He listened attentively as I tried to explain, stuttering over my consonants from nervousness, that I needed at least a year to decide what I wanted to do about Miss Peregrine's will. She had stipulated that I was to have seven days from the time of the first reading to make a firm decision about which option I wanted to take. I was already into the fourth day. How Mr. Pinckney would react to my request, I did not know, nor whether he had the power to manipulate the terms of the will to the extent I was asking. He surprised me by agreeing with everything I said, and granting everything I asked. He expressed no surprise at my request for extra time, though a puzzled look crossed his face when I told him I wanted to keep our conversation confidential, especially from Stuart.

Yet, puzzled or no, he refrained from quizzing me, and for this I was thankful.

The one thing I hadn't worked out in my mind was how to explain to Stuart the whereabouts of the missing lump sum. If I wanted him to believe I was permanently forfeiting the option of a paid job with the estate, the cornerstone of my plan, he would expect me to receive the one-hundred-thousand immediately. Mr. Pinckney helped me solve this problem by advancing me this amount out of his own funds, of which he had plenty, thanks to the largess of Miss Peregrine. He said if I decided to come back in a year to help him run the foundation, he would consider it money well invested. Besides, he assured me, he would collect twice that much in his first year's percentage bonus check from the estate's investment returns.

I stressed to him that no one was to know anything of the details surrounding our conversation. Characteristically, he didn't press for reasons. I sat quietly as he wrote out our short agreement in longhand, and made a single copy for himself. He hugged me instead of shaking my hand, and I left his office satisfied. The first phase of my plan had been put into action— the new agreement between Mr. Pinckney and myself was signed and in my possession, and I was to collect my lump-sum check the next morning. Now I could go back to the cottage to initiate the second phase.

When I arrived, Stuart had already come in from his run, showered, and shaved, and was now having a bowl of spinach salad and a raspberry wine cooler on the porch. He didn't ask where I had been, just said hello tentatively, testing to see if I would start up where I had left off yesterday. When I didn't—I had resolved never again to discuss the topic of why he was in Miss Peregrine's room at an inappropriate time, or why he had one of my prescription bottles with him, for I knew I'd never get a straight answer— he relaxed and resumed eating, pausing at intervals to comment on the weather, or offer me a bite of his salad.

"No, thank you, I ate something earlier," I said.

Then I sat down beside him and made all the correct responses while waiting for him to finish. When he did, I asked if he'd like to walk with me out to the dunes to sit and enjoy the sun. He said yes, he'd be ready as soon as he put his lunch things away. I went into the bedroom for a heavier jacket and to find Miss Peregrine's letter. I put it in my jacket pocket, wound a wool scarf about my neck, and went out to meet Stuart on the porch. He insisted on holding hands as we walked the path to the beach, which made me feel guilty about what I was getting ready to do. He laughed sweetly when the breeze put my hair into disarray. Now it was my turn to avert my eyes.

Still weak and wobbly—the truth was I hadn't eaten—I was grateful to sit down on a driftwood log and allow the sun to warm me. After a few minutes I told him I wanted to hear Miss Peregrine's letter again, would he mind reading it to me aloud? I shed a few tears while he read softly, then I took it from him, tore it into tiny pieces, and scattered them among the dunes. That act was the artful prelude to the biggest lie I would ever tell him.

He gaped at me, incredulous, as I spun my tale: I was through with the South and everything associated with it. I wanted to take the lump-sum option Miss Peregrine had described in her will, buy a new car (an idea that had sprung directly from having observed him studying those fancy brochures), and leave the area for good. The South, I complained bitterly, had almost killed me—I wanted to go back to Boston.

Naturally, Stuart would disagree with everything I said. I prepared myself for an onslaught of bitter words and was not disappointed. There, on that hard driftwood log—jittery, breathless, trembling like a captured bird—I sat for an hour and endured the first of a dozen impassioned speeches on the folly of making hasty decisions. It was more difficult than you might think to stand firm in my conviction. Stuart was nothing if not persuasive. And although I knew exactly what I was doing, and why, there were times I was so beaten down by his tireless harangues, I wanted to drop the protective façade of my lie and shout out to him and the cosmos that he was right and I was wrong. Then I could know the bless-ed relief of giving in: "Oh, Stuart. Yes, Stuart. The better choice *is* to stay in Charleston—stay and cash in indefinitely on poor dead Miss Peregrine's estate."

But I did not fold. Not then, not ever. In weak moments over the next few hours, I'd get out my handwritten agreement with Mr. Pinckney and read it word for word— "...a signature of commitment to Option Two in the document known as Fanny Lockwood Peregrine's Last Will and Testament is required within one year of this later agreement's signature dates, instead of the seven days specified in the original will. Signed: Grayson Pinckney and Arlena Prince."

I stood firm to the end, forcing Stuart to acquiesce if he wanted to realize for himself even a portion of the hundred thousand. The next morning we went to Mr. Pinckney's office together to pick up the check, the sheer amount of which salved somewhat the pain Stuart was experiencing from watching me make a dead-wrong decision.

We were free to move back north then—Massachusetts, odd consulting jobs here and there, ordinary lives, even an ordinary and inevitable separation a year down the road, when the money started running out. Stuart, I discovered, had expensive tastes when money was in the bank.

It was a strange way to spend a year, living together in the same comfortable apartment, but sharing very little. I never regained confidence in Stuart, nor he in me. We both tried for a while, and I did manage to grow less fearful of the myriad dark motives I had assigned to him after the pill bottle incident. Unfortunately, when the fear departed, it left in its wake a sort of mild revulsion that I soon realized was permanent. Neither of us ever mentioned the "incident" again. The day I confronted him at the beach cottage was the one time we discussed it. Unanswered, my question festered like an unwashed puncture wound from a rusty nail. Each time I turned it over in my mind, I added more grisly details to the skeleton of a plot only suggested by the facts.

What, exactly, did I think Stuart had done? The answer to that question isn't interesting, for I was certain Stuart had done nothing. It was what I thought he'd *intended* to do that had me on the run. Tycie had described a scene in Miss Peregrine's bedroom that told its own story, one I made a study of reconstructing in my head fifty different ways, fifty different times a day, for weeks on end, until I came to know there was only one version I would ever believe—Stuart had gone into Miss Peregrine's room to give her extra pills in the hope of hastening her death, but was interrupted before he could do the actual deed by three others more deadly than he. But why did he risk taking along a prescription bottle *with my name on it?* Did he have some nightmare of a plan to implicate me in Miss Peregrine's death? Did he know even then I was included in her will? Had Mr. Pinckney let it slip, perhaps when he made him that first loan? Did he think if I were convicted of murder, I'd be out of the way, and he could do whatever he wanted with the money?

Perhaps if Stuart had talked to me, told me the truth no matter how horrible, and not left me to my own hysterical imagination, I could have become desensitized over time to whatever madness he was about to succumb, and eventually let it go. Maybe this would have worked for me the way it works for phobics when psychiatrists make them confront the things they're afraid of in order to effect a cure. But Stuart chose avoidance over confrontation, a course of action that proved disastrous for our marriage.

I gave myself twelve months to put the horror of possibilities out of my mind, but six had not gone by before I came to the conclusion I'd have needed a hundred years to achieve such a goal. Once or twice I thought I'd made progress, but always the suspicion came slithering back, the serpentine poisonous suspicion. As weeks turned into months, I came to understand it would never go away, in fact, was getting worse. I soon realized I couldn't live with it, not indefinitely. When finally able to admit this to myself, a great burden fell away and left me with the sad truth: if I could not live with the suspicion, I could not live with Stuart.

When I told him I wanted to start the process for a divorce, he seemed almost relieved. For he had not been able to get past the idiocy of my decision about Miss Peregrine's will. His disappointment in losing the chance at what he referred to as "a real future," turned, after a time, into disappointment in me. Thus, one year less two days after we moved into the first decent apartment we'd ever had, I packed selectively, taking nothing that wouldn't fit into two oversized suitcases, and called a cab to drive me to Logan International Airport. I was going back to Charleston.

On arriving at the airport, I went straight to a pay-phone to make a call to the Boston Gynecological Group. It turned out to be the most important call of my life. It's subject was pregnancy. Not whether I was or wasn't—I already knew the answer to that— but what sex my baby was going to be. My *secret* baby. Stuart knew nothing of this development. According to the doctor's calculations, I was four months along, the earliest possible time to get an accurate reading from an amniocentesis test. This was the reason for the call—to get the results from the amnio I'd had weeks before. But my interest in the test results was not the same as my doctor's, which was to check my baby for Down's Syndrome. I knew in my heart I had a normal baby. What I wanted to know was whether it was a boy or a girl, a secondary piece of information that can be garnered from the test.

So I made the call, and was told by a nurse whose voice was all honey and warm fruit, that I was going to have a little girl. A daughter. An angel. My heart sang a melody not of this earth right there in Logan Airport. Suddenly my life had meaning. I beamed at everyone for hours—the clerk in the fast-food restaurant who sold me a bagel and an orange juice, the man in line behind me who picked up my purse when I dropped it, the clerk who issued me a boarding pass at Gate 9, the stewards and stewardesses who welcomed me aboard the plane, my seatmates, the couple across the aisle—*everyone*. Life was good, God was in His heaven, and I had found my song.

I held my arms across my abdomen as the plane banked to the right and headed south. Gradually it nosed its way upward until it broke through the gray mist of a New England winter day, and discovered in a burst of light the sun-drenched heaven above. My heart thumped with joy, my stomach fluttered in anticipation. I was on my way to claim what was rightfully mine, a gift from the universe that had passed to me mysteriously through the hands of Miss Fanny Peregrine—a chance to build a good and wholesome life. Mr. Pinckney, happy I had decided to "do the right thing," was expecting me. He had even gone to the trouble of sending Caesar out to Sullivan's Island to fix up one of the old Peregrine cottages for me to live in, and mailed me the key the week before. I smiled to myself as I considered the pleasures of touching down at Charleston Airport, renting a sporty car, and driving out to the beach. Talks with Mr. Pinckney about new job responsibilities could wait a day or two. My baby and I needed time to commune with the ocean.

My baby...*my baby, my baby, my baby*! I couldn't get enough of knowing she existed, of knowing she was all mine. I didn't want to share her with anyone just yet, especially not Stuart. He would have to wait, years perhaps, though I'd matured enough to know it might be right sometime in the future to let him be a part of her life. Not as my husband, never again that, but as an equal parent helping to care for the child we had conceived. I would not permanently deny my baby her father. I knew too much personally of the pain this could cause.

I was going to name her Raven. This I had promised God each time I'd prayed that my baby would be a girl, which was twenty or thirty times a day since I'd found out I was pregnant.

There were so many injured daughters I wanted to make things right for, so many broken relationships between parents and daughters—my own parents and myself, Miss Peregrine and baby Constantia, Jeannette FitzSimons and Raven. So many. Now my prayer reshaped itself into another more fervent plea—that God in His wisdom would help little Raven and me, for the sake of those who'd gone before us and failed, to get life right at last. On the plane that morning, on my way back to Charleston and the beginning of a new beginning, I closed my eyes and imagined that we could. I have always liked to imagine.

The End

Dr. Terry Ward Tucker is a graduate of the University of North Carolina at Chapel Hill. She is the author of the best-selling book, *Smart Women at Work*. She lives and teaches in Lancaster, South Carolina.

Elegant Sinners is her first work of fiction.

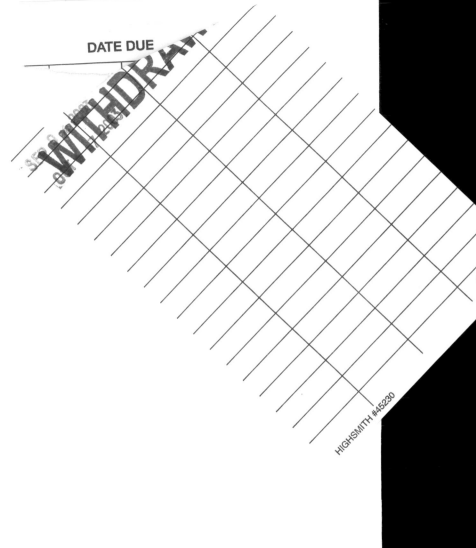